Be True

Be True

STELLA STARLING

Be True © Stella Starling 2017
Edited by Elizabeth Peters and Indica Snow
Cover design by Silver Heart Publishing
ISBN-13: 978-1542307277
ISBN-10: 1542307279

This book is a work of fiction. The names, characters, places, and
incidents are products of the writer's imagination or have been
used fictitiously and are not to be construed as real. Any resem-
blance to persons, living or dead, actual events, locale or organi-
zations is entirely coincidental.

The author has asserted his/her rights under the Copyright Designs and Patents Acts 1988 (as amended) to be identified as the
author of this book.

This book contains sexually explicit content which is suitable
only for mature readers.

Contents

Prologue

LOGAN, SEVEN YEARS AGO

Logan Carter was on top of the world, and, even though his boyfriend, Ryan, liked to tease him about not being expressive enough—*you're such a stick-in-the-mud, Logan*—as he walked across campus with a friend, he was sure that anyone who looked at him could see it.

His heart felt radiant. Everything was going right.

"All I'm saying is that if you guys get any bigger, you're going to be attending dinner parties with Bill Gates one of these days," his friend Matthew said, grinning. "Have you *seen* the share values of Rise lately? I think you owe Professor Patel one hell of a thank-you gift."

Logan choked back a laugh, sure that his own smile

must stretch from ear-to-ear. He *had* seen the share values, actually. Rise, the movie and music streaming service he and Ryan had started two years ago as a class project, was exploding. It was a dream come true... but the love he'd found with Ryan as they'd built the company was far and away the best part of that dream.

"I still can't believe Rise became what it is," Logan admitted, shaking his head.

Matthew hitched a brow, eyes bright and playful. "Believe it, baby. Your stocks have jumped *again*, and yes, I'm watching."

Logan laughed. *All* their classmates were, along with the tech and finance worlds. It was surreal.

"You're sitting at ten billion dollars right now," Matthew went on. "Billion. With a *B*—"

"Stock value isn't the same as real money," Logan interrupted, something he reminded Ryan of all the time.

"And I'm willing to bet you haven't even hit the ceiling yet," Matthew insisted, waving off Logan's comment.

Ten billion dollars. Logan laughed again. Surreal didn't even begin to describe it. Once Rise's potential had become clear, he and Ryan had both gone balls out to bring the service to market—Ryan with his knack for marketing and ability to charm investors, and Logan with everything else. Their success felt great, but, in Logan's opinion, even better was seeing how happy it made the man he loved.

If Logan were honest, it was the reason he was investing so much time into it.

Ryan may have been right about Logan not being the most expressive guy in the world, but doing his part to help take Rise all the way to the top was the best way Logan could think of to show Ryan just how much he meant to him. A few busy years of working around-the-clock seemed a small price to pay, given that Logan hoped they'd be spending the rest of their lives together. And, thanks to Rise's success, they'd be living on a level that neither one of them had ever expected to.

"You seeing Ryan tonight?" Matthew asked as they walked.

Logan nodded. "We're supposed to go out for dinner."

Although Logan and Ryan both could afford to live off-campus, they'd chosen to stay in the dorms out of convenience until they both finished their MBAs. Well, for Logan it was out of convenience, he suspected that Ryan felt differently. Even though he bitched about it, Ryan seemed to thrive on the attention he got when he was seen around the campus where it had all started.

Today, Logan's last class had unexpectedly canceled. Just one more sign that everything was going his way, he thought, grinning. He was looking forward to stealing a few extra hours with his boyfriend.

"I'm shocked," Matthew teased, shoulder bumping him. "You're actually tearing yourself away from work long enough to eat something that doesn't come in a plastic wrapper?"

Logan laughed. *Again.* He seemed to be doing that a

lot lately, and it felt good. But the truth was that Matthew was right. Logan had been working so hard over the past few months—making sure that the launch of Rise's mobile version went as smoothly as possible—that he hadn't taken the time to do much of anything else.

Ryan complained about it constantly... another reason Logan was glad to have the afternoon off.

"Honestly, Logan," Matthew said warmly. "I can't believe you two have come this far. I remember when we were all studying as undergraduates, clueless but eager, and now look at you."

"Still clueless, but no less eager," Logan joked. They arrived outside the dorms, and he turned to Matthew. "I still don't know what the hell I'm doing."

"That's not what I hear," Matthew said, laughing. "You're like some kind of business prodigy."

Logan shrugged. That part was easy, but he could never have handled the people-parts of Rise. "If Ryan weren't there to guide us into the marketplace, Rise would still be just a vague idea in a computer lab somewhere, or something that never made it off paper and into reality. The two of us are a team, but he's the better half of us. He's... everything."

Matthew's lips twitched, and he pressed his back to the red brick wall, looking Logan over. "Better half? Look at you, gushing. A few years ago, I never would've believed it of you."

Logan grinned. Was he gushing? He was in love, and he refused to feel embarrassed about it.

Growing up, his parents had constantly reminded him that his best efforts fell short of their expectations. When his sexuality had come to light, they'd written him off completely, and the rejection had caused him to build a protective shell around himself—one that only Ryan, and the immersion in the work they'd done together with Rise, had been able to break through.

"I've got to take off," Matthew said. He nodded toward the dorm, winking, "But if Ryan's up there, I'm sure you won't miss me."

"He should be. We were texting about our dinner plans earlier, and he didn't mention going anywhere else."

Matthew headed back across the campus and Logan took the stairs two at a time, suddenly impatient to see Ryan. Ryan didn't have classes this time of day, and Logan hoped he *would* find him in their room. He seemed to be in luck, because the door wasn't locked, and as Logan let himself in he decided it was just one more sign that everything was meant to be.

That feeling died, though, as soon as the door swung open.

Ryan *was* there, but he wasn't alone. He was naked, pressed facedown into the mattress of the bed they'd bought together a few months before... with another man thrusting into him from behind.

The scene before him was unmistakable, but, for an agonizing few seconds, Logan tried to convince himself that it wasn't really happening.

"Ryan?" Logan's voice sounded broken, and his stomach twisted into a sickening knot.

Ryan lifted his head from the mattress, a flash of guilt showing in his eyes before they narrowed and hardened. "I'm busy, Logan," he grunted. "You know... *busy?* Your favorite word."

The man who was fucking Ryan glanced back, but didn't stop, and, after holding Logan's gaze for another moment, Ryan buried his face back in the pillow, his moans escalating.

Logan staggered backward, feeling shattered. He wanted to tell them to stop, to have Ryan explain. To go back to how it had been. How he'd *thought* it had been. Ten billion dollars—with a B—had never been Logan's dream, and it would never be enough to buy what Logan had just lost.

What, maybe, had never really been his in the first place. Not if Ryan could do... *this.*

Logan had only been *busy* because he'd wanted to give Ryan what Ryan wanted: Rise's success. To make him happy. To show him how much Logan cared. He'd wanted Ryan to know that he loved him... but, clearly, Logan's love wasn't enough.

Logan wasn't enough.

Or, maybe... love wasn't enough.

And, as he stumbled out of the room where his heart

had just been broken, Logan vowed that believing it could be was a mistake he'd never make again.

Chapter 1

LOGAN

THE COLD CHICAGO AFTERNOON CHASED LOGAN THROUGH the doors of the bLoved headquarters building, nipping at his ankles. The wind coming off Lake Michigan was wickedly cold, and while the New York winters he was used to were equally as terrible, somehow he still never felt quite prepared for the terror that was Chicago in January.

Not that it mattered. Business was business, and personal comfort didn't play a part in it.

Investing in the popular gay dating app, bLoved, had been a move that was part smart business, part a cynical fuck-you to the idea of love. Reducing love to nothing more than an algorithm had appealed to Logan, fitting perfectly with his own disillusionment about the whole institution. His personal assistant, Hiro, liked to needle him about it— implying that since bLoved was the only company Logan had backed in whose operations he actually involved himself, there must be a part of him that *wanted* to believe in love—but Logan knew the truth.

If love existed, it wasn't for the likes of him.

In the years since Ryan's betrayal, he'd learned to content himself with the one thing that he was good at: making money. And, if some of that money happened to come from bLoved members looking for love, it wasn't his place to warn them off from the heartache that was sure to follow.

"At this rate, we'll be lucky to get out of the meeting at six. And that's assuming that Kelly's 'mysterious agenda item' doesn't hold us up even longer," Hiro said. The weather had made them late. "You may not make your... *appointment...* this evening."

"Don't start," Logan said. Why Hiro insisted on teasing him about his insistence on scheduling an appointment with his tailor every month when they flew in to Chicago was beyond him. In business, it was important to look professional. He wasn't going to let that slide, and he wasn't sure he had the patience for Hiro's brand of teasing about it today, not on top of the shit show that the weather had turned their commute from New York into. He gave Hiro a hard look. "I'm well aware that we're going to have to reschedule. It's not as though I planned for there to be delays due to inclement weather, but I'm counting on you to make sure the appointment still happens, regardless of how late this meeting runs."

Hiro's lips twitched, but he managed to keep a straight face as he asked, "I assume you'll want the appointment kept regardless of... who's available?"

"No," Logan said, the inconvenience of the whole trip making the word come out more clipped than Hiro deserved. Hiro knew Logan's priorities, and right now, his teasing was bordering on annoying. "You know I only want Trevor Rogers."

Hiro laughed, but nodded, mumbling something that sounded a lot like, "Mm-hmm, I thought so," as they reached the conference room doors.

Logan had made the mistake of commenting on Trevor's appearance to Hiro once, and ever since, Hiro had acted as if Logan's insistence on using Trevor's impeccable service might have an ulterior motive. Which was ridiculous. Logan didn't mix business with pleasure.

Ever.

Few people teased Logan and got away with it, but Hiro had worked for him for so long that Logan told himself he had no choice but to put up with it. The man did his job well, and if he insisted on getting a little more personal with Logan than was strictly necessary at times, it wasn't like Logan could afford to lose his services. Still, today, Hiro was testing his patience.

Kelly Davis, bLoved's founder, had sent a cryptic

message that morning about adding an unexpected item to the meeting's agenda. That alone had forewarned Logan that the meeting might end up running late, and now—after their flight from New York had been delayed for four hours, and then the snowfall in Chicago had slowed the driver he'd hired to get them to bLoved's headquarters—he didn't need the reminder from Hiro about how the delays would affect his plans. The one bright spot to the monthly bLoved business meeting that he attended—his standing appointment with Trevor Rogers at Ashby's department store—was in jeopardy, and the fact had his day teetering on the edge of going from inconvenient to downright miserable.

The conference room was spartan, with utilitarian gray carpet that stretched from wall to wall and office chairs positioned at even intervals, almost all of which were empty as Logan and Hiro stepped inside. So far, all profits had been poured back into the company, and between Logan's business guidance, the remarkable success of the love-match algorithms Kelly had come up with, and Kelly's engaging persona as the public face of the company, bLoved had taken off faster than any of them had expected.

They were about to launch a marketing campaign that would take them to the next level, and bLoved was poised on the brink of the kind of success that was reminiscent of Logan's early days with Rise.

Logan pushed the uncomfortable thought away. Rise—and Ryan—were his past. He preferred no reminders.

A uniformed police officer stood stiffly at one end of the room, and Logan's eyebrows shot up in surprise as he took a seat. He could only assume that the officer's presence had to do with Kelly's "unexpected agenda item."

Kelly—leaning back in one of the chairs, dressed in a solid black, fitted T-shirt that didn't even come close to business attire—gave him a strained smile. "Logan," he said in greeting, his normally cheerful voice subdued. "Hey, Hiro."

"Kelly." Logan nodded back at his business partner stiffly. He couldn't help liking and admiring Kelly, even if he doubted the other man suspected it. But today, he was feeling a bit too put-upon to make an effort at any show of friendliness.

Frank Kahele, the head of their marketing department, and Richard Lisowski, the head of finance, were also seated at the table. Both executives were dressed far more formally than Kelly was, but all three men shared a tension that was unusual for their normally upbeat monthly meetings.

Logan gestured Hiro closer and addressed him in a low voice. "Reschedule the flight back to New York for tomorrow and book us a place to stay overnight. Call to reschedule the appointment at Ashby's with Trevor to later tonight." He nodded subtly in the direction of the officer, adding, "I have a feeling that we'll be even later than anticipated."

"No disrespect, Logan," Hiro said, dropping his characteristic good cheer for a more serious professionalism that, normally, Logan would have appreciated. "But is visiting your tailor at Ashby's *that* important? Why don't you just let me cancel it, so we can make a late flight back to New York? We'll be back here in Chicago next month, anyway... or I can even book you an appointment at the Ashby's in New York for later this week, if getting a few new shirts is really that urgent."

Logan had started shaking his head before Hiro had finished talking. "Absolutely not," he said, his hard tone nonnegotiable. "Move the Ashby's appointment to later." Hiro opened his mouth, looking like he might protest, but before he could, Logan added a firm, "Later *tonight*."

Hiro's expression stretched thin, and he waited a beat as if to give Logan a chance to change his mind, but Logan wasn't going to budge. Hiro might accuse him of being stuck in his ways, but after wasting the entire day on shitty weather and now this... this... *whatever* it was, that Kelly had in store at the meeting, there was no way Logan was willing to give up the best part of his monthly trip to Chicago.

"Fine," Hiro finally murmured, nodding. "I'll step outside the conference room to handle it, but let me know if you need me."

"Thank you," Logan said stiffly. Even if Hiro thought he was being unreasonable, Logan knew he could be trusted to make it happen. "I'll be fine."

Once Hiro left the room, Logan turned his attention to Kelly and the gathered executives. "I apologize for my delay," he said into the weighted silence. "Why don't we begin by addressing the elephant in the room? Kelly, what's been happening with bLoved that involves the police?"

The officer pushed himself off the wall and walked to stand behind Kelly's left shoulder. He leaned across the table, extending his hand and introducing himself before Kelly had a chance to answer Logan's question. Logan's eyes flicked to Kelly, making note that Kelly's normally cheerful expression had been replaced by an uncharacteristic irritation.

And under that, the briefest flash of... fear?

"It's Officer Byrne, Mr. Carter," the police officer said politely. Logan rose from his seat to shake the officer's hand. "I've been assigned to watch Mr. Davis while our department investigates the death threats against him."

"*What?*" A chill went through Logan, and his attention immediately shifted from Officer Byrne back to his business partner.

Kelly was shaking his head—whatever Logan had thought he'd seen on his face a moment before replaced with an air of casual amusement that Kelly almost managed to make look real. "It's no big deal, Logan," he said. "Nothing's actually *happened*. Just some empty threats."

"The threat recovered from your bedroom is a very big deal," Officer Byrne interjected, turning to address Kelly directly. "The intruder entered your home while you and your boyfriend—"

Kelly rolled his eyes, interjecting, "He was just a hook-up."

"While you and *Mr. Wilson* were sleeping," Officer Byrne continued, correcting himself without comment. "As we've discussed, the threat is serious enough that our department is taking action, and we expect your cooperation in doing the same."

Logan stared hard at Kelly, assessing. He'd never let himself become involved in Kelly's personal life—mixing business and personal relationships, even when it came to simple friendship, was not a mistake he was likely to repeat—but hearing that Kelly had received death threats was horrific.

Kelly wasn't normally one to hide his feelings, and even though Logan could see that he was making a valiant effort to do so now—one that would have fooled most people into thinking he really wasn't bothered by the situation—Logan was an expert at keeping feelings under wraps, and saw right through him. Kelly was worried.

"It doesn't sound like Officer Byrne thinks it's an empty threat, Kelly," Logan said seriously. "You need to take care of yourself. What kind of cooperation are the police looking for?"

"For as long as the Internet has been around, there have been trolls," Kelly said dismissively, waving off Logan's concern. "It's not the first time I've received hate mail. The cops keep trying to make it into a bigger deal than it really is, but I'm not going to let it get to me, Logan... or let it interfere with bLoved."

"When that *hate mail* is being personally delivered onto your private property and sewn into the pillow next to your head, it's time to take action," Officer Byrne said sternly, his lips thinning a little as he shot Kelly an exasperated look. "Breaking and entering paired with death threats is nothing to laugh off or ignore, Mr. Davis."

Kelly shrugged. "It's par for the course when you're successful," he said flippantly, shooting Logan an apologetic look.

Despite the disruption to their normal business agenda, though, Logan didn't require an apology. He'd like to know that Kelly was safe, and if he had to couch that in terms of business success for bLoved, then so be it.

"What information can you release to us?" Logan asked Officer Byrne. "I'm assuming that the threats have something to do with bLoved, based on your presence here?"

Officer Byrne nodded. "Mr. Davis has apparently received multiple death threats over the course of the last month, although the first *reported* incident wasn't until last week." He accompanied that statement with an irritated look at Kelly, then continued. "A Mr. Eric Wilson—a guest of Mr. Davis's—discovered the latest letter sewn into one of Mr. Davis's bed pillows upon waking. I have—I mean, the *department* has reason to believe that the threats are tied to dissatisfaction with results from the bLoved dating site."

"Someone thinks I stole their boyfriend." Kelly rolled

his eyes. "Simple jealousy blown out of proportion just because I'm in the public eye. I don't even know which hookup they're upset about."

"But are you closing in on a suspect?" Logan asked Officer Byrne, not bothering to respond to Kelly's assessment. It wasn't his place to judge Kelly's love life, especially not when he understood the motivation behind Kelly's serial dating. Or, as he'd overheard Kelly joke to one of their staff once, his serial *fucking*... it was a sad irony that the creator of the dating website geared toward finding love had been let down by its failure to find it for himself, and had resigned himself to a constant stream of hookups in its stead.

Kelly leaned forward, cutting off Officer Byrne's attempt to reply. "It's not going to amount to anything, Logan," he said. "I don't understand why everyone is taking this so seriously. When you get on television, people start to recognize your face, and sometimes it gets a little crazy. It happens all the time."

It was clear to Logan that Kelly wasn't getting the message. Logan didn't let a lot of people into his life, and even though he would have claimed that his relationship with Kelly was strictly a formal one, knowing there was threat against the younger man concerned him more than he'd like to admit. In his own way, Kelly had been as unlucky in love as Logan had, and Logan would be lying if he said it didn't make him feel some kinship for the man.

"How do we keep Kelly safe?" he asked Officer Byrne.

"We have strong reason to believe that these threats

need to be taken seriously," Officer Byrne answered cryptically. "While it's true that they've been directed at Mr. Davis personally, they're definitely tied to his involvement with bLoved."

"*Everything* I do is tied to bLoved—" Kelly started to say, sounding exasperated. He cut himself off abruptly when Hiro reentered the conference room, cell phone in hand.

Hiro raised an eyebrow, clearly realizing he'd interrupted, but Kelly waved him toward Logan. "Go ahead," he said, looking grateful for an excuse to avoid dealing with the topic of his personal safety for a few minutes.

Hiro hurried to Logan's side, updating him in a low voice. "Your appointment at Ashby's has been rescheduled, but unfortunately Trevor will be off work in two hours. If we can't get there by then, he's recommended that you work with someone by the name of Jose Mendoza, instead."

"No," Logan snapped, his lips tightening. Even if it seemed petty in light of what was happening with Kelly, there was no way he was going to skip out on his one indulgence. "Make it happen, Hiro. Offer Trevor an extra day's pay if he stays late to take the appointment. If he refuses, go higher until it's worth his while."

Money may not have been able to buy happiness, but at least it could buy convenience. Logan wasn't interested in dealing with a different Ashby's employee. He wanted Trevor.

"*Really*, Logan?" Hiro asked quietly, cutting his eyes

toward Officer Byrne. He wasn't up to speed on what was happening, but his exasperated tone clearly conveyed that he suspected Logan's priorities were misplaced. "It looks like you may be needed here for a while, and with the shitty weather, it would be nice to get back home to New York tonight, don't you think? Do you really want to go to all of this trouble for one store clerk?"

"Trevor is worth the effort." Logan knew he'd put on what Hiro sometimes jokingly called his stone face, but inside, he was a complex network of emotions.

Officer Byrne had convinced him that the danger to Kelly's life wasn't to be taken lightly, and—on top of Logan's genuine concern for his business partner—the thought of having to deal with a different Ashby's employee was intolerable. The others were certainly pleasant enough, but he suspected that they would prefer to avoid him. Trevor, on the other hand, actually seemed to look forward to his visits. His cheerful, slightly irreverent personality never dulled when Logan was around, no matter how unexpressive Logan remained.

And, at the moment, Logan definitely needed some cheer in his life.

Hiro looked like he might be marshaling another argument, but Logan didn't want to hear it. "Please arrange for it, Hiro," he said in a clipped tone, knowing the other men in the room had been following every word, despite Logan and Hiro keeping their voices low.

"Yes, sir." Hiro's jaw tightened, and his reply was just as short as Logan's had been, the "sir" a clear indication that he was feeling irritated, too.

As far as Logan was concerned, though, Hiro could be upset all he wanted. Logan's appointments with Trevor were the only bright point of his monthly business trips to Chicago. Once he was back in New York, the next four weeks would be business as usual—business, *period*, since Logan didn't make time in his life for much else—and the thought of returning to the bleakness of his daily life without an injection of Trevor's vibrant, upbeat personality felt even grimmer in light of the distressing news about the threats to Kelly.

He refused to do it.

Hiro left the room again, and once the door was shut behind him, Kelly laughed. "You sure are putting your PA through the ringer, aren't you?"

"Just for today." Logan set his jaw. "Now tell me, Kelly, are the threats against your life going to affect bLoved? You've just claimed that the whole thing is due to your presence in the public eye, but Frank's got a slew of appearances scheduled for you from here until Valentine's Day for the upcoming promotion, doesn't he?"

Logan turned to their marketing head to confirm, and Frank nodded, leaning forward. "That's right," he said. "And our whole campaign is basically fucked if he *doesn't* do the appearances."

"I have strongly recommended that Mr. Davis remain

out of the public eye until the threat is resolved," Officer Byrne said, stepping forward. "If he skips town for a while, all the better. In fact, I've already recommended that he be escorted by a bodyguard since we won't be able to provide police protection once he leaves our jurisdiction. Hiring someone full-time may become expensive, but—"

"Money isn't an issue," Logan interrupted. They could call it a business expense, although Logan would arrange to personally cover the cost if bLoved couldn't. Officer Byrne exuded a grim confidence about the danger to Kelly, and Logan wasn't inclined doubt him. Kelly's safety was the most important issue at hand.

"*Money* may not be an issue, but laying low definitely is," Frank cut in. He straightened, tension radiating from him. The current promotion was Frank's baby, and Logan knew just as well as the rest of them how much of the brand's success was tied to having Kelly be the face of it. Frank continued, addressing Officer Byrne. "Like Logan just said, we have back-to-back public appearances scheduled for Kelly for the next six weeks, and the publicity is vital to bLoved's success. We're at a critical stage of growth at the moment where we're attracting all the right kinds of attention, but if we don't nurture that attention, it's going to wither. Getting Kelly out there to speak and promote the company is *essential*."

Officer Byrne's brows lowered, but before he could respond, Richard, head of finance, jumped in. "We've poured a lot of money into making sure we're in a position to cut into the top competitor's market share," he said. "If Kelly drops out, we will have wasted a significant investment that it's unlikely we'll ever be able to recover. There are other players coming to market, and timing is critical."

"But we're not *like* any of our competitors," Kelly insisted, leaning forward with passion in his eyes. Despite the seriousness of the situation, it almost made Logan want to smile. He knew Kelly's words were sincere and heartfelt, and the animated delivery that was so compelling to the public was exactly what had tipped the scales when Logan had been considering investing in bLoved in the first place. Even if love was bullshit, Kelly *believed*, and Kelly's belief—despite his own lack of love—could sell anyone on it. "bLoved isn't about just hooking up," Kelly continued. "It's about finding true, lasting *love*. And the algorithms *work*. The site has been successful at doing it, time and time again. You *know* the testimonials aren't staged. Our 'competitors' can't compete with us, because they're selling something totally different."

"And *this* is why we need you as the face during this advertising season," Frank said, smacking the table. "That passion? That dedication? You sell it, Kelly. There's no way you can skip town. Without you in front of the camera, the advertising we've got set up will fall flat."

"If Kelly had a bodyguard with him, do you think having him do the publicity would be safe?" Logan asked, directing the question to Officer Byrne. The idea didn't sit well with him, but Frank was right. From a business stand-point, bLoved really would be screwed if they lost Kelly for the next couple of months.

"No," Officer Byrne said flatly, crossing his arms.

"*Fuck*," Kelly said softly, slumping back in his chair. The fact that he didn't put up more of a fight was telling. Logan knew that bLoved meant everything to Kelly, but for all his talk, he was obviously more concerned about the death threats than he was letting on.

"We'll find a work-around," Logan said, speaking to Frank and Richard with his gaze. "We can explain Kelly's absence away somehow. Put a spin on it that we can sell. Ideas?"

Richard tapped his pen against the table, grimacing, and Frank leaned back in his chair, directing his gaze at the ceiling. He ran a hand over his face, muttering. Logan was about to prompt them when Frank suddenly bolted upright, grinning.

"A romantic retreat," he said, the despair of a moment before morphing into excitement. "We'll say that after years of looking for it... after building the whole damn site just to find it... Kelly's finally met his match. He's found real love *at last*—" Kelly winced, and Logan shot him an apologetic look as Frank went on, "—and he's retreated from the public eye to enjoy some time with his new man. The talk shows we've got scheduled will eat up the reason for his cancelation! We can come up with a profile for the mystery lover, and if anyone does discover Kelly wherever he's laying low, the story will support the presence of his bodyguard. We'll play the man off as Kelly's one true love."

Richard was nodding. "Building a narrative like that is going to drive up interest in the brand," he agreed, starting to look equally excited. "But I don't like the idea of canceling his appearances altogether. We don't want to lose that airtime. Maybe Kelly can do a live video feed without disclosing his location? We can even throw the bodyguard a bonus to show his face, ham it up as Kelly's love interest..."

As they pitched ideas, Logan watched Kelly's face sour. Chronically single Kelly, who'd spent his life looking for love—a modern day Eros whose heart was destined to be forever alone—the public ate it up, but Logan could see that Frank's scenario hit a little too close to home for the younger man.

Kelly's bLoved profile had never been matched to another user, and both Kelly and a series of independent coders had examined the algorithms and the site's coding, all but turning it inside out, trying to figure out why. They'd never found a glitch that would explain the oddity. Out of millions of users, Kelly's was the only profile not linked to any other, and Logan had heard him joke more than once that it must mean he simply wasn't lovable.

Kelly had total faith in the effectiveness of the algorithms he'd created—it's why he could sell them so well—but it also meant that their failure to find him a match had convinced him beyond a shadow of a doubt that love wasn't out there for *him*.

"Right, okay, everyone slow down." Kelly held out his hands to stop the conversation. "So let's say I get this sexy hunk of a bodyguard to follow me around, and you ship me off to somewhere out of the way so I can lay low until the storm blows over. I do everything via video feed—"

"No," Officer Byrne said flatly, interrupting. "None of you are taking this seriously enough. You need to stay completely out of the public eye, Mr. Davis. Any form of public appearance not only puts you at risk, but will hamper our investigation and your bodyguard's ability to keep you safe."

"Maybe we hire someone else to do the publicity appearances?" Richard mused, his pen tapping again. "Although... is that really going to fly?"

"I don't think so," Frank said immediately. "We've been selling bLoved as much more than just a business venture. It's something Kelly *believes* in, and our target market responds to that. If we put some talking head up there who's not connected to the company, who doesn't share that vision, it's just not going to sell."

All eyes in the room turned in Logan's direction, staring him down as Frank's words brought about a collective realization. The conference room door opened as Hiro let himself back in and took a seat next to Logan, just in time to catch the tail end of the conversation.

"No," Logan said, squaring his shoulders and narrowing his eyes. "Obviously not."

Frank grinned. "You'll have to," he insisted. "The people know you're the silent partner in bLoved, and they know *just* enough about you that you're still a mystery. You know how people love a mystery."

"My schedule won't allow it," Logan snapped, tensing up. Yes, he wanted Kelly to be safe, and of course he wanted bLoved to remain profitable, but there was no way he would allow himself to be thrust into the limelight like that. Logan didn't *do* publicity... and he certain didn't do *love*.

"Actually, I'm pretty sure the scheduling would work out just fine," Hiro said, whipping out his tablet to access Logan's calendar as he prepared to throw him under the bus. Hiro scrolled through his screen rapidly, then pinned Logan with a much-too-innocent-looking stare. "From now through the end of February, you don't have any meetings or events that couldn't be pushed back or canceled."

Was that revenge for making Hiro jump through hoops to book Trevor for his Ashby's appointment? Logan glowered at him, but Hiro just gave him a bland just-doing-my-job smile in return.

"Seriously?" Kelly broke the tension, bursting out in laughter. Once he composed himself, he brushed at the corner of his eyes to wipe away his tears and shook his head. "Okay, let's get real. There's no way Logan could do that. He doesn't even *believe* in love." He threw Logan a look with just a hint of exasperated affection in it, rolling his eyes. They'd gone round and round about the subject more times than Logan could count, finally agreeing to disagree. "Could you imagine him trying to sell our services with a straight face? We'd have people canceling their memberships left and right."

"Right. I can't do it," Logan agreed, settling back in his chair. "We're going to have to think of something else."

"You *have* to do it," Richard said. He flipped open a notebook, hastily jotting down figures that Logan couldn't make out from across the table. "Here are the numbers we've spent on booking appearances and ensuring that bLoved's name is on the media's lips. Beneath that are my estimates for the percentages of losses we will see each quarter going forward if we cancel those appearances. Keeping in mind that using someone else—someone not already connected to bLoved—will reflect just as badly on the company and produce similar results."

Richard tore the paper from his notebook and slid it across the table to Logan.

Logan scowled when he looked at it, then returned his attention to Richard. The numbers were big enough to get his attention. Even though he could readily absorb the loss on a personal level, it would hamstring the business, not to mention Kelly's future.

"And?" Logan prompted, trying to ignore the sinking feeling in his stomach. There could still be another workaround.

"And... *here* is the bare minimum I know we can afford to spend to hire on a PR coach. We'll find a professional to help you ace the publicity appearances, someone who can guarantee that you'll be able to sell the product just as well as Kelly would. It will take us over budget, but the expense will be well worth it if it means salvaging the campaign."

Another sheet of paper joined the first, and Logan tried to consider the figures unemotionally. If he could lean on the advice of a coach, would he really be able to do it?

He stifled a sigh, rubbing the bridge of his nose. It still sounded like his own personal version of hell.

"We'll send the itinerary to you, Hiro, so you can make sure Logan's schedule is cleared for the publicity appearances we've set up," Frank said decisively, steamrolling ahead as if Logan had already agreed. "As soon as we locate a suitable coach, we'll email you his or her contact details... I've got some contacts I can tap on Monday, so we should be able to get someone lined up next week. We'll have to take the loss on the first *Morning Show* appearance—" he grimaced, "—but we might actually be able to pull this off, offsetting the story we put out about Kelly with playing up the mystery of the silent partner..."

Kelly mouthed a silent "sorry" across the table at Logan as Frank, Hiro, and Richard continued making plans that Logan wanted passionately to back out of. But Officer Byrne was nodding along, too, and Logan wasn't about to tell Kelly that he couldn't stomach a few public appearances when Kelly's safety was on the line.

He gritted his teeth, settling back in his chair, and nodded.

Outside the conference room windows, the snow was coming down harder than ever, and they still had the regular business portion of the meeting to get through once the issues of the Valentine's Day campaign and Kelly's safety were out of the way.

Thank God for his appointment at Ashby's later.

"Did Trevor confirm?" Logan asked Hiro quietly as the conversation went on around them. Hiro nodded, and Logan felt some of the tension ease out of his shoulders.

It was one small kindness on an otherwise bleak day, but it was all that Logan had to look forward to, and now—faced with the daunting prospect of having to sell the public on the kind of love he no longer believed in—Logan was going to need that escape more than ever.

Chapter 2

TREVOR

"H E'S PAYING YOU OVERTIME TO STAY LATE? DUDE, where can I get me one of those reclusive wealthy businessmen types?" Jose expertly folded one of the shirts knocked askew on the display table without looking and set it back on the pile. "How much overtime are we talking? Time and a half? Double time?"

"He's literally doubling what I would have made today." Trevor shook out one of the severely wrinkled shirts, looked it over, and sighed. Whoever had decided to knock the stack and leave its shirts scattered had done the product an incredible disservice. He was going to have to steam this one to get it back to some semblance of newness. "Not that it's such a bad thing. Things got way out of hand this afternoon, and I was busting my buns to keep up with the customers. While I appreciate the fab things the cardio's going to do for my body, it wouldn't have been fair to leave the floor a mess. At least this way, you don't have to straighten it up all on your own."

"Nah, dude, it's chill." Jose shrugged a single shoulder and folded up the next shirt just as quickly as the first. "We all know what it's like. Customers always come at the worst times—like when you're trying to go home."

"Or right through the doors, seconds before you're ready to lock up," Trevor said with a grin.

"Guess your sexy Mr. Sourpuss takes the cake, though." Jose paused and rolled his shoulders back, then stretched his neck from side to side. "Asking you to stay late for a shift like that, out of the blue. I mean, money speaks, you know? But for real, I'm not sure how you handle him all the time. That guy gives vibes like he's got his own permanent raincloud over his head. I don't think I've ever seen him smile."

Trevor bit back a smile of his own. Jose was right... sort of. But every now and then Trevor managed to make Logan Carter look like he might be *thinking* about smiling, and that was... well, it was actually way more rewarding than it should be. Especially for some rich guy on whom Trevor had spent far more time than he should have making up ridiculously over-the-top scenarios about to explain his stoic behavior.

The truth was that he'd been stupidly disappointed when Logan's assistant had called to say he wouldn't make it in on time... and then a little too eager when the assistant had called back a second time saying that Mr. Carter would make it worth Trevor's while if he would stay late. Trevor was embarrassed to think about how close he'd come to saying yes, even before the extra pay had been offered. It wasn't like he actually flirted with the man—well, not any more than he flirted with anyone—but there was something satisfying about their monthly appointments that Trevor, who preferred spontaneity over routine and would deny to his dying breath that he could ever be anything as mundane as predictable, didn't want to think too hard about why he liked.

Especially because Logan most definitely never flirted back.

"He's not that bad," Trevor said, sorting through the fallen shirts and selecting another few that would need a little extra attention to be display-worthy again. He draped them over his arm so he could steam them all at once. "From time to time I see his lips twitch, and he doesn't talk too much, so it's not like he's overbearing."

"But his *energy*, dude," Jose insisted. "Man, if I could, I'd get him some crystals or, I don't know, burn some sage around him or something. Dude's got negative mojo. Big business must've gotten to him, sucked his soul out."

"You're salty." Trevor stuck his tongue out. He collected the last of the shirts and turned on his heels, determined not to let Jose get to his head. "He's really not that bad if you give him a chance. Some people are just a little bit tougher to crack than others."

"Don't lie," Jose said as Trevor wandered off to survey the rest of the aisles in search of wrinkled clothes. "You just like the tips."

"It's not *just* the tip I'm interested in." Trevor winked, falling back on innuendo to avoid thinking too hard about his instinct to jump to Logan's defense. "You should know that by now."

Jose laughed, shaking his head, and Trevor whisked himself away to run his survey of the section. With practiced ease, he swept the aisle and pulled clothes that needed a little extra care, then made his way back to the fitting rooms to pull the steamer out.

For a year now, Logan Carter had been visiting Ashby's once a month to update his wardrobe, and every time he visited, he requested Trevor's personal assistance. The first few times their paths had crossed were accidental. Trevor had just happened to be the one working the menswear department when Logan had come in, and—ever professional and eager to see the job through—Trevor hadn't let Logan's distant, dour personality scare him off. The man didn't speak much, and he emoted even less, but he was a customer all the same, and Trevor had shown him the respect and appreciation he deserved.

Not to mention that Trevor was always up for a challenge.

And not to mention *either* that yes, Logan was hella hot.

By the third time their paths had crossed, they'd exchanged names and Trevor had started to see a glimmer of the man Logan was beneath the business front. Well, either that, or he was making it all up to entertain himself. But still, when Logan started calling ahead to book Trevor's fitting services in advance, and—as far as Trevor knew—refusing to be fitted by anyone else, there was no way to deny that he'd been flattered. He'd always been a sucker for attention, but there was something about the way Logan gave it to him that made him feel appreciated. Seen. Valued.

Trevor gave himself a mental eye roll. He knew he was good at his job, and for all the time he spent putting too much thought into the mystery that was Logan Carter, the man undoubtedly appreciated good service and quite obviously had the means to pay for it, and his attention to Trevor most likely stemmed from nothing more than that. Still, there was a story behind Logan's cool personality and steely countenance, and each conversation brought Trevor a step closer to cracking the man's shell.

Humming beneath his breath, Trevor hung the shirts up and filled the steamer with water, then let it heat. Now that the Christmas rush was over, business had slowed down, and nights at the upscale department store were quiet. Trevor had been on the floor for more than nine hours, though, and if it hadn't been for the little buzz of adrenaline at the thought of Logan coming in, Trevor would have been more than ready to call it a day.

"Dude," Jose wandered over. "You know you really don't have to deal with the steaming, right? You put in your time today. Take a nap beneath the counter until your appointment shows up. Krista's not going to mind."

Jose was probably right about their shift manager, but as long as he was still there anyway, Trevor wasn't going to just sit around and leave Jose with whatever work there still was to do.

"Steaming things takes zero effort," he replied. "Just accept my help, okay? It's not my style to nap on the job, anyway. Or... is this just because you want me to leave it for you? Need some busywork to keep you distracted while Logan is in the store?" Trevor winked, brandishing the steaming wand in Jose's direction as he teased him. "You may think he's hard to get along with, but you've got to admit, he's *definitely* not hard on the eyes."

"Nah, it's not like that," Jose said, his face immediately taking on a dreamy expression that alerted Trevor to exactly what was about to happen. He stifled a groan, bracing himself internally for the sap he knew was about to spew from his friend's lips. And sure enough: "You know I got Barry, dude. I can't even *look* at other guys anymore."

"Pretty sure that other guys are still attractive, even when you're dating someone else," Trevor said. The words came across a little more stiffly than he would have liked, and he turned to the clothes he'd hooked up to start to steam the wrinkles out. He wasn't jealous. Like, not even remotely. But still, the whole "I'm so in lurrvvvvvv" thing seemed to be happening everywhere around him lately, and yeah, okay. It maybe got a little old?

"I mean, I guess so," Jose said, shrugging. "I don't know. When you're in love—" Trevor tried not to roll his eyes, "—it's different. Barry's it for me. And I guess I can still tell someone's attractive, sure, if I think about it for long enough, but... it's like it doesn't matter. Or I don't notice all that much? I can't explain it. It's really one of those things you have to live through and experience on your own."

"Guess I'll have to take your word for it, then." Being bitter wasn't like Trevor in the least, but between Jose's constant weekly updates about his love life, and their friend and former coworker, Elliott's, recent engagement to none other than Ash Ashby—heir to the same Ashby fortune that they all relied on for a paycheck—it felt like Trevor couldn't escape love, no matter which way he turned.

All his friends may have started committing themselves to long-term relationships, but Trevor preferred casual dating. Flirting with new guys was thrilling, and each night out was an adventure. And, even if there were some aspects of the stability and love that his friends' relationships seemed to abound in that might occasionally seem appealing, Trevor certainly wasn't *jealous*.

He was happy for them, and, really, he wasn't the settling-down type, anyway.

Steam rose up and loosened the wrinkles in the shirts, and Trevor focused on the task at hand while Jose sorted through the clothing abandoned in the fitting rooms and left on the sorting rack. They worked in silence, the conversation over, until the song playing from the overhead speakers ended, and another one began.

The string introduction of Etta James' song, "At Last," played, and Jose stopped what he was doing. Trevor saw him pause out of the corner of his eye, and he squared his shoulders and tried to swallow some of the sour taste in his mouth at the stupidly lovestruck expression that Jose wasn't even trying to hide.

"What?" Trevor asked at last. He turned the steamer off and hooked the wand back onto the device. "Don't tell me this is your song."

"No," Jose smiled the same dreamy smile Trevor had seen moments before. "It's just that there's a sound bite from this song that plays whenever you log into bLoved. You know, the dating app that I met Barry through? And every time I hear it, it makes me think of him. Dude, you just... You don't know. You should give the site a try if you're not having any luck with guys."

"I have plenty of luck, thank you very much."

"I mean with love, dude. The algorithms really work."

Trevor started to grimace as he turned toward the relentlessness of Jose, but then it morphed into a stupidly wide grin as he caught sight of the tall blond man in a dark gray car coat heading toward him from across the store.

"I don't need algorithms," Trevor said, grinning at Jose as he riffed off the saptastic love song that had made Jose go all gushy. "Because *at last, my* appointment *has come along.*"

He winked, adding, "Last chance for you to crystallize that bad mojo you said he had, or whatever it is you were talking about."

"Very funny." Jose rolled his eyes, but he wasted no time in ducking out of the fitting room to lose himself amongst the largely empty menswear section.

Setting aside the uncharacteristic negativity that had been stirred up inside him by their conversation, Trevor smoothed his black Ashby's shirt and fixed his black tie. Looking professional was important, even if Trevor's acquaintanceship with Logan had become a little more easy and casual as time went on. Still, even if Logan didn't ever flirt back—hell, Trevor really had no idea if the man was even gay, although he certainly didn't seem put out by *Trevor's* flirting—it never hurt to look his best around a hot man.

"I apologize for being late," Logan said stiffly, as soon as he was within conversational distance. He came to a stop an arm's length away from Trevor, brows lowered in frustration, as if he wanted to explain.

Trevor grinned. The man was paying him to stay late. No explanation necessary. And yep, he was going to stick to that story and ignore the little thrill that had shot through him the minute he saw Logan.

"You're fine, really," Trevor said, meaning it on every single possible level. "It's my pleasure to stay. What are we going to be shopping for today?"

With Logan, the question was almost rhetorical. The

man was the antithesis of spontaneity. But waiting for the answer gave Trevor a chance to reconfirm that Logan really did have the most amazingly colored eyes. Not a crazy unusual shade, like his friend Elliott's fiancé—people all around the world may have touted Ash Ashby as having the most incredible turquoise blue eyes—but Trevor thought Logan had him beat. Rich and bright in color, like cornflowers, Trevor had never seen anything quite like them, and it killed him that Logan didn't dress himself in order to make them really pop.

"Shirts," Logan answered him, somehow managing to make the clipped, impersonal answer still feel like he was happy to see Trevor, too. Or, more likely, Trevor was being ridiculous. "Perhaps, if you have any, some new ties as well."

Okay, definitely a far cry from "I want you." Well, then again, with *ties*, Trevor could imagine all sorts of ways to turn the conversation into something less professional... he cleared his throat, wondering if the long shift was getting to him after all. He really was letting his imagination get away with him this time.

"Jean Marchand came out with a new line," he said, reeling himself in. "We got them in two weeks ago. Beautiful, beautiful work. High class, woven silk, available in both solids and patterns. Let's grab some shirts first, and then we can select the ties that will best complement them. What do you think?"

"That will be fine."

Trevor's lips twitched again. There was a reason no one working menswear at Ashby's enjoyed serving Logan—he came across as detached and standoffish. Straight-laced and career driven, as far as Trevor could tell, he wasn't the walking definition of *fun*. But, fun or not, Trevor enjoyed the challenge of finding the joke that would make Logan almost smile, not to mention the secret little thrill he got on those rare instances when he managed to find a topic that incited Logan to actually engage in more than mono-syllabic conversation.

And, beyond all that of course, Logan was gorgeous.

From time to time, Trevor wondered what it might be like to go out with a man like Logan. He suspected that Logan's coldness was like an iceberg... a lot more under the surface than he ever let show. And sure, Logan may have been withdrawn, but—after all—it took a lot of energy to be as outstandingly charming and funny as Trevor was. Not everyone had it in them. Or maybe Logan just saved his energy for other things.

Trevor bit back a smile, taking the lead as he directed Logan toward a display. "Now, if I remember right, you bought a few pairs of the Hendrix Professionals last time you were in, right?"

Logan nodded.

"And how are they treating you?" Trevor asked after the slightest beat of silence, more than up to the challenge of pulling a few words out of him.

"Well," Logan answered cryptically.

"'Well' as in you'll want some shirts that we'll be able to pair with them to make an outfit, or 'well' as in you're not interested in hurting my feelings by telling me you hate them?" Trevor arched a brow and looked over his shoulder. "Let me know so I can do my job, and, together, we'll make the most out of your money."

"*Well* as in... they're pants, and they fit." Logan arched a brow in return, cutting his eyes toward the rack Trevor was leading him toward and... had he just tried not to smile? Trevor grinned as Logan added, "You know the rules."

"Blacks and grays, or, rarely, darker hues," Trevor recited. Logan's preferences never changed, nor did his measurements. With the frequency of his visits, Trevor had his numbers memorized. "But just let me point out that there are some *really* nice shirts that just came in, a little brighter than you usually go, but that—"

"No."

They came to a stop by a clothing rack, and Trevor started to pull out all the safe bets. Black. Gray. Dark gray. One by one, he draped them over his arm. "Blues would suit you, you know," he said, pulling a royal blue shirt free from the rack and held it to Logan's chest.

Yep, it totally made Logan's eyes pop, and Trevor's gaze flicked up and held Logan's, marveling anew at the incredible color.

If he was going to stay late, he was going to indulge himself a little. After all, Logan had asked for *him*. After a year, the man should know that he was going to be subjected to some mild flirting. Logan had been his customer for so long that Trevor felt comfortable enough to let the odd compliment slip in from time to time, and tonight—whether it was because he was tired or because of something in the air—it seemed to be happening with a little more frequency. As far as he could tell, though, Logan didn't mind. His apparent comfort with it, among other things, definitely pinged Trevor's gaydar, but he'd never actually asked Logan where his attractions lay.

That would have been crossing the line.

Flirting was one thing, but no matter how the familiarity of their regular appointments seemed to lower certain barriers, Trevor was still a professional. Which didn't mean he wasn't up to having a little fun...

"Not everyone can pull off a blue this intense," Trevor said, winking, "but *you*—"

"Stick to the color scheme," Logan said, cutting him off, taking a step back as if the color might somehow accidentally rub off on him.

With a sigh and a pout of his lips, Trevor returned the shirt to the rack and pulled the next one out—gray.

"I guess that's fair," he said, keeping his eyes on the rack. "You don't need color to look handsome—you're naturally attractive."

Logan said nothing about Trevor's remark, but Trevor felt Logan's eyes on him as he worked, and he wondered if the look he was getting was one of reproach or appreciation.

"I'm not going to have time to tailor these tonight, since I had to stay late," Trevor said as he sorted through the display. The last of the shirts he wanted were pulled from the rack, and the weight of them over his arm was starting to become cumbersome. "I know you usually ask for rush service, but is there any way I can maybe get the work done over the next few days? By tomorrow night, maybe?"

"No," Logan responded immediately, but then immediately, and a little softer, "You don't need to worry about it tonight. I'll bring them back with me the next time I visit."

"There are other tailors in Chicago, you know," Trevor said, grateful not to have to tack the work onto the end of the long day. "You don't have to be loyal to my service, and I can give you a few names if it's not convenient for you to come back before next month."

"I don't want anyone else," Logan said, just forcefully enough to make Trevor's eyes snap up to his. Logan's lips tightened for a moment, and he added a stiff, "Sorry, I meant, thank you for the offer of a referral. I've had a long day, too. I didn't mean to snap at you."

Trevor turned away, biting his lip. That was snapping? It had been kind of hot, actually. But Logan's apology was one of those things he'd been thinking about before, the things that made him feel appreciated in ways that—despite all the attention his outgoing personality often got him—he wasn't used to.

"I have no issues with the work you do," Logan was saying. "I'd be a fool to go somewhere else when you offer professional quality and quick turnaround times. No other tailor would suit me as well as you do."

A suggestive comment longed to part from Trevor's lips about how well they *could* suit each other, but he let it die. He was having more trouble than usual maintaining his professionalism during this appointment for some reason, but begging for more of Logan's attention would just be asking for trouble. As he'd just been thinking earlier, he had no problem with casual dating and hookups—preferred it, actually—but the truth was, it had been a while for him. The holidays had been a crazy-busy time, and with so many of his friends in relationships now, Trevor had just been... too busy.

But just because he'd been in a dry spell, it didn't mean Trevor had to start making up some story in his head about his mystery customer being something special. On the contrary, all it meant was that he probably just needed to get laid.

But right now, he needed to take care of Logan.

Logan, who'd said that he didn't want anyone but Trevor.

Trevor turned away so he could lead Logan toward the tie rack without Logan seeing the grin on his face. "It's not as though I can force you into another man's arms," he said. Then, realizing what he said, he jerked around, meeting Logan's eyes.

There was no mistaking it. Logan was almost smiling.

"Er, I mean into the arms of one of my competitors,"

Trevor amended quickly. "But if your loyalty is just some altruistic move on your part to support my tailoring business, I'll have you know that it's doing very well. Business has been growing, and not only do I get a lot of return customers, but it looks like they're telling their friends about me." Logan actually *did* smile at that, and Trevor grinned. He'd worked at Ashby's for years, and truly enjoyed the customer interaction, but he'd always kind of loved the idea of doing his own thing. He relaxed a little, letting some of his genuine excitement at the idea spill out. "The new business I've been getting is outstanding. I'm thinking that maybe, if I'm lucky, I'll be able to drop Ashby's and open up the tailoring business full time."

"Congratulations," Logan said, sounding like he really and truly meant it. The warm utterance warmed Trevor's heart, and when Logan added, "It doesn't surprise me in the least," Trevor's grin widened.

He turned with enthusiasm as they arrived at the tie rack, channeling the rush of emotion there. He gestured at the rack dramatically with one hand, announcing grandly, "Your tie selection. May I recommend... blue?"

"No." The smile had disappeared, but there was a definite lip-twitch.

"You're no fun." Trevor stuck out his tongue. "If you stick to all dark colors, it won't be long before someone stops you while you're in the store under the assumption that you're one of us." He pulled at his black tie in illustration of his point. "An Ashby's employee."

Logan cocked an eyebrow, pulling a black Jean March- and tie from the rack and draping it over Trevor's arm in retaliation.

Was that an honest-to-God hint of playfulness that sparkled in his eyes? Trevor's grin widened even more, and he felt himself growing a little cockier. Maybe his flirting wasn't as misplaced as he'd originally believed.

"If you won't try blue, then you're going to try red." Without asking for approval, Trevor snagged a bold red tie from the collection and let it join the black. "Are you ready to head back to the fitting room now, or am I going to have to force more color on you first?"

Logan's brilliant blue gaze locked on Trevor's, and Trevor found himself stunned into silence. An intensity burned in Logan's eyes that he'd never seen before, as though something had happened to him since the last time they'd met that had unhinged the stern, detached man Logan had always presented himself as, and had turned him into someone *real*.

"Let's see how they fit," Logan said after a beat of silence. "And I'll have you take my measurements again."

Their eyes remained locked for a moment too long. The moment between them was far from casual. Trevor felt it bubble up inside of him, tingling up the length of his spine and drawing him to Logan with shocking intensity.

Did Logan feel it, too?

Trevor's heart started to race, distracting him, and he swallowed hard, trying to push the thought aside. It was ridiculous. He was reading way, way too much into a simple interaction with a customer.

He really just needed to get laid.

He jerked his gaze away to break the spell and turned on his heels, ignoring the thrill of pinpricks down his back and the way his heart beat just a little faster in his chest. A little flirting didn't mean anything, even when body language was involved. Trevor had played around with enough men to know that.

But... when was the last time one of those men had made him feel anything beyond the excitement of the chase?

To fill the silence and drown out his own thoughts, Trevor let himself babble.

"Do you remember my friend, Elliott, who used to work here? Well, last Christmas there was a big to-do about him getting fired, and then it turned out that his boyfriend was the Ashby heir, undercover. You know, *Ash* Ashby?"

Logan didn't reply, but Trevor didn't let that stop his mouth from running off. Although why he suddenly wanted to talk about his friend's love story, when he'd just been thinking how *done* he was with hearing all about everyone he knew settling down and getting all happily-ever-after-ified, he did not know.

"So, anyway Elliott and Ash have been together for a year now, and the two of them just got engaged on Christmas Eve. Right *here*, in the store."

Trevor unlocked the fitting room door, ushering Logan

inside and then hanging the shirts and ties he'd selected up inside the compact space.

"I think if someone proposed to me in a store, I'd die of embarrassment, but, for Elliott, it was actually really sweet. I mean, their relationship kind of came about because of Ashby's—the store, I mean, not *Ash*—and Elliott is the biggest Christmas freak you'll ever meet, so... I guess Ash actually did a really good job with making his proposal personalized. You know, thinking of Elliott's likes, and their relationship history, and sort of going out of his way to make it special."

Logan's jaw tightened, giving Trevor pause. Would the man really care to hear about this? But then again, it was Ash Ashby. Everyone loved to gossip about Ash, and Logan wasn't offering anything—conversationally speaking—so Trevor really *did* need the distraction. At least until he got his own odd rollercoaster of feelings in check.

Trevor finished hanging everything up and swept over to the door, closing it as he thought back to Ash's proposal. "I don't know," he said, remembering. "If I were dating a man like Ash Ashby, I think that I'd want a proposal that was a little more high-profile. A little flashier, you know? I mean, don't get me wrong. I think getting us—Elliott's friends and family—involved was *good*. Super sweet. I'm definitely a huge fan of having friends involved in the proposal because it shows that they're accepting of your relationship and that's important to me, but... I don't know. I guess I'd just want something a little more..."

Logan had started unbuttoning his shirt, and—even though Trevor had seen him in all states of undress before—there was something about the slow way Logan was working through them tonight that riled him up. He let his voice trail off, looking away. Why had he been babbling about Elliott and Ash, anyway?

"Did your friend say yes?" Logan asked quietly, slipping his shirt off.

Trevor pulled his soft tape measure from his pocket and unrolled it, keeping his eyes off Logan as he answered. "Of course. He's over-the-top in love with that man. But... it's Ash *Ashby*, you know? I was just expecting a little more pizazz, maybe. Heart-wrenchingly romantic is one thing, and Ash had that in the bag, but give me something *unique*. Getting engaged at the Christmas event that brought you together? Cute, but totally predictable."

Logan folded his shirt and set it on the bench, and Trevor swept in to take his measurements, even though he already knew them by heart. It was a tradition, and Logan expected him to do it. Had *asked* for it, this time. As if Trevor would forget.

The thought of accidentally brushing his fingers across Logan's body appealed to Trevor more tonight than it should, and even if he'd ignored any surges of chemistry between them in the past, he knew there was no other way to explain the sudden rush he felt now, in Logan's presence. He stretched the tape over Logan's body, letting his fingers brush here, or draping his arms around him there. Standing so close with nothing but the soft shush of the tape as he moved around Logan, the atmosphere between them grew intimate.

Trevor wracked his brain for something to break the silence, to jolt himself out of the odd little cocoon of intimacy that they'd somehow fallen into. For once, he came up with nothing, though, and as soon as he was done, Trevor rolled the measuring tape back up and slipped it back into his pocket.

Logan's measurements hadn't changed.

Trevor didn't back away, and Logan didn't try to put distance between them.

The scant space between them was electric. When Trevor breathed in, he caught a subtle hint of basil, black leather, and cedarwood from Logan's skin.

"You're good with people, Trevor," Logan said, the low timbre of his voice making Trevor shiver, even though the comment itself felt like a non sequitur.

Still, it was true. Trevor nodded.

"Would you be open to..." Logan's voice trailed off, looking uncharacteristically hesitant, and Trevor's pulse started to race. Logan cleared his throat, finally taking a step back and saying a little more briskly, "I've got a proposition for you. Would you be free to talk for a few minutes when you get off work?"

Trevor's eyebrows shot up.

"A proposition?" The sparks between them left Trevor with no choice in the matter—he knew that he would say yes. But the uncanny chemistry was unnerving, and he deflected the intensity of what he felt with humor. "Sounds kinky. I'll have you know upfront that I'm trying to stay away from dairy, so if whipped cream is your thing..."

Logan's lips definitely twitched, but he immediately caught himself, and put even more space between them. The hint of warmth that had been in his face disappeared, and he reverted to the colder tone of voice he usually used. "I meant a business proposition."

Logan shutting him down stung, and Trevor almost snapped a very unprofessional "Thanks, but no thanks." But... he knew he'd die of curiosity if he did. "More tailoring?" he asked instead, reaching briskly for one of the shirts he'd hung.

"No," Logan said, putting a hand out to stop Trevor from dressing him. "I know you've had a long day, if you'd like, I can have my assistant call you—"

"*No*," Trevor said, ignoring the heat from Logan's hand on his arm. No matter what he felt for Logan, it wasn't as though anything was going to come of it, but still, curiosity would literally kill him if he didn't find out what this "proposition" was. And he definitely wasn't going to pass up the chance to spend extra time around his favorite piece of eye candy in favor of a phone call from Logan's assistant.

Tired or not, and even if Logan had made it clear he wasn't interested in the whipped cream option—Trevor was *not* going to let himself have hurt feelings about Logan's rejection, after all, Trevor had been a little over the line with the comment—there was no way he was going to be able to resist finding out what Logan wanted from him.

"I'll be off work as soon as I'm done here with you," he said, giving the shirt in his hand a little shake to illustrate the point. "It'll take me a handful of minutes to clock out and let the shift manager know I'm leaving, but I shouldn't be more than fifteen minutes after you check out. Wait for me?"

Logan smiled, which did all sorts of ridiculous things to Trevor's insides. "I will," he said, releasing Trevor's arm and allowing him to slide the first shirt onto his body.

Trevor cleared his throat, pulling himself back together. Logan had said a *business* proposition, and whatever it turned out to be, Trevor would be best off not letting his emotions—reciprocated or not, and Logan had pretty clearly went with the "not" option a moment ago—get in the way of the job he was hired to do. Neither this one, nor... whatever else it was Logan was thinking.

Besides, there was still fashion to be had.

"So... that red tie?" Trevor asked as he passed Logan the first of his potential purchases, determined not to let the man get to him. "It'd go great with this."

"No color," Logan said, not smiling. But Trevor couldn't help but smile for both of them, because, unless he was fooling himself—and, fine, maybe he *was*—Logan wanted to.

Chapter 3

LOGAN

LOGAN WASN'T SURE WHAT HAD POSSESSED HIM TO MAKE the offer to Trevor, but he'd always been decisive when it came to business, with good results. And this *was* business, so he wasn't going to question himself. Besides, it was an excellent idea. Trevor really was good with people. Outgoing and at ease with himself in a way that Logan could never imagine being, he was the ideal person to help Logan navigate the upcoming appearances he'd be required to make in Kelly's stead for bLoved.

As Trevor wrapped up his shift, Logan called for his car, using the brief wait to do a quick location-based search that yielded several quality restaurants. When he saw that several were within walking distance, though, he gave the driver his purchases and sent him away. The blizzard that had caused him so much scheduling grief earlier had turned Chicago into a winter wonderland, and a short walk in it would be pleasant.

He wasn't sure if Trevor had any dietary restrictions, so he picked the one that had the menu with the most variety. *I'll have you know upfront that I'm trying to stay away from dairy, so if whipped cream is your thing.* Logan shook his head, clearing the distracting thought from his mind. Trevor finally exited the building, grinning as his breath frosted the air between them. He rubbed his hands together briskly—no gloves—then shoved them into his pockets, rocking back on his heels.

"Don't tell me you're going to keep me in suspense now that I'm off the clock," he said, eyes sparkling. "What's this proposition?"

"Have you eaten?" Logan asked, ignoring the fact that he was being a little unreasonable.

The conversation could have been had in the span of ten minutes within the warmth of Ashby's, and certainly didn't require him to take Trevor out or worry about whether Trevor really was, or was not, lactose intolerant. It had been years since he'd taken a man out, or had to worry about that sort of thing when making plans. Since Ryan, Logan had stuck to brief hookups when needed, but strictly avoided anything that might resemble a date... anything that might open himself up to the kind of hurt he'd had so much trouble getting over the first time around.

Not, of course, that this was a date.

Logan held up his phone between them like a shield, screen tilted toward Trevor with the restaurant review still pulled up, and added a brisk, "RedGate sounds acceptable, and it's just three blocks away."

Trevor's eyebrows shot up. "Never been there, but I'm game." Then he grinned, and it was decidedly wicked. "Are you just into making me wait, Logan... or does this 'proposition' require that you wine and dine me first?"

Logan didn't trust himself to answer, so he pretended not to hear. Trevor had said yes to joining him for a meal, after all, which was all that mattered.

When Logan started walking, Trevor fell into step beside him without protest and making a few teasing remarks as they walked that—thankfully—he didn't seem to require a response to. It really was a beautiful walk, but by the time they arrived, Trevor's cheeks were rosy from the wind, and his body was tense from huddling in on itself to shield him from the cold. The coat he wore, Logan noticed a little too late, looked high-class and warm, but the way Trevor was shivering, he had to wonder if it was an imitation.

Logan gritted his teeth, regretting sending the car away. He hadn't been thinking.

Over the months of their acquaintance, Logan felt that he'd learned Trevor well. Always one to speak up, rarely without a brash comment or a joke, Trevor seemed perpetually confident and sure of himself. There was a resilience in him that Logan was naturally drawn to, and a genuine kindness and enthusiasm for life that underlay his teasing nature. But now, seeing him shiver, huddled tight to fight off the cold and cheeks burning as though embarrassed, Logan was catching a glimpse of another side of him.

One that was a little more vulnerable, and that sparked instincts in Logan that he would need to tamp down in order to maintain his rule about not mixing business with anything more personal.

Trevor was uncharacteristically silent as they entered RedGate. Bathed in the dim lights of the restaurant, skin reddened from the cold, he looked... tired. Still lively, but that vulnerability Logan had noted was there, showing a more delicate side to Trevor that Logan wasn't used to. One that appealed to him in ways he didn't want to think about.

"Is this okay?" Logan asked, wondering if Trevor was having second thoughts.

"Definitely," Trevor said, blowing on his hands. He winked, "Don't think you're getting out of feeding me now, Logan."

Logan turned to the hostess, startled to find that he'd had to fight off a laugh. There were no more than ten tables set for two, but as soon as he'd decided on the restaurant, Logan had called ahead and made sure that there would be one waiting for them, and as soon as he gave his name they were led to their table right away.

Trevor sank into his chair with his coat still on, still shivering, and Logan began to regret asking him out after work. He hadn't been thinking of the long day Trevor must have had, and, if he were honest with himself, it was a bit disconcerting to be with him outside the known parameters of their routine at Ashby's.

Since the first time they'd met, there had been something about Trevor that stood out and captured Logan's attention. His bright personality and his refusal to cast Logan aside because of his dour attitude had piqued Logan's interest, and now, a year later, Logan was no less drawn to him. Both business and his personal life had taught him that people weren't to be trusted, and Logan knew that the success he'd found was safeguarded by his refusal to invest himself in anyone. To let anyone get too close. But Trevor? He seemed to approach life differently, and his zest, along with that underlying kindness inside him that seeped out and colored their every interaction, pulled at Logan like a magnet.

Even though he didn't want to admit it to himself, asking Trevor to discuss their business over dinner had been selfish. An excuse for Logan to bask in that kindness for just a little longer. But there was no harm in taking a... *potential employee* to dinner. Logan had years of practice in keeping his feelings out of things, and he was very, very good at business. If being around Trevor also happened to ease something in Logan's soul and loosen the firm grip he usually kept on his composure, that was just another obstacle to be overcome.

Or, maybe, an added bonus.

"Where did your shopping go?" Trevor asked once he was settled and finally started to look a little less hypothermic. "You didn't leave it back at the store, did you?"

"No," Logan said, then stopped himself from adding more detail. Trevor was on a need-to-know basis, and even though Logan was used to his chatty ways— would have found them intrusive in anyone else—he wasn't going to let himself be opened up to anything off-topic or personal. "I took care of it."

"Mm-hmm. I bet you did." Trevor winked at him, making it sound just suggestive enough that Logan had to shift in his chair and remind himself *again* that this was not a date.

In light of why they were there, it was best not to acknowledge any attraction he might feel for Trevor. Business was safe. The rest... was not.

"Ugh," Trevor said, settling back in his chair and lifting his hands to his mouth again. His fingers were still red, and he blew on them as he added a plaintive, "When did it decide to become winter? It was almost a green Christmas, but now it feels like it's minus fifteen."

"I hear Chicago winters are often like that," Logan

commented, absurdly grateful to be talking about the weather. Something had passed between the two of them back at Ashby's that still had Logan unsettled, and he knew if he wasn't careful, it would overwhelm him.

He couldn't let that happen.

Trevor was the only person in Logan's life whom he found himself wanting to open up around, but if he put that to good use—if he could get Trevor to agree to help coach him through the next month and a half of torturous public appearances—then he could channel that tendency into something less dangerous.

And it was a good business decision.

As charismatic and sales-oriented as Trevor was, Logan was sure that he would be the perfect fit for the job. Frank could scour the earth for qualified, professional candidates, but, face-to-face with Trevor, Logan realized that none of them would end up being effective, no matter what their credentials. Logan needed to be able to appear open when he tried to sell bLoved to the world, and he wasn't going to be able to do that with anyone but Trevor at his side. For whatever reason, and despite the limitations of their acquaintance so far, Trevor was the only one who inspired that sort of openness in Logan, and he knew for sure it wasn't going to happen with someone new. Someone he didn't trust.

"So, you're not from around here?" Trevor asked, reacting to Logan's comment about Chicago's winters.

"No," Logan answered. He wasn't getting personal. This information *was* need-to-know, if Trevor agreed to work for him. "I fly in on business once a month."

Trevor undid the buttons of his jacket as they talked, shrugging it off to reveal the black shirt and tie he wore beneath. He may have an obsession with pushing color on Logan, but in Logan's opinion, Trevor certainly didn't need it. He looked fantastic in black, and with his carefully sculpted, dirty-blond hair windswept and messy, and his cheeks still tinged pink, Logan had to force his gaze not to linger.

"So you come to Chicago every month for business, and always end up at Ashby's?" Trevor's grin brightened, and he looked a little delighted at the thought. He draped his jacket over the back of his chair, then turned to face Logan again. "I mean, I *love* fashion, so don't get me wrong. I'm not saying there's anything wrong with that, but... that's a lot of clothes for a businessman. Are you trying to impress someone?"

The sly, upward turn to his words made Logan's heart race, but he ignored it and focused on the reason they were there. The conclusion he'd come to back in Ashby's had been spot-on—Trevor was a natural speaker, someone who had a way with words and was quick on his feet. More than that, he was likable. If he could help bring even a fraction of that out in Logan, the upcoming campaign would be a success.

"In business, there's always someone you're trying to

impress," Logan responded levelly, not letting himself react to the teasing sparkle that seemed ever-present in Trevor's eyes.

Who ever teased Logan? Hiro, at times, but that was different. Trevor didn't just tease him. He outright flirted.

"Hmmm," Trevor responded, a catlike smirk spreading across his face. He leaned forward, arms crossed upon the table, and proved Logan right when he added, "And... in pleasure?"

A dull ache spread through Logan's heart at the question. He didn't bother trying to impress anyone when it came to "pleasure," and fashion—which he honestly didn't give a damn about in any sense other than making himself presentable—had never been his method of trying to impress. No, instead, he'd just tried and utterly failed to give the man he thought he'd once loved everything he'd wanted. Logan wouldn't even know how to go about impressing someone he was interested in now.

So it was good that he didn't allow that sort of thing into his life.

A waiter arrived with their menus, saving him from a response, and Trevor acted as though he'd never put Logan on the spot. He uncrossed his arms, sat up straight, and accepted the menu with a bright smile.

The single-page listing was backed on a metal menu card, and although the selection was printed, Logan took note of the date across the top. The menu was rewritten and altered each day, depending on which ingredients were available. Logan afforded it only a brief glance before his eyes were drawn back to Trevor.

Trevor seemed to be reviewing each item on the menu carefully, his eyes scanning down the page with a look of delight. When he reached the bottom, he looked over the top of the menu at Logan, cocking an eyebrow up in surprise.

"Not even my dates take me places this fancy," he remarked, grinning.

Dates?

For some reason, and despite his constant flirting, the thought of Trevor *dating* had never crossed Logan's mind. He hadn't given much thought to what Trevor might do between their monthly visits, actually, but the idea of him out with other men sent a distinctly unpleasant sensation squirming through Logan's gut.

"Do you date often?" Not his business, but the words were out before he could stop himself.

"As often as I can," Trevor shot back. Confident, cocky, and totally flirtatious. And then another wink. "Like you just said, it's a long, cold winter here in Chicago. I've got to do *some*thing to keep myself warm."

There was nothing Logan could say about that. *He* certainly had no claim on Trevor. He occupied himself by looking back down at his menu, upset without any justifiable reason. Nothing bound them together apart from the professional relationship they shared, and it was better to keep it that way.

So why was he jealous?

"But, seriously," Trevor continued. "If this is a business dinner, are you paying for this as a business expense? Because these prices are a little over the top for someone on an Ashby's salary to afford. And what is 'matsutake porridge?' Based on the king crab and salmon roe with acorn squash I see listed above it, I'm going to assume whatever it is has to be extravagant."

There was charm in how forward he was, and Logan set his menu down so he could refocus his attention on Trevor once more, pushing the other feelings aside.

"I'm paying tonight," he reassured him. "Please, order whatever you'd like. According to the reviews I read, the menu features organic locally grown, caught, or foraged foods. To the best of my knowledge, a matsutake is a rare type of mushroom."

"I see." Trevor's gaze flicked from Logan to the menu, then back again. He looked like he was trying not to smile as he added a dry, "You sure make *that* sound appetizing. Delicious rare mushrooms. Mmm."

Logan narrowed his eyes, and Trevor laughed.

"I simply told you what it is," Logan said, not letting himself laugh back. "Information is useful when making decisions."

"Mm, but your 'information' was so clinical." Trevor set his menu down, too, and traced a finger along the metal ridge. "I wondered if, outside the store, maybe you'd start to let down that wall of yours. Guess I'll just have to keep chipping away at it, though."

"There's no wall," Logan lied. "This is who I am."

"Mm-hmm," Trevor said, packing the sound with enough doubt to get his disbelief across. "If you say so, Logan."

"What makes you doubt me?" Logan asked, absurdly pleased that Trevor would want to chip away at his "wall," even before Logan had made his proposal. For all of Trevor's earlier curiosity about it, so far, he seemed content to just make conversation. As if he were enjoying Logan's company, the way he often seemed to at Ashby's.

"Because *nobody* is that composed all the time."

Trevor shook his head and placed an elbow on the table, letting his chin rest in his hand while his eyes remained trained on Logan. The way he looked up at him from under his brows was sultry, but Logan couldn't tell if Trevor was flirting for the sake of flirting, or if it was intended for *Logan*. As outgoing as Trevor was, Logan suspected that his flirtatious nature and suggestive comments were more habit than anything else. Which didn't stop a small part of Logan from enjoying the attention.

"You're stony-faced and all-business, all the time," Trevor said, somehow making it sound almost funny instead of like a failing. "Even here, when we're out for dinner. I know you said that this was going to be about something business-related, but really, it's okay with me if you loosen up a little. Trust me, Logan, if there's anyone you can be yourself around, it's *me*. I've already seen you in your underwear, after all. You don't have to pretend I'm some bigwig you have to sell on your next big idea. I'm just Trevor Rogers, from Ashby's."

Until Trevor brought it up, Logan had never thought about the time they shared in the fitting room quite like that. Trevor had disarmed him, and not for the first time that night, he found himself speechless.

"I didn't mean to hurt your feelings." The grin slipped off Trevor's face, and he frowned, the vulnerability Logan had noted earlier making another appearance on his expressive face. "I was just pointing it out. Listen, if I'm getting the wrong signals, just let me know. Sometimes I get a little too wild and push things a little too far, but if I make you uncomfortable—"

"No." Single-word answers were safe. With single-word answers, Logan couldn't give Trevor any more fuel to add to the fire. Whatever Logan said, Trevor latched onto and spun into something Logan didn't recognize. Pulling him in directions he'd never intended to go. How was a man so quick on his feet not working somewhere more reputable than the floor at Ashby's?

"Well." Discomfort still twisted Trevor's features, and he let his hand slip from the menu so it could settle on his lap. "Alright, but just... don't be shy if I do. Sometimes I don't even realize I'm toeing the line until I'm all the way across it."

"You're fine." Logan straightened up, wanting to reassure Trevor and wipe the uncharacteristic look off his face but not sure how. He cleared his throat, realizing the best way was to get them both back on track. "It's probably time I cut to the chase and got to business, anyway. I'm interested in hiring you, Trevor. I have some public appearances I need to make from now until February, and, as you've already observed, I'm too businesslike. I need someone to coach me on how to loosen up and... get along with people."

Trevor furrowed his brow. "What? You mean, you need someone to help you work on your... personality?"

"Right." Logan crossed his arms upon the table, keeping his gaze on Trevor to watch his reactions.

How many times had Ryan joked with him about Logan's stick-in-the-mud personality putting Rise at risk, back when they'd been launching the company? The comments had stung at first, until Logan had convinced himself Ryan hadn't meant them the way they'd sounded. Still, he'd learned to focus on his strengths and leave the people-work to his business partner. A pattern he'd repeated—minus the personal involvement—with Kelly and bLoved. But, for the next six weeks, at least, that wasn't going to be an option.

"I need someone by my side who can turn me from the logical, detached businessman I am—" Logan ignored his irrational, small surge of hurt as he repeated one of the kinder ways Ryan had used to describe him, "—into someone the public can relate to, and I believe that you're the best fit for the job."

Trevor narrowed his eyes further, and he frowned with suspicion. "Why me?"

Because I like you. I like who I am around you. Logan cleared his throat, thankful that he hadn't blurted out *that*. "Because Ashby's has one of the best employee training guidelines known in retail," he said instead, since it was true, and made more sense than... the other truth. "With what you've learned from being trained to work the floor there, paired with your magnetic personality, I'm convinced that you'll be able to train me to appear approachable and friendly for the upcoming publicity I'll be required to do."

The answer satisfied Trevor, whose suspicious expression faded and was replaced with a more familiar, flirtatious smirk. "Well, if you want to put it that way, sure. I'm an excellent trainer, you know. I've never had a single complaint."

Logan pulled his wallet from his back pocket and produced a business card, extending it to Trevor.

"Fancy," Trevor said, sliding his fingers over the thick paper and embossed lettering. He grinned. "So you're legit, and not just trying to get in my pants?"

Logan could feel himself start to flush, but before he had to consider whether he should actually tell Trevor that he *had* crossed a line, Trevor laughed and apologized.

"I know, I know, sorry. If I'm actually going to work for you, I should get a handle on that, right? So when would this be happening?"

"I'd be looking to hire you immediately—or as soon as you were able to take the time from Ashby's—through mid-February. The contract would end on Valentine's Day, to be specific," Logan said stiffly. "My personal assistant, Hiro, will contact you with additional details about the dates, appearances, and travel details, should you be interested. You'll be flown to New York and provided with a hotel room and a meal allowance for the duration of the contract."

Trevor's eyes widened in shock. "You want to fly me to New York?"

"To New York City," Logan clarified, wondering if he'd have to offer Trevor more than bLoved was budgeting to get him to agree to temporarily relocate. "I reside there, and the majority of the publicity we have lined up is in the city."

"New York," Trevor echoed in a whisper, almost vibrating with a barely-contained excitement. His eyes lit up, and he grinned. "Yes! Yes, I'll go!"

For a moment, Logan was speechless. They hadn't even talked about salary yet, or any of the terms of the contract. What was Trevor thinking? "The compensation is a flat fee of ten thousand dollars," he said, blurting out the upper limit of the budget they'd outlined for the project. "Will this amount be adequate?"

"Shut. Up." Trevor sank back in his chair and cupped his mouth with both of his hands.

The excitement he exuded was close to palpable, and Logan assumed it meant he was in agreement. Something eased inside him, and he felt his shoulders relax, even though he hadn't been aware that they'd gotten tense.

When Trevor pulled himself together enough, he sat up in his chair, dropped his hands from his face, and gave Logan a hard look. "Let me get this right. You're willing to fly me to New York City... pay for my hotel... *and* my food... *and* pay me ten grand on top of all that?"

"Yes," Logan said, feeling something well up inside him that he didn't have a name for. Trevor was happy.

"All just so that I can turn you into a... a person?" Trevor squeaked, waving a hand toward Logan as if to encompass all of him.

"Yes," Logan repeated, the feeling inside him spreading into a smile that he didn't have the energy to hold in.

Trevor beamed back, the vivid excitement in his eyes so sincere that it made Logan catch his breath. When was the last time he'd made someone feel that way? Had it ever happened?

"Oh my God," Trevor whispered, covering his mouth. And then, louder, "Oh my *God*! Logan... I've always wanted to go to New York! The shows, the lights, the food, the fashion, the... the *every*thing! New *York*!"

Trevor's excitement was premature. Didn't he want details? But Logan couldn't help getting caught up in it. It was going to happen, and Trevor didn't seem to mind the thought of leaving Chicago. Although... Logan's smile slipped as he remembered a bit of their earlier conversation.

"Assuming you can get the time off work, you'll be free to go?"

"I will *definitely* get the time off work," Trevor answered, laughing.

"But... you're not going to miss anyone?" Logan pressed. "I won't be flying you back here until the contract is over. You'll be mine—with me, I mean—for the duration."

"For ten thousand dollars? I am *all* yours, baby." Trevor laughed. "Or was that actually a bit of fishing? Because if you're wondering, yes, I'm totally single."

Logan's heart raced. "This is solely a business proposal," he said stiffly, needing to remind them both.

"Right." Trevor was still grinning, but something like hurt, or maybe disappointment, flashed in his eyes. There and gone before Logan could identify it. Trevor laughed again, though, his excitement and that hint of natural cockiness returning. "I'm just teasing, Logan. Remember what I said about the line I tend to cross? Just push me right back over when I stray. And don't worry. I'm sure there are *plenty* of hot guys in New York, so if it turns out that the winter is just as cold there, well, I'm sure I won't be hurting for attention."

Bitterness rose in the back of Logan's throat, and he swallowed it down and did his best to push aside the sudden surge of jealousy that reared up and threatened to overwhelm him. A conflict of interests had ruined his life and changed his views of the world before, and Logan wasn't interested in having it happen again. Business was to stay business, and pleasure was to stay pleasure. What Trevor chose to do on his own time, whether here or once they were in New York, wasn't his concern.

Trevor could date whomever he wanted, as long as he did the job Logan was hiring him for. And Logan would live on as he had for years—sticking with the one part of life that had never let him down. Business.

"New York!" Trevor repeated, laughing again with a kind of delight that was contagious, regardless of the black cloud that had settled around Logan's heart at Trevor's flippant comment about his dating prospects in New York. "Oh my God, New York! Here—let me text you so that you have my number." Trevor pulled his phone out, eyes darting between the small screen and Logan's business card as he tapped in the number, still grinning.

"I'll pass it along to Hiro," Logan said stiffly, ignoring the buzz of his own phone in his pocket as the message came through. Best to minimize further personal contact between himself and Trevor. "He'll send you the contract and tie up all the business details with you."

"New York!" Trevor laughed again, waving off talk of business. "Oh my God, I promise you're not going to regret your decision, Logan. If you think I'm a good *tailor*, just wait until you see what I can do to alter your personality. You're going to be a natural, I just know it."

Logan was anything but a natural, but somehow, watching Trevor laugh with unabashed joy struck him in a curious way, making him almost believe that it could be true.

That Trevor might see something in him that he didn't know was there, and be just the man to bring it to the surface.

For the first time since his dreams had died so abruptly seven years before, Logan felt a flutter of something light in his chest. In everything Trevor did, there was tremendous sincerity and emotion, and Logan felt swept up in it. Like he'd opened a floodgate and was now being carried along on a ride he hadn't intended to board, but now couldn't stop.

Didn't want to, if he were honest, despite the emotional ups and downs that had already resulted from their brief interaction.

It reminded him of Trevor claiming he'd turn Logan into a person, and Logan bit back yet another smile, thinking it was an apt description. And that, truly, there wasn't anyone else better suited for the job. The month and a half he'd been dreading as he'd walked out of the bLoved meeting just a few hours earlier was now a month and a half that Logan found himself actually looking forward to. It would just be business, but, with Trevor in the mix, Logan already suspected that it would be night-and-day from "business as usual."

He couldn't wait.

Chapter 4

TREVOR

THE PINT OF BEER HIT THE TABLE WITH A LITTLE MORE force than Trevor had intended, and some of the head sloshed down the side and pooled on the sticky table. Grace sighed and rolled her eyes, pushing a napkin over it to soak up the worst of the spill.

"You just got here and you're already sloppy drunk?" she asked, teasing him with a wry grin. She tsked, adding, "I expect better things of you, Trevor."

"You don't even understand!" Trevor exclaimed. It was his second beer, and the first had only amplified his excitement. "I'm not *sloppy*, I'm *slaphappy*. Did you even hear what I just told you?"

"Yes." The entire table chorused at once. Trevor scowled at the lot of them playfully, then leaned back so that his head hit the back of the bench and laughed. "New York City!"

Friday nights at Reggie's were a long-standing tradition for Trevor and his Ashby's coworkers, although now that the Christmas rush had passed, they'd be dropping back to a once-a-month occurrence. Once the holidays were done for the season, there was no need for a Friday-night escape.

Trevor had showed up late, but he was still on an exhilarated high from his dinner with Logan, and his enthusiasm more than made up for his tardiness.

"Do you think Krista will let you have the time off, though?" Sean asked. "I mean, she's great and all, but taking more than a month off is probably going to cause some problems. The part-timers are back to school, and the temps are all gone now. You sure that there's enough manpower to cover your absence?"

"If they need to, they can probably call in someone from another Ashby's location," Trevor said with a shrug. "I know you guys hate the Skokie store, but someone from there can probably fill in for me. It'll only be temporary."

"What if it's Kevin?" Grace asked, aghast. "We thought we were finally rid of him."

The year before, their least-favorite coworker had been transferred to the Skokie store along with their former manager, Martin. Everyone at the Chicago Ashby's had breathed a sigh of relief, and they all agreed that the work environment was much more pleasant with those two gone. Still, nothing could dim Trevor's excitement. Not even the thought of his friends having to suffer through a month of the man they used to call "the Grinch."

"Even if it *is* Kevin, which it definitely *won't* be, it'll only be for a month, guys!" Trevor beamed. "Well, a month plus another week or two, but who's counting? You know how fast the time goes. I'll be back before you know it, a little more worldly, and with a big tick checked off my bucket list."

Grace narrowed her eyes and set her lips. "You have a bucket list?"

"I do now that I'm New York–bound!" Trevor grinned. "It's too bad I'm not heading over there during the Christmas season—I could report to the Ashby's in New York and introduce them to sexy elves. And, from there, the world."

"You're a total spazz," Grace said, rolling her eyes at the reminder of Trevor's obsession with tailoring their holiday uniforms at Ashby's renowned "North Pole" exhibit. She looked amused, though, which she tried to hide behind a long sip from her beer. Every Christmas, she was first in line to have her costume fitted by Trevor. "But I'm glad for you. Doing... whatever it is you're doing, sounds like a big deal. And New York! Maybe it'll set you up with the right connections to finally do something with fashion. I mean, who are you even working for? Did you bother to ask?"

"Of course I—" Trevor cut himself short, the unfinished sentence hanging in the air between them, "—didn't."

He *felt* like he knew Logan. Well, not really "knew," maybe, but at least like he had a good feel for the type of man Logan was. But, thinking back, Trevor hadn't really asked much of anything else, as soon as he'd heard the words *New York*.

Honestly, it had all felt like a bit of a dream, and he still kind of wanted to pinch himself. His excitement about Logan asking him to do something outside of their monthly appointments had probably led Trevor to tripping and falling over that line of propriety more than he should have, but even Logan's continued—and disappointing—lack of personal interest in him couldn't quash the electric thrill Trevor felt at the thought of spending a month with the man in New York City.

More than a month.

Six weeks of an all-expenses-paid trip to the one place on earth he wanted to go more than any other, with a hot man whom he'd had trouble getting out of his mind for the last year, *plus* ten thousand dollars?

Trevor slipped a hand under the table where no one would see and gave himself a hard pinch just to be sure. Okay... awake. He laughed, just because it was all so surreal. And yet, *true*.

But, yeah. Maybe he didn't actually know much about Logan, now that Grace pointed it out.

She was giving him a pointed look, and he shrugged sheepishly. "New York?" he repeated.

"God." Grace covered her face with her hands. "You

need to Google that shit, Trevor. What if the guy you're talking to is some creep who's going to traffic you, or... or I don't know. Maybe he's some psycho? It's always the quiet ones."

Trevor bristled a little on Logan's behalf. Sure, Logan was quiet, but there was nothing creepy about him.

"He looks legit," Trevor said, biting back any other defense. *He's too hot to be scary* probably wouldn't fly with his friends, and anything else—like the whole bit about how Logan sometimes made him feel—was too... much. He pulled out Logan's business card and passed it to Grace. "See?" Trevor said. "Ever since the first time we exchanged names, he'd insisted that his name is Logan. It matches the credit card he always uses, and now this business card. I think if he were unhinged, he'd probably have slipped up by now, and I've never caught him in any lies."

"How could you?" Sean, another coworker, asked. He pushed his glasses up the bridge of his nose, looking genuinely unsettled. "He doesn't *talk*. He's got this creepy, walled-off thing going on. He *could* be a businessman... but he could also be a serial killer."

It was Trevor's turn to bury his face in his hands. "Oh my God, you guys. I know you're concerned about me and everything, but he's *not* a bad guy, okay? He took me out to dinner at this ridiculously expensive organic sustainable whatever restaurant and paid the whole bill without even thinking about it. And as someone who's been on a *lot* of shady dates from the Internet, I know trouble when I see it. Logan is weird, but he's not trouble. He's totally the real deal."

"If he's some big hotshot able to hire you and fly you out to New York, then he should stand up to the ultimate test," Grace said sagely. She set the business card down on a clear portion of the table and pulled her phone from her pocket. With a swipe of her finger she unlocked the screen, pulling up her Internet browser. "Let's see what the Internet has to say about *Logan Carter*."

"Dun-dun-*dun*," someone intoned from across the table, making Trevor roll his eyes.

As touching as Grace's concern was, Trevor wished she wouldn't make such a big deal out of it. Logan may have had a reputation as a sourpuss around Ashby's, but that was only because no one else had taken the time to get to know him. Tonight, Logan had been more open than Trevor had ever seen him. Still not *open* open, but compared to Logan's regular personality, the change had been noticeable. At least, to Trevor.

He liked Logan, and it wasn't just the tips the man usually included with his tailoring bill or even how ridiculously sexy he was, despite his reserve. Logan had said that Trevor was good with people, and it was true. He was also a good *judge* of people, and there was something about Logan that was attractive to Trevor on more levels than were probably good for him.

He grinned. The man may keep insisting that their New York thing was going to be all business, but since he'd already proven open to Trevor's flirting, as far as Trevor was concerned, that was an open invitation to keep it up. If nothing ever came of it, well, at least it was fun.

"Hmmmmmmm," Grace said, drawing the sound out as she swiped through the Google results on her screen.

Trevor waited a beat, watching her face, but she gave him nothing. The brat.

"*And?*" he finally insisted, curious despite himself.

"And... not much." Grace pursed her lips and squinted at the screen, looking a bit frustrated at whatever she was finding. Or, more likely, not finding, based on that comment. "It looks like Logan *is* a businessman... there are some really old stories about him being excessively private. Which, I guess, makes sense, right? With what we've seen of him."

Sean snorted, nodding, and muttered under his breath, "Understatement of the century."

Grace ignored him, continuing to scroll through the results.

"Hey, dudes," Jose said, approaching the table with his boyfriend, Barry, in tow. "You all sloppy yet?"

Jose pulled a chair up and offered it to Barry, and Barry sat and pulled the next chair out for Jose in return. Trevor just shook his head, unable to wipe the smile off his face. For once, his friends' ooey-gooey love fest toward each other didn't even bother him.

"*Trevor* is," Grace answered Jose, waving a hand in Trevor's direction without taking her eyes off whatever she was reading on screen. "You wouldn't believe what's happened to him since he left Ashby's a few hours ago."

"Let me guess," Jose said, grinning. "You met up with Mr. Sexy Sourpuss, he took you to dinner, and now you're going to work for him in New York City?"

Trevor bit down on his bottom lip to chase away a smirk, and as he did, Grace slowly looked over her phone and directly across the table at Jose. "...What?"

"Trevor sent out a mass text a while ago to the people in his address book who weren't going to be at Reggie's tonight, talking about how he was going to New York City." Jose laughed. "Pretty sure half of Trevor's social world must know by now." He turned to Trevor. "But what are you going to be *doing* in New York, anyway? I guessed that it had to do with Big Business, but I wasn't sure."

"You're right." Trevor leaned across the table, only trying to keep his voice down because everyone else had already heard his story, and he was sure they were growing sick of it. "Logan asked me if I'd go to New York with him to coach him on being a person, or... something. I think I'll be sort of like a PR manager and a speech writer, combined."

"Dude, that's great. You're going to rock that. You can sell just about anything." Jose held out his hand, and Trevor clasped it. "New York's awesome. Broadway and fashion and big lights. You gonna see the sights?"

Their hands parted, and Trevor sat up a little straighter in his seat and lifted his chin, hamming it up. "I'm going to be living big, of course. I'll have to *schedule in* sightseeing around my business itinerary."

"God, he's not even on the plane yet and he's already full of himself." Grace elbowed Trevor in the side, and Trevor collapsed from his place of poise, laughing. "Well, Mr. Bigshot Jr., do you want to hear what you're in for? Because I just found the dirt."

"Give it to me." Trevor bounced right back up and turned to face Grace, doing his best to look serious. He *was* curious, but he trusted his instincts. He highly doubted there was actual *dirt*. "Who is Logan Carter, and what are his motives?"

"Welllllllllll," Grace said, drawing out the word for full dramatic effect. "According to this ancient article, Logan Carter was a business graduate who started up a little music and video streaming service in his spare time. You know, just a little company called... *Rise*."

Trevor's eyes widened, and he stared at Grace in shock. "What... the actual... *fuck*?" he squeaked. Sure, Logan obviously had money, but... *Rise*? She might as well have said Google. Or Facebook. "Are you being serious right now? *My* Logan Carter?"

Well, fine, not *Trevor's*, but whatever. Grace knew what he meant.

"That's what the article says," Grace flipped her phone around to show Trevor the screen, and Trevor found himself staring at a candid picture of a stony-faced Logan as he stepped out of the back of a car. Blond hair carefully styled, blue eyes piercing and cold... usually, Trevor saw a hint of something warmer underneath all that ice. It was missing in the picture, but still, there was no mistaking him. "This your man, Trevor?"

"That's him," Trevor confirmed, breathless. Logan wore an expensive suit, and the shoe visible in the shot was polished and likely designer. What was a man like that doing shopping at Ashby's? "Oh my God. *Rise*? Seriously?"

"It says he was one of two founders," Grace said. She turned the phone back around and scrolled through the article. "It looks like he was the silent partner, for the most part. Not like his existence was secret, but it sounds like he was more involved behind the scenes."

"Isn't Rise owned by the out-and-proud guy, Ryan-something, who was dating that French tennis player for a while?" Barry asked, joining in on the conversation.

Grace nodded, tapping her phone. "Yeah, Ryan Grisham. He was the other founder. The one who's always been the face of the company."

Trevor recognized the name, and could easily pull up a mental picture of his face. In general, he loved the idea of openly gay public success stories, but—if he remembered correctly—Ryan Grisham always seemed to be smiling just a little too widely to come across as anyone Trevor would care to hang with. The man seemed a little full of himself, honestly.

"And..." Grace's face grew serious, and she fell silent to keep reading. Trevor picked up on the change immediately, and he furrowed his brow and leaned toward her to try to read over her shoulder. Grace snatched her phone away and leaned back to stop him.

It must have been something serious.

"What?" Trevor demanded, anxiety starting to build. "Why are you leaning away from me like that? I want to read it, too."

"Trevor," Grace said unevenly, turning the phone screen down onto her lap to stop him from peeking. "Are you sure that Logan's interested in bringing you to New York and paying you this hefty salary for strictly business-related reasons?"

"Uh, *yeah*." Well, Trevor wouldn't mind being wrong. But he was determined not to let his interest in more sour the whole, amazing deal. Especially not since Logan had shut him down twice already. But none of that was Grace's business. "Logan needs someone to coach him on being more approachable," Trevor reminded her. "Hello, I'm the king of approachable."

Grace frowned, then said, "Well, according to this article he wasn't just business partners with Ryan Grisham... they were boyfriends when they started the business. And the reason we don't hear about Logan in relation to Rise? It sounds like it's because the two of them had a really nasty break-up. One that, according to some cryptic comments on record from Ryan, makes it sound like Logan was a real ass."

Trevor bristled. "Comments on record from *Ryan*? What did Logan have to say about it?"

"Nothing I can find," Grace said. "As far as I can tell, he's fallen off the radar since then. At least, from anything public. But, if he had a tendency to mix up business and... more. And then hang his boyfriend out to dry—"

"Are you even serious?" Trevor's irritation turned to anger. "He wouldn't need to fly me out to New York if he wanted to, I don't know. I don't even know what you're implying. Screw me over somehow? Mess with my head? He wouldn't need to do this whole, elaborate, New York thing if that was the case. And besides..."

Logan had repeatedly shut down Trevor's flirting, making it clear time and again he was only interested in a business relationship, but that felt a little too embarrassing to admit. But regardless, no matter how much flirting Logan let Trevor get away with, there was no way that Trevor could believe Logan had some sort of weird, nefarious designs on him. Logan was too... good inside. Trevor trusted that, despite the man's reserved nature.

"No," he said, realizing Grace was waiting for him to finish his argument. "No way. Logan is a better man than that, and if you ask me, those one-sided media reports are a little too weighted in Ryan Grisham's favor to sound believable. Logan isn't like that. I know you don't believe it, but it's *true*."

Grace shook her head, obviously not buying it. She was his best friend, but sometimes she was a little too cynical for her own good. Trevor crossed his arms and turned away from her, outraged. None of them were willing to give Logan a chance. When it came to Logan as a customer, Trevor had never minded. But now that Logan was his... employer? Now that they'd taken their relationship, such as it was, outside the bounds of the Ashby's fitting rooms and Logan had spent a little time with the man?

And, fine, maybe Trevor was going a little OTT with his newfound, fierce loyalty to the man, but he'd always been one to trust his gut, and right now it was screaming in protest at the way Grace was trying to characterize Logan.

Grace tugged on his arm, making him turn to face her again.

"Fine. Sorry. I just want you to be safe, and you've got to admit, none of us know this man, and now he's going to fly you away for six weeks?" Her lips twitched with humor, even though the concern in her eyes remained. "What if he gets you all the way to New York, and then it turns out it was all just some convoluted strategy to get you in bed and make you his love-slave or something?"

Trevor grinned, wiping it off his face as fast as he could. *Um, yes, please?* But no, that's not what Grace wanted to hear. Her worry about him was actually kind of sweet.

"If that's what he thinks is going to happen, then I'm going to tell him to shove the deal up his ass and leave," Trevor lied. He could walk away from New York and ten thousand dollars if somehow the whole deal ended up being creptastic, but over Logan trying to get him in bed? Not a chance. Still, for Grace's sake, he added, "But he *won't*, Grace, because Logan is a *good guy*—" and, no matter how

Trevor tried to spin it in his own head, not interested, "— and, besides, he has no reason to go to all that trouble over some Ashby's employee from Chicago."

"I'm just worried about you, Trevor," Grace said. "You'll be going all the way out there without any support. Hopefully Elliott and Ash will be in New York at the same time, so you have some kind of lifeline. It's a long way to go on your own without a solid backup plan."

Their friends Elliott and Ash had an apartment in New York, and Trevor had to admit, it would be pretty awesome if they *were* there at the same time. He honestly didn't think he'd need "backup," but it would be great to have friends in the city. He may have slipped in his little dig about hooking up with hot guys in New York to Logan earlier—more of a retaliation to Logan's repeated lack of interest—but the truth was, Trevor wasn't planning on it.

Not that he wouldn't mind getting laid, but... well, okay. No "buts." He could really use some sex, but if Logan was off the table, faceless strangers didn't sound that appealing, either.

"Dudes, calm down about the whole is-Logan-a-bad-guy issue," Jose cut in, tapping the screen of Barry's phone. He grinned. "Do you know what Barry just found out? Logan Carter sold his shares of Rise after the messy breakup and went and invested in some other companies. One of which is..."

"*What*, already?" Grace asked, rolling her eyes at Jose's attempt at drama.

"Logan Carter is one of the two founders of bLoved," Barry said, putting Grace out of her misery. "The man clearly has a knack for backing the right horse."

Grace paused to think, then she laughed. "So what you're telling me is, there's no chance he's hiring Trevor for illicit reasons when he has access to a whole network of single gay men at his fingertips?"

"Nah," Jose said, shaking his head. He glanced at Barry, giving him the kind of private love-smile that seemed to pack a whole conversation into it. Jose turned back to Grace. "What Barry's saying is, bLoved is all about falling in love and finding your true match. If Logan is one of the founders, it's gotta mean that he believes in love. He's not going to lure Trevor out to New York for some casual, six-week hookup."

Trevor frowned, not sure how he felt about that reasoning. Good? *He* wasn't looking for love, but maybe it was a good thing that Logan was onboard with the kind of company that helped find it.

Did Logan have a boyfriend? He'd been fishing all over the place about Trevor, but he hadn't actually said.

Maybe he was already taken.

But if he wasn't, and if Jose and Barry were right, he'd probably be looking for the type of long-term commitment that Trevor had always shied away from. He sighed, wanting to get off the subject and go back to the part where he was just excited about the crazy, once-in-a-lifetime New York City opportunity.

"Well," Grace said, picking up her beer. "If you go to New York and Logan *does* turn out to be a certified creep—bLoved or not—you know you can call me, right? I'll drive down right then and there to pick you up, okay?"

"Thanks, Grace," Trevor said, picking up his own beer and clinking it against hers. "And same goes, if you end up getting into any trouble while I'm gone. You need me? I'll be back in a flash."

"Yeah... about that. You might not wanna abandon ship on New York right away, though," Heidi, another coworker of theirs, called from down the table. She winked at him "Trev, do you realize it's going to be *Fashion Week* while you're there?"

Trevor sat straight up in his chair and locked eyes with Heidi from down the table, the tension from the earlier conversation disappearing as a wave of fresh excitement prickled through his chest, rising up inside him like bubbles through champagne until it burst out in a disbelieving laugh.

"Fashion Week?"

Heidi waved her phone at him, tapping the screen as if that proved it and laughing along with him.

"You're not serious!" Trevor exclaimed, wanting to squeal but holding it in through a valiant effort. Could life get any better?

"I am *so* serious," Heidi cooed back. "Fashion Week, baby. You're a *star*."

There was no way Trevor would ever get in to watch

any of the shows, but just the thought that he'd be sharing New York with hundreds of celebrated models and designers made the unknown so much better.

Trevor was going to be in New York City during Fashion Week. If there was ever a sign that the trip was meant to be, this was it.

"Fashion Week, you guys!" Trevor cried. "It's going to be *Fashion Week*! Oh my God, what am I even going to wear?"

"And so it begins," Grace said with a playful roll of her eyes. "You couldn't have told him about Fashion Week while we were walking out the doors at the end of the night, Heidi?"

Heidi stuck out her tongue, and conversation at the Ashby's table resumed, but Trevor's heart and mind were filled with New York.

And, if he were honest, with the gorgeous man he was about to share it with.

Chapter 5

LOGAN

By silhouette, Chicago was breathtaking. Staggering skyscrapers reminded Logan of New York City, but, even then, the flavor of the architecture was wrong. When he'd seen the lights of Chicago by night, they were different than the lights in New York. The flashy, look-at-me vibe was absent. Chicago was sure of itself, understated, and yet beautiful for it. And now, at midday, without any lights to help it along, Chicago was all class and modernity.

Somewhere in that city was Trevor.

Logan turned away from the window in his hotel suite, pushing the thought aside. It had been a week since Trevor had said yes to his business proposal, and he'd promptly handed off the task of arranging the details to Hiro. There hadn't been any reason to contact Trevor directly in the interim, and—since Trevor hadn't been available yet to help him with the talk-show appearance he'd flown in for that morning—there still wasn't any reason.

Hiro had reported that Trevor had confirmed he'd been granted the time off work from Ashby's, and Trevor was scheduled to start the contract on Monday, just three days away. Logan was planning on staying in Chicago over the weekend so that he could fly back to New York with Trevor then, and he'd brought enough work with him to keep him occupied in his hotel suite for the duration, now that the morning's media appearance was completed.

The one Trevor hadn't yet been available to help him with.

Frank had insisted that they couldn't afford to skip it, regardless of Logan's lack of coaching, and Logan had agreed. He'd even been hopeful that he might be able to carry it off, even without coaching. Somehow having gained an unfounded sense of... not confidence. Possibility, maybe? ...after hiring Trevor.

Logan had been wrong, though. He grimaced, fiddling with the clasp on his briefcase absently as it replayed in his mind. He simply wasn't a people person, and there was no way to sugarcoat the fact that he'd bombed it. The host had been as uncomfortable with him as he'd been with her.

She'd obviously been expecting someone with Kelly's grace and charm, and had been unprepared to deal with Logan's total lack of either.

The shame of the botched television appearance weighed heavily on his heart.

Over the entire course of his life, Logan had always striven for perfection. It had been drilled into him from childhood, and the fact that he'd never managed to attain it in his parents' eyes—not to mention the loss of their love when he'd come out—had hurt him more deeply than he let on. He'd failed again with Ryan—the only time he'd ever opened himself up to a long-term relationship—but he wasn't used to failing in business. Business was his escape, and the one area that he felt utterly confident in. He threw himself into it not only to prove his worth to those who had wronged him—but to prove his worth to himself. The fact that he'd failed that morning so miserably almost knocked the wind out of him, even though, logically, he knew it wasn't unexpected.

He didn't know what he'd been thinking when he'd imagined he could pull it off alone.

After so many incredible steps forward in his professional life, the look on the morning show host's face had made him feel like he was right back to where he'd been when he left his parents' house for the last time.

Empty. Cold. Alone.

A failure.

Logan turned away from his briefcase, leaving it un-opened, and went back to stand at the floor-to-ceiling win-dows again. Antsy, when usually work allowed him to lose himself with a focused intensity that had served him well over the years. Hopefully, Trevor's energy would counteract the gut-twisting emotions inside him for the next appear-ance he was scheduled to make on Monday afternoon, back in New York.

Logan knew he was putting a lot on the line by not hiring a trained professional—not just for himself, but for Kelly, for whom bLoved was everything he had. But Logan trusted that he'd made the right decision. Trusted *Trevor*, on a gut level that he had no rational explanation for. But he knew that Trevor was the kind of person who invested himself into whatever it was he was doing. His personable attitude at Ashby's and the attention to detail evident in his tailoring work made Logan sure of it.

As his public-appearance coach, Logan was sure that Trevor would do a fine job. Better than fine. Despite the morning's failure, the sense of hopeful possibility that Trevor had inspired in him—the idea that the future might be different than the past—remained. And, in a small, self-ish way, Logan knew he simply wanted to feel more of the things Trevor stirred up inside him. The carefully con-structed walls Logan maintained to keep people out so he could focus on work were ineffective in Trevor's presence, and even though Logan would retain his commitment to keeping their relationship professional, there was no reason to lie to himself about the fact that he was looking forward to spending time with him.

And... he thought Trevor might be, too. Yes, Trevor was over-the-moon excited about the chance to broaden his horizons by taking on the job, but Logan thought there was something more to his eagerness.

Or maybe he just hoped.

Which was silly—not a word anyone would normally apply to Logan—because, again, he had no intention of getting involved on a personal level.

The sharp, rhythmic beep of his phone pulled him away from the floor-to-ceiling windows of the hotel room and back to the side of the bed. Logan took his phone from where it was charging on his nightstand and answered the call.

"Logan Carter speaking."

"Logan." Kelly followed the greeting with a strained laugh, and Logan pinched the bridge of his nose, knowing just from that that Kelly must have seen the broadcast. A fact Kelly confirmed when he added, "I just saw the *Chicago Morning Show* broadcast and... ouch."

"That bad?" Logan sank onto the edge of the bed and stared out the window from where he sat. He knew the answer, but it would have been nice, for once, to have been wrong.

"That bad." The stress in Kelly's voice came through loud and clear. "The hostess looked like she would rather have been anywhere else than in her little barrel chair.

And the awkward silences? Man. I think even the audience wished that it could have attended another studio session. It was *bad*."

Logan winced. Worse than his own failure was the fact that he'd let Kelly down. "My coach will be available starting Monday," he said, hoping the news would reassure Kelly. "He's finishing up another contract, and then he'll be joining me in New York so that he can get to work on fixing my problem."

"Your *problems*. With an *'s'*. Logan, you looked so damn stiff on the set that you might as well have been a robot—and not even one of those fancy Japanese ones. We're talking like... knockoff tin-man types. And your personality matched." Kelly paused, sighing, and Logan forced himself to relax his grip on the phone. Kelly's words were all too reminiscent of other conversations Logan had had in the past. With Ryan.

"I'm sorry," Logan said stiffly. Robotically. Kelly was right, but it was what he reverted to when he was uncomfortable.

"I know, Logan," Kelly said, sounding discouraged. "We both knew you weren't, um..."

"I'm not cut out for it," Logan said, saving Kelly the awkwardness.

"There's just no way you're going to be able to sell *love*," Kelly said, a tacit agreement. "Not like that. I hope this coach you've got coming in is worth his salt. What are his qualifications?"

Logan stiffened up again, and he stared at a point in the distance as he tried to reason out how to best explain why he'd selected Trevor to the man who was counting on him not to let their business fail. Wealthy enough from his past endeavors, Logan's life wasn't contingent on bLoved's success—but Kelly's was. With all his eggs in one basket, if bLoved tanked, so did Kelly.

"Logan?" Kelly prompted.

"He made me laugh," Logan answered without thinking.

"Holy fucking shit," Kelly blurted, laughing himself. "Put him on the permanent payroll. *Done*."

Logan felt his own lips twitch in response to the relief in Kelly's voice, but, really... was he *that* dour?

"I think the only time I've ever seen you laugh was when we went out to Salt Lake for that conference that turned out to be a total bust, and we decided to skip out and spend our time more wisely by getting drunk instead," Kelly said. "By the time I got you back to your hotel room, you were a person again. If this coach can pry that out of you without turning your blood to booze, then he must be big league. I'm surprised you're getting expertise like that on the shoestring budget we arranged. So we're talking... what? Celebrity PR maven? World class comedian and life coach? I know that Frank and Richard were worried about being able to find someone who could handle the job on such short notice."

Was there any way Logan could fib his way out of revealing Trevor's lack of qualifications? If he told Kelly that he was trusting in an untried retail employee with a sparkling personality to iron out *his* personality issues, and—more importantly—guide him in knocking their current publicity campaign out of the park, he knew Kelly would have a fit. In fact, he might even make a stink about trying to come back and do the publicity himself.

The officer assigned to the case had managed to convince Kelly to leave almost immediately after the meeting they'd had, and Kelly had already been whisked out of town with his new bodyguard, under strict directive not to return under any circumstance until the police had a handle on the threats against him.

"I guess I just got lucky when I found him," Logan finally said, hoping that the fact that it was true—even if not the way Kelly would assume—would sell it. If Logan refused to commit to specifics about Trevor, he wouldn't have to lie about them. "It turned out that I was in the right place at the right time, and the pieces fit together in just the right way."

"Here's hoping. Sounds like you found a good match, though." There was shuffling on the other end of the phone, and Logan heard as Kelly said something in the distance. When he returned to the phone and spoke next, he sounded exasperated. "Sorry about that."

"What's happening over there?" Logan asked, not sure where "there" actually was. Officer Byrne, Kelly, and Kelly's bodyguard were the only ones who had that information. "Is everything okay?"

"No," Kelly grumbled. "The bodyguard they stuck me with is some friend of that police officer who was at the meeting. I mean, I'm grateful that he's keeping me alive, I guess, but he's so fucking annoying, Logan. Constantly prying into my business like it's *his*... tailing me... watching me wherever I go... I am *not* having a good time."

"You wouldn't be having a good time here, either," Logan replied, sternly. "Death threats are serious business, Kelly."

"This has gotten blown out of proportion," Kelly groused. "You know I get hate mail all the time as the public face for bLoved. It's not that big of a deal. People write derogatory things to me because I promote *sinful* lifestyles. It's par for the course when you're vocal about who you are."

"Hate mail is one thing, Kelly. Threats are another."

Kelly scoffed, but Logan remembered the flash of fear he'd seen on his face.

"The police never should have gotten involved," Kelly said. "I had taken some guy home, just a hookup, and he got spooked and called them when that stupid note showed up on my pillow—" Sewn into it, Logan remembered, "—but it's not any worse than anything else that's been happening. I mean... not *happening*. But, you know, the scare tactics and such."

"Wait." Logan paused, taking a moment to choose his words carefully. Outside their monthly business meetings in Chicago, he and Kelly didn't typically stay in touch on a personal level, and while Kelly had occasionally brought up some of the more over-the-top hate mail bLoved received, he'd never mentioned "scare tactics" before. "There was more going on? Incidents that you didn't call in to the police?"

"Yeah," Kelly said, sighing. "Minor shit. My car's been vandalized, and one time I arrived at the office and found the window smashed. Just petty acts of damage. I had everything fixed up, then I moved on. There's no sense in wasting resources on negativity."

A chill ran down Logan's spine, and, more than ever, he was glad that Kelly had agreed to stay out of the public eye. Logan would figure out whatever he had to in regard to his own limitations to keep the business moving in the right direction so that Kelly could stay safe.

"Did you tell the police about those incidents after the death threats were reported?" he asked.

"Nah. No point. I'm pretty sure they're all the same guy, given the kind of notes left, so, you know, the police are already on it."

Logan rubbed at the bridge of his nose, trying to stop the onset of a tension headache. Kelly's failure to take it seriously bothered him more than he'd like to admit, but at least something was being done about it.

"This bodyguard you're with, is he the real deal?" Logan asked. "He's not just some gym rat who looks intimidating, is he?"

"No, he's real," Kelly said, sounding exasperated again.

"Annoying as shit, but definitely legit. You'd think a guy with a body that incredible would loosen up a little, but no. He's got a serious stick up his ass, and... ugh. I don't really want to talk about it."

"That's fine," Logan said. He was happy to respect Kelly's privacy, and doubted Kelly considered him a friend. As long as Kelly was safe, that was all that mattered.

"What I *do* want to bring up is the media appearance you've got on Monday," Kelly said. "I've got a few tips on how you can come across a little more personable. Hopefully, your coach will be on top of it, but just in case, here are some simple things, okay?"

"Sure," Logan said, feeling himself tense at the reminder. Even though Trevor would be with him for the appearance on Monday, his failure that morning had drained some of the optimism out of him.

"First of all," Kelly said. "Don't be afraid to talk with your hands, and it's actually advisable to smile and, you know, look like a *real* person... not a robot. Try to be the nice, down-to-earth kind of guy you'd want to leave your dog with if you had to go away for two weeks."

"I don't have a dog," Logan said stiffly.

Kelly laughed. "I know, Logan, but pretend that you do. And that you *love* that dog, and you want to make sure he's going to be cared for. Do you want to leave your beloved dog with some cold, calculated robot, who doesn't look like he'll pet him on the head in just the right way, or do you want to leave him with Mr. Warm-and-Approachable, who's smiling and speaking casually, but with passion? Remember that we're selling *love*, Logan. It's not music or videos or long board meetings or—"

Kelly stopped speaking abruptly, and Logan heard voices in the distance again. One belonged to Kelly—whose annoyance from earlier in the conversation escalated into sounding pissed beyond belief—and the voice was low and deep and seemed to be arguing, even though it didn't sound like the other man was losing his temper. After a few seconds, the man with the deep voice came on the line.

"Mr. Davis has been asked not to use his phone for prolonged personal use, and I'm afraid he'll have to let you go. My apologies."

In the background, Logan could hear Kelly cussing and insisting that it *wasn't* personal use. The bodyguard sounded unperturbed, and Logan realized he was actually smiling as he tried to picture Kelly—emotional and prone to act before thinking—putting up with that.

"No need to apologize," Logan said to the bodyguard. "Please wish Kelly my best. And... thank you. For keeping him safe."

"Just doing my job." The bodyguard terminated the call, and Logan set the phone back on the bedside table to finish charging.

Kelly was physically safe, and now it was up to Logan to make sure he was financially safe as well. With a frustrated sigh, he fell back on the mattress and stared up at the ceiling. A smoke detector's red light blinked on and off in the center of it, and Logan focused his eyes on the flash as his mind raced. What was he going to do if he turned out to be wrong about Trevor, and he wasn't coach material, after all?

Or, worse, if Logan proved to be uncoachable?

Business was about taking calculated risks, but after the fiasco on the *Chicago Morning Show*, Logan was beginning to doubt his calculations. Perhaps it would have been better to hire someone who'd been coaching individuals through public appearances for years, instead of the young man whom he'd impulsively made the offer to. Trevor, who'd already started breaking him out of his shell, but who, really, Logan knew very little about.

But there was something in Trevor that spoke to a part of Logan that had long been dormant. The personable, sensitive part of his soul that he'd hidden away for so long. By doing nothing more than being himself, Trevor had broken through the barriers Logan had in place, a little bit more each time they'd met, chipping away with humor and his incessant flirting and his relentless optimism and spirit.

Maybe, with a little time, Trevor would be able to break through them completely, freeing Logan from the shackles he'd forced himself into after Ryan's betrayal. Setting him free from years of introspection and the lifelong feeling that, no matter what he accomplished, it would never be good enough.

Logan closed his eyes, sighing. That was... outside the parameters of the contract. His lips curved up of their own volition, as he thought about how well that phrase suited most things about Trevor. Logan had absolute faith that Trevor would do everything he'd agreed to—his professionalism and work ethic weren't in question—but that he would also bring his own flare to it. And that, from what Logan had experienced of him so far, would *definitely* push things "outside the parameters of the contract."

Logan's mind started to wander down dangerous corridors, chasing that thought. With his winning smile and quick wit, Trevor was the complete package. The week before, at dinner, when Trevor had lit up at the table upon hearing Logan's invitation to work for him in New York... Logan smiled.

He wanted to see that light in Trevor's eyes again.

When Trevor smiled like that, the corners of his eyes wrinkled a little, and his nose scrunched up in a subtle, but impossibly adorable, way. Trevor wasn't the *adorable* type— it certainly wasn't a word Logan would have thought to apply to him before. Competent, yes. Outgoing, definitely.

Sexy.

Logan groaned, pushing the thought away. There was no denying that Trevor's confidence made him impossibly attractive, but also, having seen him so full of joy when he'd accepted the New York offer had made Logan... happy.

And it had been a long time since anyone had made Logan feel happy like that.

As his mind wandered, contemplating Trevor and what he might be doing at that moment, he let himself wonder what type of man Trevor was outside Ashby's. He'd seen a glimpse of it when he'd taken him to dinner, and Trevor's zest for life and enthusiasm in all things was contagious, and the hint of his flamboyance—even at work—spoke to a developed sense of self. Trevor knew who he was, and he wasn't afraid to let others know it, too. Logan admired that about him as much as he marveled at it.

It was exactly that confidence that made Trevor so damn attractive.

Logan's cock throbbed, begging for attention.

He denied it.

He'd never let himself fantasize about Trevor before, and doing so now would be a bad precedent to set if he planned on getting through the next six weeks without, as Trevor had said, crossing the line. He glanced over at his briefcase, thinking of the work he'd brought with him. That was where his attention needed to be.

Instead, he traced his palm along the bulge in his slacks, Trevor's cocky grin in his mind's eye. *Fuck.* Logan's lips parted on a little gust of desire, and he stroked himself through the front of his pants as his cock strained against the fabric. He spread his knees apart, and it was all too easy to picture Trevor in front of him, Trevor holding eye contact as he sank to his knees, daring Logan to stop him with some kind of sassy comment...

Logan groaned, forcing his hand off himself. He had no problem with sex, and none whatsoever with self-satisfaction, but if he let himself go there with Trevor—even in fantasy—he knew it was going to be damn hard to close the lid on those desires again.

Logan stood up abruptly, the motion causing his cock to rub against the smooth fabric of his pants with just enough friction to make him realize he was going to have to do something other than ignore it. He fumbled at his belt. His erection would only get in the way of his ability to concentrate if he didn't do something about it. It made sense to handle it quickly and efficiently so he could shut off the train of thought that his traitorous brain kept insisting on riding.

He shoved his pants just far enough down on his hips to free himself, his cock slapping against his stomach as soon as he freed it. The image that had started to form earlier appeared in his mind's eye again, fully formed, and he wrapped his fist around his hard length even as he made one last effort to deny what he was fantasizing about.

Trevor, on his knees and looking up at him from under those long lashes.

Trevor, his laughing mouth stretching wide as Logan guided himself inside it.

Logan gave up trying to justify what he was doing. He'd already decided it would be too risky to get involved with Trevor on a personal level—Trevor drew him in too easily, stirred too many things inside him—but fantasizing wasn't getting involved. This was private, and it was... necessary.

Trevor had been on his mind far too much, and the

attraction he'd never acted on—the one that had simmered under the surface from the first day Trevor had turned that bright smile on him—was too strong to deny. Best to do something about it here, now, and get it out of the way. He needed to be able to interact with Trevor for the next six weeks without letting these sorts of feelings interfere.

His hand tightened on his cock, but there was no going back. If he were being honest with himself, there hadn't been from the first. It was why he always returned to the Chicago Ashby's, after all. In his heart, Logan knew it was the truth. The thinly veiled excuses about his wardrobe needs that he'd pawned off on Hiro were just that: excuses.

The truth was, he wanted Trevor.

He groaned, sinking back onto the bed as he worked his cock. Fuck, he was hard. He usually took care of himself in the shower, where cleanup was fast and it was simply a superficial satisfaction of a physical need.

This was different.

He knew he should take off his clothes. At this rate, he was going to make a mess. He should at least unbutton his shirt... or pause and get a hand towel from the hotel bathroom... or finish taking his pants off. But he was past that point, his balls already starting to tighten as he imagined that it wasn't his own hand at all, but Trevor's dirty mouth wrapped around his cock.

That he wasn't thrusting into his fist, but fucking deep into the heat of Trevor's throat.

Logan groaned, his breath starting to come in short,

hard bursts as his hips drove up into his clenched hand. He was going to have Trevor for six weeks, and it was all too easy for him to imagine what it *could* be like in New York... Trevor's full lips and expressive eyes, flirting with him from the wings while Logan made each TV appearance... waiting in the green room beforehand, Trevor on his lap, grinding down on him as he whispered sassy, dirty comments that made Logan laugh even as they made him... so... fucking... hard...

Logan groaned. Long and loud and with absolutely no ability to stop it. He didn't even recognize the deep, almost desperate sounds coming from his throat. He closed his eyes, lost. Past the point of holding himself back. Knowing that if the fantasy were real, Trevor would tease him to the point that he'd have no choice but to take control. To bend Trevor over the arm of the couch and fuck him senseless.

But Trevor would never be a passive sex partner.

It was all too easy to imagine him gasping as Logan pounded into him, to picture Trevor pushing back against him, giving him one of those teasing looks over his shoulder as he egged Logan on for more.

Logan's arm trembled as his breath started to grow even more ragged. He bucked up into his hand, then, with a low curse, rolled over onto his stomach to thrust down into it. Fuck, it was filthy of him, but he couldn't help it. His vision of Trevor was irresistible, and the sooner he worked it out of his system, the better.

Sweat beaded Logan's brow, and he fucked into his fist

with abandon. He'd need Trevor to be naked. He wanted to see the bare length of his slender back stretched out in front of him, wanted to hold him down, run his hand over the long curve of his spine, take total possession of Trevor's sweet, round little ass.

Wanted to watch his own cock disappear inside it... again and again. Driving them both toward the kind of ecstasy he could feel rising within him now. Logan grunted and squeezed his eyes shut, losing himself to the fantasy.

Not just fucking Trevor, but being *connected* to him. Taming all that cocky sass and burying himself inside Trevor's heat, inside the welcoming goodness that was... that was... just... *Trevor*...

"Fuck fuck *fuuuuuuuuuckkkk*."

The panted words devolved into a long, low moan, and Logan slammed his hips forward one more time, coming into his hand. He'd been bracing himself with one arm on the firm mattress, but as he gasped out the last of his release, he collapsed down onto it, burying his face in the crook of his elbow.

A soothing warmth rushed through him as he spent himself, and for a moment, he just lay there, not letting himself think.

Trevor was his newest employee. Trevor was *business*. Anything more was as tempting as it was terrifying, because Logan hadn't just imagined fucking Trevor... he'd imagined all the feelings that might go along with it, too.

And letting himself go down *that* road was a sure-fire

path to the kind of heartache he'd been protecting himself from for years.

Trevor had made it clear he was all about casual dating. He flirted with Logan... but not *just* with Logan. And, even if Logan ever found the courage to open up to a man the way he had with Ryan once before, he didn't have it in him to deal with the aftermath when that man inevitably found Logan lacking.

...you're like a robot... all you care about is work... good thing you've got that body to make up for what's lacking in your personality... Logan, you're just no fun...

He shoved Ryan's voice out of his mind firmly, rolling off the bed and shedding his clothes on the way to the shower. He'd allow himself the fantasy in the privacy of his hotel room just this once, but, now that he'd enjoyed it, that was it.

There was to be no more indulging in Trevor.

Whatever would happen between the two of them in New York would be business, and business only. Mixing pleasure into his professional life had burned him once before, and Logan wasn't willing to let it happen again. No matter what he felt—no matter what he might *want*—there was no room for Trevor in his bed... and most certainly not in his heart.

It wouldn't be worth the pain that came with it... no matter how tempting the idea felt at the moment.

Chapter 6

TREVOR

TREVOR HADN'T REALIZED THAT bLOVED'S HEADQUARTERS were located in Chicago, but Hiro, Logan's personal assistant, had called him and asked him if he could drop by for an emergency meeting, a few hours before his flight was scheduled to leave for New York. Hiro had also said that he and Logan were in town, and would be flying back to New York with Trevor.

Trevor had no particular reason to be happy about that... except, hello, stuck sitting next to his hot, new boss-slash-fantasy-fodder for an hour and a half while they flew the friendly skies? Yes, please.

The address Hiro had given him was located off

Madison, in the Loop. The stuffy business district was perfectly suited to the way Logan presented himself, even if Trevor might have imagined a warmer, more hip location for the vibe bLoved was usually presented as having. Still, wasn't it his job to make sure Logan lost some of the stuffiness, at least on air?

Trevor laughed as he pushed open the door of the old brick building. Fine, not *just* on the air, if he had his way. No way he was going to spend six weeks in New York City and not have a little fun... and, yes, he had no trouble admitting to himself that he was half-hoping to convince Logan to have some of that fun with him. Trevor would manage, regardless, because... New *York*. But he'd always been one to seize opportunity when it came his way, and since he'd be spending so much time with Logan anyway, and Logan had yet to tell him to back off the flirting...

Trevor sighed softly, reining himself in. No, Logan hadn't told him to back off, but he *had* made it clear—repeatedly—that he wanted nothing more from Trevor than what he'd asked for: a business relationship. Which was fine. Golden. Trevor didn't need some man who didn't actively *want* him. There were plenty of fish in the sea.

The first-floor offices housing bLoved's headquarters boasted their own, unique street entrance: small, but respectable. Still, for a moment, Trevor had to wonder if he was in the right place. The offices were closed to the public, and there was no receptionist to offer guidance. Before he could second-guess himself, though, Logan swept in through the front doors, looking slightly harried and hella hot.

Trevor relaxed, his mood brightening instantly.

"Have you been waiting long?" Logan asked. He stomped the bottoms of his shoes on the carpet near the door and looked Trevor over clinically.

Hmm. So much for hoping Logan would be happy to see him, too.

"Nope," Trevor answered, looking around the sedate office.

The building they were in didn't span a city block or ooze sophistication, but Hiro had let drop that Logan—not bLoved—*owned* it. Trevor struggled to pay rent on his studio apartment some months; the thought of owning property was as exciting as it was out of his reach. Logan moved in entirely different circles than he did, but—Trevor grinned—he'd still seen Logan in his underwear.

"So this is it, huh?" he asked, sweeping an arm out to take in the bland room. "The bustling hub of Love, Inc.?"

"No," Logan said dryly. "There are other rooms. People, too."

Trevor grinned. Logan *did* have a sense of humor, even if he didn't want anyone to know it.

Logan gestured to a door almost directly across from the front door. "The conference room is through there, and Hiro and Frank are likely already waiting on us. Come along."

Trevor followed Logan to the darkly paneled doors, feeling an uncharacteristic moment of trepidation. Was he dressed well enough for this meeting?

He wasn't even entirely sure what it was about, since he'd taken care of whatever paperwork Hiro had needed electronically the week before. And Hiro hadn't mentioned a dress code, so Trevor had assumed that business-professional was a safe bet. Beneath his heavy winter jacket, Logan certainly seemed put together, which pointed toward that being a good choice. Still, Trevor had opted to wear a tie, but not a suit jacket, and he hoped it was enough. He'd never rubbed elbows with a man as rich as Logan, and he was still figuring out the rules as he went.

When they entered the conference room, two men were seated at the boardroom table—one, Trevor assumed was Hiro, based on his obviously Asian heritage, and the other was an aging man who must have been the Frank that Logan had referred to. Both men wore jackets, and Trevor internally cussed himself out for not having the foresight to bring one, just in case. Then he took a breath, letting it out slowly. Feelings of fashion inadequacy were just nerves, and he knew it.

It would be fine.

Logan nodded at the two men briskly, but there were no hellos or introductions, and when Logan took a seat in one of the office chairs pulled up to the table, Trevor rallied, quashing the nerves and pulling up his more comfortable take-me-as-I-am confidence. He leaned across the table, offering his open hand to Hiro and Frank. "Trevor Rogers," he said. "It's a pleasure to meet you."

"Likewise." Hiro rose and shook his hand, but Frank just responded with a brisk nod, reminiscent of Logan's. Other than that, he ignored Trevor and launched into a verbal attack on Logan.

"Do you know how much time and energy, not to mention *dollars*, we've put into this campaign, Logan?" Frank demanded. His eyes flicked toward Trevor, and he added a heavily laden, "What are you *thinking*?"

Trevor scowled. He wasn't dumb, and although he hadn't been briefed on what the meeting was about, he could put two and two together. Frank was referring to *him*... and definitely not favorably.

"Excuse me?" Trevor interjected, his earlier bout of nerves disappearing as a wave of what-the-fuck swamped him. Uh-uh. If this *Frank*, with his ill-fitted suit and knock-off watch, thought he got to shit all over Trevor and his chance to spend six weeks in New York with Logan, Trevor had no problem setting him straight.

Frank ignored Trevor, continuing to address Logan. "We gave you the budget to hire a professional. This campaign isn't a joke. If you botch these appearances, we're sunk, and all of us are out of a job. Do you really think this is the time to be squandering resources and making risky bets?"

Oh, *hell* no, he wasn't. Trevor was on his feet before he'd realized he'd moved. Frank was talking about him like he wasn't even there, and Trevor wasn't going to stand for it.

"I'm sorry," he said, pouring every ounce of fuck-you he had available into the two words. "I didn't realize you'd asked me here so you could trash-talk me as if I don't exist. Next time, I'll do you a favor and stand out in the lobby while you tear into me like that. I mean, really?"

Frank's eyebrows shot up in surprise, and Hiro sent Trevor an apologetic look, but it was Logan who spoke next. And the tone of voice—cold and hard and absolutely nonnegotiable as he addressed Frank—sent a little thrill through Trevor, despite his current and totally justified outrage.

"I *do* know what this campaign means to bLoved, Frank," Logan said. "And I have selected the best man to assist us in meeting those goals."

Trevor shivered. When had icy become so fucking hot?

"Trevor Rogers is a talented individual who will perform to the highest industry standards," Logan continued, his eyes boring into Frank. "And most likely, beyond that. More importantly, as he has just pointed out, he's right here. You will refer to him, and address him, with respect."

Frank's jaw tightened, but for all his questionable fashion sense, he clearly had balls of steel. He didn't back down. "We didn't even know about—" he waved a hand in Trevor's direction, shaking his head, "—this, Logan. We've already found you a professional, straight out of a Hollywood PR agency," he said. "The man is waiting on our signature to finalize the contract. What the hell did you think you were doing, signing this kid on through Hiro without running him by us?"

"I am *not* a child," Trevor said, clenching his fists as he seethed at Frank's continued, condescending dismissal. "I'm twenty-seven, and I'm a *person*, just like you are... albeit one who has clearly had more experience playing nice with others. If you have an issue with me, would you kindly speak it to my face? I do *not* appreciate being talked about like this."

Logan stood, placing a firm hand on Trevor's shoulder, and Trevor snapped his attention away from Frank to look up at him. That ice he'd heard in Logan's voice when he'd addressed Frank had frozen his gorgeous blue eyes into hard chips, and his lips were set in a thin line that betrayed his anger. But it wasn't at Trevor.

"Sit," Logan said. Not a question. "Let me deal with this."

Trevor's gaze flicked across Logan's face, and he found himself unable to speak. Not only did Logan look dangerous in that moment, as though he were a sprung viper, ready to strike, but there was power in his voice that... well, fine. It was turning Trevor the fuck on, if he were honest.

It wasn't like him to feel attracted toward a man who ordered him around. On the contrary, Trevor's personality was strong enough that more than one person had accused him of bowling them over with it, but the idea of someone else taking control for once. No, not "someone else"... *Logan*... It was hot.

Trevor had zero patience for the kind of shade Frank was throwing, and normally wouldn't think he'd react well to someone else taking charge, but apparently—if the little surge of heat in his dick that he was doing his best to ignore was any indication—Logan was the exception.

Although he'd spoken firmly to Trevor, the tone of his voice wasn't patronizing. The control Logan assumed over the meeting was powerful without being self-absorbed or superior. He understood the weight of his words and how to use them effectively. The display of dominance made his mind start to move in distinctly not-safe-for-work directions, and it was an effort to drag his attention off the other ways he could think of for Logan to use that confidence outside of the boardroom and refocus on the dressing down Logan was unleashing on Frank.

For Trevor.

"First of all," Logan said, the words lashing out like a whip. "Don't make me remind you again that you will speak with respect to bLoved's newest hire. Trevor may not have Hollywood PR experience, but what he lacks for in formal training, he makes up for in extensive knowledge of *me* and my idiosyncrasies. Secondly, let me assure you that whatever peppy, overly positive PR trainer you could find wouldn't be worth the expense, because I know who I am as a person, and that person would *not* take that kind of chipper attitude seriously."

"You *would* take it seriously, because if you don't, this whole thing will spiral right down the drain," Frank shot back. "The formal training you would receive from *a professional* is the only hope we have of turning this thing around. We *all* saw the disaster that was your *Chicago Morning Show* appearance on Friday. A day, I might add, when we had our first day in *twelve quarters* with more canceled memberships than new subscriptions! I'm talking about the first time since we *launched*, Logan. If you don't think there's a direct correlation, you're out of your mind."

Most of the business talk went over Trevor's head, but he didn't miss the way Frank's attack made Logan's jaw clench. And, by the impassioned way Frank spoke, obviously whatever the business situation was, was serious. Trevor hadn't seen Logan on the *Morning Show*—most days, if he wasn't working, Trevor's "morning" tended to start around one in the afternoon—but based on what he was hearing here, he could only imagine how terribly it must have gone.

If Frank hadn't just been such a massive asshat toward him, Trevor might have felt badly for him. Frank was just trying to do his job, and—having seen Logan's lack of people skills—a part of Trevor could sympathize with the man's frustration.

Still, he was a dick, and the whole thing just gave Trevor one more reason to want to knock it out of the park.

"There is no one else I'm willing to work with," Logan said to Frank in a clipped voice. "Trevor's the one I want.

The one I *need*, if we're going to accomplish what we need to with this campaign."

Trevor's dick had reacted to the whole "the one I want, the one I need" bit, and he knew he was going to have to get a handle on that if he was going to make it through the next six weeks with any semblance of professionalism. For God's sake, he'd been dressing and undressing the man every month for the last year without slipping anything more than a few flirtatious comments in here and there. Somehow, everything felt different now, though.

Or maybe it was just a side effect of that dry spell he was really going to have to do something about, one of these days.

"Our budget—" Frank started to say, only to be cut off by Logan.

"The money, ultimately, is mine and Kelly's to decide what to do with, Frank. And I'm more than happy to invest ten thousand of my own funds into this project, if Kelly has any objections to my choice. I have every confidence that Trevor is the right man for the job, and you need to understand, the issue is nonnegotiable."

Trevor blinked. Logan would spend ten thousand of his own dollars on *him*? Sure, as one of the co-founders of Rise, he had to be hella rich, but... dammmmmn.

"What if I told you that *somehow*," Frank's gaze flickered to Trevor for a second before returning to Logan, "word was leached to the media about how you need a PR handler in order to represent bLoved? If you don't select someone discreet, someone with insider knowledge about how to spin—or *hide*—their involvement, this is all going to blow up in our faces, no matter who pays for it. bLoved has done as well as it has in large part because Kelly makes people believe in love, Logan, and we all know it. There's no chance that our target market is going to buy it from you… especially if they think you're just a talking head who doesn't buy it him*self*."

Trevor sat, twisting slowly back and forth in his chair as a creeping sense of guilt built within him. He *had* texted quite a few people about his exciting new position, and not all of them had been close friends. Through word of mouth, the message had been passed around a little too far—but it wasn't as though he'd known who Logan was when he'd shared the news. Or what it might do to the campaign he'd been hired to help with, if word got out.

Logan hadn't looked at him, but Trevor could see that Frank's last words had had an effect on him. *Did* Logan believe in love? Trevor could definitely coach him on personality—Trevor had it in spades, and was more than happy to share—but love? The kind that bLoved's users were looking for—white picket fences and happily-ever-after and the kind of sappy, dreamy-eyed mush that his friends Jose and Elliott had found with their men—that wasn't something that Trevor could help Logan sell. He'd always been more Grindr than bLoved, and even if he did occasionally get a twinge of longing, watching what his friends had, overall,

Trevor wasn't at all convinced that being tied down like that was the way to go.

"I've talked to Kelly," Frank said, sighing. "And he agrees. The whole coached versus authentic thing isn't the image we want to project. Beyond everything else, we need to sell the world on love, and the fact that our product can help find it. If you go out there trained by a literal salesman, one who works retail at one of the biggest department stores in the world, how do you think that's going to come across? Face it, Logan. You need a professional."

"But it's true," Logan protested. "*All* of this is just publicity. What we're selling is hope and algorithms."

"True or not, it doesn't matter," Frank said dismissively. "People don't want to know that the shine on the apples they buy from the store is a wax, and people don't want to know that the man we're sending out into the world whose dating app can give them the love they crave is a fraud who's only trying to get into their wallets. Bottom line is, *you* aren't someone anyone would buy love from, Logan. This is *business*, so I'm not going to sugarcoat it. You won't be able to sell this without help, and the coach you've selected can't give you the kind of help you need."

Logan had instructed him to stay out of the conversation, but when Trevor stole a glance at Logan, he noticed something he'd seen before. From time to time, when Logan visited Ashby's, Trevor would catch sight of him before their appointments began. Days when Logan was like *this*—holding his shoulders stiff and high, eyes drained of his commanding presence, jaw clenched—Trevor always tried to step up his banter. Worked a little harder to try to win a smile, or teased him more about his monochromatic wardrobe choices. Turned up the flirt.

Now, something about the conversation had given Logan the same thousand-mile stare, and the same squared, stiff shoulders. Tension.

Hurt.

"Are you kidding me?" Trevor said, unable to keep silent in the face of it. He didn't rise from his chair, but he gestured at Logan with one hand while he kept his gaze fixed on Frank. He may not be able to address the business and financial issues Frank was concerned about, but he could definitely do royally pissed off and impassioned when it came to what Logan could or could not sell to the public. "You're trying to say that people wouldn't buy the concept of love from Logan? Are you blind? In my hands, he's going to *shine*. What you are looking at is a *living billboard*. Do you see that face?"

Logan still looked tense as hell, but Frank didn't interrupt. His attention shifted to Logan's face, then back to Trevor.

"A jawline for *days*," Trevor said, letting his own eyes roam over Logan freely. Not a hardship. "Beautiful, sultry eyes that ooze mystery... that hint of bad boy under his icy demeanor... enough of a hidden past that he's mysterious and appealing, but, *hello*, also single, and ready to mingle.

By the time I get through with him, he won't only *sell* love, you'll have new members signing up right and left, trying to match *his* profile."

"Trevor," Logan said, looking at him oddly. "I don't think that's—"

"It *is*," Trevor said, cutting him off.

He wasn't really sure how Logan had intended to finish that sentence, but Trevor knew for sure that he was right. Anyone, if given the chance, would want to hook up with Logan. Would want *more* than a hookup, which was exactly what bLoved was trying to sell. He swiveled in his chair to face Logan directly.

"I know we can do this," he said, reaching for Logan's hands and squeezing them tightly. Staring into his remarkable eyes and willing him to believe it, too. And, sure, Trevor didn't want to give up his ten grand or the trip to New York, but he also didn't want to walk out of there with Logan still looking like Frank's words had gut-punched him. The man had every reason to ooze confidence. And, usually, he *did*. When it had come to defending Trevor, Logan had been all over it. But the minute Frank had called into question Logan's ability to represent bLoved, it was like something inside him had broken. Not okay. "Logan, trust me. Everyone's going to want you. Want what you're selling, I mean. Have I ever steered you wrong?"

Logan's lip twitched, just a bit, and some life came back into his eyes. "The red tie..."

"Would have looked incredible on you," Trevor insisted,

grinning. He turned to Frank, adding, "See, look at him? Single and ready to mingle. You should set him up with an account on bLoved, like a whole, 'mega-rich super hottie looking for love right now!' sort of thing, and bam! You've got yourself an advertising campaign. I mean, it's true, I didn't go to school for anything like this, but it's a no-brainer that when you've got a man like this to work with, selling your market on falling in love is going to be a piece of cake."

"Trevor," Logan said, a note of warning in his voice.

Trevor was on a roll, though, as he started to imagine it. "If you *really* want to play it up? We can show Logan defrosting as time goes on, make it look like all his icy-sexy-pants thing is starting to crack because of *love*... update the bLoved profile you set up for him to make it look like he *is* dating—" Trevor paused, deciding he maybe wasn't as sold on his own idea as he'd thought, but Frank, Logan, and Hiro were all hanging on his words, so he swallowed, recovering in a slightly less enthusiastic tone. "Um, you can make it look like it just took the right man to bring it out in him. You know, exactly what half your market base is probably looking for. And, at the very end, you can say he found his man. And... they'll make it official. No one in the world will be thinking about how standoffish he was in the beginning, they'll just be talking about how true love managed to change him."

Trevor let his voice fade off into silence, looking between the three men. Hiro was staring back at him with a twinkle in his eyes that belied the passive expression on his face, and Logan was looking... closed off. *Shit*. Had Trevor just blown it?

Frank looked Trevor over carefully, then crossed his arms and sat back in the chair, tilting his head back and staring blankly at a corner of the ceiling, lost in thought.

"Maybe you're right," Frank said at last. "Maybe Logan *can* pull it off."

"See, I *told* you." Shaken out of his own uncharacteristic uncertainty, Trevor tore himself away from looking at Logan and sat back in his chair, feeling a little smug despite himself. "We can definitely pull this off—"

"You'll need to be by his side at all times, though," Frank continued, talking over him. "What I just saw between you two? Magical. Not something I would have expected from Logan. And you're right, the audience is going to eat it up. No one's going to be thinking about his failure here in Chicago, because everyone's going to be too busy eating up Logan's new relationship." He clapped his hands together, rubbing them briskly as he grinned. "And if they *do* ask about what the hell happened on the morning show here? We'll just say that the two of you had a fight about moving to New York together, and Logan wasn't himself."

"Um, excuse me?" Trevor swallowed. That didn't sound quite like the idea he'd just shared. "What?"

"We'll mock this up as a love match off the site," Frank explained, leaning forward enthusiastically. "I'm sure I can get Kelly or one of the IT guys to create fake profiles with some retroactive activity on them for both of you. We'll say that the two of you were paired up while Logan was here in Chicago on business, and he's been flying back once a month ever since, not just for the bLoved meetings, but to spend time with *his* beloved, too."

Logan's posture had gone even stiffer, and Trevor felt something shrivel inside him. Okay. He *did* see where Frank was going with the whole thing, but clearly, when Logan had told Trevor he wanted to keep it just business between them, he hadn't counted on "business" taking *this* turn. And just as clearly, he wasn't interested.

"People will buy the chemistry between the two of you," Hiro offered blandly, looking back and forth between Logan and Trevor. His lip quirked up in a smile. "I see what Frank is saying."

"*Exactly,*" Frank said, slapping the table and chortling. "We can make the morning show snafu from last week work *for* us. The public will be able to see how different Logan is while you're around, Trevor, and they'll have to believe that bLoved can work for them, too. You'll be able to escort Logan to his public appearances and coach him directly without anyone blinking an eye. It gives you the chance to be that much more hands-on... it's *perfect.*"

With a body like Logan's, it wouldn't take much convincing for Trevor to be hands-on, but then again, maybe not. No matter how attracted *he* might be, he wasn't going to throw himself at someone who didn't want him. Besides, there was a big difference between physical attraction and something deeper. Trevor had been on a lot of dates—hot ones, bad ones, forgettable ones, casual ones—but he'd never been in love before, and wasn't at all sure he could pull off the act, even if Logan *had* been on board.

"You want Logan and me to pretend to fall in love over the next month and a half?" Trevor asked Frank, just to clarify.

"That's right," Frank said. "It was your idea."

"Not exactly," Trevor mumbled, wishing Logan would say something. That he would jump in as decisively as he had earlier, and quit just sitting there like a statue.

Like the idea had frozen him with distaste.

"I'm sure we're paying you enough that you'll find a way to pull it off," Frank said, eyes narrowing at Trevor from across the table. "Isn't that what you're here for?"

Trevor bristled. "I'm sorry, but *what* is it you think he's paying me for?" he asked, seeing red. *What* was that man's problem? Trevor leaned forward, taking the little twinge of hurt at Logan's reaction and ramping it right up into a case of pissed-the-fuck-off. He jerked to his feet, totally happy at this point to rip Frank a new asshole, but Logan stopped him.

"No, Frank. Trevor's *not* here for that," Logan said coldly, grabbing Trevor's arm and pulling him back down into his seat. "Forget it."

The total shutdown in Logan's voice hurt, and Trevor sank back into his chair and tried to convince himself that he didn't need to take it personally. He'd accepted the job because of the chance to go to New York, hadn't he? He'd *always* wanted to go to New York. His excitement hadn't been about spending time with Logan, a man he barely knew. And, of course, there was all the money that went along with it... it really and truly didn't matter if Logan found him attractive, or not, did it? If Logan couldn't stand the idea of pretending to be with him for a few weeks?

Trevor had been thinking with his dick instead of his head. A sure recipe for disaster. But... if it was just his dick that wanted Logan so badly, why was it that the rejection felt like a sick ache inside his chest?

Just another sign that he for damn sure wasn't cut out for the kind of thing that bLoved was selling.

Frank cursed, then sat back in his chair, crossing his arms. "Fine," he said tightly. "You're not letting me do my job, Logan. You're shutting me down on all fronts. But, since you're so knowledgeable about the best way forward for the company, have at it. Use Trevor however you see fit. I'm done trying to direct you toward something that will actually *work*."

The air felt thick with simmering anger, but, thankfully, Hiro cut in with some kind of Zen calm radiating from his voice.

"Why don't you and I step outside for a few minutes, Frank?" he said, standing and gesturing toward the conference room door. "We'll give Logan some time to think about your suggestions, okay? He can talk them over with his chosen PR coach, and you and I can take a minute to review the schedule once again for New York."

Like he was breaking apart a group of squabbling children, Hiro spoke in a slow, reassuring tone. He waited patiently until Frank stood, too—accompanying the move with a long-suffering sigh and some muttered things that Trevor was sure he was happier not hearing—and then led him toward the door.

Trevor watched the two of them from where he sat, livid and hurt and spiteful all at once. Frank didn't apologize as he left, and when the door closed behind him, Trevor felt the same kind of frost he saw so often in Logan start to creep through his own body, hardening him to what had just happened. Protecting him from the rejection.

It was just business.

But he didn't know how that actually worked for Logan, since no matter how many times he repeated it, the sting remained.

"I'm sorry," Logan's voice rang out through the empty conference room, but Trevor refused to turn toward him. If Logan felt that strongly that Trevor was repulsive, Trevor had to learn to harden himself toward him. He still wanted the job.

He could still do it.

And... there was no sense in prolonging the hurt. He needed to get over it and talk business. Not that he had any right to be hurting in the first place, of course. Trevor sighed, forcing some of the tension out of his shoulders. All of it was quickly becoming muddled in his mind, and the faster he shut down his emotions, the better.

Logan grabbed the arm of Trevor's chair, spinning him around so that they faced each other, and the abrupt move sent Trevor's heart into his throat.

Logan looked... sorry.

Trevor's anger evaporated. He really *didn't* have a claim on this man, and he'd let a bunch of jumbled feelings and excitement and his own hot-headed nature turn a business meeting into a fiasco. It was totally fine that Logan didn't want him like that. Logan *did* want him to do what he'd asked—to help coach him through the publicity appearances—and he'd been nothing but wonderful to Trevor, in his own, Logan-like, reserved way.

"I'm sorry," Trevor said, swallowing his pride. "I shouldn't have suggested—"

"*I'm* sorry, Trevor," Logan said, cutting him off as he looked into Trevor's eyes. "Frank was totally out of line for lashing out at you like that. If I'd had any idea that he would treat you that way, this meeting would never have happened."

Trevor ducked his gaze, trying to convince himself that the warm, cottony feeling in his chest didn't exist. Logan was so damn appealing. So... nice. Hot as fuck, and yet, always making Trevor feel like he appreciated him, valued him, like no one else ever had.

"I'm going to have a strongly worded talk with Frank about his behavior," Logan went on. "There is no universe in which you deserved that, or deserved to have him suggest that you were here to act like my—"

"Shutting him down like you did was short-sighted," Trevor interrupted, some of his hurt bubbling to the surface again. No matter how Logan made him feel, he was there to do a job, and it *was* a good idea, given the goals bLoved had for the campaign. "It's actually brilliant. And if the problem is *me*—" Trevor swallowed, forcing himself to go ahead and give Logan the just-business he wanted, "—then you can always use someone else for that part. To pretend to be the guy you fall for. I'll still coach you, either way."

"What?" Logan asked, looking confused. "Trevor—"

"It's *fine*, Logan," Trevor interrupted, trying to convince himself. "You've made it clear now—*several* times—that you're not interested in anything other than a work relationship with me." Trevor stated it flatly, keeping his feelings out of it. It was the truth, after all, and saying it out loud allowed him to commit to the notion that he was fundamentally incompatible with Logan, no matter how hot Logan was. "And that's fine. I keep flirting, you keep shutting me down, whatever. With an attitude like that, we could never have pulled it off, anyway. So, just tell me what you want me to do, how you want me to coach you, and we'll work on it from there."

Logan was staring at him as if he'd suddenly grown a second head, and something dangerous flashed in his cornflower-blue eyes.

"You don't think we could pull it off?" Logan repeated quietly, pinning Trevor with his eyes.

Trevor swallowed, but refused to be intimidated. "It's not worth forcing something that will never look natural. We could never sell it—"

Several things happened at once. Trevor heard the shush of wheels on carpet as Logan rose from his chair, saw the flash of black as Logan closed the space between them, felt the firm grip of Logan's fingers, holding his chin steady. And then, before Trevor had time to pull away, Logan's lips crushed against his, stealing the breath from his lungs and catapulting his heart into a kind of mad rush that almost made him dizzy.

Adrenaline hit Trevor square in the chest, and for a split-second Trevor's pride almost got in the way of what he wanted. He tensed and tried to push away, but the heat of Logan's demanding lips, his overpowering presence and his sheer intensity were overwhelming. Trevor forgot about his hurt feelings and made an embarrassingly needy sound, submitting to all of it.

Hunger. Lust. *Need*. Primitive, erotic emotions thickened the air around them, connecting them through passion. Teeth clacked. Logan's hands tightened against Trevor's jaw, and Trevor moaned into the kiss as his arousal went from zero to sixty.

Fuck, was Logan a good kisser.

It wasn't fair that a man could kiss that well. Especially when he pulled away abruptly, leaving Trevor dazed by the force of what had just passed between them. Straining to catch his breath, he looked up into Logan's half-lidded eyes, willing Logan to come back for seconds.

"You still don't think we could pull it off?" Logan asked, voice pitched low with his own arousal. Trevor shuddered at the tone. *Wanting.*

Logan was hot. Way, way too hot.

"N-no," Trevor whispered. "I mean. Yes?" He cleared his throat. Had that been just a demonstration, then? "So... you want to do this?" Trevor asked. "To be boyfriends?"

Fake boyfriends, he meant, of course. But before he clarified, Logan answered.

"*Yes.*" Logan had stopped kissing him, but he hadn't moved away. Hadn't released his grip on Trevor's jaw. Was still close enough that Trevor could taste his breath.

"But... just for business, right?" Trevor asked, licking his lips as his eyes dropped back to Logan's. "Or—"

"Right," Logan said, releasing Trevor and taking a step back. "Just in public. Of course. But we *are* going to sell it, Trevor. We're going to make this work."

Trevor nodded jerkily, the hurt coming back and mingling with the raging heat in his blood to put him in an uncharacteristically dark mood. But he could shake it off.

"Okay," he said, agreeing.

And, as Logan turned to head to the conference room

doors, he noted that Logan had to discreetly adjust himself.

And he reached up to touch his bruised lips, thinking of the fierce passion in Logan's kiss.

And the intoxicating flavor of it...

Trevor smiled, glad Logan's back was turned, as his lingering hurt feelings at Logan's rejection evaporated. That hadn't been acting... Logan *wanted* him. And, come what may on the business side of things, Trevor could definitely work with *that*.

Chapter 7

LOGAN

"WE NEED TO GET TO KNOW EACH OTHER A LITTLE better," Trevor said, grinning at Logan with such an abundance of vivacious *life* in his eyes that, even though the plane was at a standstill on the tarmac, for a moment Logan almost felt like they'd already taken off. They sat side by side in the first-class seats that Hiro had booked for them, and Hiro was passed out in the next aisle back, already snoring.

Four hours later, and the rush of kissing Trevor hadn't died yet. It came in waves, receding until it was nothing more than a distant murmur before amping itself back up into a pressing need that harkened back to the fantasy

Logan had indulged in three days prior in the privacy of his hotel room.

Trevor had kissed him back.

"How?" Logan asked, swallowing as his own mind supplied a variety of ways that the two of them could "get to know each other." But, regardless of what he'd felt back at bLoved's headquarters—was *still* feeling—Trevor was still business. He met Trevor's eyes steadily, making sure to school his features to keep his thoughts off his face, and silently repeated the mantra of "just business" in his head as Trevor slanted him a wicked look that was anything but.

Logan hadn't meant to kiss him, but—*we could never pull it off... forcing something... we could never sell it*—Trevor's words back in the conference room had been like waving a red flag in front of a bull. There had been a lot of very good reasons that Logan had tried to shut down the plan to present Trevor to the world as his boyfriend instead of his PR coach, none of which had been even close to the reasons Trevor had spouted. Not by a long shot.

The plane started moving, and Trevor grinned at him, which made Logan want to kiss him *again*.

But of course not.

Earlier, he'd acted without thinking, giving in to something he had already been set on denying himself... with explosive results. The fervent reluctance in Trevor's touch had melted almost instantly, and he'd given in to the pressure of Logan's lips and devoted himself to their cause with an enthusiasm that had proven just how off the mark the bullshit he'd rattled off about the two of them not being able to pull it off had been.

But Logan hadn't just been trying to prove Trevor wrong. He hadn't been *trying* to do anything; in that moment, he'd *needed* to kiss Trevor, the way he needed air. And the way feisty, sassy Trevor—who was always pushing him, and who Logan had no doubt would never let anyone walk all over him—had submitted so hungrily to the force of Logan's passion had stirred something in Logan that he hadn't known was there.

Something he'd never felt with anyone else.

Principles he'd clung to for years had burned away in a flash, and business had blurred into pleasure, and—for the first time he could remember in much too long—he'd let himself go. For a few seconds, past hurts and embarrassments and the deep-rooted beliefs that he wasn't good enough had ceased to exist. For that all-too-brief moment, there had only been the heat of Trevor's body, and the taste of his lips, and a sense of utter *rightness* that Logan hadn't even realized he yearned for.

"We should go over the stupid things any couple would know about each other," Trevor said, twisting around in his seat and looking Logan over with a raking glance that made his blood boil. "Like... the question that's been plaguing me for the last year.... what's your favorite color?"

Trevor's innocuous question was so far from the direction Logan's thoughts had been going that it startled a laugh out of him. Trevor's eyebrows shot up in obvious surprise, and Logan realized he was really going to have to get a handle on himself if he was going to make it through the next six weeks.

"Black," Logan answered dryly, refusing to admit to himself that he knew the answer would goad color-adoring Trevor into needling him even more.

After seven years of denying himself the kind of connection with another person that might leave him vulnerable to the kind of pain he'd experienced before, Logan's protective shield had cracked and Trevor had blasted his way inside it. It should have been terrifying, but instead, Logan found himself absurdly grateful that the cascade of events that had led him to this moment gave him a legitimate excuse to foster the electric connection he couldn't deny he felt with Trevor. Logically, he knew that what they were about to embark on *was* just business... but also, labeling it "business" allowed him to justify walking far too close to a line that he knew he'd be foolish to step over.

Trevor made him feel like the kind of future he'd once dreamed of could be possible, and that kind of hope was dangerous.

"Black is *not* a color," Trevor insisted, pouncing on the information exactly the way Logan had suspected he would. "Neither is gray, or dark gray, or silver, or any variation along those lines."

He tried not to smile as Trevor ticked off the monochromatic options that Logan always insisted on buying. There was no doubt in his mind that as soon as he revealed his favorite color that Trevor would begin slipping it into his wardrobe once he returned to Ashby's. A tie here, a cufflink there, until he'd worn Logan down enough that he'd buy something other than the always-safe black or gray.

"Pick a real color, Logan," Trevor said, leaning in and waggling his eyebrows. "You can't hide what you like from me forever."

You. Logan clamped his lips closed to avoid blurting the incriminating word out, reaching deep to find his usual reserve. He was still a little in shock about how Trevor had jumped to his defense earlier, with Frank. He couldn't remember anyone doing such a thing in... well, *ever*. And that, combined with the intensity of Trevor's spirit and the constant, playful teasing made Logan want to keep him close.

If he wasn't careful, pretending to be Trevor's boyfriend might become all too addicting. Might blur the lines of what he *wanted* to do and what he *should* do, until he completely lost sight of the latter. Getting involved on a personal level wasn't something he could allow himself... but, at the same time, he already knew he wouldn't be able to deny himself the indulgence of whatever Trevor was willing to give him, for the few weeks they'd have together.

He just had to remember that he was doing it for bLoved—that, in fact, bLoved *needed* him to do it—so that he could walk away unscathed when they were through.

His stomach dropped a little as the plane tilted steeply, gaining altitude, and Trevor nudged him, the touch sending a jolt through Logan's body. He was still waiting on

Logan's answer, and Logan had to play along, didn't he? For the business.

"...Chartreuse," he finally said, trying to remember the last time he'd teased someone.

Trevor scowled. "No one's favorite color is chartreuse. I call bullshit. If you want to play this game, you're going to play it right! It's important. For *business*."

Trevor's Cheshire grin grew, and Logan felt a smile tug at his own lips in response, despite his best efforts at keeping a straight face. Trevor was giving him exactly the same justification he'd been using himself, and it was the perfect excuse to let his defenses down.

"Isn't that rude to chartreuse?" he asked, feeling playful for the first time in years. "It's a color, just like the rest. Who's to say I can't like it?"

"It's a yellow-green," Trevor scrunched up his nose, which should have been either funny or adorable looking, but which, instead, Logan found disarmingly sexy. "It's not exactly top-favorite-color material. Passable, in the right circumstances, but there's not enough to justify anyone *favoriting* it. For example, my favorite color is purple, because it can be both fun and sophisticated given the right circumstances."

Slowly, Logan looked Trevor over while Trevor was distracted with the game he'd set out to play. Totally devoted to the moment, he brought the same kind of vivacity to their little bit of silliness that Logan had seen in him while he'd been working the floor at Ashby's. The life in his eyes and the emotion on his face lent him a striking, masculine beauty that Trevor didn't seem aware of, but that Logan was having trouble looking away from.

"You've convinced me," Logan said. "I change my answer to green. What's next?"

Looking smugly pleased that he'd received an acceptable answer, Trevor lifted his chin. "Favorite food?"

"Lasagna."

"Sushi," Trevor replied in rapid fire. "I guess lasagna's okay, too. All that cheese though."

"You have something against cheese?" Logan hitched a brow.

Trevor rolled his eyes, but grinned. "I *told* you, I'm trying to avoid dairy."

"Right," Logan bit off the word, Trevor's seemingly innocent answer shooting straight to his cock.

He could still recall the conversation they'd had back at Ashby's in vivid detail. Right now, though, the thought of Trevor and whipped cream was a little too much to handle, and Logan shifted his legs to mask a growing erection. This game with Trevor was about *business*. Loosening up was advantageous for publicity, but even if he let himself enjoy it, getting too close wouldn't be smart.

Too wrapped up in his questioning to notice Logan's shifting position, Trevor launched into another round of questions about trivial likes and dislikes. Logan kept his replies limited to single word answers, but even so, he couldn't deny that he was having fun—largely because of Trevor's undying enthusiasm.

"Okay, okay. Serious question time," Trevor said quite suddenly. He'd undone his seatbelt and had scooted around in his chair so his back was to the window. Logan sat in the aisle seat. "How many guys have you slept with?"

Logan flinched. "What?" Trevor had lulled him in with a series of basic, silly questions, but now it seemed he was skirting back toward a line that was blurring all too rapidly.

Trevor raised an eyebrow. "What?" he quoted back, his lips twitching in amusement. "It's not really that hard of a question, is it, Logan? I'm not sure how I can clarify... but if you don't want to answer that, because I'm getting some major grump vibes from you right now, we can tone it back a little. How many guys have you dated?"

Trevor was right. He could feel the familiar shape of a scowl pulling his lips down, but he couldn't seem to get back to the easy playfulness of a moment before. It was a sore subject.

"Just one," he bit out when it became clear that Trevor was going to wait him out. Logan sat back in his chair, his mood ruined.

"Just one?" Trevor asked, incredulous. "You're so hot, though. What the hell?"

"I'm not a fan of dating," Logan replied. He wished Trevor would drop the subject. Talking about the failures of his past destroyed the easygoing energy between them, and Logan could feel himself withdrawing back into his shell.

Which was fine. Even good. He'd forgotten himself, but Trevor's new line of questioning was a reminder that Logan hadn't been enough for Ryan, whom he'd loved, just as he hadn't been enough to his parents. This whole business with bLoved was just PR. Clearly, Logan wasn't cut out for love.

Trevor wasn't going to let it die, though. "...So that means that you've missed out on a *ton* of pet names, haven't you?" he asked, grinning like everything was still the same. "What did that one guy you dated used to call you, hm? Babe? Baby? Hunk? Sweetheart?"

"Oh, Lord," Logan muttered. The man was irrepressible.

"Kinky," Trevor responded, taking it and running with it. "Lord and Master? I can almost see that. You can be a bit... forceful."

Logan laughed before he could stop himself, scrubbing a hand over his face to hide his reaction to the thought of Trevor letting him take control. "You know that's not what I meant."

"No? Then, something more like... sweetie pie?" Trevor guessed, doing that eyebrow waggle again. "Schmookums? Pumpkin? Babelicious?"

Logan parted his fingers so he could look at Trevor through them. "Are you going to stop?" he asked, a little shocked to find that Trevor's relentless playfulness was pulling him out of his black mood again.

"Stop? No way, cupcake." Trevor beamed. "I mean, we're a couple now, right? So we should have cutesy nicknames for each other. Do you want a super sappy emotional one, like 'sugar dumpling cutesy-poo,' or something a little more low-key like, 'superbabe?'"

"How about none of those," Logan suggested. "My name is perfectly serviceable."

"Gonna leave it to me, then?" Trevor asked, smirking. "Because I can just keep dreaming them up until we find something you like, sweetums."

"Is there a way off this plane?" Logan asked dryly. The recollection of Ryan's betrayal eased away the more Trevor joked around, and he found himself resisting a chuckle the longer Trevor pressed on.

"Why would you ever want to do that, lumpkins?" Trevor cooed. "My baby sister's gonna want to meet you. Don't run away from my love."

Logan barked a dry laugh, which Trevor seemed to take as license to push for more information.

"Alright, babyboo, let's move on. If we're dating, it's only right that I know certain private things about you, so..."

Logan glanced at Trevor out of the corner of his eye to find Trevor smirking again. Whatever he was about to ask, it was guaranteed to be trouble.

"Do you like to top or bottom?"

Logan's throat tightened, and his heart skipped a beat.

"Why is that important?" he ground out, doing his best to ignore the way the question had just made his cock jerk back to life.

Trevor looked him up and down slowly, the heat in his eyes not helping in the slightest as Logan tried to get his physical reaction under control.

"Because," Trevor said after a moment, his gaze settling on Logan's lips for a lingering moment before moving up to meet his eyes again. "If we're going to be appearing in public together, I need to know if I should be limping or not. And if you're a bottom, then I'm definitely going to have to tone down some of my personality, because no one's going to think that I top when I'm so incredibly fabulous."

"That's bullshit," Logan said flatly.

"Sure, but that's also straight America," Trevor replied, shrugging a single shoulder. "And, hell, let's be honest. Half of gay America, too. Our job is to sell it. The last thing you want is people doubting the validity of our story... and if that means I've got to play a role, well, isn't that what I'm here for?" He winked.

Logan's teeth grazed his lower lip, knowing he should appreciate the reminder that this was all acting, but unable to shake the image Trevor's question had put in his mind. Or forget how readily Trevor had let him take charge back in the conference room, when he'd submitted to Logan's kiss.

He needed to change the subject. "I prefer to top," he found himself saying instead.

"Then we're already a good match, because I *do* like to bottom," Trevor shot back, grinning.

Logan stifled a groan.

"Favorite position?"

Logan let out an explosive breath of air that might have been a laugh. "Really?" he asked, not sure if he was charmed or turned on by Trevor's brash self-confidence. *Both.*

"Gotta know exactly *how* I should be limping," Trevor said with a wink.

Logan was sure that Trevor was well beyond the line Trevor had warned him about before, but he couldn't bring himself to care. An uncharacteristic recklessness was brewing inside him. For the past year, he'd been finding excuses to visit Trevor while denying the pull Logan actually felt toward him. If they were going to pretend to be a couple to save bLoved, Logan knew he would need to find a balance between giving in to that pull, and keeping himself guarded.

He just wasn't quite sure how he was supposed to accomplish that.

"Missionary?" Trevor prompted. "No. Doggy... mmm. Bulldog? Spoons?"

"Cowgirl," Logan cut him off, trying to adjust himself discreetly.

"Cow*boy*, I'd guess," Trevor's smirk grew. There was just no way to be discreet when they were sitting side-by-side. "Naughty. I like it."

"So exactly *how* are you going to be limping, now that

you know?" Logan asked, goading him. "What's the technique?"

Trevor reclined so that his back was pressed against the cabin wall. When he spoke, it was slow and sultry, spoken just loud enough so that Logan could hear. "I'm going to have one hell of an all-over limp, because when I'm in control, I go *hard*."

Trevor's words sent any hope of fighting his erection straight out the window. Trevor thought *he'd* be in control? Logan went rock hard at the picture of Trevor riding him, breathing in slowly and steadily, for balance, then focusing on the exhalation that followed. *That* had definitely been over the line, but he didn't want to push Trevor back into safe territory.

"You wouldn't be the only one hard," he murmured at last.

"Is that so?" Trevor glanced to the front of the cabin, then to the curtain separating them from the economy seats. Slowly, he extended a leg and ran his foot up Logan's calf, to the knee. His shoes were abandoned on the floor in front of his seat. "Maybe we should test out how that'd go? You know. For research purposes. So we can make it look authentic."

Logan's heart jumped into his throat. Probably a good thing, since it prevented him from saying yes. In fact, he couldn't seem to speak at all.

"Well, think about it," Trevor said after a beat of silence, drawing his foot away and tucking his legs up against his chest. He gazed at Logan from over his knees. "After all, this is important business, and we both need to... do our part."

"Right," Logan said, the word coming out raspy and low. He cleared his throat, wondering what he'd gotten himself into.

Trevor stayed silent, and Logan wasn't sure if he was grateful or disappointed. Was Trevor just playing, or would he actually follow through?

Not that Logan could let himself go there.

It wouldn't be smart... at all.

He urged his pulse to slow and his heart to come off its high, and, while he did, Trevor stretched. Yawning and glancing over the back of the seat at where Hiro was still sleeping.

"What about your family?" Trevor asked at last, settling into a position that an airplane seat shouldn't have allowed. He looked comfortable. At ease. "I mentioned my sister, but what about you?"

"I'm an only child," Logan replied, the shift in topic doing a fair job of cooling his arousal. "I don't speak with my parents anymore. They weren't... comfortable... with me, after I came out."

The understatement would have been almost laughable, if it had been even remotely funny. Logan clenched his jaw tightly, wondering if there would come a day when the memory of his parents' rejection would stop twisting his stomach into knots. He was a grown man, and a successful one. It shouldn't matter.

"Then you don't need them," Trevor said forcefully. He crossed his arms, shaking his head as the teasing heat from a few moments ago was replaced by something softer. "*Look* at you, Logan. Successful in business, drop dead gorgeous, probably funny or something beneath all that ice..." Trevor winked, and Logan's heart did an odd flip in his chest. Trevor was so quick to jump to his defense, earlier, with Frank, and now against his absentee parents. "If they're dumb enough to drop you because of who you love, they're obviously not worth your time."

Logan gave a jerky nod. Trevor was right. Someday, maybe he'd bring himself to believe it, too.

"Sounds like you have experience with that kind of reaction?" Logan asked, hoping to deflect their conversation back toward Trevor. Talking about himself was too uncomfortable, and, besides, getting to know Trevor was important for their public appearances. Trevor had been right about that. And the fact that it allowed him to indulge his genuine curiosity to know more about Trevor was just an added perk.

"No, not really. I mean, not personal experience, at least. But that doesn't mean I don't have opinions on the subject."

Trevor? Opinionated? Logan laughed, startling himself. How did Trevor keep *doing* that? Every time Logan went into a dark place, Trevor yanked him right back out.

"My mom and dad are great people," Trevor said, grinning. "They've been very supportive of me since the beginning. I was more or less born flamboyant, so I'm sure they figured it out when my first word was 'shoes'. You know how it goes."

"Your first word was shoes?" Logan asked, arching a brow although, really, the idea made him want to laugh *again*. When had he ever laughed as much as he did around Trevor?

Trevor rolled his eyes. "No, poopsie, my first word was *mama*, like pretty much every other English speaking baby out there. But it might as well have been shoes, for how out I was pretty much right away. So when I came out, my parents already had years to prepare for it, and they were like, 'yeah, we know.'"

"And your sister?" Logan asked.

"She's a sweetheart and she's awesome. She's in college studying to be a lawyer. Can you believe that?"

A corner of Logan's lip twitched upward. "With a mouth like you have?" he shot back, unable to keep his eyes from dropping to it for a second. "If that's genetic, I think it's a perfect fit."

"Shut up!" Trevor laughed. "You're just jealous that I'm so charismatic and outgoing."

"Maybe I am." Logan leaned a little closer. "But maybe I just like to see you put on the spot."

Was it a trick of his eye, or did Trevor's cheeks redden just a little bit? Before Logan could get a good read on what was happening, Trevor's attention refocused on something right behind Logan, and Logan turned to see what it was.

A young flight attendant stood next to them, smiling and cheerful. His short brown hair was styled away from his face, and his eyes were bright and—Logan noticed—lingering on Trevor for longer than they needed to. A surge of raw jealousy shot through him, as hard and fast as it was unexpected, and he sat up a little straighter in his seat, turning his back toward Trevor to partially block him from the flight attendant's view.

He let out a slow breath, trying to contain his reaction. But... in public, they were dating, weren't they? In public, it was okay to feel jealous that another man's eyes were on Trevor. To stake his claim.

"Can I get you gentlemen anything to drink?" the too-attentive flight attendant asked.

"No," Logan's reply was curt.

"Mm, maybe," Trevor said, leaning around Logan and making eye contact with the flight attendant. "Tell me, what's *your* favorite thing on the menu?"

The playful, flirty way Trevor spoke only amplified Logan's jealousy. What was he *doing*? He'd just spent the last hour giving Logan all his attention, was he really that fickle? Was this how Ryan had acted around other men, when Logan had been too blinded by "love" to notice?

The flight attendant had instantly brightened at Trevor's question. "Well—"

"No drinks," Logan said, cutting the flight attendant off. "My boyfriend must be tired from all the flying we've done recently. As soon as we land, we're heading to the studio for a television interview. He needs to keep his wits about him."

The interest in the flight attendant's eyes dimmed as soon as Logan used the word "boyfriend," and he nodded politely, toning down his flirt into something more professional.

"Of course, sir. If you want anything—water, juice, snacks, whatever it might be—just let me know." He pointed to his name tag—*Jacob*—and added, "My name's Jake."

"Thank you, Jake," Trevor said tightly, turning to Logan as soon as Jake walked away. Logan raised an eyebrow, ignoring the little surge of adrenaline that the interaction had caused as he took in Trevor's narrowed eyes. His full lips, more suited to his usual smile, were drawn into a thin, angry line. "What the hell was that, Logan?"

"In public, you're *mine*," Logan bit out. "You agreed to do it, and you're going to stick to it."

The anger on Trevor's face eased, and he broke into a grin that did treacherous things in the vicinity of Logan's heart. He reached forward, running his hand along Logan's arm and lacing their fingers together. The fine hair on Logan's skin stood up, skin tingling from Trevor's touch, and he tightened his hand around Trevor's without thinking.

"Got it, pookie," Trevor said. "Yours... in public. I'll play nice. I'm sorry."

"And can you stop calling me by stupid nicknames?"

Logan grumbled. Trevor's small signs of affection, physical or verbal, made him feel far too connected. Still, he couldn't bring himself to let go of his hand. "Just 'Logan' is fine. Or... baby. Anything else is overkill."

"You're right, baby." Trevor leaned over and kissed Logan on the cheek, and Logan's heart sped up anew. "I'll tone back my natural charm, even if it does mean that men like Jake are going to be missing out. You just tell me what to do, and I'll do it. Not something I normally let a man get away with, but, from you, I've gotta admit, it's kind of hot."

Trevor played his role all too well, and it was all too tempting to take him up on that. To tell him *exactly* what Logan wanted him to do. But, even harder—Logan bit back a sound, not sure if it would have come out a groan or a laugh—he'd have to remember that Trevor's affection was part of the act.

For just a little while, though, it felt good to pretend that Trevor cared for him. That Trevor really *was* his, and that he didn't find Logan lacking, the way others had.

That Logan was worthy of love.

Logan leaned his head back against the seat, closing his eyes as Trevor's voice washed over him, prattling on about the things he wanted to see and do and taste and *experience* in New York. Trevor was both the best and the worst choice he could have made to fill the position as his PR coach. It was only the first day of their arrangement, but—as the warmth of Trevor's hand in his seeped deep inside him, warming places he hadn't realized were cold—he already knew that pretending to be Trevor's boyfriend wasn't going to be any struggle.

Or, if you wanted to look at it another way, "pretending" might just end up being the biggest struggle of his life.

Chapter 8

TREVOR

TREVOR WAS BUZZING WITH ALL SORTS OF EXCITEMENT AS they landed. The fact that he was arriving in *New York* and excited about it was no surprise, but, if he were honest, the man he was with added a whole extra layer of interest to the trip. Still, the moment they'd touched down and Hiro had woken up, Logan's face had slipped back into business-mask mode. Not that he was going to let a little thing like that fool him. Flying—and flirting—with Logan had been... fun. *Hot as fuck*, was maybe more accurate. But in general, basically a win. Even LaGuardia didn't seem to be the hellhole that Trevor had heard it was. Their flight arrived on time, they deplaned without issue, and the terminal they arrived at wasn't all that far from the exit.

Everything was coming up roses.

"Which way to baggage claim?" Trevor asked, scanning the concourse for the appropriate signs as his lips twitched in memory of Logan's reaction to his three overstuffed suitcases back when they'd left Chicago. But, *hello*, New York City. Even with what he'd managed to bring, he wasn't sure he'd be fully prepared to unleash his full fabulousness on the city of his dreams.

"Hiro will pick your bags up and bring them to your hotel room," Logan said, wrapping a hand around Trevor's upper arm and steering him toward the exits. The dominant edge Trevor had heard in his voice earlier had returned, and Trevor's skin prickled at the tone.

It should have prickled with irritation—Trevor never dated possessive assholes—but the hot surge in his blood was definitely something else.

Usually, at the first sign of aggression or territorial behavior from a guy, Trevor was done. There were more than enough gay men in the world to go around, and Trevor never wasted his time with the kind who wanted to treat him like property. He had no interest in being owned. Casual dating was more his speed. It was fun. Temporary. *Safe.* It allowed him to enjoy himself without the danger of getting stuck with a white picket fence and a doting, but boring, husband.

The world was a big place, and Trevor wanted to experience all of it, not be shackled into a long-term relationship with someone who wanted to stifle him from being himself. And a man who wanted Trevor to play the role of submissive partner? Instant turn-off.

Except, apparently, when it came to Logan.

But that was probably because it was just pretend. Or, maybe, because for all of Logan's sudden show of caveman style possessiveness, there was no stifling in sight. Trevor being Trevor seemed to work for Logan, and, if Trevor were being honest, Logan going all dominant and bossy was turning him the fuck on.

Trevor let out a breath, knowing he'd gone way, way over the line during the flight.

He wanted Logan, and, for a moment, he'd forgotten what he was supposed to be doing with him. Logan had brought him to New York to do a job, and turning into a walking hard-on around the man was not going to get that job done.

"Are we going to the hotel now?" he asked, digging in his heels for a moment and bringing Logan to a standstill, since the man still had a firm grip on his upper arm. The bossy routine may have been working for Trevor in a way he'd never suspected, but it wasn't the kind of working that was supposed to be happening, and he had to get his head in the game if he was going to do what Logan had hired him for. Which was *not* to goad Logan into bending him over and fucking him. Trevor let out a slow breath, trying to refocus. "Will we have time to go over some ideas before the television appearance this afternoon?"

Skilled and capable in business, it was obvious to Trevor that Logan was a born leader. Even without knowing all the details, the fact that he'd found such success in the business world didn't seem surprising at all. He was firm without being insulting. In their meeting that morning with Frank, Logan had taken clear control and asserted himself. With the flight attendant, Logan had stepped in to keep Trevor from botching their "dating" deal.

As a person, though? Trevor still needed to figure out how to reroute Logan's professional confidence into personal confidence, the kind that would come across as natural and engaging on camera. If he could do that, Trevor was sure that Logan wouldn't struggle with talking to others or presenting himself well in public anymore. And, yes, it was what Logan was paying Trevor to do. But, if Trevor was honest with himself, he *wanted* to see Logan come out of his shell.

And, selfishly, if he were really going balls out with the self-honesty, Trevor wanted to be the one to bring him there.

"The publicity piece is being recorded live today," Logan said, releasing his grip on Trevor's arm but sliding his hand down to lace their fingers together again. Trevor swallowed, reminding himself that Logan had been the one determined for them to stay in character in public. It didn't mean anything. Logan added, "We'll head to the studio immediately. We're on a tight schedule."

Trevor nodded. He was more than capable of rolling with a tight schedule, and Logan almost smiled—fucking gorgeous—but then turned and headed toward the exit again, keeping a grip on Trevor's hand.

The smart snap of Logan's dress shoes echoed through the halls, and Trevor eyed him critically as they walked, trying to look at him in a strictly professional capacity as opposed to the drooling he'd been close to doing earlier. Beneath Logan's jacket, he wore a sharp suit, tailored to fit his body. He would look fantastic on camera. Trevor looked presentable, as always, but nowhere near as put together. The shirt and slacks he wore would definitely be considered casual in comparison to Logan's outfit, but he reminded himself that that was fine. *He* wasn't going to be the one on television.

"They'll let me come with you backstage and stand in the wings while you're interviewing, right?" he asked, double-checking. Logan nodded, and Trevor did a quick mental review of the details Hiro had supplied about the upcoming appearance. "There isn't much time for me to coach you for this one, but we can still talk about some strategies in the car. Are we taking a cab?"

Instead of answering, Logan ducked under a velvet rope and headed through a sliding door to exit to the pick-up point where a black stretch limousine waited. Trevor skidded to a stop, eyes wide. A smile spread across his face before he could stop it.

"Shut. *Up*."

Logan pulled the door open, revealing the limo's spacious interior, and threw Trevor a look over his shoulder that *might* have included a teasing twinkle in his eyes. Maybe.

"No. A cab would be inconvenient. Now hurry and get in," he said imperiously, not cracking a smile. Bossy again. *Hot*. "We don't have all day."

Trevor had never been in a limo before. Back in high school, he'd gone to his senior prom with Grace, just for shits and giggles. They'd gotten all dressed up and then taken her old beater car, laughing the whole way there about all the better uses they could put their money to than having sprung for a limo. Never had Trevor imagined that he'd be climbing in the back of one years later with a man to whom it seemed that dropping several hundred dollars on a quick ride from the airport was the equivalent of pocket change.

There were two seats in the limo to the left of the door, just as there would be in any other vehicle. What set the limo apart was the long bench stretched across the opposite wall beneath the windows. It faced a bar.

Logan settled comfortably in one of the two seats in the back, looking for all the world like the upscale ride was no big deal. Which, okay, for him, it obviously wasn't.

"There's a bar in there," Trevor said, holding in the shit-eating grin that threatened to break loose. He still hadn't climbed in, and he kind of wanted to pinch himself.

"Right." Logan arched a brow. "And *you* should be in here, too. Come on. Sit."

Trevor's cock twitched at the command, but he ignored that. He was *working*. He took a seat beside Logan, taking it all in and totally failing at holding in the grin. After a beat, Logan sighed, reaching across him to close the door and doing a poor job of hiding the amusement in his eyes.

Trevor's grin grew even bigger.

The bar's polished wooden surface gleamed beneath display lights. Sliding glass panels revealed the contents stored beneath, and Trevor took note of everything from champagne to tequila. Glasses, both lowball and stemmed, were stored on a lower shelf.

He really had stepped into a different world.

The limo pulled away from the curb smoothly, and Trevor sat back and tried to process what had gone on so far with his day. He'd gone from being Logan's coach to being his pretend boyfriend, had milked the pretend boyfriend into a ramped up state of arousal that, for a few minutes back on the plane, he'd honestly thought might either kill him or make him start begging, and now they were in New York as a "couple," destined for the first of several television interviews hoping to sell the world on love. And, more specifically, finding that love with the help of bLoved.

Trevor grinned. Talk about a one-eighty from his day-to-day life.

He'd take it.

Logan was watching him. "Enjoying yourself?" he asked, somehow managing to combine the dry words and an expressionless face into something that felt distinctly intimate. The man had skills.

Trevor nodded, clearing his throat. Time to focus and get his mind out of his pants. Or, Logan's pants. His new, temporary career as a PR coach was officially beginning, and it involved more than just a license to flirt with his hot boss. He sat up straighter in his seat and launched into strategy. He wasn't sure how long the drive would be, but Trevor was determined to make the most of it. He knew that Logan was well-versed in the content he had to deliver; it was the delivery itself that was going to need some work.

"Okay so, let's start with the basics. When you get on stage, you really need to smile," he said, knowing for sure that if Logan followed his directions, half of gay America would be rushing to sign up for bLoved on the spot, and frantically searching the site for Logan's profile. Did Logan *have* a profile on bLoved? Not Trevor's business. He pushed the thought aside, refocusing. "Even if the host is annoying you, you've still got to make it look like you're having a good time, got it? Looking approachable is rule number one for selling anything, so you've got to... well... basically, come across as the exact opposite of how you do most of the time."

"Gee, thanks," Logan said dryly.

Trevor grinned at the sarcasm. Whatever. He was there to do a job. Sugarcoating was only going to waste time, and—despite the much more interesting side Logan had started to show Trevor on the plane—it was true.

"Realize that there's a difference between work-you, and *you*-you, okay?" he said, plowing ahead. "You've got to be able to slip into professional mode whenever needed, regardless of who you really are, or even how you're feeling. So why don't we work on that now? We'll start by pretending that you're alternate-dimension Logan, the one who loves life and always has a great time? Hmm?"

Logan scowled.

"Perfect." Trevor teased, almost buzzing with the rush of it all. He was in New York City with a hot man who pushed every one of his buttons, riding in the back of a limo. He'd never been one to back away from a challenge, and the challenge that was Logan only served to fire him up. He winked, adding, "Now just do that in reverse, and we'll be onto something."

Logan barked out one of those startled laughs, and something in the vicinity of Trevor's heart swelled with a warm satisfaction. He could do this. *Logan* could do this. Together, they were going to be unstoppable, Trevor had no doubt.

"THANK YOU FOR BEING ON THE SHOW, MR. CARTER," THE perky hostess said with a glittering smile. "We're so glad to have you here with us today."

"You're welcome," Logan said... full stop. Trevor winced and crossed his arms, running his hands along his sleeves as he silently willed Logan to give the woman something more to work with. Or at the very least, one of his rare, but heart-stopping, smiles. Hadn't they just talked about this? Conversation was a two-way street, and the hostess would only able to pull so much out of Logan if he refused to open up to her.

By the look on the poor woman's face, Trevor knew she was thinking the same thing. Just as the silence from Logan's abrupt response started to tip over into the realm of awkward, she turned a bright smile directly on the camera.

"Logan Carter is one of the two founders of the popular new gay dating app, bLoved," she gushed. "Kelly Davis, who we're all familiar with from previous television appearances and events, has so far been the face of the operation, but Mr. Carter has remained somewhat of a mystery." She turned back to Logan, her eyes pleading with him to work with her. "Can you share the reason you're representing bLoved here today, Mr. Carter?"

Logan blinked, stone faced, and Trevor bit back a groan. God, it was *so* uncomfortable. He shuffled his feet, watching from his place in the wings and wishing he could rush in to smooth things over. This version of Logan was exactly why the other employees at Ashby's shied away from him, but Trevor *knew* there was more to him than he was showing. He'd done his best to prepare Logan for the interview, but a half-hour just wasn't a lot of time.

There were so many things that Trevor wanted to fix. And, worse, a lot of them were things he'd thought wouldn't be a problem. Between the plane ride and the limo ride, Logan *had* seemed to be relaxing, letting his guard down, opening up. He'd *laughed*, for God's sake. Even Trevor, who was almost allergic to the idea of settling down, would have bought the idea of love from him... in a heartbeat.

But they weren't even thirty seconds into it, and he was already bombing, big time.

The first thing Logan had to do was invite the poor hostess to call him by his first name. Hearing her call him Mr. Carter over and over was awkward as hell, and it wasn't helping to sell the public on Logan *or* on bLoved.

"Kelly is off on a romantic getaway with his new boyfriend," Logan replied, sounding stilted. "Through bLoved, he's finally found love, and he's taking some time off so they can enjoy their new relationship."

Right before Trevor's eyes, the future of bLoved and his own success as Logan's PR coach were imploding... and there was nothing he could do about it. No wonder why Frank had been so adamant about professional help. Would a trained publicity coach be able to pull some sort of magic out of their pocket right about now and save everything?

Trevor's back stiffened, and he gritted his teeth. He'd never been one to give up, and as he wracked his brains for how to save the situation, he seriously contemplated causing a scene that would force them off air for a few moments.

If he could just get his hands on Logan, he *knew* he could bring out the man he'd just spent the last few hours with. The one anyone would want to fall in love with.

The hostess looked Logan over, a fake smile plastered on her face that couldn't quite hide the resigned look in her eyes.

Did Logan know he was bombing his performance? The rigid way he held his posture and the tight, square way his shoulders sat beneath his suit jacket told Trevor it was likely. He was so confident and commanding in every other situation. Trevor didn't understand it. The man had everything going for him; he should have been a shoe-in for this role.

Logan had seemed cool and collected backstage while the crew had hooked him up with his microphone and prepped him on how his appearance was going to work. He hadn't said much, but he'd demonstrated signs of understanding.

Trevor should have picked up on his anxiousness.

He should have done... something. Anything. There was no way he was going to leave Logan out there to dry.

"Well," the hostess said, turning the wattage of her smile up to blinding levels as she spoon-fed Logan with a palpable undercurrent of desperation. "Kelly's story certainly *is* romantic, Mr. Carter. And you said he met his boyfriend through bLoved?"

"Yes."

The hostess was beginning to sweat. Her fingers twitched, picking at the hem of her skirt, and she crossed and recrossed her legs. The resignation in her eyes was deteriorating into full out panic, and her eyes flicked toward the film crews, no doubt wondering how much longer she had before she could shoo Logan off her stage.

It was obvious she'd been expecting a personality like Kelly's notoriously outgoing one, and instead had received the equivalent of a brick wall.

"That's... incredible," she said gamely. "I'm so glad to hear things are working out so well for the two of them."

The woman deserved an Oscar for her chipper performance and maintaining some semblance of an easy smile. In the face of such hardship, Trevor knew he'd have been hard-pressed to have pulled that off. He shifted his weight, hoping the movement would catch Logan's attention so that Trevor could somehow do... *something.* Smoke signals or a mind-meld or, hell, full-blown charades if necessary. Anything to jolt Logan into action.

"Why don't you tell us... Mr. Carter... have *you* ever had luck finding a love match with bLoved?" the TV hostess asked.

Logan turned his head to look at Trevor—*finally*—and

Trevor nodded his head vigorously, pantomiming an over-the-top wide smile and then gesturing between Logan and himself, throwing kissy lips at him.

Come on, Logan.

Some of the tension went out of Logan's shoulders, and he did that so-sexy almost smile thing. "Yes," he answered the hostess, keeping his eyes on Trevor. "bLoved is where I met my... boyfriend."

The hostess perked right up, swiveling around to face Trevor with a comically grateful look. Without her having to say a word, the entire stage crew jumped into action. The mobile cameramen swept into the wing like SWAT members on a bust, surrounding Trevor before he had a chance to react. One of the audio interns slipped through the crowd on her hands and knees and hooked Trevor up with a sound pack from behind, and, before he knew it, she'd snaked the microphone up his back and clipped it to a discreet place on his collar.

"Your boyfriend is with us today?" the hostess exclaimed excitedly, her voice brimming over with relief. Trevor's image suddenly lit up all the screens lining the back wall, broadcast live from the camera feeds as they focused in on him, and the audience clapped and cheered. "We'd *love* to meet him! Why don't we bring him on out?"

"Go," the audio intern hissed, definitely not a request. She pushed at Trevor's hips, and Trevor stumbled forward, breaking through the ring of cameramen to the fervent applause of the audience. He walked across the stage, his heart racing, and shook hands with the hostess.

Any nerves he felt at the unexpected turn of events flew out the door at the ecstatic look she gave him. There had never been a woman so happy to see him before, and Trevor was more than up to the challenge. He grinned, air kissing her cheek.

"Welcome to *What's Now?*" she said, looking like she would have gladly handed over her first born child in gratitude. "It's *so* great to have you here, um…"

"Trevor. Trevor Rogers."

"Trevor!" she said, making his name sound like it was her new favorite word. She beamed, guiding him to sit next to Logan. "Really, *really* great to have you here."

"It's great, and totally unexpected, to *be* here," Trevor replied.

The couch Logan sat on was wide enough to accommodate three, but Trevor didn't allow himself any space. He pressed up against Logan and slipped a hand comfortably onto his thigh—maybe a little higher than he should have, but he didn't want anyone to mistake what his intentions were. There was a lot of damage he had to repair in the brief time that Logan had been on the air, and Trevor wasn't going to mess around. Once he was given a role, he took it seriously.

Plus—*in public, you're mine*—as far as he was concerned, Logan's claim was a two-way street.

"Here I was, thinking I'd just be hanging out in the wings, cheering my man on," he said, grinning at the cameras. "I'm still getting used to the whole 'dating a minor celebrity' thing. But I'm always happy to talk about bLoved and how it's changed my life."

Trevor knew his words rang with sincerity, because, after all, it was *true*. The heat of Logan's body pressed against his side, and when he slanted a glance at him, Logan looked more like... *Logan*. Trevor's Logan, who'd kissed him in the conference room like a drowning man finding water, and joked with him on the plane, and taken charge of things in a way that Trevor would have loved to find out whether or not carried through to the bedroom. He smiled, covering Trevor's hand with his, and Trevor forgot to breathe.

"I can't even imagine how exciting it must be for you," the hostess said, looking between the two of them with a smile that looked genuine, instead of forced. Her gaze settled on Trevor, and her eyes warmed with gratitude. Trevor knew how to give prompts, and he wasn't about to leave her hanging when she had an interview to conduct. "So, Trevor, you're saying that you're just an average man who happened to meet up with someone successful and accomplished like Mr. Carter?"

"Trevor isn't average," Logan said, his cheeks taking on the faintest hint of pink when the audience went "*awwww*."

"You can call him Logan," Trevor said to the hostess with a wink, doing his best to ignore his own reaction to Logan's comment. "He only gets to be Mr. Carter between ten and eleven at night, and only if he's been a good boy that day."

The hostess and audience laughed, and Trevor beamed. Logan turned his head to look at him, eyebrow raised with a challenging look that really, truly, should not have been on daytime television, and Trevor stroked his hand along Logan's thigh, giving him a saucy smile.

"Isn't that right, baby?"

"I'm not sure we should be talking like that on television... sweetheart," Logan replied, his dry tone at odds with the flare of heat in his eyes.

Trevor looked back to the hostess and grinned. "He's shy."

The chemistry crackled between the two of them. Logan's shoulders had relaxed, his posture loosening up and his face losing that stony, cold look. He looked... hot. Even more so, in Trevor's opinion, because he couldn't seem to take his eyes off Trevor.

Was it because Trevor was his lifeline right now?

"The two of you are incredible together," the hostess said. "Can you tell us a little bit about how you were matched up? How does bLoved work? I've heard that the algorithms were designed in-house."

"That's correct," Logan said. The speech he used was formal, but his tone had softened considerably, now that Trevor was by his side. "Kelly coded them himself, alongside a small IT team. bLoved is about far more than just hooking up. The algorithms facilitate finding a partner who you'll not only be attracted to, but who will *match* you in every way that's important. It allows our members to find true, lasting love."

"*At last*," the hostess sang, winking at the two of them as she went a cappella on the first verse of bLoved's signature song. "*My love has come along... My lonely days are over...*"

"That was the case for us," Trevor said with a small smile, wondering why the cheesy lyrics gave him a twinge in his chest. *He* wasn't one to be lonely. And even if he happened to be panting after Logan at the moment, he wasn't looking for *that*. He cleared his throat, pushing it away. This was *acting*. He ramped up his smile, adding, "Physical attraction is definitely important, but it's only a small part of what makes a relationship great. Logan *gets* me. I've never had a boyfriend who understands me like Logan does. Or one who made me feel so appreciated. *Valued*. Like I matter to him, and..."

Trevor let his voice trail off, realizing he was saying things that were maybe a tad bit too real for comfort. The audience *awwed* again, not seeming to mind that he hadn't finished the sentence, and Logan pulled him more tightly against his side, their fingers still linked together on his thigh.

Touching Logan like that was starting to get to Trevor. Earlier, he'd felt like a walking hard-on around the man, but now... this was something else. Pretending that they were really in a relationship—the kind Trevor had never had and had always been sure he didn't want—was starting to feel too damn easy. And they had just started... could he really survive six weeks of this?

Logan's hand tightened around his, and Trevor's heart soared, making it a moot point.

He had to, didn't he? That's what he was there for.

"I can't get over how adorable the two of you are together," the hostess said with a small shake of her head. "But we're getting way off topic. What's your background, Trevor? May I call you Trevor?"

"Of course." Trevor rallied, rattling off the cover story they'd agreed on. It would help to remind himself that it *wasn't* real. "I met Logan when our bLoved profiles were connected, thanks to that sophisticated algorithm. He lives here in New York, and I was living in Chicago at the time, but he'd expanded his search radius because he flies into O'Hare all the time to do business at the bLoved headquarters. We'd been chatting online for a while, and he told me he was coming into town and invited me out to dinner."

"We went to this little restaurant called RedGate, downtown," Logan interrupted, taking over the course of the story and sounding—for Logan—animated. "Over dinner, we talked about ourselves and got to know each other a little better, and... there was an instant connection."

"I've never felt anything like it," Trevor said. If Logan wanted to play off their back and forth, he was game. "It was just... *wow*, you know? And when he's not on camera, Logan's this completely different kind of guy. I guess he must have stage fright."

The hostess watched, content to let them speak, and as long as she wasn't going to corral them back on track, Trevor was going to run with it. There was no better way to sell bLoved than to speak about it so sincerely, and he was thankful that Jose had droned on about it so many times. Trevor was familiar with how the app worked, at least, even though he'd never visited the website.

And they really *had* had that first date at RedGate. Well, okay, fine, not a "date," but still... inspiration that Trevor could draw on to give a sense of realism to their backstory.

"It's not the cameras," Logan said, shifting in his seat to look at Trevor. "It's that you weren't here with me."

Trevor's heart skipped a beat, and his lips parted on a soft sigh. The investment in Logan's words sounded too real, and even Trevor couldn't detect the lie in them.

Did he mean it?

"So... are you just visiting Logan in New York, Trevor?" the hostess cut in. "How are the two of you navigating the waters of a long-distance relationship?"

"Trevor's recently agreed to move in with me," Logan said firmly, that dominant confidence that was like Viagra for Trevor back in his voice as he turned back to face her.

Trevor felt all sorts of flustered, and he sat back in his seat, letting Logan run with it while he tried to get a handle on what they were doing. Flirting? Acting? Foreplay? Was it still just business?

"We'd actually just disembarked from his last flight here to New York from Chicago before coming to the studio,"

Logan was saying. "We'll be living in the city together from here on out."

"Congratulations!" the hostess cooed. "It's *so* nice to see love working in this day and age. I'm beyond happy for the two of you."

"Thank you," Logan said. He smiled like he meant it. "I am, too."

Trevor cleared his throat. "bLoved saw us through the long-distance portion of our relationship, though," he elaborated. As distracted as he was by Logan's sudden show of affection and sincerity, he wasn't going to forget that his job was to help Logan sell the product. Pretending to be boyfriends was a tactic to promote bLoved, not... anything else. "Not everyone is going to find their one and only right next door, and the app has a great chatting system built in, like an instant messenger. Logan and I used it exclusively, allowing us to stay in touch while we were apart. It has all these fun online activities you can do together... games, quizzes, tests, all sorts of stuff to test your compatibility, find common interests, spark important conversations, or just have fun with each other. And it also enables you to stream movies through Rise on two devices simultaneously, as long as your accounts are connected, so Logan and I were able to watch movies together from different states and chat about them in real time, just like going on a date."

"Whether relationships are based in the same city or based internationally, bLoved is a way to find them, nurture them, and strengthen them," Logan concluded. "Love is love, no matter where you are."

Logan had gone from boring to engaged in the span of a few minutes, and Trevor couldn't have been happier with the results. The hostess played off the two of them for a few more minutes, getting in some great plugs for the business, and when they finally left the stage, Trevor was confident that they'd managed to turn around what could have been a serious disaster for the business into a major win.

The same audio intern rushed over once they were in the wings, unhooking their mics and disconnecting their sound packs. Logan stood, proud and handsome in his suit, as she worked, and Trevor ate him up with his eyes. He'd always found Logan attractive, but the more facets of his personality emerged, the more drawn to him Trevor was. And here, now, seeing Logan succeed did more than make Trevor just feel accomplished as a PR coach—it fulfilled him on a level that he wasn't sure he wanted to think about.

He was as happy for Logan's victory as he would have been for his own.

"You did great," Trevor said, trying to distract himself from what he felt. "I think that Frank's going to be proud of you."

"I did great because of *you*, Trevor," Logan replied, the sincerity in his voice making Trevor feel all sorts of things he wasn't used to, even though they'd been coming up around Logan repeatedly. Logan smiled at him, looking for all the world like he wasn't aware of anything but Trevor in that moment. "Thank you. Having you by my side made all the difference."

"Well, of course." Trevor puffed up with pride and something else that he wasn't ready to think too hard about, grinning ear to ear. He winked. "When you surround yourself with greatness, you become great, too."

"Humble, as always," Logan said dryly, hitching up an eyebrow with a teasing glint in his eyes that mirrored the slight twitch in his lips.

Logan's lips. Trevor lost his train of thought, eyes flickering down to Logan's mouth. The kiss they'd shared that morning played in his mind over again, and Trevor wondered when he could taste those lips in earnest again.

If, not when.

It wasn't a given.

"I am who I am." Trevor cast a quick glance at the intern, both to distract himself from Logan's mouth and to remind himself that this was the public act they'd agreed to put on. For the intern's benefit, he added, "That's why you fell in love with me, after all."

"That's exactly why," Logan murmured, stepping in closer and pressing a chaste kiss against Trevor's lips.

Trevor couldn't help it. He melted into him, knowing that—whatever Logan might intend with that kiss—for Trevor, the lines were blurring. But, at that moment, he didn't care. Logan was hot as hell, and Trevor was attracted to him, and that's all there was to it.

All the warm, fluttery feelings were just... a side effect.

The intern cleared her throat and finished up her job. On stage, the commercials had come to an end and the next interview had begun. Logan took Trevor by the hand and led him through the back of the studio.

"The car should be waiting," Logan said. "I'll have it drop you at the hotel so you can settle in."

Trevor nodded automatically, even though he felt a little too keyed up for anything as mundane as "settling in." By the back doors were corkboards loaded with advertisements for things in and around the city, and a flash of green from the corner of Trevor's eye drew his attention as they passed.

He dug his heels into the floor and brought Logan to a stop, gasping and not even caring if it sounded overly dramatic. There, among fliers for symphonic orchestra performances and comedy acts, was Trevor's first taste of the New York City he'd always dreamed of.

"Oh. My. *God*."

"What?" Logan asked, furrowing his brow as if he didn't see it.

"*Wicked* is playing right now," Trevor said, flinging a hand toward the poster. "The Broadway musical. It won three Tony awards, Logan. *Three*. We have to go! I've always wanted to see it. I'm in New York City, I was just on live TV, and *I need to go see* Wicked. I can't even think of a more perfect day."

The fact that Logan was probably the hottest guy he'd ever dated figured pretty heavily into that equation, actually—even if their relationship *was* just fake—but Trevor didn't bring it up. Even though no one was around to hear them, they were still technically in public. And, as far as the rules went, until they were in private, he was Logan's.

A delicious shiver went through him, and he spun around to face Logan. He didn't want to go to the hotel. He wanted to stay out with Logan. In *public*.

"Take me out on a date tonight," Trevor said urgently. "I *need* to see a Broadway show while I'm here."

"Okay," Logan said, smiling down at him. Trevor's heart had one of those side effect moments. Someone bumped into them, passing by, and Logan broke eye contact, adding, "Sounds like a good move for PR, especially if we happened to get noticed. And I can write the tickets off as a business expense."

A business expense. Right.

Trevor's shoulders stiffened. For a second, caught up in their chemistry, he'd let himself forget that, outside of their television appearances and the live publicity events Frank had scheduled, the time they spent together was still just... business.

Some of Trevor's enthusiasm slipped, but then he took a deep breath and shook off his disappointment. Logan was paying him to play a role, not to actually be his boyfriend. No matter how much Trevor might enjoy flirting with Logan, or how far Logan let him push things, he'd known from the beginning that that was the deal.

Besides, who cared if Logan wasn't really interested in him? If Logan was really just that good of an actor? Wasn't that all the better for the job Trevor had been hired to do? Trevor certainly wasn't looking for anything like what they'd been spouting off about on the talk show. He didn't *want* to be tied down. He never had... right?

He was in New York City, and that was plenty of dream-come-true for anyone.

Logan pulled his phone from his pocket and dialed a number, but then covered the receiver and sent Trevor a questioning look. "Everything okay?"

"Absolutely," Trevor lied. No, not lied. Everything *was* okay. It was fabulous. Great, in fact. "I'm not ready to go to the hotel, though," he said. "Show me the city, Logan. I want to just *be* here. I want to see *every*thing."

"Then let's do it," Logan said, putting a possessive hand on the small of his back as he guided him out toward the waiting limo.

And Trevor grinned, coming out of his momentary funk. Logan wasn't *that* good of an actor. Sure, playing at being boyfriends might have been a business play, but there was no denying that Logan *reacted* to Trevor.

And, if he thought about it in a certain light, wasn't getting Logan to react basically Trevor's job?

Chapter 9

LOGAN

Front row seats to *Wicked* had been sold out, but Hiro had managed to obtain center stage seating, three rows back from the stage. To Logan, who wasn't invested in theater, it was all just logistics. To Trevor, who sat starry eyed and riveted, it seemed to mean the world.

"I can't even begin to process that we're sitting here right now," Trevor gushed. "We're seeing *Wicked* live on Broadway in New York City. Is this even real life? Am I dreaming?"

"If you are, it's a dream with some of the best production value I've ever seen," Logan teased, and to his surprise, Trevor laughed. It wasn't a chuckle, or a snort, or even a roll of his eyes—it was a genuine laugh, as though Logan had managed to say something funny.

Was it just the high of having appeared on television, or the thrill he seemed to feel about being in New York City, that gave Trevor the added zest he seemed to have as they settled in at the theater? Trevor had always been fun and energetic, but there was something extra that sparkled in his eye now. He seemed even quicker to laugh, quicker to smile, and, while the show of his affections had remained constant throughout the day, he'd lost some of the edgy flirtatiousness he'd been so fond of falling back on in Chicago and replaced it with something softer.

Something that almost felt real.

"If it's a dream, then I don't want to wake up." Trevor slipped his hand over Logan's and laced their fingers together, something that was already feeling entirely too natural. "I'm having a really great time, and I don't ever want today to end."

Logan looked away, not sure what to say. The whole day had him feeling off-kilter. He'd blown off an entire afternoon of work without a second thought when Trevor had asked him to show him the city, and now, with Trevor holding his hand and practically vibrating with excitement about what they were about to see, Logan was hard-pressed to remind himself that they were not, in fact, on a real date.

Trevor smiled and leaned forward as though to whisper something else to Logan, but as he did, the lights dimmed and a pre-recorded message played, asking the audience to turn off their cellphones, and Trevor sat back in his seat without making whatever provocative or funny or sassy comment he'd been about to share.

Logan was oddly disappointed.

He silenced his phone, slipping it into his back pocket. Since their television appearance, Frank had been trying to call almost nonstop, and when Logan wouldn't answer, he'd resorted to texting... nonstop. Frank was pleased. Memberships had spiked during the broadcast, and had continued to rise every hour since.

Trevor was breathing a kind of life into bLoved that it had never had before. Not only that, but Trevor was breathing life back into *Logan*.

The moments on the stage together had felt like a revelation. There was nothing motivating Trevor to commit himself to bLoved's cause as he had. Joining Logan on the set and playing up their fake relationship as well as he had was above and beyond the terms of their contract. He'd saved Logan from another botched interview—saved him from another failure—and it had felt like he'd done it because he'd cared in ways that weren't tied to a paycheck.

Logan was used to going through life on his own, but suddenly, he'd felt like he *wasn't*. Like he had been facing a challenging moment on stage with a true partner... a feeling that had been more solid than anything he'd ever had with Ryan, in either a business or a personal partnership sense, despite the brief time he'd actually known Trevor.

And in addition to the television appearance, the day

with Trevor had been... *fun*. Another thing Logan wasn't used to experiencing on a regular basis.

He glanced over at Trevor, biting back a smile. Trevor squirmed in his seat, grinning like mad as the show progressed, totally engrossed. He squeezed Logan's hand and leaned in close to whisper facts or opinions into his ear, and, eventually, Logan found himself whispering back.

"But why green?" Logan asked, keeping his voice low. "I mean... of all the colors?"

"It gets explained. You just have to wait for it," Trevor whispered back.

"I'm not a patient man," Logan murmured.

Trevor took his eyes away from the stage long enough to fix Logan with a heated stare. "Sometimes, it pays to be."

Logan didn't have time to ask Trevor what he meant by that. Before he could open his mouth to ask the question, Trevor leaned forward and claimed his lips. Logan's heart pounded, and he closed his eyes and kissed Trevor back, giving in to his own hunger and, for once, not second-guessing it.

All day they'd been fooling around with each other like that. Walking through the city, Trevor's touch had been near constant. The warmth of Trevor's hand in his had become expected, and even in the few hours that they'd been together, Logan found the intimacy between them had become organic. When they stood together, Trevor tucked himself beneath Logan's arm and cuddled close. And sometimes, when there were eyes on them, Trevor made a point of kissing him, always careful to keep it short, sweet, and respectable. There was nothing short, sweet, or respectable about the way Trevor kissed him now, though.

Their lips met softly enough... at first. But then Trevor prolonged the kiss, increasing the heat.

It wasn't the kind of kiss couples shared in public. Sensuous, lustful, and darkened with desire, it spoke to the same kind of need that Logan felt building in his groin. Before Trevor drew away, he traced his tongue across Logan's bottom lip, then sat back with a sly smile on his face that Logan wanted nothing more than to taste. Again. Immediately. *Always.*

"Patience," Trevor whispered, his eyes locked on Logan's mouth for just long enough to make Logan go from hungry to rock-hard. Trevor's eyes dropped to Logan's lap. He'd noticed, and his smile turned even naughtier. "Tonight, you're going to have to wait until we get back home to do anything else about... that."

Logan sucked in a sharp breath. If that was an act, Trevor deserved to be up on stage with the rest of the performers.

The line between business and pleasure, between should and *want*, had become so blurred for Logan that it was almost nonexistent. Was Trevor trying to tempt Logan into taking their business relationship further, or was he just making sure the job got done the way it was supposed to?

The rest of the show didn't interest Logan half as much as the answers to that. But, after their kiss, Trevor slipped back easily into the magic of the performance and lost himself in the magic happening on stage. Logan, however, couldn't seem to tear his attention away from the vibrant man next to him.

Full of light and life, Trevor was unafraid to be himself, confident in all regards. Fashionable and forward, bold to an extreme, he was one of the most remarkable men that Logan had ever met. The thought that a man like that would agree to be his pretend boyfriend, and then invest so much of himself into the role, was almost unfathomable. Yes, Logan was successful in a certain realm of life—business—but never in matters of the heart. He'd internalized the belief that he couldn't be. That it was the one area of his life he didn't measure up.

Trevor's attention almost made him want to question that belief... but then again, Trevor had been hired to do exactly what he was doing. To sell the world on the fact that the two of them were in love.

Was it so surprising that he would start to sell Logan on it, too?

One day, Trevor would treat another man the way he was treating Logan. The tender touches and stolen kisses would belong to someone Trevor truly cared for. Someone Trevor *loved*.

Clearly, Logan himself lacked the thing that made love possible. His shortcomings had been constantly pointed out by his parents, he'd failed to hold Ryan's love, despite all

Logan had poured into the success of Rise and how thoroughly he'd given his heart, and his inability to open up and be relatable had threatened to cripple bLoved, if Trevor hadn't been there to save him.

What had he done?

The results had been far too painful when he'd opened up to Ryan all those years ago, and yet, here he was, on the verge of risking the same kind of mistake with someone else. Someone who he was having a hard time remembering was being *paid* to be with him. Logan scrubbed a hand over his face, wanting to groan.

No, it wasn't like that. Trevor had flirted with him even before Logan had offered him the contract. Trevor had been welcoming and warm, every time Logan had visited the Chicago Ashby's over the last year.

When intermission came, Trevor excused himself and left to use the bathroom, and Logan took the time alone to try to settle his roiling emotions. Spending the day with Trevor had been like jumping into the deep end of the pool, and he still wasn't sure whether he'd end up sinking or swimming.

Ryan may have been the one who'd betrayed him all those years ago, but, in his heart, Logan knew that the end of their relationship had been his own fault. It had come to an end because of Logan's devotion to work and because of his inability to loosen up. Because Logan had wanted to prove his worth, only to take it too far. Rise had been important to Logan because of what it had meant for his future with *Ryan*, and in the end, dedicating himself to the business they'd built together had cost him everything.

With Trevor, though, Logan didn't feel like he had to prove anything. Trevor made him feel like he was *already* worthy of the attention Trevor bestowed upon him. Trevor had him loosening up without Logan even trying, and, even though he didn't share Logan's drive or his passion for business—the common grounds between them were few, in fact, and in many ways Trevor was his opposite—when they spent time together, Logan started to feel like he might become a version of himself that he'd always wanted to be.

That, once, he *had* been.

There had been days in Logan's past, carefree and happy, where he hadn't been so rigid with his life. Before Rise took off, and before his parents decided that their son's heteronormativity was worth more than maintaining a relationship with him, when Logan had laughed. Smiled. *Loved*.

Trevor effortlessly reminded him of the times before life had hardened Logan's spirit and left him with nothing. Trevor hadn't given up on him like Logan's college friends had. To Trevor, the injured part of who Logan was, was just another facet of his being, rather than a deterrent.

It was what made Trevor so special.

"Back." Trevor slipped into his seat and got comfortable just as the house lights flickered, indicating that the show was about to resume. He threw Logan a cheeky grin. "Did you miss me, cuddle muffin?"

"I'm practicing my patience," Logan reminded him, Trevor's teasing pulling yet another a smile out of him. "So... no."

"Oh, that's so cold it burned." Trevor grinned. He slipped his hand back into Logan's, his attention immediately going back to the stage.

Logan frowned. Then he laughed. He was... jealous. Of a Broadway show. His lips twitched in the darkened theater, knowing he was being ridiculous. "And I thought we weren't going to do cutesy nicknames anymore," he whispered, leaning in, just for an excuse to get closer to Trevor. "What happened to you being good?"

"Changed my mind," Trevor whispered back, dragging his eyes off the stage just long enough to give Logan a naughty wink. Trevor looked back at the show, but not before adding, "It's just too much fun to tease you. Besides, if I'm bad enough, maybe you'll have to punish me."

Logan's hand tightened convulsively around Trevor's, and when Trevor afforded him a sly look out of the corner of his eye and raised his eyebrow in a silent challenge, Logan gave a quiet groan, assaulted by a vision that made his cock harden yet again. He shifted in his seat, mind filled with the picture of Trevor laid across his lap, tight little ass bare and pink as he goaded Logan into spanking him for his transgressions.

Logan stared blindly at the stage, the production value unable to hold a candle to the images in his own head.

"I'm pretty sure that one of these days I'm going to get around by bubble, too," Trevor whispered in Logan's ear after a bit, as, on stage, Galinda the Good Witch descended from above in an opalescent bubble.

Trevor had gone from provocative back to playful, slipping between the different facets of his magnetic personality with an ease that reflected just how comfortable he was in his own skin. He was attractive on so many levels that it left Logan reeling, and despite his own strict rules about mixing business with pleasure, Logan was having trouble remembering why he should fight it.

"You'll need to earn your wings first," Logan responded, wondering when the last time he'd actually felt playful had been. "I'll be sure to put in a good word or two for you with the wizard."

"Ooooh, you've got *connections*," Trevor teased back, grinning at him. "You're the best, stud muffin. I'll have to thank you properly... later."

"Cuddle muffin... stud muffin... either you really do want me to punish you, or you're hungry," Logan murmured. "Should we go to dinner after this?"

"No," Trevor whispered back, rewarding Logan's playfulness with another cheeky grin. "I'm only interested in dessert, sugar pop. But whatever you've got in mind for me... no whipped cream, remember?"

Logan snorted back a laugh, not sure whether he should

be amused or aroused. *Both* seemed like a good answer. He may have been able to keep Trevor from adding color to his wardrobe for the last year, but, after less than twenty-four hours together, it was already clear that Logan wouldn't be able to stop him from adding color to his *life*.

And Logan didn't have it in him to resist.

THE SHOW HAD ENDED HALF AN HOUR AGO, BUT TREVOR AND Logan had been walking, enjoying the bite of the night air while Trevor babbled on about *Wicked* and related stories. The bright lights of the city lit their way, and the passing cars and chatter of pedestrians drowned their conversation out to the rest of the world. In that moment they were surrounded by life, and yet Logan felt as though the world was made just for the two of them. As if they were alone, and yet Logan had never felt less lonely. Their small sphere of existence simply felt... perfect.

"And if *Rent* is going to be performed while I'm in town, then we need to get tickets for that, too," Trevor insisted. He'd shoved his hands into his pockets to project his skin from the cold, but as he walked, he brushed against Logan's arm to make up for the loss of contact. "And *Les Mis*? Um, sign me up for some Jean Valjean, please."

"It's like you're speaking another language," Logan grumbled. Despite his tone of voice, he smiled. Trevor's excitement was contagious, and the longer they spent together, the less Logan wanted the night to come to an end.

Being with Trevor made it feel simple to let go of the brooding darkness of his past and live in the light Trevor brought to his present. "You really think that highly of musicals?"

"Um... *yes*," Trevor said, laughing and shaking his head as if the answer should have been obvious. "The whole reason I got into sewing was because I wanted to design costumes. There's so much going on in terms of fashion history and understanding shapes and weights and nontraditional body types... don't get me wrong—I *love* fashion. I love the runway walks and the models and the haute couture and the catalog material... but why stop there when you can work in any time period you want, challenging yourself each and every day to tackle the unusual?"

"But instead, you're working at Ashby's and altering clothes on the side. Why didn't you pursue something like that?" Logan asked, genuinely curious.

"Maybe someday I will," Trevor replied, shrugging with an easy smile. "It's not that easy to pack up and move when you've got no savings to speak of, though. I mean, yes, it's a dream of mine, but as much as I dream, and as outspoken and, I don't know... *outrageous* as I know I can get, I'm not out of touch with reality. It's hard to get a toe in the door for that kind of thing, and, even then, the pay's not fantastic. For now, it's easier to stay at Ashby's than to try my luck behind the scenes here, on Broadway, or with movie production out in Hollywood."

"You should do it," Logan said, smiling down at him.

If anyone had what it took to accomplish his goals in life, he would bank on it being Trevor. "I have no doubt you'd succeed."

Trevor blinked up at him, looking surprised for a moment. Then, like the sun breaking through clouds, a smile spread across his face that was yet another facet of the many faces he'd shown Logan. This one looked... radiant.

"Maybe I will," he said, and the tone of his voice made Logan's heart do a slow roll in his chest.

Which scared the shit out of him.

Logan had been buffeted by feelings all day—stronger emotions than he'd allowed himself in years—and as irresistibly tempting as Trevor was, the feeling Logan was experiencing was too dangerous. He was setting himself up for something he couldn't handle going through again, and even though, if he were honest with himself, the seeds of it had been slowly building for the last year, the speed at which everything had ramped up since he'd brought Trevor into his life more fully was terrifying.

He took a step back, pulling out his phone. "You'll need your rest," he said abruptly. "I've got another publicity appearance tomorrow that you'll need to coach me through. I'll call Hiro and get him to send over your hotel itinerary so we can get you home."

Beneath the orange glow of the streetlights, Trevor's eyes flashed with impish intent, as if he wasn't at all put off by Logan's suddenly cold demeanor. But then again, he never had been. He closed the space Logan had put between them and wrapped his arms around Logan's neck. "You're really going to end our date here?" he asked. "*Now?*"

"It wasn't..." Logan's words snagged in his throat. It hadn't been a date, had it? It had been business. He froze, staring down at Trevor, and Trevor smirked at him. Their noses nearly brushed. Logan cleared his throat. "Trevor, I—"

"We've just come out on national TV as a cohabiting couple, baby," Trevor said, cutting him off. "What's the media going to think if you don't take me home with you?"

Once more, the line between what was an act and what was truth blurred in Logan's mind. He wrapped his arms around Trevor's waist and pulled him in, flush against his body. It was only when Trevor was pressed against him that he realized how hard he was.

Trevor felt it, too.

Eyes flashing with sly, cat-like delight, he pushed his hips forward so that the pressure against Logan's crotch increased. "More importantly, what's *he* going to think if you don't take me home?"

Logan groaned. The thrum of his pulse drowned out the sounds of the night and the last vestiges of his self-preservation. "We're only boyfriends in public," he said, his resistance already eroding.

"We don't have to be boyfriends to go back to your place." Bold, Trevor tilted his head to the side and leaned in so that their lips brushed. When he spoke again, he whispered the words against Logan's mouth, so that they were more felt than heard. "Tonight can be a one-time deal, if that's all you want. But the truth is, pretending to be your boyfriend has had me hard all day. I don't want to go to bed alone tonight, Logan. You're the hottest guy I've ever gone out with, and I *want* you. We can work out the hotel arrangements in the morning."

Could Trevor feel the way Logan's cock throbbed in response? The thought of bringing Trevor into his bedroom made Logan's heart go haywire, and his brain processed his thoughts like he was drunk. All day, Logan had been debating what he felt for Trevor, and whether or not it was acceptable to feel anything for him at all.

No, not just "acceptable"... whether it was *safe*.

Logan doubted he'd be able to fuck Trevor without feeling things that he hadn't let himself feel in far too long, and even though Trevor was playing along at monogamy now, he'd made it clear in their past conversations that in real life, he was only interested in casual dating. Hell, he'd just said that he'd be perfectly fine with tonight as a one-off... the question was, could Logan be?

"You're thinking too much," Trevor whispered. When he spoke, his lips moved against Logan's. "You wouldn't even need to hire me anymore if you just learned to let yourself go."

"I can't," Logan whispered back. "It's not—"

"You *can*," Trevor insisted. The sound of his voice barely carried over the noise of the traffic. "Practice with me tonight. I want you, Logan. Take me home and let it all go. I want it, you want it, it doesn't have to be more complicated than that."

Trevor's arms tightened around his neck, and he kissed Logan in the same, slow, lustful way as he had back in the theater. Logan's arms tightened around Trevor in response, and the city faded away from around them. Trevor was right; it didn't have to be complicated. In fact, the only kind of sex Logan had allowed himself since Ryan was the uncomplicated kind.

But being with Trevor felt different.

Trevor moaned gently and deepened the kiss, and when the kiss broke, Logan's lungs were starved for air. Trevor took him by the hand and led him to the side of the street, flagging down a taxi as though he'd lived in New York for years. Logan may have been conflicted about what they were about to do, but Trevor clearly was not.

In a matter of minutes, they were seated side by side in the back of a car. Trevor's hand settled dangerously far up Logan's thigh, and he groaned, remembering the thought he'd had the week before, when he *had* let himself go in the privacy of his hotel room.

Trevor would definitely not be a passive sex partner.

"West 18th Street. The Parker Tower building," Logan said to the cabbie, a split-second before Trevor's free hand pulled him back for another kiss that only served to prove him right.

The driver cut into traffic and the city passed by around

them, streetlights showering them in momentary light that raced up their thighs and over their torsos, only to be left behind as the taxi sped onward. Trevor was all over him, and even though Logan had never been one for public displays of affection, there was no way he was going to push him away. It was *so* Trevor. No holding back.

The kiss they shared grew quicker and needier. Trevor's hand wandered inward, and his fingertips played discreetly with Logan's bulge. Every fantasy Logan had indulged in about Trevor was nothing compared to the reality. Trevor was as confident and demanding during passion as he was in real life, and Logan couldn't get enough of him.

When the taxi came to a stop outside of Parker Tower, Logan paid the fare and stumbled out, and Trevor followed him. Hand in hand, they crossed the sidewalk and entered the lobby. Logan fumbled with his keys. At the back of the lobby were three elevators. The one on the left belonged exclusively to Logan, its only destination the penthouse he owned.

"C'mon," Trevor murmured, pulling him toward the call buttons for the standard elevators. "What are you—"

"Not there." Logan tugged him to the side and slipped his key into the lock. "Up here."

Trevor's eyes widened, and he looked between Logan and the newly opened elevator. "You really *are* rich, aren't you?"

"A little," Logan said, feeling his lips quirk up.

Trevor's enjoyment of the things Logan's money could

buy—like the first class seating on the plane and the limo earlier—was refreshing and genuine, but at the same time, the way Trevor treated him left him no doubt that Trevor didn't really care. Or, more specifically, that he'd want Logan anyway, even if "rich" hadn't been a factor.

Trevor wasn't moving fast enough for Logan's taste... now that he'd set this course of action, he wanted Trevor as soon as possible. He put a hand on the small of Trevor's back, wondering how Trevor's brash confidence would mix with Logan's own need to be in charge in the bedroom. Eager to find out.

"Get in," he said, giving him a little push into the elevator.

"Bossy," Trevor said, and the wicked smile that accompanied the words made Logan's heart rate almost go through the roof. As soon as the elevator doors closed behind them, Trevor pinned Logan to the wall and kissed him hard. Logan's hands held Trevor by the jaw as their kiss turned ferocious. Their teeth clacked. Their tongues met. Trevor nipped Logan's bottom lip and tugged it, and Logan seriously considered flipping him around and fucking him right there. Instead, he tugged Trevor's hair, forcing his head back so he could take more of his mouth. In retaliation, Trevor reached between them and squeezed Logan's cock through his pants.

"Dirty," Trevor panted. "When'd you get so fucking dirty, getting hard like this for someone like me?"

The gentle pressure of his hand tightened, and Logan

tossed his head back and hissed out a gasp. A full day of flirting, of touching, and of teasing was finally culminating in something tangible. There was nothing left to agonize over or regret. Business hours were over, and as long as he kept his heart firmly in check, Logan knew he had nothing to worry about. Trevor would be his.

The elevator doors opened onto the twenty-fourth floor, and Logan didn't waste any time—he grabbed Trevor by the hand and dragged him into his penthouse. They stumbled through the expansive art deco inspired living room, down the hall, and into Logan's bedroom. Riled, Logan pushed Trevor down onto the bed and crowded him back across it, chasing Trevor on his hands and knees while Trevor crept backward, facing him.

The lights in the bedroom were out, but they'd left the door open, and the light from the hall fell across the bed so Logan could still see him. Trevor's arousal was evident in the size of his dark pupils, the flush in his cheeks, the short, panting breaths... but that was just physical. What pushed it over the edge for Logan was that it was *Trevor*. He didn't just look turned on, he looked like he was having *fun*. It was the sexiest thing Logan had ever seen.

Trevor reached up and grabbed Logan by the tie. He yanked on it so that Logan sank onto his body, and the kiss started again. Hot. Needy. Wild. Logan was hard and aching for more, and he was going to take it. For the moment, at least, every carefully guarded emotion was left unattended, and every wall he'd built to keep himself safe was demolished. Being with Trevor wiped away his past, made him feel like nothing had ever happened to harden his views on the world. Trevor made him feel *right*.

Clothes were shed. Logan barely felt it as Trevor undid the buttons of his shirt and pushed his jacket down his arms. Shoes were kicked off, and with them, socks. Logan's fingers undid each of Trevor's buttons and left his pale chest bare.

Trevor's lips were swollen when the kiss broke, and his eyes were partially lidded. He traced a single finger down Logan's cheek. A smirk quirked his lips almost imperceptibly.

"Do you have a condom, baby?"

The primitive part of Logan's brain wanted to push Trevor into his mattress and forget about safety for the night, but the calculated, logical part of him urged him to take the request seriously. He'd never been lax about it, and despite rarely bringing men to his penthouse, he was fully stocked.

He jerked away from Trevor and scrambled across the bed to grab one from the nightstand drawer. When Logan turned around, both condom and a bottle of lube retrieved, he found Trevor had already lifted his hips and was sliding his pants and briefs down his thighs. Willowy and slight, Trevor's body looked almost fragile. The elastic band of his underwear caught the shaft of his cock on the way down, and, when freed, his cock slapped against his stomach— hardened and beaded with precum—leaving no doubt that Trevor wanted him just as much as he wanted Trevor.

Pants removed, Trevor sank back down onto the bed and wrapped his cock with his palm, stroking himself as he watched Logan with hungry eyes. Logan's cock throbbed in response.

"Why don't you take off those pants and show me what dessert looks like?" Trevor asked in a low voice. "I've been waiting all day for this."

"Weren't you the one counseling patience?" Logan asked, his voice husky and raw sounding in his own ears. He tossed the condom and the lube onto the bed and pushed his pants down his hips, then crossed the bed on his hands and knees.

"That was then," Trevor said. "But now I'm all out of patience. Do you want me to ride you? I can do it all night if you want me to. I'm so fucking horny for you right now." Trevor let go of his cock, sitting upright and reaching for Logan as he spoke, but as much as Logan adored Trevor's forthrightness, he was taking charge that night.

"No." Not caring how rough he was, Logan grabbed Trevor and flipped him so he was face down against the mattress. "Lift your hips. I want you to present yourself for me."

Trevor moaned, looking back over his shoulder as he sucked in a breath and did as he was told. Something hot and fierce surged through Logan. One part possession, one part arousal. Trevor was perfect. Perfect for *him*.

Trevor lifted his hips and supported himself on his knees while keeping his torso flush with the mattress.

After that one, hot look, he pressed his face into a pillow, the modest rounds of his ass perked and on display for Logan's pleasure.

Logan ran his palm over one of Trevor's cheeks, and Trevor shuddered at his touch. He'd never been a selfish lover, but something about Trevor made it tempting to just *take*. Not least of which was Trevor's own impatience.

"I was bad today," Trevor said, the words muffled by the pillow. Still, Logan could hear the smile in his voice, a playful complement to the way Trevor's skin flushed at the taunt.

"Oh, I remember," Logan said, his cock throbbing as the vision he'd had before flooded through him again. "I told you to stop with the nicknames, and what did you do?" He continued to caress Trevor's soft skin, waiting for his response.

"I kept using them." Trevor's voice trembled and nearly broke, his body strung taut. The air between them thickened with arousal, and Logan wanted more than ever to take him immediately. But, like Trevor had said, patience...

"So you know why you have to be punished," he said, barely recognizing his own voice. He certainly hadn't denied himself sex since Ryan, but it had always been just the fulfillment of his body's need. This was something different.

"Y-yes," Trevor said, pushing back against Logan's hand. "I was bad, Logan. You need to do something about it. *Please*."

Where was his dominance coming from? Trevor's influence was twisting Logan in strange ways, creating a man far more sure of himself than he'd ever been before... at least, in *this* environment. He'd always preferred to top, but taking it this far? Logan had never been so in control outside of business. The new grounds they explored together were opening facets of Logan's personality he wasn't sure he'd ever acknowledged.

Trevor was right—letting go really was empowering.

He caressed the smooth curve of Trevor's ass one last time, then he drew his hand back sharply and spanked him. Trevor cried out, the startled sound making Logan's cock jerk against his stomach when it devolved into a low, needy moan.

"Are you going to do it again?" Logan asked. He smoothed his hand over the freshly irritated skin, hoping to cool it. Ridiculously aroused by the sight of the bright pink stain spreading out from the point of contact.

"I might forget," Trevor said, his voice muffled and panting. He kept his hips lifted, waiting. "I'm sorry."

Logan groaned. Trevor would *always* push him, wouldn't he? He spanked him again, his own breath coming in short, hard bursts as Trevor writhed under his hand. Logan wanted to fuck him, but he didn't want to give this up, either.

"How many times did you slip?" he asked, his voice thick with need.

"Three?" Trevor said, trembling the third time Logan's hand cracked against his ass. "F-four?"

"*Fuck*, Trevor," Logan said, grinding his erection against Trevor's hips as he spanked him. He needed to fuck. *Now*. He reached around Trevor's hip, finding the base of his cock. His fingers traced through the coarse hair there, then up the length of Trevor's hardened shaft. "You're going to take everything I give you, aren't you?"

"Y-yes," Trevor panted, thrusting into Logan's hand as it worked his cock. He moaned—such a delicious, tempting sound—and pressed his face deeper into the pillows. Logan reached for the condom with his free hand, ripping the packaging with his teeth and then smoothing it down his own cock.

How long had it been since he'd had a man in his bed? Since he'd been so aroused?

Trevor was experienced, wasn't he? With the way he flirted, and the way he'd alluded to dating other men who'd keep his bed warm during Chicago winters, Logan didn't think he needed to be gentle. Trevor didn't seem to want it. He drizzled lube down between Trevor's cheeks, mesmerized for a moment as it pooled against his hole. He tossed the bottle aside, working it in momentarily as Trevor panted and moved back against him, begging so prettily that Logan almost came right there.

"Please. *Please*, Logan, *hurry*. I need—"

Logan needed it, too. He positioned himself behind Trevor and held his cock steady, then pushed inward and sank as deep as Trevor's body would allow him to.

For a moment, his vision whited out. Nothing could

have prepared him for how tight Trevor felt around him. How *right*.

"F-Fuck!" Trevor howled. A sharp press of his hips back against Logan's body swallowed Logan's cock deeper, and Logan grunted and pushed into him harder. Deeper. "H-Holy *fuck*, Logan. So good, baby. *Fuck* me."

Logan drew his hips back sharply and bucked into Trevor while Trevor gasped and panted, shifting his position to take as much as he could. The tight embrace of his body urged Logan to work him deep and hard, and he fucked him mercilessly, spurred on by the graphic evidence that Trevor was loving every second of it.

Crying out in ecstasy, Trevor ground back against him, the litany of his dirty begging going on and on and *on*, encouraging Logan to fuck him even harder. Logan did it, letting himself go the way Trevor had urged him to.

The long dip of Trevor's spine was on display for him, drawing Logan's eyes down Trevor's body to the fantastic ass he dominated. With each thrust of his hips, he watched his cock disappear into Trevor's body, and the sight was almost too much. Logan felt the swell of orgasm approach. Desperate to ward it off, he sank down across Trevor's body to force his gaze from the erotic vision.

"You like it rough?" he whispered, burying his face in the heat of Trevor's neck. Logan nipped at the skin there, earning another full-body shudder underneath him. Every cell in Logan's body was attuned to Trevor, and every breath, every move, every sexy-as-sin sound that fell from his lips ramped up Logan's arousal to the point that he doubted he'd be able to hold on much longer, regardless of what distraction-tactics he employed.

But no matter how much Trevor turned him on, he was going to make damn sure Trevor came for him, first.

"Mmm, fuck, yeah I do," Trevor moaned, turning his head to the side. "*So* rough. Pound me, baby. I want it bad."

Logan's hips snapped forward at that, making Trevor cry out. He buried his face against the pillows, but Logan wanted to hear him. He wanted to hear every gasp, cry, and whimper that parted from Trevor's lips. Wanted to force even more of the heady sounds from him. Taking him at his word, Logan fisted his hand in Trevor's hair and tugged his head back.

Trevor sucked in a startled breath and tried to turn his head to the side to look at Logan, but Logan's fingers tightened their grip and held him firmly in place. "Let me hear you," he ordered. "I'm going to give you exactly what you want, Trevor. And I want to hear how much you like it."

Another hard thrust of his hips rattled the bed frame, and Trevor cried out in unbridled pleasure. "Logan! Fuccckkkk. *Yes.*"

Logan didn't stop. Trevor cried out his name until his voice grew hoarse, and Logan ached from the need to release. It was a decadent torture to hold himself back, but sex had *never* been so good, and he wasn't ready to end it.

Trevor moved, reaching toward his cock, and Logan

released Trevor's hair to slap a hand over his wrist, pinning it to the mattress before he could reach himself.

"No," he growled. "You'll come when I say, Trevor. Not before. I'll get you there."

"Oh *fuck*, Logan," Trevor panted. "I need it, baby, *please*, I need... oh fuckoh*fuck*oh*fuck* Logan I need to come I need it *fuckkkkkk Logan*."

Logan's entire world narrowed to the tight heat of Trevor's body, the wet slap of their skin together, the frantic desperation in Trevor's voice that mirrored the rising tide of erotic tension building inside him.

Trevor started to tremble, still begging, and even before he said it, Logan knew he'd reached the edge.

"*Logan*," Trevor moaned. "I'm gonna—"

"*Come*," Logan demanded, slamming into him. He'd never wanted anything as badly, and when Trevor did it—letting himself go with a deep, shuddering gasp that Logan felt with his entire body—Logan gave in, too. Trevor's walls embraced his cock, milking it, and even if he'd wanted to, there wouldn't have been any way for him to hold himself back any longer. Pleasure burst inside of him, and he bucked deep inside of Trevor, fucking him through the course of his own release.

So good.

So. Fucking. *Good*.

Trevor collapsed underneath him, and Logan rolled to the side, refusing to let them separate. He buried his face against Trevor's neck again, feeling the warm afterglow steal through him as he breathed in the scent of sex and heat and *Trevor*.

"Mmmm... fuck," Trevor purred, melting back against him. "You're so dirty, Logan. Where did *that* come from? Because I definitely want to sign up for more."

Trevor had said they'd just do tonight, and with Logan's mind clearing from the erotic haze he'd been in all day, Trevor's words made his walls start to come back up.

Trevor was getting to him.

Letting himself go had been one of the most exciting things he'd ever done, but it might have been one of the stupidest, too. Mixing business and pleasure had ruined him once, and already, Logan could tell that something similar with Trevor would be even harder to recover from.

But if Trevor wanted more, he doubted he'd have the ability to resist. Trevor was going to rip him to pieces, and Logan was fearful that he wouldn't be able to pull himself back together once he was through.

"Goodnight, baby," Trevor murmured, his body already relaxing into sleep in Logan's arms, as if orgasm had sucked every ounce of Trevor's incredible stamina out of him, quickly and completely.

Logan pressed his lips against Trevor's skin, wondering why that little bit of intimate knowledge made him want to smile. "Goodnight," he said, even though he could tell Trevor was already out.

And the problem was... it *had* been a good night. Too

good. So good, that—in Logan's experience—nothing might ever match up to it again.

Even if Trevor wanted "more," Logan was sure that *more* would still come with an end date. Their contract, Trevor's dating preferences, and Logan's history all pointed toward it. Which basically meant Logan was fucked, because he wanted more, too. But, the way he was feeling at that moment, he doubted *more* would ever be enough.

Logan wanted it *all*.

Chapter 10

TREVOR

LOGAN SNORED WHEN HE SLEPT. IT WASN'T THE KIND OF loud, rattling rumbles that Trevor despised, but a far gentler sound that edged on delicate. Still, *no* variation of snoring should be attractive. It was stupidly ridiculous that he would like the sound, and he rolled over, forcing himself off the warmth of Logan's chest, determined to stop liking it.

After a year of regular visits to Ashby's and one hell of a first date in New York City, Logan had full-on rocked his world the night before. There were times in the past when Trevor had woken up in a strange bed and felt guilty, or gross, or otherwise negative.

But waking up beside Logan felt... perfect.

The cold winter light was bright enough that it was definitely morning, and even though Trevor was by no means a morning person, he was willing to bet it was also still early. Stifling a yawn, Trevor stretched out and kicked his legs over the side of the bed, refusing to let the warmth and general loveliness of snuggling up to Logan keep him there. Sleeping in a strange bed *always* managed to wake him up early—which was usually a good thing. After most one-night stands, Trevor preferred to get out before his host woke up, but then again, most one-night stands didn't include six more weeks of working together.

Was Trevor really going to be able to do the full six weeks and not have more of what had happened the night before?

Could Logan?

He shook off the thought. He was beyond experienced with casual dating, and he needed to keep his head straight about what was and was not happening between him and Logan. Throwing himself wholeheartedly into the role of loving boyfriend had been much too easy—shockingly so, given how out of character it was for Trevor in real life—and he was pretty sure that the overabundance of warm fuzziness he kept feeling toward Logan was a side effect of all that pretending.

He grimaced as he left the warm covers, but Logan was slated for a series of public appearances a little later that morning, and Trevor figured that meant they'd be leaving together, directly from the penthouse. Without any of his luggage there to fall back on, he would have to make do, and he might as well get started on that now.

He grinned. It was a good thing he knew Logan's closet inside out.

With a gentle hum, Trevor padded his way across the bedroom and entered the attached bathroom. He ran a shower and washed, helping himself to Logan's soaps and shampoos and refusing to wonder if Logan would wake up and join him.

The high from the night before still raced through his veins, making everything seem bright. So far, New York was everything he'd ever dreamed it would be, and sharing the night with Logan had made it even better. In one day, Trevor had appeared on live television, seen a Broadway show, and had sex with one of the hottest men he'd ever met.

Life didn't get much better than that.

Trevor pushed aside the memory of how tempting it had been to stay in bed with Logan. And not just for more sex.

There were clean towels stored on a freestanding towel rack near the door of the bathroom, and he helped himself to one. After drying off, he slipped into one of Logan's plush white robes. LC was embroidered in black thread on the pocket, and while it was a little too pretentious for Trevor's taste, he couldn't help but smile as he drew the robe snug against his body. He was wearing Logan's robe, in Logan's multi-million dollar New York penthouse, in Logan's dreadfully plain bedroom.

Logan, the brooding hottie that everyone at Ashby's had dismissed as a total stick in the mud. Trevor grinned, a ripple of heat moving through him. *Logan*, who'd tossed him down on the bed and spanked him for being naughty the night before.

No Broadway show could compare to a thrill like that.

Trevor exited the bathroom and claimed his phone from his discarded pants. There was enough battery in it to last for a while longer. Pocketing it, he glanced over at the bed. Logan was still sleeping, looking far more relaxed than he usually did in waking life, and the sight gave Trevor's heart a little flutter. He turned away, worried with himself. He needed to keep it casual, the way he always did with men. No matter what he might think he felt, it was too soon, and Logan was too quick to remind him it was just business.

I'm going to give you exactly what you want, Trevor. And I want to hear how much you like it.

Trevor shivered, his cock swelling at the memory. But no matter how many of Trevor's buttons Logan managed to push, Trevor wasn't looking for love. He'd never wanted to be tied down—he snickered, slapping a hand over his mouth to muffle the sound—well, not like *that*, at least. He should be more than happy with what he had with Logan. Especially if it turned out that Logan *was* up for more.

He exited the bedroom, deciding to investigate the penthouse while Logan slept. The place was *huge*. Trevor had barely had time to make note of the art deco living room Logan had dragged him through the night before, on their way to the bedroom. The open-concept area likely covered as much floorspace as some of the houses he'd lived in. Floor-to-ceiling windows stretched the entire length of one wall, offering a stunning view of the city.

Trevor recognized the Empire State Building when he saw it, even from a distance, and another thrill went through him as he took in New York City in all its glory, stretched out before him.

The furniture in the living room was sparse but modern, and if Trevor had to guess, he'd say Logan had hired an interior decorator to pull it together. While it was stylish, it was also a little plain, and Trevor already saw dozens of ways to improve it. To give the room not just more style, but more *life*. With an accent piece of artwork there, and a pop of color...

He sighed and shook his head, turning away. It wasn't like Logan was going to take him up on his suggestions. Trevor hadn't even been able to convince him to *wear* color over the last year; the man certainly wasn't going to be interested in Trevor's home decorating ideas.

A hall to the right of the living room led to several smaller rooms, including Logan's bedroom. Nosy, Trevor peeked in through each door. Apart from a study—which was exceptionally minimal and stripped of character— there were three bedrooms and two bathrooms, one at either end of the hall. At the end was a dining room, and beyond that, a kitchen.

No one could say the penthouse wasn't stunning, but it reminded Trevor too much of the way Logan had been the day before, for those first few moments on the stage of the morning show. There was so much more to the man than he'd shown to the television audience, and his home was the same. It could be so much more. So much more *Logan*.

Trevor wanted that for him, even though he reminded himself that it wasn't his place to want anything of the sort. But everyone should have a place where they could let go completely and just be themselves, and this... this wasn't the Logan that Trevor was getting to know.

As Trevor investigated some of the cabinets beneath the lava stone counters—an early morning like this would definitely require a coffee fix—his phone rang. He recognized the cheery ringtone at once and answered immediately, a smile spreading across his face.

"Bri!" His sister, Brigid, was one of his favorite people in the world.

"Trevor, what the hell is going on?" she barked, not bothering with a greeting.

Trevor frowned, caught off-guard. "Um, I'm in New York, like I told you?"

"Where did you wake up this morning?"

Trevor blinked, then grinned. He finally found a kettle in one of the cabinets and brought it to the sink to fill with water. There was a French press already on the counter, and he assumed there had to be coffee somewhere. Just another sign that Logan was the perfect man.

"In bed," he answered cheekily.

"In *whose* bed?" Brigid asked. "Because one of Mom and Dad's friends saw the television interview you did yesterday—which, by the way, what the hell? You never told us you were going to be on TV—and now they're saying that you've moved to New York so you can live with *Logan Carter*? Like, I stalked him online for a little, and he keeps a low profile, but I read that he founded Rise *and* bLoved? Are you sugar babying for him? Because you told us you were offered a job in New York, but I thought you meant something legit."

The kettle filled with water. Trevor turned off the faucet and carried it to the stove. He turned the burner on. "Bri, it's okay, I promise. I'm not a sugar baby. Logan and I are just... having some fun."

"You're at his place right now, aren't you?" Brigid asked.

"...Maybe." Trevor bit down on his bottom lip to hold back a grin. "He was so good, Bri. Oh my God. We went out yesterday after we made our TV appearance, and he took me to see *Wicked*, and then I kind of turned on the charm, and—"

"You need to be careful," Brigid warned, cutting him off and sounding not in the least impressed with his excited gushing. "Mom and Dad worry about you sometimes, you know. And I know you're having fun and enjoying yourself, but, until now, you've been doing that in a city you're familiar with. One where you have support. Now, you're out in New York where none of us can get you, and if you lead this man on and make him think the two of you share something you don't, I don't know what's going to happen."

Trevor laughed, even though it was a little strained. Brigid had always been a bit of a mother hen, and, normally, he appreciated the fact that she liked to look out for him. He knew Frank didn't want the fact that Trevor and Logan's relationship was fake to get out, but he trusted his sister not to let that happen, and if he *didn't* tell her, she'd just keep worrying.

"It's all acting," he said. "The job *is* legit, but the bLoved people don't want the world to know I'm coaching him on his public personality, Bri. So they came up with this ruse to make it look like we were a couple."

Brigid was silent for a long moment, then she sighed. "You were gushing a minute ago, Trevor."

He opened a few more cupboards, looking in vain for the coffee. "Acting plus maybe a bit of fun on the side," he admitted, ruthlessly ignoring all those warm, fuzzy side effects. Brigid really would think something was off if he let her in on that part of it. It wasn't like him.

"Well, you need to make sure *he* knows you're just having fun," she said. "Because the look on his face in that clip? Trev, that wasn't acting."

Trevor's heart raced. He wasn't sure if that made him get his hopes up, or scared the shit out of him. Sure, he felt... things... around Logan. But he *was* just the casual dating type. And Logan... well, he wasn't really sure what type Logan was.

Mine, his traitorous brain immediately supplied.

"If you thought it looked real, just remember, Bri... I'm *that* good at my job," he quipped to his sister, doing his best to ignore that little bit of editorial commentary from a part of himself he wasn't ready to hear from. "Logan knows where we stand."

"I'm serious." Brigid's somber tone made Trevor frown. "The way he looks at you isn't like how you'd look at some casual fling. You're far away from friends and family, Trev, and you're playing with the heartstrings of a powerful man. You need to be careful, okay?"

"Sure," he said, giving up on the coffee hunt and leaning back against the counter. He pinched the bridge of his nose, wanting to be done with the conversation. Just another reason to avoid actual relationships.

"Promise?"

"I promise."

"Good." Brigid paused. "That's all I wanted to say. I've got to get to class, but I love you, baby brother. I'm just not used to seeing you like this."

"Me?"

"Logan Carter wasn't the only one who didn't look like he was acting."

"I've gotta go, Bri," he said. "Lots of work today."

"Okay, but..." Brigid hesitated. "Call me whenever you

need to, okay? I'm here for you. And if something goes wrong, we'll figure it out together. Love you."

"Nothing's going to go wrong. Love you, too," Trevor replied, eager to get off the phone. "Bye."

"Bye."

Trevor took the phone from his ear and stared down at the screen after the call ended. Brigid's picture smiled back up at him, her blond hair swept away from her face and her blue eyes sparkling. Everyone back home thought it looked like he was legitimately dating Logan, and they were worried about him.

Trevor, who'd never had a serious boyfriend in his life.

Could they really all believe that he was ready to settle down—unannounced to his family—out of state? What Brigid said haunted him.

The way he looks at you isn't like how you'd look at some casual fling.

Last night, a casual fling was all it had been, wasn't it? The business arrangement between them was clear, and, regardless of the surge of unaccounted for feelings that Logan brought up in him—which, really, could all be attributed to the excitement of being in New York and the rush of starting this new job, right?—Trevor had been upfront the night before about being okay with no-strings-attached sex.

Because he always was.

He didn't do anything deeper than that.

So why did the conversation with Brigid bother him?

When Logan laughed, Trevor felt that much more alive.

When he got bossy, both in and out of the bedroom, Trevor felt cared for, rather than dominated. And the touch of his lips...

"Coffee's up there," Logan remarked from across the room. Trevor jumped and nearly dropped his phone. Once he'd recovered it, he slid it into the pocket of the robe and crossed his arms over his chest, telling himself that his heart was pounding because *Logan* had surprised him. Certainly not just because he was... there.

"You scared me."

"It's my house," Logan said, raising an eyebrow. He was dressed in a robe identical to the one Trevor wore, and he looked... amazing. "I'm allowed to be wherever I want to be in it."

Trevor's lips twitched. Logan was acting stiff. More like the man he'd been from their Ashby's days. Had he not had to suffer through awkward morning-afters before? But Trevor wasn't going to let this be that.

He crossed the room, wrapping his arms around Logan's waist and leaning up to kiss him.

"You're *allowed* to do whatever you want, baby, but you still scared me. You can make it up to me by getting the coffee down."

Logan relaxed and kissed him back. Trevor grinned, refusing to think about what *this* was. Not acting for the public, because, hello, they were in private. And not hot sex that they were both too wound up to resist. This was just... nice. Logan crowded him up against the counter, still kissing him, and Trevor laughed, a kind of happiness bubbling up inside him that he wasn't used to.

"What?" Logan asked, pulling back far enough to look down into his eyes. His big hands were on either side of Trevor's face, and his thumbs brushed against the line of his jaw in a deliciously distracting rhythm.

Trevor cleared his throat, not even remotely willing to admit that he was just happy to be there. That was too sappy. Too... much.

"I'm just glad you woke up in time," he deflected. "Who knew you were such a sleepyhead? You've got a morning appearance, you know."

The kettle started to boil, and Logan stepped away from him, taking down the coffee and measuring it into the French press. "It's something at a campus pride event for... some university," he said. "I don't remember the details."

"Well, leave it to me to make you look hot as hell today," Trevor said, grinning as he found the mugs and set two of them out. He poured them each a cup. "Let me dress you. I'm going to make you look sexier than you've ever been before. If there's a gay guy on campus who doesn't fall in love with you after I'm done, then I'll resign on the spot and fly back to Chicago."

"I'm not going to let you do that," Logan said, the hint of a smile playing over his lips as he accepted his mug. "You signed up for six weeks, Trevor, and I want all of it."

Trevor gulped his coffee, belatedly remembering he'd forgotten to add sugar—yuck—but needing it anyway to stop the stupidly wide smile that tried to spread across his face at that.

He cleared his throat, gesturing back toward Logan's bedroom. "Well, you can have it," he said, winking. *Anything.* He waggled his eyebrows at Logan, determined to keep things a little lighter. This. Was. Casual. "But first, I'm going to get that robe off you."

He turned Logan around and pushed him through the dining room and back down the hall. As soon as they entered Logan's bedroom, Trevor set his coffee down on Logan's bedside table and made his way to his closet. Double slated doors promised a big space, and when Trevor pulled them open, he wasn't disappointed. Behind the doors was a walk-in closet filled with every piece of clothing Logan had bought at Ashby's. But, toward the back, pops of color caught Trevor's eye.

He grinned, throwing Logan a look over his shoulder. "Strip, baby, now."

Logan raised an eyebrow, his gorgeous eyes heating, but Trevor didn't let himself get sucked in. He really did have a job to do. He turned his back on temptation and walked into the closet. It hadn't just been his imagination... past the legions of dark clothes were shirts with real, honest-to-God *color*. Whites, blues, greens, reds, and patterned prints waited. Trevor inspected a royal blue shirt, testing the fabric of the sleeve between his thumb and middle finger.

The quality was respectable. The style was right. Why didn't Logan wear any of them?

He unhooked the blue shirt and tucked it over his arm, then selected one of the lighter colored patterned shirts for himself. Logan was bigger than he was, but as long as there were clips in the kitchen, Trevor was good to go. He'd clipped enough mannequins while working at Ashby's to know how to make clothing that was too big look good—and he figured he'd be spending most of his day in a coat, anyway. Who knew where his luggage was, or when he'd get it.

Would Logan want him to stay at the hotel bLoved had arranged for him that night?

Trevor pushed the thought away, searching for the set of gray Hendrix Professionals slacks he knew would best complement the shirt he'd chosen for Logan. Dressing his boyfriend was fun. Well, fine, fake boyfriend. But if Logan thought he got to be the bossy one in bed—Trevor shivered, his cock starting to rise at the memory—Trevor was definitely going to use his boyfriend-status to finally take charge of Logan's wardrobe, the way he'd always wanted to.

He heard conversation from the bedroom and frowned, speeding up his search. Finally done, he emerged from the closet to find Hiro standing not far from the bed.

"We have an hour?" Logan was asking him.

"Right," Hiro said, looking efficient and put together as he consulted his ever-present tablet. "It should be less pressure than the television interview, but it's still important that you act casual and mingle. Really focus on selling the product, without coming across as too strong." Logan's face started to do the stony thing that Trevor had figured out masked a little anxiety, and Hiro, apparently also knowing Logan well, quickly added, "As long as you have Trevor there, I'm confident it will go well. Yesterday's interview was a tremendous success, thanks to him. Don't worry, Logan."

"I'm kind of the best," Trevor said, grinning at Hiro when the other man jumped at his voice. "Morning."

"Good morning, Trevor," Hiro said, managing not to smile even though a distinct sparkle appeared in his eyes. "I noticed that you never called to get directions to your hotel last night."

Trevor grinned, unrepentant.

"Your luggage was sent there, and I can email the details to you now, so that you can head over after the publicity appearance."

Trevor opened his mouth to thank Hiro, but Logan cut him off before he could get a word out.

"With just an hour left, it's not prudent to waste time on that, Hiro," he said, not meeting Trevor's eye. "Right now we need to get ready. Hotel arrangements can be dealt with later, and as a back-up plan, Trevor can always stay here again. I have... plenty of guest bedrooms."

Trevor grinned. Guest bedroom. Mm-hmm. Only if Logan joined him. There was no way he was going to stay under Logan's roof without going for round two of the night before.

Hiro arched a brow and pressed his lips tightly together,

obviously holding back a laugh. He clearly wasn't buying the guest room thing any more than Trevor did. Under his amusement, though, Trevor could also see a softness in Hiro's expression that sent fuzzy affection coursing through Trevor's chest. He was glad that Logan had someone like Hiro looking after him. It was clear that Hiro cared, and Trevor was getting the impression that Logan didn't have a lot of that in his life.

He deserved more of it.

"It might be better if we just moved my stuff over here, anyway," Trevor offered, hoping it came off as nonchalant. Despite Brigid's warning, there was no way Trevor was going to give up the chance for more Logan if he could get it. He swept over to Logan's side and held up the blue shirt. It really did bring out his eyes in the best way. Trevor cleared his throat, reminding himself not to get distracted. He turned back to Hiro, adding, "The media expects us to live together. Isn't that what Logan told them yesterday? If someone saw me in a hotel now, it'd break the illusion that we're really a couple."

"The two of you... play the role well," Hiro said straight-faced, his eyes briefly flickering to Trevor's robe.

"It's not that hard to pretend when you've got a boss as hot as Logan," Trevor replied. He looked into Logan's eyes as he spoke. The glint of something affectionate crossed Logan's gaze, and Trevor couldn't help but thinking back on Brigid's observation.

...that wasn't acting...

Could there actually be something more between them? When Logan looked at him like... now wasn't the time to think about it, though. Instead, he flashed Logan a smile and held up the unbuttoned blue shirt. "It's time I get you into some color, baby. You have no idea how long I've been waiting for this moment."

"I'm surprised that Logan even *owns* any colored shirts," Hiro joked. "Must be from before he started working with Kelly on bLoved. I've been his assistant since the beginning, and I've never seen him out of black or gray."

"Or very dark blue," Logan grumbled, even though Trevor recognized the way his lips tightened at the seam. He wanted to smile, but he wasn't letting himself.

Trevor didn't miss how Logan's eyes stayed on him, and now that Brigid had mentioned something, he paid attention to the emotion in them.

She had to be crazy.

Still, thinking about Logan warming to him, smiling for him, and laughing because of *him* made Trevor want... more.

Maybe *he* was the one who was crazy. Trevor resisted the urge to shake his head. Instead, he prepared his own outfit for the day while Logan dressed.

Hiro turned his back while they changed, saying, "I think it's a positive sign. A new Logan needs a new wardrobe. A little bit of color is going to make all the difference."

"My thoughts exactly." Trevor buttoned up the shirt he'd chosen for himself and pinched the loose fabric back.

With a few clips, he could definitely make it work. Beneath a jacket, no one would notice. "I think this is the start of something great."

They finished dressing. Trevor swept around and fiddled with Logan's tie, loosening it a little to lend him a more relaxed, casual appearance. If their demographic for today was college-aged kids, he'd need to look more approachable and down to earth than ever.

"Are the two of you ready to go?" Hiro asked.

"Did you pick up the things I asked for?" Logan asked.

Hiro bobbed his head. "Of course. The new coat is in the car." He winked at Trevor. "There's no way we'd let a key player like Trevor brave the elements today without something properly warm."

Trevor narrowed his eyes and looked at Logan, and Logan dodged his gaze and shrugged a little too casually—like he was hiding what he really felt.

"I got you a new coat," Logan said, brushing at some nonexistent lint on his sleeve. "Yours isn't warm enough."

A smile crept along Trevor's lips, and the warmth inside of him returned. Logan had noticed?

"I'll have to tell everyone today what a caring boyfriend you are, to be thinking of me like that." Trevor's grin felt like it would never die. A small, stubborn part of his brain screamed at him to reject the kindness—that he was getting in too deep, wandering into dangerous territory.

He ignored that part.

Logan's attention warmed him and fulfilled him in a

way Trevor hadn't been aware existed. He put his hands on either side of Logan's face, forcing him to meet his eyes.

"Thank you," he said, stretching up to press a chaste kiss against his lips. Practice, if Hiro asked.

"It's just a coat," Logan mumbled.

"The important part of a gift isn't what it is, but what it *means*. Let me boast about your thoughtfulness, alright? It'll be good for our image." With a playful swat, he slapped Logan's butt. Logan's eyes widened, then narrowed. "Now go get 'em, babyboo. I believe in you!"

"Was that really necessary?" Logan grumbled. He took Trevor's hand as Hiro laughed at them, and the three of them headed to the elevator.

"Of course it was. Am I good at staying in character or what?"

Logan's grip tightened, holding him back just a tad as Hiro led the way.

"Babyboo?" Logan whispered, his breath hot against Trevor's neck.

"Mmm," Trevor said, slanting a look up at him as his heart raced. So he'd caught that, had he? "I told you I might forget."

"Then it's a good thing you'll be coming back here tonight, isn't it?" Logan asked.

Trevor bit his lip. Hard. And somehow managed to keep in the embarrassing sound Logan's implied promise had almost wrenched out of him.

Yes. Yes, it was a very, very good thing that he'd be coming.

Back here.

Tonight.

In fact, tonight couldn't get there soon enough, as far as he was concerned.

Chapter 11

LOGAN

Telling the public that Trevor was not only his boyfriend, but had come to New York to move in with him, had been a brilliant move in Logan's normally much more humble opinion. As Trevor had pointed out, it would have looked odd to have him at a hotel after that announcement, and as the days went on and their public appearances started to garner more and more media attention, their relationship was starting to get scrutinized, gossiped over, and speculated about on a daily basis.

It was fantastic for bLoved, and the surge in both their membership and revenue had Frank and Richard on cloud nine. It should have thrilled the businessman in Logan, too, but, if he were honest, that wasn't the part that he was so pleased with.

"You do this on purpose, don't you?" Trevor asked, winking at him as he tapped the knot of Logan's tie.

"What?" Logan asked, attempting to look innocent. He'd tied his tie correctly. He looked professional. He pressed his lips together to keep them from twitching with amusement as Trevor rolled his eyes.

"It's too tight. You look stuffy. *Sit*."

They were in the green room of *Cool Talk*, another New York-based talk show. Since their appearance on *What's Now?* the week before, they'd done a series of live events on the East Coast and into the Midwest, jetting out and back in a single day, but this was only the second time he'd be appearing on television. Well, the second time with Trevor to support him.

Logan would prefer not to think about that first time.

He sat, and—just as he'd anticipated—Trevor immediately sank down onto his lap, knees straddling Logan's thighs. He fussed with Logan's tie, bringing the knot down a bit and pretending to ignore the fact that Logan's hands were all over his ass.

"Nervous?" Trevor asked, smoothing out his handiwork but making no move to stand.

"No," Logan lied.

The truth was that every public appearance with Trevor had gone well so far. Tremendously well. The public was eating up their romance, and Trevor was a natural public speaker. Witty and sharp and full of just enough sass to keep them in the headlines. This time, though, Trevor wasn't scheduled to be on stage with him, and Trevor was most definitely the best part of... *everything*, his mind readily supplied, even though he'd been thinking "the campaign."

"You're going to do fine, baby," Trevor said, the teasing sparkle in his eyes softening into something else. "All you've got to do is loosen up just like we've practiced, okay?"

"Loosening up is not my forté," Logan admitted, his hands, which had been happily kneading one of his favorite parts of his boyf—of *Trevor*—going still. "At least, not without you."

"Well, lucky for you that you've *got* me," Trevor said. The words were cheeky, but he held both sides of Logan's face in his hands and met his eyes with a look that Logan was hard-pressed to not take as real. Even when Trevor grinned and added, "Remember? Whenever we're in public, I'm yours, Logan. And today, I'll make them put me in the audience where you can see me."

They *weren't* in public, though. Not at the moment. They were alone in the green room and there was no one Trevor needed to put on the fake boyfriend act for... but there was no way in hell Logan was going to argue that point. Especially not when Trevor leaned forward and kissed him, more sweet than heat. Logan closed his eyes and did his best to ignore the voice in his head that wondered if Trevor was just doing his job—doing whatever it took to get Logan to relax before he went on air—and let himself enjoy it.

With Trevor firmly ensconced in his penthouse for the last seven days, they'd both stayed "in character" pretty much full-time. At night, Trevor slept beside him. Behind closed doors, they kissed and touched each other, even though there was no one around to see. When they slept late, Trevor showered with him to save time, and now, the scent of rosewood and amber clung to his skin. It was a scent Logan usually associated with himself, but his body wash had never smelled so good before.

Trevor teased him and pushed him and made him laugh more than he ever had in his life. And he was *attuned* to Logan, attentive in a myriad of little ways that made Logan feel, for the first time in his life, truly cared for.

Like now, when Trevor had seen right through Logan's facade to the hint of nerves beneath.

Trevor was still kissing him, which was doing a fantastic job of dealing with that issue. After years of keeping his distance from people, afraid to be faced with the heartache of knowing he was a disappointment to someone he cared for yet again, Trevor was Logan's reprieve. In public, they played off each other expertly. In private, this easy flowing affection was always present, making it hard to remember that it was supposed to be temporary... making it feel like Trevor had always been a part of his life. Like he *should* be.

Logan's phone rang.

"Ignore it," Trevor said, pulling away just far enough to grin at him. "You really need to focus on—" Trevor rocked against him, and, yes, as sweet as it had been, there had definitely been some heat in that kiss, too, by the feel of things, "—getting loosened up for the show."

Logan laughed, and Trevor's eyes lit up at the sound. He glanced down at the screen, fully onboard with swiping the "ignore" button, but then he saw the caller ID.

"It's Frank," he said. "I should pick it up in case he needs to give me any data for the show."

Trevor pouted, but then he grinned. "Okay, but put it on speakerphone, baby," he murmured. "You need to be hands-free so we can practice multitasking."

With a tap of his finger, Logan answered the call, tempted to mute his side of it when Trevor got busy "multitasking." Instead, he swallowed, answering with, "Hello, Frank. You're on speakerphone."

"Logan!" Frank said, not—thankfully—commenting on the husky timbre of Logan's voice. "Just a quick call to touch base. Do you have a minute?"

"Only a few of them. I'm about to go live on *Cool Talk*." Trevor leaned forward, the chaste kiss he pressed against Logan's lips at odds with the extremely un-chaste activities he was engaged in below the belt. Logan's heart rate sped up, and he tried to ignore Trevor's wicked grin as he went for a nonchalant tone and asked Frank, "What's up?"

"The fake boyfriend thing?" Logan could hear the shit-eating grin in Frank's voice. "The two of you are *killing* it. The media is eating it up, the consumers are eating it up, hell, there are fan pages dedicated to the two of you now."

"Fan pages?" Trevor asked, pressing a hot kiss against

the base of Logan's throat. Logan heard the subtle change in his voice that occurred whenever Trevor was aroused, and he grinned at the languid, sultry tone. Trevor did love attention.

"Is that Trevor?" Frank asked.

"Mm-hmm," Trevor said, turning his attention to the phone. "Are they saying good things about me, Frank? Because, if they're not..."

"Everyone loves you," Frank said, laughing. "Everyone loves Logan, too. They love the two of you, as a couple. The press is going around calling you 'Tregan' now. Like Brangelina or TomKat."

"Neither of those ended well," Trevor said dryly.

Frank laughed. "It's the publicity that counts. The fact that there's reporting being done about you at all is phenomenal for business."

Trevor pulled back a little from Logan and grinned. "So what you're saying is that I'm single-handedly rescuing bLoved? How could that be, when I'm not even a Hollywood professional? Hmmm?"

The cheeky response brought a smile to Logan's lips. He slid his hands from Trevor's ass around to his thighs, wondering if he should have skipped the call after all. At least, a part of him was wondering.

Logan stifled a laugh. Trevor was turning him into a horny teenager.

"Are you still sore about that?" Frank asked, oblivious to the... multitasking. "You have no reason to be. Logan, give the man a bonus. Keep him happy, because we *need* him to stick around for the next little while."

"Yes, you need to keep me happy, baby," Trevor whispered, leaning in close so he could whisper into Logan's ear without being heard. "And I'll take my bonus in cock, thank you very much."

Logan wanted to laugh at that, but it came out more like a groan. His cock—already interested—stiffened, and Trevor gave him an evil grin, clearly satisfied with the response. He nestled down on top of him and started to rock his hips steadily, his own color rising as he found a rhythm that... really... worked... for Logan.

"I'm about to go on TV," Logan whispered, all the protest he could muster. He'd moved the phone away from them, and his other hand had somehow found its way back onto Trevor's ass, urging him on.

"I know." Trevor smirked, grinding against him even more. "Have fun with that... pookie."

"Are you two still there?" Frank asked. "I hear your voices, but they sound distant."

"We're here." Logan stood up—an amazing feat of willpower—which dumped Trevor onto the couch. He sank back against the cushions, giggling, and Logan's heart did a slow roll in his chest. He was hard as a rock, but he was also—always, with Trevor—having *fun*. He cleared his throat, addressing Frank. "Trevor was just trying to... negotiate his bonus. But we're listening."

"Give him whatever he wants," Frank said

magnanimously, making Trevor nod vigorously and mouth something dirty that Logan pretended not to catch. "Now that we've got the media focused on you as a cute new couple, you've got to bring it back to bLoved, bring it back to *love*. Make sure that you're setting bLoved apart from the hookup apps, especially this close to Valentine's Day. People want to believe in what they're seeing between you two. Believe it's *real*, that it can happen for them... and you need to sell them on the fact that it can, and bLoved is their ticket to finding it."

Squirming up from where he'd landed, Trevor pressed himself close to Logan. "I agree," he said. "I'm all about that upsell, Frank. Logan can totally do this."

"Then I expect good results following this broadcast," Frank said. "Measurable ones. I'll let the two of you get back to preparing for Logan's appearance."

Trevor snickered, but Logan's nerves came back.

"Bye, Frank," Trevor said, reaching out and jabbing the end-call button. Then, to Logan, "We need to get back to preparing—what's wrong?"

"Nothing."

"Logan..."

Selling love? Logan sucked in a breath, a creeping dread tightening his stomach. After everything Trevor had done to loosen him up, he felt the first stirrings of doubt start to draw him back into his shell. What did he know about love, really? He'd only had Trevor for a week, and no matter how good it felt, he didn't know how to convince other people they could have it, too. Especially when what he had *wasn't* real.

Trevor was looking at him like it might be, though.

"What am I supposed to say?" Logan asked.

Trevor grinned. "Well, you're more than welcome to tell your adoring public how crazy you are about *me*."

Logan laughed, the sound easing some of the tension inside him. "I can talk about you easily, but how do I make people believe bLoved will help them be just as lucky?" He frowned, mulling it over. "Maybe I should talk about the most effective information to include in their profiles so that the algorithms can—"

"No," Trevor said, laughing. "Logan, no one cares about how it works... you've got to make them *believe*. And believing is all about feelings. When I sell a shirt, I don't sell fabric and stitching, I sell the customer on how great they feel when they wear it. And when I say talk about me out on that stage, I mean it. Talk about what you *feel* for me. Or, what you're, um, pretending to feel, I mean." He looked away, brushing some invisible lint off his sleeve and then smoothing Logan's hair. Not meeting his eyes. After a moment, Trevor cleared his throat, adding, "Your job is to inspire them. Talk about how being with someone you care about, finding love, is different from just hooking up. Maybe not everyone wants it, or is ready for it, but for those that do, you're going to follow up all those feelings with a plug for bLoved, and they're going to jump on it."

He adjusted Logan's jacket and set his tie straight. He'd

convinced Logan to wear one with a pop of blue in it, and Logan had to admit, it really did bring out his eyes. Trevor was right.

"People are lonely," Trevor said, still fussing with Logan's outfit even though he'd adjusted just about every inch of it. Was *Trevor* nervous? He looked up, meeting Logan's eyes. "It's in the song the bLoved app plays when you start it up, right? *At last, my love has come along. My lonely days are over.* That's the whole point of why this... fake relationship... appeals to people, I think," Trevor said. "They think that people like us could actually exist in real life, and that, maybe, if they sign up for bLoved, they'll be able to find the same kind of happiness that we have, too."

The same kind of happiness that we have. Logan's heart bled at the statement, and he looked at Trevor in silence, trying to determine whether he meant it. Logan *was* happy. In fact, the last week with Trevor had probably been the happiest of his life. But... for Trevor? It seemed silly to ask. Or, not silly. Terrifying?

It was too soon.

He didn't want to jinx it.

Trevor had just *said* it was fake.

He opened his mouth anyway. "Trevor, I—"

"Mr. Carter?" an intern popped his head into the room, eyes zeroing in on Logan. "We need you on set, sir. We're about to go live. If your boyfriend would kindly take his place in the audience now, we need to get started."

Without Trevor as a safety net, Logan was all on his

own. Trevor pressed a quick kiss to his lips, then went to exit the green room. He hesitated at the door for a moment, gazing back at Logan. "You're going to do great, baby. I believe in you."

"I love you," Logan said, since the intern watching gave him a good excuse to.

Trevor smiled, fully in character. "Love you, too."

"WE'RE HERE TODAY WITH GAY DATING APP, BLOVED'S, CO-founder, Logan Carter. Logan, thank you for being here with us today." Mariposa Otis, host of *Cool Talk*, leaned forward in her chair to grin at Logan, and after a split-second of feeling frozen, Logan summoned a return smile. Out of the corner of his eye, he caught a glimpse of Trevor in the audience.

Right. He could do this.

"It's my pleasure to be here," he said, trying to make the words sound sincere. An image of Trevor straddling him in the green room flashed through his mind, and he felt his smile grow into something real.

"Trust me, the pleasure is all ours," Mariposa responded, sitting back in her chair and trilling with laughter.

Logan wasn't sure what the joke was—was she just one of those women who followed up every statement with a laugh?—but he maintained his smile, shifting in his seat slightly to face Trevor more directly. Trevor winked, and Logan was pretty sure Trevor's plan was going to work.

As long as he kept sight of Trevor, he was going to be able to keep his smiles looking genuine and, hopefully, say the right things.

"You've been blowing up on social media after you introduced your boyfriend, Trevor Rogers, to the world last week," Mariposa said, leaning forward with a look of delight. "Everyone with an Internet connection has seen #Tregan trending. Tell me, has your sudden popularity detracted from your relationship at all?"

Frank had asked him to sell the product, but Logan trusted Trevor's advice when it came to how to do that. The question didn't lend itself to plugging bLoved directly, but Logan could surely spin it into an opportunity to talk about Trevor.

He shook his head, making sure to keep smiling. "It's been... fun." And wasn't *that* true about every day he'd spent as one half of *Tregan*? "The two of us are having a great time getting out in the world and meeting as many of our supporters as we can. Trevor makes friends wherever he goes, so it comes easily. I think he's loving the attention."

"And you?" Mariposa asked. "You certainly haven't been one to seek out attention in the past, Mr. Carter."

"Call me Logan," he said, earning a discreet thumbs-up from his boyfriend. "And it's true, I'm not used to the limelight, but as long as Trevor is happy, I'm happy."

The answer had come out without Logan having to think about it, and he realized it was true. Out in the audience, Trevor beamed at him.

"And the two of you met through bLoved?" Mariposa brushed her hair back over her shoulder, watching Logan eagerly. Clearly, she was a fan of love. "You two seem so well matched, but from what I understand, it was unlikely that your paths would have crossed without the app. Love is a tricky thing to find."

Over the last week, Trevor had been coaching him in the art of conversation and how to turn it in the direction he needed when necessary. In this case though, Mariposa seemed to be spoon-feeding him exactly the opportunity Frank had pushed him to find: an opportunity to sell the benefits of bLoved.

"Love is incredibly complex," Logan agreed. "A lot of bLoved's most vocal critics argue that love can't be boiled down to an algorithm, and that people are too individual and varied for it to be of any use. But I disagree. Our results speak for themselves... and you're right. It allows people to come together who might not otherwise meet."

Even though he and Trevor didn't have the algorithms to thank for their relationship, they *did* owe it to bLoved. It had brought them together, and talking about love no longer made Logan feel like a sham. Even if they were both just acting the part, opening himself up to others no longer felt quite as dangerous. Over the course of one week, Logan had started to regain himself.

"The truth is, bLoved exists because there are lonely souls in the world who need that reassurance that there really is someone out there for them. Love *is* complex, and,

sometimes, we need a little help to find it... and to let it in."
Logan's gaze wandered to Trevor, meeting his eyes. "Sometimes, we're so caught up in our own heads that we forget what love really is—a celebration of another person. A selfless extension of the self. Love—real love—turns that other person's happiness into our own."

Trevor's eyes were bright, and he was smiling ear-to-ear. Through his expression alone, Logan knew he was doing a fantastic job. That he *was* making Trevor happy. Trevor was lit up with pride, and Logan wondered how much of it was because Logan wasn't bombing, and how much—if any—was because of what he was actually saying.

Because he was doing what Trevor had suggested, thanks to having the safety net of staying-in-character... he was talking about how Trevor made him *feel*.

"Do the bLoved algorithms *really* work?" Mariposa asked, leaning forward. "Do you think you would have connected with Trevor without them?"

"Yes," Logan said firmly. Trevor blew him a kiss. "Trevor is my ideal match, and even without an algorithm to confirm it, I don't think I would have been able to stay away, once we'd met. But—" he swallowed, reminding himself that bLoved's future required him to bare his soul... and that the people who mattered would think it was just an act, anyway, "—not everyone believes in love. Believes they're *worthy* of it, or that it's out there for them. I want to speak to those men today, because bLoved is for them."

He turned away from Trevor, but he could still feel his

eyes on him. A connection that had been between them from the first, but that had only gotten stronger with the time they'd spent together... thanks to bLoved.

Facing the camera directly, Logan said, "For the lonely hearts out there who have been scorned, or cast aside, bLoved is for *you*. It's for the men who know what heartbreak is, who have been scarred by it. Shut down. Alone, and afraid to try again. Please, give bLoved a try, because love is worth it, and it's possible, for *all* of us.

"There are other apps out there, and I'm not disparaging them, but for the men who bounce from hookup to hookup, enjoying themselves but wishing there was something more for them... if only they knew how to find it. No matter who you are, love exists for you. All of us are connected by the same thing—we all want to feel appreciated, we all want to feel safe. We want to feel like there is someone out there who understands us, and loves us anyway." The audience laughed, and Mariposa nodded, wiping at her eyes. Logan grinned, looking back at Trevor as he added, "Someone who can make us laugh, and whose laughter in return brightens up... everything. Whether you believe in the algorithms or not, I am a living testament to the fact that love is real. It takes a man like me, once hollow and empty, and turns me into something so much more than that."

The audience *awwed*. Trevor flashed Logan a smile that made his heart fill until it felt as though it would burst. Everything that Logan did, he was only capable of because of

Trevor's influence. He'd come so far. *They'd* come so far. The celebrity nickname they'd been tagged with—Tregan—was ridiculous, but he really did feel like they were something new, something greater, together.

A couple. Two halves of a whole.

"Well, I can definitely see why the two of you are trending," Mariposa said, laughing. She refocused the conversation. "Why don't you tell us all a little bit more about this fantastic app? I'm sure that gay men everywhere are looking at you and Trevor and wondering what steps to take to get to where you two are."

The rest of the interview went easily, and through it all, Logan kept Trevor in his sights as a reminder not to let himself go into the more familiar, businesslike mode that Trevor told him came across as too stiff. Trevor's support was almost palpable, despite the space between them, and to his surprise, Logan found it easy to stay relaxed with the perky host. Knowing that he had such tremendous support made it feel almost natural. With Trevor, there were no expectations or demands—Logan was free to be himself, and to express himself. And, shockingly, when he did so from the heart, instead of disappointing the people who were counting on him, it seemed to turn out well.

As soon as the segment was over, Logan slipped backstage and Trevor popped up from his seat and ran after him, pushing past security with a single-minded focus. As soon as he was close enough, Trevor tackled Logan with a jumping hug, almost knocking him over.

Logan laughed, wobbling on his feet before righting Trevor.

"You *slayed* out there!" Trevor crowed. "That speech about love? Oh my God, I thought that *I* was good at staying in character. That was *fantastic*."

Staying in character? Logan's face fell, but Trevor didn't seem to notice.

"I mean, I know I helped coach you on it, but still... today? I totally bought it. *Everyone* bought it. The sparkle in your eyes and the way your lips lifted in that dreamy, contented sort of way? I swear, you must have been channeling some of that Broadway talent we caught last week. Frank is going to go *crazy* when he sees this clip."

"Yeah." Logan's mouth was dry, and the reality of their relationship hit him like a sledgehammer, almost crushing his chest. Trevor was glowing, but his words made it clear that it was with pride in a job well done, not... what Logan had thought. What they'd *agreed* to. He swallowed, summoning a smile to mask the foolish death of his hopes. "It was a great performance, wasn't it?"

"*Yes*," Trevor said enthusiastically, throwing his arms around Logan and kissing him again before babbling on about his success on stage and what Logan should focus on for his next appearance.

And, fool that he was, Logan kissed him back. He'd set himself up for this moment since the beginning, but, like he'd said for the cameras, he wasn't going to be able to stay away from Trevor now that he'd found him... or deny himself the few, short weeks of "staying in character."

Of pretending that love really *could* exist for him, now that he'd made the mistake of letting himself want it again.

Chapter 12

TREVOR

"THIS IS THE PLACE." TREVOR'S FRIEND ELLIOTT SWEPT his arms outward as he welcomed Trevor into the apartment he shared with his fiancé, the reformed billionaire playboy, Ash Ashby.

"*Damnnnnnn*, Elliott," Trevor said, pulling him in for a brief hug while he scanned his gorgeous surroundings. "You got him to move to Chicago and give up this? If I didn't already know Ash loved you..."

Elliott went pink as he shrugged at the good-natured teasing, looking around as if to see what Trevor was talking about. Trevor knew it wasn't that his friend was immune to the luxury, more like it didn't register much on Elliott's scale of what was important in life.

"Well, you know, the two of us are in and out of New York all the time for meetings at Ashby headquarters, anyway, so keeping it made more sense than staying at hotels," Elliott said, sounding almost apologetic. "I wanted to rent it out while we're not here, but Ash isn't too fond of the idea."

Trevor could see why that was. Elliott might not have been sensitive to the quality of the apartment, but it wasn't lost on Trevor. In the main hallway alone, just the interior decorating must have been worth tens of thousands of dollars. From the reclaimed wooden floors to the modern paintings hung from the walls, Ash had invested a small fortune in the place. Renting it wouldn't be worth the gamble.

"It's nice," Trevor said, tongue-in-cheek.

The truth was, Logan's sprawling penthouse was far more impressive from a luxury-living standpoint—Ash's condo was compact, and no amount of interior decorating would change that—but it was definitely light-years above anything he or Elliott could have afforded when they'd both been salesclerks at Ashby's together. Still, something felt off. He squinted, looking around to figure out what it was. A delicious smell was coming from the kitchen, and in the small space, he could see right down the hall where the kitchen table was visible from the front door. Another hall off to the left must be the bedroom, and... oh.

"Where's Donner?" Trevor asked, grinning. It was rare to visit Elliott anywhere and not immediately be greeted by the click of eager dog toenails racing to greet him. The little rescue dog Elliott and Ash had adopted the year before went with them everywhere.

"We're just here overnight," Elliott said. "I wanted to bring him, but it didn't feel right to make Donner come all that way for a few hours, so we hired a dog sitter."

Trevor grinned. Donner was a notoriously bad flyer.

Elliott had been leading him back to the kitchen as they talked, and Trevor's eyebrows shot up in surprise to find Ash there... cooking. The heir to the Ashby's fortune, Ash would one day be just as rich as Logan was, if not richer, and Trevor clearly remembered Elliott laughing about Ash's overuse of food delivery services back when the two of them had gotten together. As far as Trevor had been aware, Ash couldn't boil water.

"Don't tell me your invitation to visit was an evil plan to poison me," Trevor teased, leaning against the counter. "Ash, *cooking*?"

"How are you doing, Trevor?" Ash asked, looking back over his shoulder with a grin but not leaving the stove. He looked... focused.

"Ask me after I've tried whatever you're making," Trevor shot back, laughing. "But seriously, how did this miracle come about?" He waved a hand at the direction of the... okay, *delicious* smelling pots bubbling on the stovetop.

"Elliott gave me an ultimatum," Ash said. "If I want to

marry him, apparently I'm going to have to supply breakfast in bed. I thought I had a pretty good counteroffer, since I'd rather give him—"

"Ash!" Elliott flushed, cutting his fiancé off from saying something that Trevor had no doubt would have been loaded with innuendo.

"Breakfast in bed is definitely a prerequisite for marriage," Trevor said, grinning at Elliott in solidarity. "I'm surprised Elliott even accepted your proposal without some kind of confirmation you'd be able to provide it."

Ash laughed. "I *have* been providing it. I figured out Elliott's favorite breakfast place and convinced them to set up a delivery route for us back in Chicago." Ash swung a wooden spoon in Trevor's direction. Hot water flew, and Trevor and Elliott both took a step back. It looked like Ash was cooking pasta. "I tried to convince him that knowing how to cook is less important than a proper allotment of your resources. The same can be said about business."

"Stop right there," Trevor said, holding up a hand. "It's my day off, and I am *not* talking about business."

Logan had no media appearances that day, just a bunch of board meetings scheduled or something equally boring for other companies that he was apparently invested in, and Trevor couldn't have been happier that the timing had worked out so he could visit his friends while they were in the city. Still, the very mention of "business" stirred up his own uncertainty about where he and Logan stood, and he'd rather not think about it.

Although, good luck with that. He didn't seem to be able to think of anything *but.*

Lately, he'd taken to dropping more and more references to their business arrangement into conversation, hoping that Logan would seize the opportunity to... what? Declare his undying love? Sweep Trevor off his feet? Tell him that yes, it may have started that way, but he was actually falling for Trevor now?

That all the things they'd shared, the sweet moments and hot sex and tiny little shows of affection... the things he said in public about his feelings... that all of that was real?

But he hadn't. And Trevor, normally not the least bit shy about clearing the air when it came to his love life, didn't want to hear Logan's shock if he brought it up.

What? You actually thought this was real? Weren't you right there back in Chicago when we all agreed to fake it? Didn't you hear Frank praise how well our FAKE relationship is working? Didn't I tell you from the get-go that I didn't mix business and pleasure? This is just business, Trevor, businessbusinessbusinesss...

Trevor huffed out a breath, knowing he was being a drama queen. He had an amazing thing going with Logan, and there was no way he was going to ruin it right in the middle. He'd never had a real boyfriend—never wanted one and had always been cautious about anything that might mistakenly give a partner the idea that there was more of an attachment between them than the casual sex he excelled at—but knowing that it *was* just a business arrangement with Logan had given him permission to go all in.

Not just in terms of physical attraction, but making it safe to give voice to all the... warm feelings, he was *definitely* not going to say love because hello, that wasn't... Trevor didn't do love... didn't *want* it... but still, with Logan, he could—

"Everything okay, Trevor?" Ash asked, quirking up an eyebrow as he went back to stirring some kind of sauce. "Business a... touchy subject right now?"

"No," Trevor lied, mustering a wide smile. "I'm just saying, can't we just talk about your wedding plans, or how many babies you're going to end up with, or how fun New York is?"

Trevor folded himself into a chair by the table and Elliott sat down across from him, concern marred his features.

"What's wrong, Trevor?" Elliott asked gingerly. "All of us have been a little... confused about what's happening with you out here. And you haven't been talking, which, come on, that's just not like you. We've all seen, you know, the TV clips about bLoved. Is there really something going on with you and Logan?"

Logan. Hearing his name made Trevor deflate, and he sighed as he crossed his arms on the table, hunching down to rest his chin upon them. He didn't want to talk about it. Except, he kind of did, too.

"There *is* something going on," Elliott murmured. He reached out to put his hand atop Trevor's in solidarity. "Grace has been calling me, asking me if you've said anything about him. The way you two are together—"

"Tregan," Ash said, snort-laughing.

"—I've never seen you like that with a guy you're dating, Trev," Elliott said, ignoring Ash. "I half-expected you to bounce in here spouting love sonnets or something, but you don't look happy."

"I'm totally happy," Trevor argued. "Logan is great. *Amazing.*"

"So you flew out here to work for him and just... fell in love?"

Trevor frowned, knowing the charade was supposed to be kept under wraps, but also needing to talk to someone. And it was Elliott. And, well, Ash. Elliott he'd trust with any secret, and Ash's high-profile life—not to mention his devotion to Elliott—made Trevor think he'd keep it private, too.

Ash had turned away from the stove and was leaning against the counter beside it, clearly waiting for Trevor's answer, too. "Are you really a couple, like the news is reporting?" he asked bluntly when Trevor's hesitation dragged out.

"No." Trevor pursed his lips, not liking the answer. He *felt* like they were a couple, and even though it was never something he'd wanted—was, in fact, something he'd actively shied away from for fear of getting tied down—he liked it far, far more than he would have expected. He felt the hot prick of tears behind his eyes, but blinked them away before his friends could see. Clearing his throat, he said, "I mean... we're pretending to be. The guy who heads his marketing department wanted us to pretend to be boy-friends to give me an excuse to be seen with him, and when it started to take off, it turned out to be a great way to hype bLoved as a service. The real reason I'm in New York is like I told you in that text message—I'm here to work some PR for Logan, coaching him on being more personable for his publicity appearances."

Ash sniffed at the idea, turning back to the stove. "Well, you're doing one hell of a job. Logan Carter is one of the most insufferable men I've ever met."

Trevor bristled. "You just don't know him."

"Ash!" Elliott turned in his chair to shoot Ash an admonishing look. "Be nice. Obviously Trevor, um, cares about him."

"I just told you, it's an act," Trevor said weakly.

Elliott looked back at him, shaking his head like he didn't believe it. "Trev, I know you. Sure, you're great with people and outgoing and all that, but you're not fake. I mean, the way you look at him..."

"Please, babe, let's get real," Ash said, jumping in. "Logan is well known for being as cold and calculating as an ice sculpture. We're talking one-word answers, expression-less, and totally heartless. All he cares about is his bottom line."

"That's not what I see when he looks at *Trevor*," Elliott insisted.

Ash snorted. "I'd bet money that it's just a testament to how well Trevor's doing at his job. No surprise, knowing

Trevor. Sure, the media's been eating Logan up, now that Trevor's defrosted him, but that's not gonna change who the man is."

Trevor frowned. Ash's certainty was not helping his state of mind in the least.

"I think I'm in over my head," he mumbled, sighing. "The truth is, I've always thought Logan was hot. I came on to him as soon as we got to New York and... all the fake boyfriend stuff we do in public doesn't stop when we go home, even though it's just supposed to be a show for the public."

"Do you love him?" Elliott asked carefully.

"Of course not." As soon as he answered, Trevor felt sick. He lifted his head and crossed his arms over his chest as if to protect himself. Love was off the table. Love was something he refused to do. Sleeping with guys was fine—sometimes, Trevor even went on second or third dates. But being in a relationship? Being domestic?

He didn't want a white picket fence.

Ash left the stove, moving to stand behind Elliott. Elliott reached up without looking, and they laced their fingers together. Trevor looked at the two of them—stronger together than they were alone—and had to blink back those stupid tears again.

"I know you're not someone who wants a relationship," Elliott said carefully. "But I've got to disagree with Ash. I don't think it looks fake. The way you look at him, Trevor..."

Trevor rubbed at the bridge of his nose. It didn't feel

fake, but he never would have let himself be so open and...
loving... toward Logan if he hadn't had the excuse of their
fake relationship. He was always telling *Logan* to let himself
go a little, but the truth was, their arrangement had given
Trevor permission to let go, too. He hadn't been holding
back, and even when he tried to focus on the materialistic
stuff—the great sex, the perks of living in a luxury penthouse, the feeling, even for just a short time, that he didn't
have to worry about money and the life-altering amount
of weight that lifted from his shoulders—he always came
back to that warm, fuzzy feeling that he got when Logan
smiled at him.

Which, of course, couldn't be *love.*

"I don't *look* at Logan in any kind of way."

"You do," Elliott said.

"If you saw how big his cock is, you'd look at him like
that, too," Trevor shot back, suddenly needing to deny all of
it. Because if he was in love and Logan wasn't, that would...
suck. So hard. So, so hard. He pulled up a cocky grin, adding, "It's not my fault that the man's hung and knows how
to use it."

Neither Elliott nor Ash laughed, and Trevor felt himself
slipping. Not even his humor was saving him.

"There's nothing wrong in changing your mind, you
know," Elliott said softly. "Just because you've always said
you don't want a long-term commitment doesn't mean you
can't have one. Circumstances change. No one is going to
think twice if you want something real with him."

No one was going to think twice about it, but Trevor knew that *he* would. All his life he'd clung to the notion that he'd take adventure over security, that he'd live life to the fullest. The idea of going through the motions just because it was safe and known scared the shit out of him. His parents had a great relationship, hell, Ash and Elliott were the poster-children of the glories of love, but Trevor had lived his whole life determined not to be boxed in by anything. Determined not to settle down into something mundane and dull and *routine*.

But now he *had* a routine. In just a few short weeks, his life had become predictable and... comfortable. Every morning, he woke up next to Logan... and he liked it. He knew how Logan took his coffee, and what music he liked, and that for all his general tidiness, he would not, for the life of him, remember to kick his shoes off anywhere but right in the middle of the front hall.

When they got ready to go out, they shaved together in Logan's bathroom over the sink, sharing the same mirror. And at night, when it was time for bed, Trevor would yawn and stretch and get up, and Logan would give him an already-familiar smile, and take him into the bedroom. They'd undress and curl up beneath the sheets together, and then...

No. He had to stop.

"I'm just not interested," Trevor said stiffly. All of the small rituals he shared with Logan warmed him, the moments that *weren't* for the public. Being with him already felt like being home, and that was going to hurt like a bitch when his contract was up and he went back to Chicago.

"Well, I can't see Logan as the type of guy you'd want to end up with," Ash said. Elliott turned to glare up at him, and Ash grinned, hastily adding, "*But*, I can confirm that the whole happily-ever-after thing... isn't that bad."

"You romantic, you," Elliott laughed, but the look they shared was almost *too* intimate.

Trevor kind of wished he hadn't seen it. That he didn't *want* it. No... that wasn't it. Logan did look at him like that. He just wished it could be real.

Then Elliott narrowed his eyes and sniffed. "Do you guys smell that?"

Something was burning.

"Oh, shit!" Ash gasped. "The pasta!"

"You didn't turn the burner down, did you?" Elliott asked, lips twitching with suppressed mirth. Ash bolted back to the stove, but it was clearly too late. He moved the offending pot off the heat and prodded at its contents with his wooden spoon.

"So, I'm guessing pasta's not supposed to be... uh... a gelatinous, melted mess, right?"

Elliott covered his face with his hands and laughed. "No. How do you guys feel about going to the restaurant down the block? We can get pizza."

Ash and Elliott were perfectly fitted to each other,

Trevor thought. Neither of them were perfect, but their flaws were balanced by the other's strengths. Together, they were a force.

It was what the media had been saying about himself and Logan, wasn't it? Trevor pushed the thought aside.

"Going out sounds great," he said, thankful that Ash's lack of skill in the kitchen had at least gotten them off the subject. Still, he had felt compelled to add: "Um, the public needs to believe that Logan and I really *are* together, so no bringing any of what we just talked about up, okay?"

Elliott nodded, looking like he wanted to get right back into it and push Trevor until he broke down and admitted that he'd gone and fallen for a man who only wanted him for... business. But, thankfully, whatever he saw in Trevor's face kept Elliott's mouth closed.

Trevor eased out of his chair, stretching until the pastel pink shirt he wore beneath his jacket threatened to untuck from his pants. Logan had bought it for him from one of the more expensive boutiques one day during their free time.

Another business expense, Trevor reminded himself.

Like his new, thick winter coat.

Like the Broadway tickets.

Like every other small thing Logan had bought him to keep the illusion they were a couple alive. After all, hadn't Trevor been the one who'd told Logan that he could spin Logan's thoughtfulness into even more media coverage?

They headed out, and as they hit the sidewalk, Ash

moved up beside Trevor and leaned in close. "If you need to talk to someone who lived loose and easy for most of his life, give me a call any time. I was never interested in settling down, either, you know, but—"

Trevor rolled his eyes and huffed a breath. The air froze as it left his body and fogged the space in front of him. "Forget I even said anything. It's not... real."

Ash looked like he was going to argue, but then, from the other side of the street, a bright flash went off, then another. Ash lifted his head, grimacing. "Fucking paparazzi," he said, shaking his head.

Sure enough, two men sprang out of the back of an idling car and rushed in their direction. Elliott fell back, clustering close to Ash for safety, and Ash took a protective position between Elliott and the cameras. Trevor walked behind them, observing.

From time to time, he saw Ash and Elliott on gossip sites. Ash had been one of the world's hottest bachelors before Elliott tied him down, and the media loved to scrutinize every part of their relationship.

But it wasn't Ash and Elliott the paparazzi were coming for.

They rushed past Ash and closed in on Trevor instead.

"Trevor! Where's Logan today? The two of you haven't been spotted apart since your relationship went public."

"What's your connection to Ash Ashby? Is this an affair?"

Trevor furrowed his brow. The brilliant flash of the

cameras blinded him, and the rapid-fire questions left him momentarily stunned.

"Are you crazy?" he demanded. "I'm just going to eat lunch with some friends. What are you—"

Ash pulled Trevor forward by the arm and winked at the paparazzi. "No comment," he said loudly, cutting off Trevor's protest. "Sorry, guys. We've gotta run."

"I'm already calling a car," Elliott mumbled. He had his phone out. Trevor caught what was happening in small fragments of clarity between camera flashes. How were the flashbulbs so bright? No wonder celebrities wore sunglasses all the time. Ash picked up the pace, dragging Trevor along with him, but the paparazzi didn't give up, following and shouting questions at Trevor as they did.

"They're here for *me*?" Trevor asked, stunned. "I thought they were coming for you. I'm not... I'm not *that* newsworthy, am I?"

"Now that you're dating Logan Carter, you are," Ash said. A nondescript car pulled up and idled along the side of the street, and Elliott jogged for it and tugged open the door. Ash ushered Trevor inside, and Trevor folded into the seat, taken aback by what had just happened. "Better start getting used to it," Ash added.

But wasn't that exactly what he needed to *avoid* doing? Getting used to it?

Trevor scooted across the seat so Ash and Elliott could climb in next to him, and as soon as the door was closed, the car pulled away from the curb and merged with traffic. Ash leaned forward to give the driver directions, and Elliott laughed, shoulder bumping Trevor.

"I'm sure you'll deal with it better than I did, right, Trevor?" he asked, grinning.

Trevor laughed. Fine, so he liked attention. Maybe he could just focus on that, and get over wanting anything more.

"Sure," he said, making himself smile back at Elliott. "I'm in New York City, I'm living in a luxury penthouse, I got to see a Broadway show, I'm making television appearances... and now I'm being chased by paparazzi like I'm some big name celebrity? Life doesn't get any better, right?"

"Wait until they start reporting that you've been having an affair with your fiancé's deadbeat dad," Ash said with a wink. "Or that your partner is actually a woman."

Mouth hanging open, Trevor looked between the two of them. "Someone reported that Elliott is a woman?"

"I know, right?" Ash smirked. "Just wait until you see some of the crazy things they'll come up with about you. They really are shameless."

Let the crazy stories come—Trevor would laugh every one of them off. There were only a few weeks remaining in his contract with Logan, and, once it expired, so too would his stardom. The chaos would end, and he'd be on his own again.

Alone. Without Logan.

"It stops hurting, after a while," Elliott said softly.

Trevor jumped. "W-what?" He'd thought Elliott was going to let the subject drop.

"The gossip magazines," Elliott said. "The awful things they say stops getting to you after you've read enough of them. I promise."

Right. Of course. Elliott hadn't been talking about Logan.

No, Trevor was the one who couldn't seem to get the man out of his mind.

Chapter 13

TREVOR

"Logan?" Trevor called as he entered the penthouse and almost tripped over Logan's shoes. His jacket was hung neatly on the coat rack and his briefcase tucked away in the spot he kept it by the door, and Trevor grinned as he picked up the shoes and lined them up on the shoe rack that was *right there*. It cracked him up.

He'd thought Logan was scheduled to be in meetings all day, and coming home to the evidence that Logan was there, too, shot a surge of excitement through him that he really wished he could pretend didn't happen, especially on the heels of all of the thoughts that had been stirred up by his conversation with Elliott and Ash.

Logan hadn't answered, and Trevor heard the faint sound of the shower running from Logan's bedroom. He slipped out of his shoes, shrugged out of his new jacket, and headed across the living room for the bedroom. On the way home—*no*, not "home"... to *Logan's place*—he'd worked hard to convince himself that the attachment he felt for Logan was simply a side-effect of the constant, mind-blowing sex they'd been having. What better opportunity to prove it than now?

The shower stopped running, and Trevor pushed the bedroom door open just as Logan stepped out of the attached bathroom. He was nude, wet, and mouthwatering.

"Honey, I'm home," Trevor said, grinning from ear-to-ear.

Logan's cornflower-blue eyes locked with Trevor's, and the answering smile that spread across his face and lit them up like the sun made Trevor suck in a sharp breath, struggling to pull himself together.

Logan was *hot*. That was it. That was why he felt this way. As if to prove it, Trevor's cock stirred to life, and he shifted his hips to avoid tenting.

"Trevor," Logan said, dropping the towel he'd been drying his short hair with and crossing the room in two strides. He wrapped his arms around Trevor and greeted him with a swoon-worthy kiss, then pulled back just enough to ask, "Did you have a good time out with your friends?"

"Um, yeah. I did." Trevor cleared his throat, definitely

not in love. "I thought you weren't going to be home until late."

"Turns out my meetings were canceled. I showed up and no one was there. I would have called, but I knew you were out."

He would have called? That was... unnecessary. From a business standpoint. Wasn't it? It was a very boyfriend-y thing to do. Trevor ruthlessly pushed the thought aside, reminding himself that even if what was between him and Logan *wasn't* all business—and clearly, it wasn't—it was definitely rooted in *sex*, not anything deeper.

Sex, he could get over.

"You're home just in time to join me, then," he said, coming up with it on the fly as he felt Logan's cock start to swell against him. "I was planning on lying in bed all afternoon and watching porn."

Logan choked on a laugh, his eyebrows shooting up. "Really?"

Trevor shrugged, doing his best to keep a straight face. "You left too early, baby. We didn't get to have sex this morning, and I've been horny since I got up. You know me."

"I don't think we need porn to take care of that," Logan teased, giving Trevor one of those looks that made him want to believe there really *was* more than just heat between them. The fucker. He was messing with Trevor's plan.

"You have on-demand, don't you?" Trevor insisted, pushing away from Logan and snatching the remote from the bedside table. He flicked the television on, sinking down to sit on Logan's side of the bed. THE bed, he meant. Obviously, the whole thing was Logan's. A few weeks of sharing it didn't give him the right to claim a side, and He Needed To Keep That In Mind. Paneling on the far side of the room opened, revealing the fifty-inch television behind it. The screen blinked to life, and Trevor brought up the menu selection. Logan was still standing there... naked and hot and looking at Trevor like Logan didn't want to be any-where else but with him, porn or not, and Trevor added a desperate, "Or... pay-per-view, or... whatever it is."

"I do, but—"

"Great. Then you can write it off as a business expense." Trevor patted the bed next to him. "You can claim it as re-search. If we're going to keep selling people on *Tregan*, we'll need to get inspiration from somewhere, right?"

Logan hesitated, giving him an odd look, then he smiled and shook his head. He tossed the towel aside and joined Trevor on the bed, not arguing the point.

"If you're going to watch porn with me, then you're going to have to abide by the house rules," Logan said, the playful tone of voice making Trevor wonder how anyone could ever think him cold. He was anything but. He was... wonderful.

"House rules?" Trevor grinned. The hunger in Logan's eyes was real, and the foolish heartache Trevor had been battling all day started to fade as the sheer pleasure of being with the man he lov— with *Logan*, overtook him. "Tell me more, Sir Bossypants."

"In my house, we only watch porn naked," Logan said, lip twitching at the ridiculous nickname. He leaned down and brushed his lips against Trevor's, and Trevor's cock pulsed in response. "You're going to need to strip."

"Are these rules you need to, um, enforce often?" Trevor asked, sure that Logan was making it up to tease him but more than ready to defend his territory if necessary. "Or am I a special case?"

"Are you never *not* a special case?" Logan asked, grinning. Button by button, he started to undo Trevor's shirt. When it hung open, Logan started to work his belt undone. "It's not your place to question my rules. Your job is just to follow them."

Trevor bit back a moan. With Logan in control, following was what Trevor did best. He lifted his hips, and before he knew it, Logan had enforced the rule completely.

"Do you have something in mind?" Logan asked, his voice doing that low and husky thing that never failed to turn Trevor on. He slid a hand over Trevor's erection, stroking him slowly as he waited for an answer.

"Fuck me?" Trevor suggested, his brain slowing down in direct proportion to his growing cock.

Logan laughed, but Trevor felt how his cock—pressed against the side of Trevor's thigh—jerked in response. Still, instead of flipping him over and following through, Logan grinned. "Wouldn't that ruin your... plans? I thought we were going to watch porn together."

"Right," Trevor said. He laughed, the sound coming out sort of breathless since Logan wasn't letting up, and tried to focus on... porn. "I've never paid for it," he said, passing the remote to Logan. "Hell, I've never even paid for *television*. You pick something."

"I'm just going to put on the first thing I find. You know that, right?" Logan let go of his cock and used the remote to scroll down the list, and Trevor read the titles as they went.

BBC Stuffs and Breeds Tiny Twink Ass.

Give Me That Creampie.

Sexy Twink Xtreme Fuck.

He snickered, looking over at Logan. The first thing he found? Nuh-uh. His man was looking for something that would do it for him, and Trevor was suddenly intensely eager to see what he chose. Logan finally selected something, but Trevor had missed the title.

Two attractive men were in bed together, fully clothed, and Trevor cocked his head to the side, contemplating them.

"Why even bother with clothes?" he asked, working his cock slowly since Logan was currently neglecting it. "It's *porn*. Anyone who tunes in knows exactly what's going to happen."

"Some people find storyline sexy," Logan argued. He dropped the remote and pulled Trevor back on the bed with him, propping himself up on the pillows against the headboard so he could see. Logan's fist closed around his own cock, and the sight of him stroking himself distracted Trevor from the screen.

Storyline, huh?

"Like you?" Trevor asked, vaguely aware that on screen, the porn stars had started to make out. "Are you saying I should be whispering my backstory in your ear while you take me? Would it be better for you if we came up with some kind of... role playing?"

Logan laughed, and Trevor noted how his hand sped up on his oh-fuck-yes now very hard cock. "With the way you make me come, Trevor, clearly that's not necessary."

A delicious tension coiled in Trevor's gut, and he slowed his hand to stop from pushing himself too far. Logan really had opened up in the weeks they'd spent together, still hearing him speak so boldly about their time in bed together took him by surprise... and turned him on even more. The Logan he'd known from his time at Ashby's had been so closed off, Trevor had barely been able to get him to remark upon the weather, forget sexual situations. But now look at them, watching something that would hopefully be dirty as fuck, and joking in bed together.

Trevor's heart... *no.*

It affected his *cock*, not his heart.

"So, you're saying you're hot for me?" he asked, determined to keep it about just sex.

"If there's a gay man on this planet who *isn't* hot for

you, I'd be surprised," Logan said, grinning over at him. "I don't know how anyone could see you and not want you, Trevor."

"But you're *hot* hot for me," Trevor insisted, his hand resuming its original speed and his heart definitely *not* reacting to that statement. "You just said the way I make you come... a clear testament to my tight, fabulous ass."

"Your tight ass isn't what I'm talking about." Logan groaned and closed his eyes momentarily, arching up into his hand.

On screen, both of the actors were naked now, and they'd started sucking each other off. Trevor fixed his eyes on them, his heart racing. What was Logan saying?

"This is moving too slow," Trevor said, not sure if he was terrified or excited. "Blowjobs in porn? Snoozefest. I wanna see them fuck."

Logan laughed—a sound Trevor was already addicted to and, honestly, hadn't associated with sex all that much, before Logan—and grabbed the remote. "For someone so sweet and chipper out in public, you have a dirty mouth on you, you know that?" he asked, skipping forward a scene, just because Trevor had said so.

He was always doing that, giving Trevor what he wanted.

On screen, oral sex had turned into full-on anal, but in one of the most uncomfortable positions Trevor had ever seen. The top was on his back, legs pulled back farther than should have been humanly possible, and the bottom was squatting over him and riding his cock in reverse. For balance, he gripped the top's leg, and his thighs strained as he fucked himself on the truly impressive cock of the man below him.

It was hot, and under most circumstances he would have had no problem getting off on it, but with Logan next to him, he couldn't help wondering how *they* would pull off a stunt like that. A low grunt of pleasure from Logan as he worked his hand into his fist made Trevor want to find out.

Why were they settling for just jacking off when they had each other?

"I want to do that," Trevor announced. He abandoned his erection and sat up on the bed, boldly reaching for a condom from the pile that they'd scattered over the bedside table the night before in the dark.

Logan gave a disbelieving laugh. "You want... wait." Logan grabbed Trevor's arm. "You want us to do *that*?"

Trevor grinned. "Yeah, why not?" With his own desire pulsing through him and Logan's big cock—much more impressive, in Trevor's opinion, than the one on screen—so close and tempting, Trevor suddenly wanted it *badly*.

But, more than that, he wanted to prove to himself that sex with Logan was only sex. If they could treat sex like a sport, then he could convince himself once and for all that there were no feelings involved. This wasn't going to include kissing or sweet talking. They weren't going to be pretend boyfriends.

They were going to fuck like porn stars.

"You're going to hurt yourself if we try that," Logan protested, still laughing. Not at all a porn star thing to say.

"Me?" Trevor arched an eyebrow. Challenge accepted. "I may have fallen off the wagon since arriving in New York, but back home in Chicago, I go with Grace to hot yoga three times a week. We *stretch* like it's none of your business. If anyone is going to be hurt, it's *you*, babycakes." He poked Logan in the hip, resisting the temptation to turn the light touch into something else. Instead, he tossed out, "Those old joints aren't quite as flexible as they used to be, hmmm? Don't think you can pull it off?"

Logan scowled, but it wasn't Logan's formerly-standard, detached expression. It was playful. Logan... *playful*. Trevor honestly had never seen a sexier sight. He swallowed.

"I'm plenty flexible," Logan argued, sitting upright.

"Then hurry up and wrap your dick and get those legs back as far as they go," Trevor retaliated, shoving a condom into Logan's hand. "I'm going to get lubed up, and then I'm going to fuck you like the star I am."

Logan's gaze lingered on him for a second, his expression a mixture of arousal and concern. Did he feel the way Trevor was trying to pull away from him? Did he care? Trevor wasn't going to let himself think about it. They were going to fuck, and it was going to be fucking epic.

He grabbed their bottle of lube and prepped himself, the action spurring Logan to rip the little packet open and do as Trevor had suggested. He loved watching Logan get ready for him. Loved the sight of those big hands smoothing the condom over that cock that felt like it had been made for him. Trevor bit his lip, holding in a moan, and worked his fingers into himself deeper and let his eyes drift closed with pleasure. The stretch felt fantastic, and his own cock throbbed in response.

Damn. He really had been horny, hadn't he? That was where all this was coming from.

"I'm ready." The playfulness in Logan's voice had been replaced by raw lust, and when Trevor opened his eyes, Logan was looking at him like watching him might have been enough to get him off, all on its own.

Logan was planted firmly on his back, his rock-hard cock sheathed and—yes, *very* ready—and he'd pulled his legs back so far that Trevor saw the muscles on the backside of his thighs straining. Was Logan really going to do this? The position was ridiculous, and the absurdity of it forced a grin to cross Trevor's lips. He slipped his fingers out and crawled across the bed, cocking his head to the side to assess the situation as desire was momentarily trumped by logistics.

How had those porn stars gotten *into* that position?

Trevor would have to get his feet planted wide apart, and then squat as far down as he could go. How the hell was he going to do that, though, without toppling them both over? He braced one hand on the mattress for support and tried to inch his feet away from each other, but the softness of the mattress and the way it shifted under his weight quickly made it clear that that was going to be a no-go.

"Maybe you could—"

"*Shh*," he flapped a hand at Logan as he shushed him, trying to figure out the best angle of approach. If he wanted to do this, he was going to have to stand, then lower himself.

Which, he suspected, might not end well.

Wobbly due to the mattress, Trevor stood and widened his stance. When his feet were in the right position, he carefully began to lower himself down. Step one, squat. Step two, fuck. His legs trembled as his body swayed, and he clutched at Logan's legs for support. Logan laughed, almost tipping them both over.

How in the hell had those porn stars *done* it? Had the bottom been lowered by crane?

"Steady!" Logan insisted, still laughing. He was too busy holding his legs back to be any more help in guiding Trevor down.

"*You* wanna try this?" Trevor shot back. "*Steady* isn't exactly an option."

"Just don't hurt yourself."

It wasn't a phrase Trevor had heard used all that often—okay, *ever*—in the bedroom, and he snorted, determined not to laugh. He was totally going to get this. Still, his lips twitched, and he said, "Phrases you hear when you know sex is going wrong... *Stop* laughing, Logan. You're bouncing."

Against all odds, Trevor finally succeeded in his squat without either of them falling over. His thighs were starting to burn, though, and he took a look behind him to figure out how far he had left to go to actually make it onto Logan's cock.

Fuck. He was nowhere close.

"What the hell," Trevor muttered under his breath. Logan's legs were as far back as he could get them, and he obviously had to keep a firm grip on them to keep them that way, but there was no way Trevor could accomplish his end of the position on his own. If he let go of Logan's legs, he'd tip over, but someone was definitely going to have to guide that cock home if this was going to happen.

Was that what the porn stars did? Some director or camera guy helped with insertion?

Yeah, no. There was *no way* Trevor wanted some other guy sharing Logan's bed.

"You're going to have to get lower," Logan said unhelpfully.

Trevor resisted the urge to glare at him. Logan laughing was not helping in the least, but it *was* filling Trevor with those currently unwelcome warm fuzzy feelings that only served to heighten his arousal. They had to fuck, and fast, or else he was liable to forget that he wasn't going to fall in love with the man.

"I'm *trying*! But any lower, and I'm going to fall over."

"Widen your stance," Logan said, apparently determined to be a backseat driver. "You just need to get your ass all the way down, and then—"

It was impossible, and Trevor twisted around to flop down on the bed.

"Screw it," he said, working Logan's condom off and tossing it across the room in frustration. "I don't need to have sex like a porn star. I like my cock uncomplicated. Blowjobs it is." Trevor punctuated the remark by running his tongue up Logan's hard length and swallowing his cock. Tongue swirling, lips tightening, he invested himself in Logan's pleasure.

Logan's cock throbbed for him, and Trevor pressed his hips against the mattress as fresh arousal filled him.

Logan was... laughing.

"Trevor," he said, hands stroking Trevor's head tenderly as he thrust up into his mouth. "You're amazing."

Trevor squeezed his eyes closed, determined to get Logan off as fast as he could. He made his way back up Logan's cock, tonguing at his slit before he sunk back down again, but when Logan groaned and his fingers tightened against Trevor's skull, he couldn't resist opening his eyes and looking up to catch the expression on his face. Sprawled out on the bed with his skin still pink and warm from his shower and something that could only be joy pouring off him in waves, Logan was gorgeous.

"That's it," he said, starting to pant as he fucked Trevor's mouth. "Oh, fuck, Trevor, so good... always so good with you."

Trevor moaned, the sound muffled by the hot length pressing against the back of his throat, and he reached beneath himself as he worked Logan closer and closer, fisting his cock as he stared up into Logan's eyes.

Trevor had been an idiot to waste time trying to convince himself not to fall for him. What he needed to do—as a sweet tenderness blossomed inside his heart even as his own cock started to swell with his impending release—was put all that energy into something more worthwhile.

"Oh, fuck," Logan moaned, his head tipping back against the pillows and breaking their eye contact. "Oh, *fuckkkk* yes, Trevor, *yesssssss*. I'm going to... *nnnnnnnggghhhhhh...* I'm going to come."

Logan's cock swelled in his mouth, almost choking him, as the hot burst of his release accompanied the words. Trevor closed his eyes, swallowing it down and moaning his own satisfaction as he spilled over his fist, coming right along with him. And then Logan was pulling him up into his arms, licking his way inside Trevor's mouth and murmuring words that were everything Trevor wanted to hear.... if they were true.

Words that gave him hope that, if he put his mind to it, before the contract was over, he might just be able to convince Logan to love him right back.

Chapter 14

LOGAN

"Profit margins are up for this quarter, as you can see in figure 4.3. We attribute this increase to..."

The board meeting for one of the other companies that Logan held shares in—the one that had been canceled the week before—was now in full swing. Logan's eyes drifted across the presentation on the projector, coming to rest on figure 4.3. The graph was drab. Last year's figures were recorded in red, and this year's were done in black. How boring. Trevor would have whispered something snarky and hilarious into his ear about how the presenters needed to brighten things up if they wanted to keep the audience's attention.

It was the line that had convinced Logan to give in and wear color for the first time since he'd lost Ryan. For six years his soul had ached over the loss, and he'd been in mourning for what felt like the biggest failure of his life.

But with Trevor in his life, that pain had all but disappeared, and color no longer felt like an insult to his emotions.

"Mr. Carter?"

Logan jerked to attention, blinking rapidly as his eyes regained focus. "Yes?"

"Did you not hear the question?" The presenter spoke in slow monotone, like a teacher who'd spent the last twenty years repeating the same lecture verbatim.

"No, I'm sorry. My mind must have been stuck on the... profit margins."

If he were in any less professional of an environment, Logan was sure that the other men around the table would have snickered at him. God, did none of them know how to have fun? It was yet another good thing Trevor had brought into his life, and one that he was no less inclined to give up than any other part of Trevor.

He just had to figure out how to make that happen.

"Is your opinion that we should continue to push in the same way we've been pushing, or are there new market trends that you think we should pursue?"

Often, due to his experience, Logan was asked questions like that, but market trends were outside of his realm of expertise. His master's degree was in business, not marketing, and while markets could be predicted and trends analyzed, there was never a surefire guarantee that a sudden shift in direction wouldn't ruin an entire campaign. He bit back a grin, giving in to the devilish urge to answer with an ambitious, "Yes."

Beside him, Hiro shot him a look, but Logan ignored him. Other board members had jumped in to argue the question, and Logan settled back in his chair and let his mind wander again. Would Trevor have scolded him for replying with a single word? Replying so shortly didn't lend itself well to conversation, and it made him look hostile. On the other hand, he had no doubt that Trevor would have found it funny.

For the first time in years, Logan was struck by the thought that looking over figures and discussing sales strategies was... boring. Trevor had shown him that there was more to life than financial success. After all, Trevor had next to no money, and he led one of the most compelling existences that Logan had ever seen.

Passions. Dreams. Ambitions. For Logan, all of those had fallen by the wayside since his breakup with Ryan. He'd buried his head in his work and cut the outside world out. He'd made safe investments. He'd led his life according to a narrow set of rules.

Trevor lived by certain rules, too, but there was an element of unpredictability to his life that made it exciting. *Fun.*

During their down time, when they could bring

themselves to get out of bed, Trevor had taken to dragging Logan around the city to see the sights. Logan had lived in New York all his life, but he'd never gone to see the Statue of Liberty before Trevor had insisted on taking him there. The harsh cold of January had bitten at them, but they'd stood before her and looked up as the wind whipped and the damp air froze them to the core. The statue was closed for the winter, so they weren't able to go up, but standing there, marveling in the artistry in silence, was something Logan didn't think he'd ever forget.

Over coffee, warming their hands and their frozen cores, Trevor had rattled on and on about Chicago. Navy Pier. The museums. The festivals. The Bean. Logan had been content to let him talk, admiring the way his lips moved and the musicality of his words. There was passion in him about life, and about his city. For now, Trevor's passion spilled over into New York.

Into Logan.

Logan found himself hanging on Trevor's words lately, trying to pick them apart and analyze them and look for some sign that Trevor wasn't just "staying in character." That he might want to turn what was supposed to be temporary into something more permanent.

There was no doubt that having Trevor on as a full-time boyfriend was the best arrangement Logan had ever been involved in. Not even his relationship with Ryan compared. The common interests he and Ryan had once shared, and the successful company they'd built together in Rise, paled in comparison to the way Trevor's eyes lit up when Logan did something small for him, or how he laughed without reserve as they navigated New York together despite the frigidity of winter.

Even New York's notorious subway—which Logan avoided like the plague—had made Trevor happy.

Logan loved to see him smile.

Logan loved... *him*.

He gritted his teeth, fending off the surge of fear that came with that admission. For all of Trevor's outgoing, flirtatious nature, Logan didn't fear that things would end with him the way they had with Ryan. Trevor was *his*, and Logan didn't doubt for a moment that he wouldn't stray. But still, for all of Trevor's zestful enthusiasm for being with him, he'd never once talked about anything beyond the end of their contract.

"If we're thinking of advertising on that grand a scale, why don't we go all the way?" One of the other board members, Estelle Lowe, said in response to something Logan had missed. She pulled a file folder from her briefcase, opening it to reveal a collection of photographs. Logan's eyes regained focus.

They were pictures of... runways?

"Fashion Week is in New York," Estelle said, looking around the table. "If we're interested in stirring up international interest without straying far from home, then we need to book advertisement space in the venue. With our newest ads, as sleek and sophisticated as they are, we could easily advertise along the bottom of the catwalk. Thousands of photographs. Millions of eyes. And the direct presence of the ad to the audience?"

The table was silent, listening, but Logan's thoughts had jumped in a completely different direction. Apart from his love of Broadway, Trevor had been on-and-off talking about Fashion Week ever since he'd arrived. If Estelle had connections...

Logan grinned. He needed to show Trevor everything New York had to offer. Needed to make him fall in love with the idea of staying.

Fall in love with *Logan*.

"We're talking about an extremely influential group of people," Estelle continued. "Top fashion reporters. The who's who of the industry. If we're interested in selling a luxury product, we need to target those who can afford to pay for luxury."

"Or those so desperate to emulate that kind of wealth that they'll go out of their way to afford whatever products are associated with the elite."

"Bingo." Estelle arched one of her perfectly groomed brows. "I have connections. We'll need to rush production for the ads, but if you can get it done, I can have it arranged to be displayed for a reasonable price—well within our discussed budget."

"All opposed?"

There were none.

"All in favor?"

Logan's voice joined the rest—it was a smart move for the business—but his gaze was glued to the photographs in the folder. The catwalk. The lights. The fashion. The rest of the meeting went by in a haze, and as the room emptied out, he approached Estelle as she packed up her briefcase.

"You said you had connections, Estelle. Is there any chance you have passes to any of the Fashion Week events you'd be willing to part with?" he asked. "Price isn't important."

Estelle paused as she packed, looking up at him in surprise. "I never took you as a man interested in fashion, Mr. Carter. This new boyfriend really *is* changing you, isn't he?"

Was it that obvious? Logan grinned, not bothering to deny it. Apparently *#Tregan* really was trending, since he'd never mentioned Trevor to the members of this company's board.

From the same folder with the pictures of the catwalk, Estelle produced two embossed tickets dated with today's date. She handed them over, winking. "Is tonight too soon? Because these are *highly* coveted... and we could always call it payback for the time you saved my ass a few quarters back and floated me that advance. What do you say?"

Logan had no idea what the cost of two tickets to a fashion event would go for, but he suspected it wasn't anywhere close to the amount of financial support Logan had thrown Estelle's way when she'd botched a decision that had come close to dragging her business under.

But when Trevor saw the passes, he was going to lose it.

He grinned, taking them. "It's a deal."

She gave a disbelieving laugh, shooting Logan a look. "Are you sure? I was kidding, Logan. The tickets—"

"He's worth it, Estelle."

Her face softened. "So it *is* true."

Was the secret out? Logan's face hardened. If he had to, he'd deny it. So far, no one had caught on that their relationship had started out as a marketing ploy, but Estelle was an astute businesswoman and a marketing genius. She also knew him, well enough to know how cynical and hardened he'd been about love.

Logan gave a stiff nod. Would bLoved suffer if the truth came to light? Probably. But—other than the blow to his business partner, Kelly, which would be significant—Logan couldn't bring himself to care too much about that. Even if bLoved failed utterly, it would be a minor blip on his financial spectrum. What would be far worse was losing Trevor if the nature of their relationship was revealed and the campaign prematurely ended.

He needed all the time he could get to come up with a way to convince Trevor to stay... but "all the time he could get," at best, was still only two weeks. Valentine's Day—and the end of their contract—was bearing down on them like a freight train.

"Congratulations," Estelle said, giving him a genuine smile. "I'm really happy for you, Logan. And I have no doubt, with your connection to bLoved, that you're planning on sweeping him off his feet on Valentine's Day, aren't you? The two of you are tremendously cute together, and I wish you all the best."

"Thank you," Logan said automatically. He'd been thinking of Valentine's Day in terms of the dreaded end date, but Estelle was right. It might be his last opportunity to come up with a gesture grand enough to make Trevor fall in love with him.

If only he had a clue what that might be.

Cheerful, Estelle collected her briefcase and stood. "I'll see you sometime next month. Take care."

He wished her well, picking up his own briefcase and following her out. He had no idea how to make a grand gesture, or make someone fall in love with him. He'd failed miserably at both, once before.

But Trevor was different than Ryan.

Logan was different, when he was with Trevor.

This time would be different.

He wouldn't get his heart broken. Somehow, he would find a way to hold onto the best thing that had ever happened to him. He glanced down at the tickets Estelle had given him, smiling as he anticipated Trevor's reaction. There was nothing he enjoyed more than making Trevor happy. And, one way or another, he was determined to find a way to keep doing it.

Ideally, for the rest of his life.

Chapter 15

TREVOR

"THIS IS WEST SOHO," TREVOR SAID, HIS NOSE NEARLY plastered to the window of Logan's town car.

They sat together in the back seat, Logan's hand resting possessively on Trevor's thigh. Trevor loved it, continually surprising himself with how much it worked for him. Nothing about Logan's dominance struck him in the wrong way. From the firm, authoritative touch of Logan's hand to the way Logan took control while they were in public, Trevor reveled in the attention. On their way to the car, paparazzi had been waiting by Parker Tower's door, and Logan had expertly placed himself in between them and Trevor, much in the same way that Ash shielded Elliott.

With any other man, Trevor would have felt caged. With Logan, he felt protected.

Valued.

When was the last time he'd felt so valued? In other areas of his life—as a friend, as a son and brother, as an employee at Ashby's—Trevor knew that he was appreciated and loved. But as something more than that? No one had ever made him feel the way Logan did, and Logan's initial possessive statement when they'd flown into New York the month before—*you're mine*—felt just as right for Trevor as his hand did now, high on Trevor's thigh.

Of course, as far as he was concerned, it was a two-way street. He tore his eyes away from the window, looking at his man. "Logan, we're in West Soho," he repeated.

Logan's eyes were sparkling, but he just shrugged, visibly holding in one of his killer smiles. "Mmhm," he replied, clearly determined to continue to torture Trevor by not telling him their plans.

"West Soho like..." Trevor opened the GPS on his cellphone, tracking their location. "Logan. We're in West Soho near Skylight Clarkson SQ."

"Are we?" Logan asked innocently. "Not a part of town I usually visit."

Trevor's heart started to race, but he forced his excitement down. Were they just passing through?

Logan grinned, pulling two long, embossed tickets out and fanning them in his direction. "Maybe we'll be able to make use of these, since we're in the neighborhood."

"What are they?" Trevor demanded, not letting himself hope that they could really... could they... he squinted, but the glossy finish prevented him from reading the printed text on the tickets as Logan waved them in front of him enticingly. "*Logan*."

Logan laughed, but finally had mercy and handed one of them over. Trevor's hand was shaking as he took it, tilting it so he could read the words plastered across the thick, elegant paper.

New York Fashion Week — Men's

"No!" Trevor's head shot up, and he stared at Logan. Logan grinned. "Shut up!"

"I'm not even speaking."

"Just!" Frantic energy coursed through his veins. Trevor rocked forward in his seat and sunk his fingers into the front of Logan's coat, pulling him forward until he could kiss him hard. The pass was clutched tightly in his other hand.

"So... is *shut up* a good thing?" Logan asked as the kiss broke, smiling down at him.

The driver pulled up outside of Skylight Clarkson SQ— the same venue that had hosted New York Fashion Week the year before. The men's segment, occurring a few days before traditional Fashion Week began, was just as new as the venue.

"Shut up is a *great* thing." Trevor's heart swelled so big, so fast, that for a moment he thought it might burst. Questions tumbled out of him in his excitement. "Have long have you been keeping this from me? How did you get invites? They don't hand these out to *anybody*."

Trevor lingered close, hand still hooked on Logan's jacket as he tried to wrap his mind around it. His heart pounded, and more than anything, he wanted to run. To shout. To let the world know that his dreams were coming true.

He was in love, and he was in New York City, and his boyfriend had managed a miracle and was taking him to Fashion Week.

"Logan..." Trevor released his grip and sat back in his seat, pulse thudding in his ears. He read over the pass again, marveling at the little details. They were guests of a woman named Estelle Lowe, and while her name wasn't familiar to Trevor, he was sure that somewhere within the industry, she was an influential figure. He looked up, feeling his eyes well up. "Logan..." he swallowed back *I love you*, since that was something they only said in public—*in character*—settling for an equally true, "Thank you."

It wasn't like him to say words that simple—without flair, life was boring—yet, there was nothing Trevor could hope to say that would adequately convey what Logan's gesture meant to him. He knew without a doubt that *Logan* didn't want to attend Fashion Week—he was about as fashionable as a potato, at least, without Trevor's influence—but he clearly understood what it meant for Trevor.

He'd listened. He'd remembered. Most importantly, he'd cared enough to act.

Love blossomed and filled Trevor with its glow. It was love, unavoidably and undeniably. He'd stopped pretending that it was anything else. It *never* had been. He'd felt an attraction for Logan from the start, and even back during his Ashby's days, a part of him had known it wasn't just physical. There was a connection between them, and he'd looked forward to Logan's visits because of it, and he suspected that Logan had come back time and time again because he'd felt the same.

He looked down at the ticket in his hand. The appeal wasn't how expensive it was, or how exclusive the event was, or the fact that Logan was richer than Trevor could ever dream of being. The appeal was that Logan wanted him for who he was—flamboyant, fashionable, outspoken Trevor Rogers—and that, no matter how he played it off, he'd meant what he'd said on air.

He wanted Trevor to be happy.

And with Logan, Trevor was very, very happy.

"You're welcome," Logan said, the look in his eyes proving Trevor right. Logan grinned. "I have no idea what to expect, but I trust you to guide me through."

Logan unbuckled his seatbelt and nodded toward Trevor's door. The two of them would exit together, Trevor realized, and Trevor would lead the way. It was like they were a Hollywood power couple, and Trevor had to laugh at how radically different his life had become since Logan had swept him out of his humdrum existence back in Chicago.

The area in front of Skylight Clarkson SQ was cordoned off and secured, but there were plenty of cameras in the crowd, waiting to capture famous faces. Apparently, based on the number of flashes that went off and the excited shouting, *Tregan* qualified.

"You could have prepared me. Thank God I always dress well," Trevor whispered, making Logan laugh.

The sound reverberated in Trevor's bones and shook him to his core with a quiet joy. Sincere, relaxed, and genuinely happy, Logan had become a different man in public than the one who'd hired Trevor to help him come out of his shell all those weeks before. And in private, he was breathtaking.

Logan slipped his hand into Trevor's and squeezed, and Trevor looked up at him. Cameras flashed. Logan stole a kiss from his lips, and Trevor closed his eyes and gave into it as his heart raced. Not even sex felt as good as what he shared with Logan in that instant. The frost in the New York air couldn't rob him of the fuzzy heat that warmed him from the inside, filling all the parts of him that he'd long insisted didn't exist.

The parts that needed someone to love.

Someone who would love him back.

When their lips parted, Trevor looked up into Logan's eyes, realizing he needed to tell him. Logan smiled back at him, his warm gaze making a cocoon of intimacy despite the noise and excitement around them.

"Trevor! Trevor! Logan! Over here!"

Trevor glanced over his shoulder, laughing in delight at the attention.

"You've never looked happier," Logan said, wrapping an arm around Trevor's waist and turning to wave at the reporters on the sideline, the way Trevor had coached him. "The media is going to eat this up. Good job."

Job? Disappointment began to curl the edges of Trevor's affection. Was this just another business expense after all, a publicity opportunity to get more people buzzing about bLoved, despite the thoughtfulness and everything Trevor had thought he'd seen in Logan's eyes?

But then they were through the doors, and he was surrounded by one of his personal dreams—*Fashion Week*—and he shook it off. He knew what he'd seen in Logan's eyes; he saw the same thing every time he looked in the mirror. Unless the man looked him right in the eye and told him otherwise, he was going to go ahead and let himself believe that what had started out as business had, in fact, turned into something far more.

But, just in case, it was probably a good thing he hadn't blurted out his own feelings.

He'd hold off rocking the boat until the end of their contract.

Because if he was wrong, God help him, he wasn't willing to ruin the last two weeks of fantasy with a hard dose of reality.

Chapter 16

LOGAN

Despite his hectic publicity schedule, Logan still needed to report to bLoved headquarters in Chicago for the monthly meeting. The company was simply too small to do without him, especially with Kelly still out of touch while the police narrowed in on the perpetrator of the death threats he'd received.

This month, though, Hiro had been unable to book Logan's regular flight, which meant that Logan would have to stay in Chicago overnight.

Trevor wasn't coming with him.

"I'm not going to be able to sleep without you," Logan

grumbled as their car pulled into the lane leading to O'Hare departures.

"You've been sleeping without me for thirty-three years," Trevor reminded him, laughing. Still, he snuggled a little closer and wrapped his arm around Logan's waist. "Besides, you've still got my number, right?"

"Of course I do." Logan knew he was being unreasonable—it was just one night—but there was no denying that the idea of so much distance between them was making him cranky. How did all of those bLoved users who were involved in long-distance relationships survive it?

"So call me." Trevor smiled. "Easy peasy. I'll keep my phone charged so you can get in touch any time."

"Right."

Trevor laughed. "Stop pouting, baby," he teased. "One night without me to warm your bed isn't going to kill you. You remember how to use your hand still, don't you? Besides, phone sex might be fun."

For once, Trevor's playful grin didn't lift Logan's mood. Missing Trevor wasn't just about sex. Their end date would be there before he knew it, and Logan still hadn't figured out how to ask Trevor to stay.

He needed to come up with a convincing argument, but—for all Trevor's uninhibited enjoyment of the city and the perks of Logan's money—Logan suspected those alone wouldn't be enough to keep him. And, without those things as enticement, what did he have to offer?

Just his love... which, in the past, had never been enough.

"Can I walk you to your gate?" Trevor asked as the car came to a stop, his playful mood becoming a bit more subdued. "I'm going to miss you, too, you know."

Logan's heart surged, and he nodded, directing the driver toward a lot he could wait in while Trevor came inside the airport.

Trevor grinned. "*Great,*" he said, looking happy again. Then he cleared his throat, his eyes skittering away from Logan's. "It'll be, um, good for publicity. You know, that's something boyfriends do for each other all the time."

"Of course." Logan swallowed back his disappointment. Leaving Trevor now was much more challenging than he'd anticipated. What would he feel when he was the one seeing Trevor off to Chicago in a couple of weeks?

There was no way he could let that happen. His heart would break, and, this time, he didn't think it would recover.

They left the car together, and Logan pulled his carry-on out of the trunk and rolled it across the pavement. Trevor's hand slipped into his as they walked through the broad rotating doors and into the massive maze that was LaGuardia.

Trevor no longer looked quite as happy.

"Are you upset you're not coming back to Chicago with me?" Logan asked. "You spoke about it fondly while we were sightseeing the other week. You must miss it."

Trevor had been the one who'd insisted it was silly for Logan to incur the extra expense of including him on the trip, especially when there was absolutely no publicity scheduled for him to be a part of.

Yet another reminder that Trevor was still thinking of their time together in terms of publicity.

"Miss Chicago? No, not really." Trevor shrugged, not meeting his eyes. "I mean, sure, Chicago is great, but New York has grown on me. I like it here. The culture, the pace, the atmosphere... I'm actually going to be, um, sad when I have to leave."

Hope was dangerous, but in that moment, Logan let himself cling to it. If Trevor wanted to stay, then his chances were that much better.

"What about your family?" he asked, remembering that Trevor had said they all lived in the Chicago area. Unlike Logan's own estrangement from his parents, he'd gotten the impression that Trevor was close to them.

"What gate are you leaving from?" Trevor asked, looking at the overhead signs.

Logan told him, leading the way down the proper concourse, then pressed him again about his family. "You're not eager to get back and see them?" he asked.

Trevor flashed him a strained smile. "Trying to get rid of me?"

"No," Logan said, biting off the word. "But they must miss *you*." Not that Logan could blame them.

Trevor laughed, giving him a more genuine smile.

"Well, I guess, but I mean, it's not like I see them *that* often. I've been living on my own for years, and sure, I love them, but honestly, you know I've toyed with the idea of packing it all up to move to New York or Hollywood for a while now. I *would* miss them if I was gone more permanently, but sometimes you have to follow your dreams, right?" He cleared his throat, his smile dimming, and added, "Besides, this is just a couple more weeks, so..." His voice trailed off, and he sighed, looking away.

Logan's hand tightened, stopping Trevor in his tracks. He had to let him know how he felt before he left. He wanted to straighten things out between them. To know that there was hope for a future beyond a mere two more weeks.

"Trevor, I'm hoping that—"

"Excuse me," a voice cut in politely from behind them.

Logan stopped himself and turned, the momentum behind his words lost. What had he been thinking? They were in public, after all. If anyone had overheard him asking Trevor if there was a chance they could try a real relationship, it would have outed that their relationship was fake... no doubt undermining all the positive publicity that *Tregan* had generated for bLoved.

"Are you Logan and Trevor?"

"Tregan, reporting for duty," Trevor said brightly as he turned around, too. "That's us."

The middle-aged couple who had stopped them beamed at them. One of the men stood tall, graying hair cut short. A few wrinkles crept across his forehead and framed the corners of his mouth, but his eyes were vibrant and ageless. His partner, a shorter man, close to Trevor's height, came across as a little younger, but Logan suspected it was simply a matter of being well-preserved. He could read the age in the man's hands.

"We're sorry to bother you," the shorter one said, practically glowing as his eyes bounced between Logan and Trevor excitedly. "I'm Eric, and this is Pierce, and we've been following the two of you."

Logan stiffened, moving in front of Trevor slightly. So far, the attention they'd received in public had been almost universally positive, but...

"On the Internet," Pierce rushed in to say quickly, eyes tracking Logan's subtle movement. "Not in real life."

Trevor laughed, and Logan relaxed.

"We just wanted to say thank you for what you're doing," Eric said, wrapping an arm around Pierce's waist and smiling down at him for a moment before turning his attention back to Logan and Trevor. "We met through bLoved two years ago, and now we're about to fly out on our honeymoon. Seeing the two of you on television... well, it's been reminding us of *us*."

Trevor's hand tightened in Logan's, and he felt Trevor draw closer. Public performance or not, Logan's heart skipped a beat. Trevor was reacting to the palpable love between the two older men the same way he was.

"Congratulations," Logan said, meaning it. "You two look very happy."

"Oh, we are," Pierce said, his smile growing impossibly wider. "At first, despite what the algorithms said, neither one of us really believed it could work out. But the first time we met in person—"

"—there was an instant connection," Eric said, cutting in so smoothly to finish his husband's sentence that it felt like they were speaking from one mind. "There was this kind of heaviness in the air, and this rushing feeling through my chest, like I was coming down from the peak of a roller coaster."

Pierce kissed his husband's cheek, clearly unable to keep his affection from overflowing. He turned back to Logan and Trevor. "And when we look at the two of *you*, and how you treat each other in public, we get the feeling that you're feeling it, too. It's a blessing."

"A gift."

"We're so happy to see that you've found it, too. You deserve it, and more, for all that you've brought us."

"And every other bLoved user."

Logan half expected Trevor to jump in with a witty comment or a charming comeback, but he was silent. Logan, too, felt speechless as the sincerity of Pierce and Eric's words sunk in. They were right... for him.

What was Trevor thinking, though?

"There aren't enough people like you, who stand up for the gay community like this," Eric said. "When we were younger, things like bLoved didn't exist. You have no idea how precious a resource like that is to us."

"Well, maybe you do." Pierce smiled, and Logan knew exactly what he meant. Both men were clearly sold on the notion of Trevor and Logan as a couple.

"Anyway," Eric said, taking a step back and laughing self-consciously. "We didn't mean to keep you. We just wanted to say, thank you for making us possible, and for promoting love above all else. We want to wish the two of you the best. We're rooting for your love to last forever."

Trevor's grip tightened almost painfully in Logan's hand for a split-second, then eased. "Thank you," he said to Eric and Pierce, leaning against Logan's side. "It's really amazing to hear stories like yours. I'm so proud of Logan and everything he does to make the world a little better. Everyone deserves to feel like you two do." He cleared his throat, adding, "Like... we do."

Logan blinked away something that came dangerously close to tears.

"It was great meeting you," Eric said, smiling. "Take care."

"We'll be keeping you in our thoughts," Pierce promised.

"Thank you so much for saying hello." Some of Trevor's bubbly charm had returned, but his voice was still much more subdued than usual. "I hope you two have a fantastic time on your honeymoon. If you take some great pictures, send them to us through bLoved's contact page. I'll, um, make sure Logan passes them my way."

"We've got to get going, but really, thank you." Logan couldn't express how much he meant it. The cynicism he'd once had about bLoved's services was gone, and as he and Trevor continued down the concourse toward the security check point, he cast one last glance in Eric and Pierce's direction. The happiness they shared with each other was the same kind of happiness he felt whenever he was with Trevor; the same kind of happiness he hoped he was seeing in Trevor's eyes, too.

If Eric and Pierce had overheard him referring to the business side of their relationship, it would have crushed their belief... even though the business side was exactly what Logan was hoping to change. Still, he'd wait and do it right. As they reached the point where they'd have to part, just before security, he stopped and drew Trevor into his arms.

"On the last night you're here, I want to take you out to dinner."

"You mean, the day before Valentine's Day?" Trevor asked. Hiro had booked his flight back to Chicago for the afternoon of February 14th, directly after their final television appearance. Trevor grinned. "That will probably be easier than getting reservations *on* Valentine's Day."

"Find someplace you want to go, someplace special, and have Hiro book it," Logan said, wondering if he should ask Trevor to stay an extra day instead. If he'd be messing up by missing out on the romance of declaring himself on Valentine's Day itself. Was he being stupid not to take every advantage he could get?

"Okay," Trevor said, biting his lip and looking like he

wanted to say more. But then he glanced at the huge digital clock on the wall near security. "You'd better get going, baby. Security looks like it might be a bitch today, and you don't want to miss your flight."

"What if I do?" Logan teased, half meaning it.

Trevor laughed, and his cheeks turned a satisfying shade of pink. "Go," he said, stretching up to kiss Logan and holding on tight enough that going was, for a moment, impossible.

Not that Logan minded.

And, when he finally broke away, Trevor called after him. "I love you, Logan."

Logan turned back, wondering if he was the first person in the history of all relationships to wish he could hear those words in private, rather than public... so he'd know they were true.

"I love you, too," he said.

And Trevor smiled like the sun, the brilliance of it already making Logan count down the hours until he could come back and see it again.

Chapter 17

TREVOR

THERE WAS NO WAY TREVOR WANTED TO LEAVE NEW YORK City without visiting Canal Street. Well, if he were honest, at this point, he didn't want to leave New York at all... but still—since Logan, who was otherwise the first to make things happen if Trevor so much as mentioned an interest—refused to budge on the matter, being stuck on his own for a day while Logan was in Chicago seemed like the perfect opportunity to go. Logan insisted that he didn't want to have any part of buying counterfeit goods, and that, with the money he had, there was no reason why Trevor would need to, either.

As if Logan wouldn't give a second thought to spoiling

the shit out of Trevor if given the chance. Which, frankly, he *did*. And while Trevor didn't say no, he also had zero expectations in that regard. Honestly, as fun as it was, he would take time with Logan over *things*, any day.

Which had made it hard for him to explain to Logan why a trip to Canal Street was a necessity when it came to making his time in New York City complete. As a lifelong resident, it was clear that Logan didn't understand the touristic appeal.

Trevor cared as much as the next fashion-savvy consumer about counterfeits. Poor quality products ruined reputations and diluted brands. People who worked hard to produce high-end fashion deserved to be paid for their time and efforts, and he knew that sewing a leather bag using fine leather was *not* easy, nor was it cheap. But Trevor wasn't interested in the shopping, so much as he was interested in the *experience*.

Logan had given him instructions on how to call for his personal driver while Logan was out of town, but Trevor didn't bother. There was nothing that screamed New York more than arriving at the south end of Canal Street by taxi, and Trevor wasn't going to pass it up.

The Canal Street he arrived at wasn't the one he had imagined, though. The wide sidewalks were jammed with stalls selling fruits and vegetables, their vendors wrapped up in winter coats and scarves. Pedestrians browsed the selection, but the crowds were nowhere near what Trevor assumed they would be. It was... well, not quite disappointing, but after spending so much of his time with Logan, it hit him that—while, yes, New York would *always* be magical, no matter what—it was just that much more so when he got to share it with Logan.

Still, in a small way, he enjoyed the quiet. Trevor *liked* attention, and he was definitely on the far end of the outgoing spectrum, but it was still true that keeping a constantly cheery attitude could be exhausting at times... especially when so much of his life felt uncertain.

Well, okay. Maybe not "so much," but... the part that currently felt most important.

Did he have a future with Logan, or not?

He wove between the light crowds on the sidewalk, barely taking note of his surroundings. The entirety of his adult life had been spent bouncing from man to man, refusing to settle. Even when some of his closest friends—Jose with Barry, and Elliott with Ash—had found love, he still hadn't really seen the attraction of tying himself down to one man, long-term. But now, the thought that he might, in fact, only have two more weeks of being one half of Tregan... hurt.

As he headed north on Canal Street, he fished his phone out of his pocket and unlocked the screen. He had no reason to call Logan. His flight would be leaving Chicago in a matter of hours, and Trevor would see him not long after. Besides, they'd spoken the night before. Even though Trevor had teased Logan about phone sex before he'd left, they'd ended up just talking... for hours. Still, it had been a long night without him, and, in the morning, bleary and half-asleep, when Trevor had reached for him out of habit and come up with nothing but cold, empty bed on Logan's side, Logan's absence had made him ache.

Trevor rolled his eyes, trying to talk himself out of it. He didn't want to come across as needy. His plan to make Logan fall in love with him for real had so far consisted of nothing more than continuing to stay "in character"... but Logan *still* hadn't argued the point, the few times Trevor had dropped references to their fake relationship, and a surge of anxiety went through him as it hit him that the clock was ticking.

His phone buzzed in his hand, but instead of Logan's killer blue eyes popping up on screen, it was a shot he'd taken of Brigid over Thanksgiving, mugging for the camera with their parents' eighty-year-old-in-dog-years poodle.

"Hey, Bri," he said, smiling as he answered. He hadn't talked to his sister in close to a month—not all that unusual—but hearing from her now was just what he'd needed to combat his uncharacteristic attack of loneliness.

"You still in New York, Trev?" she asked in lieu of a greeting.

"Yep."

"Well, shoot. I've just been invited to a thing—"

"A thing?" he interrupted, laughing.

"You know, a *thing*. One that I need you to dress me for."

"Oh, a party, you mean."

"Not just a *party*—" he snickered, swearing he could

hear her eye roll, "—this is important, Trev! My faculty advisor will be there. When will you be back, because if I have to figure out what to wear without you..."

"We don't want that," he agreed hastily. His smile faded. It figured that her call would bring up the very subject he was feeling so torn up about. "Two weeks."

"What's wrong?" she asked immediately, zeroing in on the change in his voice.

"Nothing."

"Trevor..."

"*Nothing*, Bri. I'm still in New York. I'm on Canal Street right now, for God's sake," he said, letting his gaze wander the stalls around him. "I'm having a really good time. In fact, um, I think that I might want to... stay."

Silence.

He pulled the phone away from his ear, wondering if the call had dropped. Nope.

"Brigid?"

She sighed. "Trevor, you want to move to New York? I mean, I know you've always talked about it, but... does this have something to do with Logan Carter?"

"Maybe."

"Don't lie."

"Okay. I... like him, and I'm thinking that he actually likes me." Saying it out loud was freeing, even if he had chickened out on using the other L word.

"You've never even had a boyfriend before," Brigid said carefully. "Not one who matters. And you told me this thing with him was just for fun. You're seriously considering moving all the way out there just to be with him?"

"Yes?"

"Is that a question?"

Trevor sighed, finally spotting the first of the fashion stalls down the street. He angled toward them, deciding to go for broke. After all, it would be good practice. "I think, maybe, that I actually sort of love him, Bri."

"Oh, Trevor," Brigid murmured. "Are you that serious about him?"

"Yeah."

Displays of purses spilled out from open storefronts into the streets. Booths full of scarves and graphic t-shirts and souvenirs were dotted in between, and Trevor scanned them to find one hawking sunglasses. Normally he loved attention, but with the crowds increasing in size, he didn't really feel like getting recognized for once. He wedged his phone between his shoulder and ear, still waiting for his sister to say something as he bought himself the most fabulous, oversized pair he could find. He popped them on, realizing she was going to wait him out until he gave her something more than "yeah."

"I mean, I've known him for over a year, Bri, so it's not like this is sudden." He ignored her dismissive snort. "But since getting to know him better here, I... I can't explain it. He's what I never knew I wanted, if that makes any sense."

"But does he want you, too? He's a powerful man, Trevor..."

"Please," he scoffed. "Not want *me*? Honey, how could he not?"

She laughed, apparently buying it. Maybe not all that hard, since it was exactly what the old Trevor would say. The one who had never been in love. But Logan *did* want him. That much was obvious every day, and Trevor came to a sudden standstill in the middle of the sidewalk, forcing the crowds to part around him, as dozens of small moments flashed through his memory.

Not the big ones, like the tickets to Fashion Week or Logan's sort-of declaration of love on live TV, but all the little ones. The way Logan's eyes lit up whenever Trevor walked in the room. The way he'd switched coffee brands after Trevor had mentioned his favorite. The way he always took Trevor's hand when they were walking, and the way he always smiled down at him like they were the only two people in the world, and the way he looked when he laughed...

Logan loved him.

Trevor's uncertainty disappeared, and he laughed out loud.

"He loves me," he said, grinning from ear-to-ear, and then saying it again, just to hear it. "Bri, he *loves* me."

His phone beeped with another call, cutting off her response.

"What was that?" he asked.

"I'm... happy for you, Trev," she said, sounding like she meant it, even though her tone wasn't nearly as enthusiastic as his. Whatever, though. He was bubbling over with it, so he had no problem being happy enough for the both of them. "Just be careful with your heart, okay? I've never had to worry about you before because you never put your emotions out there before, but... just make sure you take care of you."

"Sure thing," he said, grinning. Was the other caller Logan? "Bri, I've gotta go."

"Okay, love you. And I really *am* happy for you, Trevor."

He was still smiling as he said a quick goodbye and accepted the other call without looking. "Miss me already, sugarpop?" he asked, figuring that with as awesome as he was feeling, it pretty much *had* to be Logan.

"Counting down the days until you're back, loverboy," came the rapid-fire reply.

"Grace," he said, still smiling. He *had* missed his friends from Chicago. Not enough to want to give up a future in New York with Logan, but it was still good to hear her voice. "What's up?"

"Just checking in," she said in a high-pitched voice that immediately alerted him to the fact that she was lying. "You'll be home on Valentine's Day, right?'

"*What*, Grace?"

"What do you mean *what*? It's a simple question."

He rolled his eyes, realizing he was blocking foot traffic and that, really, he wasn't all that interested in wandering the stalls by himself, after all. He'd need to try a little harder to convince Logan to come down here with him, but—his smile split his face again, making his cheeks ache—he was sure he'd be able to, because Logan *loved* him. He headed for the street, ready to practice his New York skills and flag down another taxi.

"Hiro has a ticket booked for me on Valentine's Day, yeah," he answered Grace, not bothering to add that he was hoping not to use it. She was being weird.

His phone vibrated, and he pulled it away from his ear long enough to see that she'd just sent him a link.

"What's that?" he asked.

"Look, maybe nothing?" she said, even though the way she made it into a question meant she thought it was Something. "But I'm just... I'm worried about you, babe. The way you and that Logan Carter look on TV, well, remember when we Googled him?"

"And found nothing bad?" he retaliated. "Grace, he's a good guy. He's amazing. Actually, I—"

"Stop right there," she said, cutting him off. "Just hear me out. Remember how the guy he started Rise with, that Ryan Grisham, had some comments on record about Logan being a real ass."

"*He's* the ass," Trevor snapped back, even though, honestly, Logan had never mentioned the guy and Trevor hadn't asked. Talking about exes? Um, no thanks.

"Well, I had a Google alert set in case both names came up in the same article—Ryan Grisham and Logan Carter— just for, you know, shits and giggles, and apparently he was giving an interview the other day in which he was asked about his relationship with Logan, and how it feels to see his ex—Logan—so much in love."

"Jesus, Grace. Old news, anyone? Wasn't that like, a hundred years ago?"

"Well, in my experience, people don't change. And you know what Ryan said when he was asked?"

"No, and I don't care," Trevor said, irritated that she'd gone and ruined his happy. "Grace, I've gotta go. Thanks for caring, but trust me, I have zero interest in hearing what someone who was dumb enough to let Logan go thinks about my love life."

"Trevor—"

"Nope, sorry. Look, I really do have to go. I'll talk to you soon, 'k?"

He ignored her squawk of protest as a bright yellow cab stopped in front of him, popping his phone in his pocket and settling into the backseat.

He drummed his fingers on the cracked upholstery as the cabbie swung back into traffic, telling himself he didn't care.

Did not.

It meant nothing.

He lasted three blocks.

With a sigh, Trevor pulled out his phone and opened the link, skimming through it for mention of Logan. There it was, in the interviewer's own words.

"Logan Carter, in love?"

Ryan Grisham laughs for a solid minute before sobering up and shaking his head.

"Look, that man doesn't do love. Anything and everything he does has one purpose, and one only: increasing the bottom line. He bleeds green, and business is the only thing that matters to him."

Ryan's eyes grow misty, and he pauses to wipe them, turning his head as if I might not see.

"I did love him," he continues softly. "But he sacrificed that for the success of Rise. Logan will always put business before anything else. And this... Tregan? Nah. Have you seen bLoved's numbers since Logan 'fell in love?' Really, I think they say it all. I just hope the kid doesn't fall for it, like I once did, because, unlike me, he's not going to walk away with a few billion in the bank, right?"

Ryan laughs, but there's no humor in it, and even though it should be hard to feel sorry for a billionaire, I do.

"No," Ryan says, answering his own question as he gives me a soulful gaze. "Anyone who falls for Logan's act is only going to walk away with a broken heart."

Trevor narrowed his eyes. What a dick. Both Ryan Grisham, and whoever the reporter was who'd been stupid enough to buy his sob story. Sure, Logan was good at business, but this Ryan was probably just bitter because, after buying Logan out back in the day, apparently the loss of Logan's expertise had sent Rise into a few rocky years that had taken a serious chunk out of those billions.

Trevor had always gotten a bad vibe from the guy's smarmy, smiling face.

He stabbed at his phone's off button, staring out the window blankly.

Ryan Grisham didn't know what he was talking about.

Logan may have *said* that he planned on keeping it just business between the two of them, but he clearly hadn't.

Logan just wasn't that good of an actor.

Logan loved him.

It was *real*.

But maybe it would be best to wait and talk to him about it until after the contract was up... after Valentine's Day. When Logan didn't need Trevor anymore, in a business sense, it would be damn clear to Ryan Fucking Grisham and anyone else who doubted it that Logan wanted Trevor for himself, not just for what he could do for bLoved's bottom line.

Chapter 18

LOGAN

S TANDING IN FRONT OF THE BATHROOM'S VANITY MIRROR, naked except for the towel around his waist, Trevor looked—in Logan's completely unbiased opinion—amazing. His hair was wet from the shower and beads of water still clung to his skin. If he hadn't been so adamant about their reservations, Logan would have given in and kissed him.

Instead, he leaned back against the counter, content to watch.

"We're going to be late," Trevor said, shooting Logan a look that made him want to laugh. *Logan* was ready. Trevor stretched his head to the side and applied shaving lather to his skin, giving a dramatic sigh. "Why does being stunning take so much time?"

Logan's lips twitched despite himself, but still, just to be clear: "It doesn't have to. You look incredible even when you don't shave."

"But I look *better* with smooth skin," Trevor shot back, grinning. "And I know you like it, baby. I've noticed how you stroke my face when I'm fresh from a shave."

"Mmmm," Logan offered noncommittally.

He did, but really, he'd take Trevor any way he could get him. Besides, *he* knew for a fact that *Trevor* liked it when Logan stroked his face. Win-win. Trevor preened like a cat, and Logan... he shifted, adjusting himself discreetly. Damn, would he ever not get turned on by each and every little thing Trevor did?

He was very much hoping that, after tonight, he'd get a chance to find out.

The closer Valentine's Day had gotten, the more often he'd caught Trevor's normal cheer slipping. Logan could relate, but tonight, their last night together unless Trevor said yes to staying—to being Logan's boyfriend for real—he was determined that they'd both have a good time.

He glanced around his bathroom—a space he'd always considered spacious. It was amazing, though, how much room the toiletries Trevor had amassed took up. They clogged the shower bar, and the shelves, and filled three full drawers in the vanity. And, even though the truth was that Logan liked it best when Trevor smelled of *his* body wash and cologne, the sight of them there made him happy.

Trevor had to stay.

Logan wasn't sure what he'd do if he lost him.

He caught Trevor giving him an odd look in the mirror, and pushed his worries aside, smiling at the man he loved. "Where are we going tonight again?"

"It's called Blackout," Trevor reminded him, rinsing his hands now that he was finished lathering his face. With care, he ran his razor in a straight line along his neck and under his chin, his eyes sparkling as they met Logan's in the mirror. "The idea is, your senses are amplified when one of your senses is taken away, right? So what they do is deprive you of your sight. The restaurant is pitch black on the inside, and the waiters are all visually impaired, so they're skilled at navigating through any terrain. They don't tell you what you're eating, either. Then, when you eat it, your taste is stronger than it was before and it leads to an incredible culinary experience."

"But what if it's something you don't like?" Logan asked with a wry grin. "Does it taste worse than usual?"

"It *won't* be bad," Trevor insisted. He ran the razor over a new section. "Blackout is highly acclaimed. I don't think they could make something bad, even if they made a dish out of all the things I can't stand. Besides, they tell you what's on the menu so you can make an informed decision."

A restaurant like Blackout would never have been on

Logan's radar. Dining at a place so untraditional didn't speak to his sensibilities, but with Trevor's sense of adventure and his thirst for new experiences, Logan was eager to go. Navigating through the dark to eat their meal, fumbling with food, laughing together...

He grinned, already eager to make yet another unforgettable memory with Trevor. Even if the food was awful, Logan had no doubt that he'd enjoy himself.

Trevor finished shaving, rinsed his razor clean, and toweled off the lather that remained on his skin. He turned his jaw this way and that, examining himself in the mirror while Logan watched.

Could this be his every day? There was a simple joy in watching Trevor get ready for their night out. In sharing his home and his bed and his *life*. Trevor seemed to like it, too, and the more time they'd spent together, the more Logan's doubts had quieted. It was impossible to imagine *not* having Trevor around... not sharing these moments with him. Logan refused to let himself believe that Trevor might not feel it, too.

"You'll like it, baby," Trevor said to him now, and for a moment, Logan thought he was referring to the future Logan was hoping to make with him. Trevor winked. "There's at least one boring menu choice, so if you're not up for trying mango chutney or duck confit, you're not going to go hungry. I think there's some roast with potatoes on the menu. I glanced at it before making reservations."

"I'm not worried," Logan said, meaning it.

He trusted Trevor's judgment. Every time Trevor pushed him out of his comfort zone, Logan's life got a little bit better. And, he liked to think, Trevor felt free to venture that much further, knowing he had Logan to lean on.

Trevor pulled his towel away and slung it over the bar on the shower door, and Logan grinned and reached for him.

"So, if the place is pitch black, does that mean you can go naked? Because as stylish as you are, I like what I see."

"Hah," Trevor said, rolling his eyes and swatting at Logan's hands, even though he grinned back. "I came to New York to enjoy the city, not to get arrested, baby. I'll rock all the Emperor's New Clothes fashion you want in the penthouse, but outside, you're getting actual *style*."

Trevor had to walk past him to reach the clothes he'd hung on the back of the bathroom door, and, as he went by, Logan snaked an arm around his waist and pulled him close. Trevor gave a sexy little squeak, laughing as he staggered, then braced himself against Logan's body, not making much of a protest at all as Logan's hand explored the dip of his back, then moved lower to cup Trevor's ass.

"Logan," he mumbled, pressing himself closer for a second and wrapping his arms around Logan's neck. "Stop. I actually *want* to go out to dinner tonight."

"So you're saying that I have to take you out before I can get in your pants?" Logan asked, leaning down to press a kiss against the side of his neck, just below his ear.

Trevor melted against him for a split-second, then

squirmed out of his grip and arched a defiant eyebrow, laughing. "*You* don't have to take me anywhere. We're going out *together*. I don't want this to be just another business expense. I've got some savings of my own, thank you very much. Why don't I take *you* out this time?"

The request touched Logan. He'd heard a frisson of tension in Trevor's voice at the words "business expense," and Logan understood it completely. As much as he hated the idea that Trevor might feel hurt by the same uncertainty about their relationship status that Logan had struggled with, it gave him hope. If he was reading Trevor right—and God help him, he wasn't sure how he'd bear it if he was wrong—Trevor wanted more out of their relationship, too.

"Hmmm?" Trevor prompted him, arching a brow. Still completely naked and tempting as hell. "Dinner tonight... my treat. Okay?"

Logan pulled Trevor back into his arms, smiling down at him. "Okay, but I hope that doesn't mean you're not going to let me buy you something pretty."

Trevor blushed, shaking his head. "You don't have to spoil me to get me to..." He let his voice trail off, clearing his throat as he pulled away from Logan completely. "Why don't we focus on getting ready to go out? I want to talk about this after we've eaten, and when I'm not naked."

Logan leaned back against the counter again, not arguing. They had the whole night together, and—as Trevor had teased him about on their first night together—he trusted that good things would come from a little patience.

"Why are you smiling?" Trevor asked, unhooking his shirt from its hanger and threading his arm through one of the sleeves. As he did, Logan's phone rang.

"You," Logan answered, because, really, that was all the reason he needed. He glanced down at his phone. "It's Frank."

"Put it on speakerphone," Trevor said, grinning as he continued dressing.

Lately, all Frank's news had been fantastic. bLoved's membership and revenue numbers had both skyrocketed over the last six weeks, and the success of the campaign had exceeded even Frank's most optimistic projections.

"Hi, Frank," Logan answered the call, smiling as he hit the speaker button and set the phone on the counter. Trevor joined him there, ducking down to reach the drawers below the sink as he rifled through Logan's cologne collection.

"Logan," Frank's voice boomed out of the speaker enthusiastically. "Glad I caught you. I know your final campaign appearance tomorrow is pretty early, so I took a chance that you wouldn't have called it a night yet."

"Me, quit work early?" Logan joked, earning a hearty laugh from Frank.

In the past, managing the various businesses he had his fingers in had been a 24/7 pursuit, and Frank knew it. The truth was, though, that ever since Trevor had come with Logan to New York, he *had* been working less. Case in point, tonight. His dinner with Trevor was definitely not about business. For the first time in years, Logan had a life... and if he was lucky, after tonight, that life was going to include Trevor for the long-term.

"I know, I know," Frank said, still laughing. "Which is why I thought you might want to hear *this*: bLoved is getting *massive* amounts of new members. I just totaled the figures for the first time since the current campaign started, and we're talking tremendous increases. The only thing it can be attributed to is your publicity efforts. I'm floored."

This wasn't news, but as Trevor straightened up, a bottle of cologne in his hand, the look of glee on his face made it worth hearing again, as far as Logan was concerned. Logan was glad for bLoved's success, too, of course, but honestly, knowing how happy it made Trevor—not to mention what the success would mean for Kelly—meant far more to him than adding a few more zeroes to his wealth.

"That's great, Frank," Logan said, running a hand down Trevor's back just because he could. "Was there anything else?"

"Yes," Frank said, his voice going from gushing to all-business in a heartbeat. "We need to keep this momentum going, Logan. I can't reach Kelly, but if I can get your okay, I'm going to set the ball in motion tomorrow."

"For what?" Logan asked, handing Trevor the hair gel without being asked as soon as Trevor finished applying his cologne. Trevor winked at him, blowing him a kiss.

"I want to launch a new campaign after this one ends," Frank said. "I know Trevor's supposed to head back to

Chicago tomorrow, but we need to get him to agree to another publicity appearance... hopefully as early as next week."

"I don't think that will be a problem," Logan said, grinning at Trevor in the mirror.

"Perfect. He's served his purpose, and now we need to schedule a big breakup, and we need to make sure it's somewhere public. Very high profile, so it gets some coverage. We're talking screaming, maybe some tears, some... I don't know what. Profanity? That's always good. Something *really* emotional, which I'm guessing Trevor will handle like a pro, since he's done such an Oscar-worthy performance with the being-in-love job."

"What?" Logan asked, forcing the word out past his frozen lips.

Frank had caught him totally off-guard. What was he *talking* about? A *breakup*?

Hell no.

Beside him, Trevor had gone still, too. He was holding the hair gel in one hand, and as he met Logan's eyes in the mirror, Logan saw that his hand was trembling.

"I know, I know. It seems counterintuitive," Frank said, laughing.

Laughing? Next to Logan, Trevor set the gel down on the counter slowly, and the look on his face made Logan want to kill Frank.

"Sure, we're selling love, Logan, but listen," Frank's voice boomed out of the speaker, grating and raw in the total silence of the bathroom. "What we want are *repeat* customers. Kelly's algorithms are great for making these love matches, but let's face it, when you've got two people involved, sometimes love just goes wrong. That's life. But that doesn't mean that bLoved can't help find our members someone *else*."

"No," Logan said. Or tried to. His mouth was dry, and he wasn't sure if the word had made it past his lips. He didn't want someone else, he wanted *Trevor*.

"Let's face it, Logan," Frank said, seeming not to have heard him. "The current business model means that every time bLoved works, we lose two members. We've got to have more to offer them."

"No, Frank," Logan said more forcefully. "The current business model isn't about losing members, it's about delivering on bLoved's promise. And that promise is love, not loss."

"Loss is part of life," Frank said dismissively. "The important thing is that our members know we can always find someone to replace the guy who broke their heart, right? I've already been reaching out to a few other public figures for our next campaign. The plan is, after you break up with Trevor, you'll go into mourning for a few weeks— eh, maybe a month, tops, but we really need to get you back in the public eye quickly—and then, once you're done grieving over your heartache, you'll bounce back by dating someone who's already famous, so we can leverage their publicity, too. Not to mention we'll make sure that your next Mr. Right is hotter. Not all of our target market wants to date the ones like Trevor, you know, so flamboyant? But I'm working on lining up someone with a much higher cross-appeal, based on the preferences our members list in their profiles."

Trevor went pale, and Logan's blood boiled. He pressed his lips together, knowing if he said something to Frank before cooling down, it might not be reversible.

"I've been talking with Tallon Croft's manager," Frank rattled on, oblivious. "You know, the underwear model? He's on board to date you publicly. Wes Jenkins, the football player who came out as gay last year, is down to do it, too. I tried to get Ash Ashby on board, but his people said he's not interested in putting things on hold with his fiancé."

"*Jesus*, Frank," Logan said explosively. "This is not going to happen."

"Sure it is. Leave it to me, it's almost a done deal," Frank shot back, laughing. "And it's going to be perfect, Logan. We're talking exponential growth. You're all over the media now. Hell, people are responding to you more than they ever did to Kelly and his poor-me-I've-got-nobody-to-love angst. Trust me, this is the smartest business decision you'll ever make, and—" he barked out another laugh, then continued, "—who would have thought I'd be hitting *you* up for this role? You surprised me, Logan, but I'm more than happy to say you were right. Trevor really brought it out of you. I would've bought your performance myself—hook, line, and sinker—if I hadn't known you were just hamming it up for the bottom line."

Logan reached for Trevor, who was trembling all over now, but Trevor jerked away, sending an icy shaft through Logan's heart.

"Frank, let me be clear," Logan said, clenching his jaw so hard that he could barely get the words out. He took a breath, searching for a way to get through to the man when all he wanted to do was rip his throat out for putting that look on Trevor's face. "I will *only* do this with Trevor. You're right when you said he brought it out of me. You didn't think he could do it, but he's the one you have to thank for our numbers. He made this whole campaign work, and I'm not willing to work with anyone else, because—"

"Look, I'll admit the kid is good," Frank said, cutting him off before he could explain that it was because Logan had fallen in love with Trevor, not because of some PR magic. "But don't worry about hurting his feelings. You won't. He knew what he was getting himself into. Just buy him something pretty and move on. It's not like he's expecting anything more than the paltry amount we signed him on for, and from the looks of things, he's had a ball playing house with you along the way. Toss him a bonus and wrap it up, and let's move on to someone who's going to help us take things to the next level."

"Buy me something pretty?" Trevor whispered, swallowing hard as he finally met Logan's eyes in the mirror. Frank's words were an ugly echo of the happy banter that

Logan and Trevor had exchanged just before the call, and hearing them now, repeated in a broken tone that Logan had never heard from Trevor before, cut him to the core.

Frank was hurting Trevor, and Logan wasn't going to stand for it.

"You still there, Logan? Just give me a heads up on whether to go with Tallon Croft or Wes Jenkins, and I'll set things in motion."

Trevor's eyes welled up, and he rushed out of the bathroom, slamming the door behind him. Logan snatched his phone up and followed.

"Neither, Frank," he hissed, seething as he stabbed the button to take it off speakerphone. Frank's words had already done enough damage. "Trevor is the only one I want, do you understand? The *only* one."

He made it out of the bathroom just as the bedroom door slammed shut across the room. From the other side of it, he heard Trevor's rapid footfalls bolting toward the front of the penthouse.

"Trevor is as expendable as any of the temporary IT workers you and Kelly hired to get the algorithms up to snuff," Frank said, his exasperated voice sounding tinny without the speakerphone as Logan dashed across the room, his heart pounding. "*What* is your problem, Logan? Sure, the two of you have great chemistry, but that's really no reason to keep him on. You'll find someone else you have chemistry with. That's the whole point of the campaign."

Except it wasn't a campaign. Not anymore. Trevor had

opened up Logan's heart, making it his own, and Logan didn't want anyone else. Love had found Logan at last. He was sick of being lonely, and of mourning his failure with Ryan—a man who had never been worth his time—and a love that, *finally*, Logan understood, had never been true.

Trevor had healed his heart. Made him whole. There was no going back from that. The relationship they shared wasn't fake. Despite Frank's praise, Logan simply wasn't that good of an actor. He and Trevor hadn't "fooled" anybody; they'd simply let the world see the miracle that they'd found in each other.

Love.

Logan wrenched open the bedroom door, but the hallway was already empty.

From the phone he still clutched in his hand: "Logan?"

Logan jerked it up to his ear again. "I'm not doing another fake-dating campaign, Frank," he growled. "Not with some football player, not some hot underwear model, not even a prince. Trevor is *it* for me. *Fuck* your campaign."

The mechanical whir of the elevator doors parting echoed through the penthouse, and Logan's heart shot up into his throat. He raced down the hall toward the living room, but it was too late. The elevator doors were already closed, and Trevor's shoes and coat were gone.

"*Shit!* God *damm*it!"

"Logan?" Frank asked. "What's—"

Logan cut the call off without apology and shoved the phone in his pocket as he jammed on the button for the elevator. But it was on its way down, carrying Trevor away, and wouldn't return until he was already long gone.

There were a set of emergency stairs leading to an exit-only door below, and for a crazed second, Logan whirled around and headed for it. But the door attached to Logan's penthouse was alarmed, and if he went through it, half of New York's emergency responders would arrive before he could clear the halfway point.

That would only slow him up more.

What the hell was he going to do?

He jammed on the elevator button until his thumb hurt, then stalked away from it like a caged animal. When his phone beeped a moment later, a shot of adrenaline surged through him and he scrambled to pull it from his pocket.

It was a text message from Trevor.

> *Don't worry, I know what my job is. I'll be at the studio by 8:00 a.m. to finish out my contract, and then we're done.*

Logan swallowed and stared at the message, reading it over and over to look for an in. What was he supposed to say to that? How was he supposed to make a convincing apology after all the damage Frank's words had done? And, most importantly, why the hell hadn't he told Trevor he loved him the moment he'd first realized it?

Well, technically, he *had*... but the fucking campaign had made the words both too easy to say, and too hard to believe in.

For both of them.

Logan's finger hovered over the keypad as he wracked his brain for something that would bring Trevor back to him. Would Trevor believe him if he told him he loved him *now*, after hearing Frank crow about how well Logan had faked it to boost the business?

His phone beeped again.

> *And you don't need to buy me anything "pretty," Logan. Frank was right. I'm not expecting anything more than what we agreed on.*

Trevor was hurting, and it killed Logan. In desperation, he texted him back.

> *Frank is an ass. Call me, please. I need to know that you're ok.*

Logan swallowed, waiting for a response. The elevator doors swished open, but where would he go now? Trevor was already gone. Logan tapped out another text.

> *Where are you, Trevor? Please come home.*

He had no idea where Trevor had run off to, and he couldn't stand the thought of Trevor out there, alone, with his heart broken. He stared at his silent phone without blinking until his eyes started to water, willing Trevor to reply.

But he didn't.

Chapter 19

TREVOR

New York was beautiful at night, but the bright lights and vibrant energy of the city that had enchanted Trevor since day one now felt like a slap in the face. Isolating, as though the pulsing life of the city that he'd fallen in love with didn't give one single shit that his heart was broken.

He's served his purpose... we'll make sure that your next Mr. Right is hotter... I would've bought your performance myself, Logan—hook, line, and sinker—if I hadn't known you were just hamming it up for the bottom line...

Snippets of Frank's conversation replayed in his mind, stabbing through it like vicious little daggers. After all that had happened between him and Logan, every sign he was so sure he'd seen that Logan had really loved him, Trevor had been wrong.

But it hadn't been *Frank's* words that had hurt the most, it had been Logan's.

Trevor had been so quick to dismiss Ryan Grisham's take on whether or not Logan loved him when he'd read that stupid fucking article Grace had sent him a couple of weeks ago, but it turned out, Logan's former partner had been right about him all along.

Out on the street, Trevor swiped at his phone, since apparently he wasn't already in enough pain, and re-read the last line:

> *"Anyone who falls for Logan's act is only going to walk away with a broken heart."*

He couldn't stand it. He shot off a text to Logan, and then another, then flagged down a taxi, giving the driver the only address he could think of. Sinking down into the back seat, he let New York pass him by, wishing he could turn off his mind.

He swiped at his eyes, letting his head flop back onto the back of the seat. The bitch of it was, Logan had never lied to him. Logan was *not* a bad guy. They'd had fun, and there was no doubt that Logan liked him. It was Trevor who'd lost sight of reality. Who'd let himself believe in something he'd never even wanted before.

It was Trevor who'd fallen in love, and now it was

Trevor who'd had his heart broken.

From time to time, Trevor had regretted ending things with one of his flings, but he'd never actually let himself get attached to the guys he'd hooked up with in the past. He'd never felt like *this*, like he'd been on top of the world and then, with no warning whatsoever, been shattered into a million pieces, every one of which was jagged and painful and broken beyond repair.

Trevor's phone buzzed for what must have been the dozenth time since he'd left Parker Tower. He switched it off. For good measure, he removed the battery and kept them in separate pockets. He knew himself too well—if he left the phone in one piece, he'd check it before he had time to talk himself out of it. And, God help him and his self-respect, even knowing Logan's primary interest in him was business, he was so far gone for the man that he'd go back.

He wasn't proud of it, but even now, even hurting, he wanted nothing more than to be in Logan's arms.

"We're here," the cabbie said, pulling up to the curb.

Trevor lifted his head, slid his credit card through the reader on the back of the seat, and exited the taxi. He was eight hundred miles from home, but he wasn't alone. There was still someone he could turn to.

With a dull sigh, he approached the building, nodding at the doorman and praying he remembered the right con-do number. As soon as he knocked on the door, he heard a familiar, rapid scurrying from the other side. The click of tiny claws against wood and a few huffed barks of excitement told him he was in the right place, and his lips lifted the tiniest bit at the sound.

"Trevor?" Ash asked, his eyes widening in surprise when he pulled open the door. He'd scooped up his and Elliott's little rescue dog, Donner, before answering, and had the little guy tucked against his chest, tail wagging and tongue lolling. "What are you doing here?"

Trevor opened his mouth, but instead of answering—to his utter embarrassment—his throat closed and tears rushed into his eyes. He turned away, sniffling and running his arm beneath his eyes, and Ash pulled him inside.

"Are you hurt?" Ash asked urgently, closing the door behind him and looking Trevor over carefully. "Did someone try to force themselves on you? Should I call the police?"

"No." Trevor tried to smile, but he could tell by the look on Ash's face that he was failing. "I'm sorry. I didn't have anywhere else to go, and I knew you were in town because Elliott was texting me about it, and..."

"Trevor, what's wrong?" Ash asked soberly, his serious demeanor at odds with Donner's ongoing excitement as the little dog squirmed in the football-hold Ash held him in.

"I... I..." Trevor shook his head, not wanting to cry again. "I just need someplace to stay."

"Of course," Ash said, nodding.

Trevor swallowed as Ash waited patiently for more of an explanation, and Trevor noted that Ash was well-dressed, as though he were about to head to a cocktail party. The suit jacket he wore was designer—Trevor recognized it right away. Paired with a white dress shirt and a blue patterned tie, he was exceedingly handsome.

Ash glanced back over his shoulder, down the hall, and Trevor followed his gaze.

"Shit," Trevor said, feeling like an ass. He backed up, only to find himself hitting the door. At the end of the hall, sitting on their kitchen table, Elliott was dressed in the same style as Ash. His shirt hung open, and his fly was undone. Behind him were empty boxes of Chinese take-out. When their eyes met, Elliott squeaked and hurried to button his pants.

"You guys are... busy," Trevor mumbled. "I'm sorry. I'll go."

"No." Ash grabbed Trevor's arm and held him in place. "I know that something's wrong with you, and if you need a place to stay, I want it to be here. I know Elliott feels the same way."

With his fly finally done up, Elliott hopped off the table and made his way down the hall as he buttoned his shirt. A red mark had started to darken on his neck, and Trevor could tell it would turn into a bruise before long. Trevor's hand drifted up to his collarbone, and another hot prick of tears started behind his eyes as the sight reminded him of Logan.

The man did like to mark him.

He'd been so possessive. So... loving.

Trevor drew in a shuddering breath, forcing the thought away. It hurt too much.

"Ash is right," Elliott said as he walked up. "If you're here, Trevor, it's for a reason. Did something happen with Logan?"

Ash set Donner down, and Donner took it as his chance to skitter around Trevor's legs, nosing his calves and stepping on his feet.

Trevor choked out a sob and shook his head. "No. I-I'm just being a b-baby about it, and now I've r-ruined your night."

"Trevor," Elliott whispered. He pushed past Ash and swept Trevor tenderly into his arms. "No. Stop. Come sit down with me in the living room, okay? You didn't ruin anything. I'm so thankful you consider me a good enough friend that you'd come here after something happened."

"Did *he* hurt you?" Ash demanded, his brows lowering. "If that fuckhead did something to you, I'll kick his ass and destroy his company from the ground up."

Trevor buried his face into Elliott's shoulder and hugged him back tightly, shaking his head. Fucking heartache. When had *Trevor* ever been at a loss for words? But now he couldn't seem to get any out, at least, not without an accompanying waterfall of tears.

"Ash, baby, maybe just let Trevor get it out before you vow to destroy Logan, okay?" Elliott ran a hand comfortingly through Trevor's hair, then pulled back and guided him down the hall and into the living room. Trevor allowed himself to be led—his knees felt like they'd give out if he walked on his own, and he was beyond thankful to be able to put himself into the hands of a friend.

Elliott made sure that Trevor was settled and comfortable on the couch before sitting down beside him. He curled his legs up beneath him and faced Trevor as Trevor fought back more tears—would they ever end? He really *was* being a baby,—and then, after waiting patiently for a long moment, Elliott finally asked, "You ready to share what's going on, honey?"

Trevor shook his head no, then blurted out anyway: "I'm in l-love with Logan."

Elliott's eyebrows shot up, and behind him, Ash frowned. Trevor ran the back of his hand beneath his eyes to wipe away a fresh onset of tears.

"Tonight, um, we were getting ready to go out to dinner, and he got a call from bLoved's marketing guy," Trevor said, his stomach clenching at the memory.

...Trevor's served his purpose... served his purpose... served his purpose...

Trevor drew in a shuddering breath, and went on. "Frank wanted to congratulate Logan on how well the campaign was going. He told him to break up with me so he could fake-date some underwear model instead, and Logan..."

"What the *fuck*?" Ash spat, looking pissed. "He's dropping you for an *underwear* model?"

Trevor swallowed. Logan hadn't said yes.

But he also hadn't said no.

Well, okay, he had said no. But not... *fuck* no. Not, *hell* no. Not, "No, Frank, I'm in love with Trevor you small-dicked prick, of course I don't want to date someone hotter and more famous."

Nope. Logan had just let Frank go on and on and *on*, and then, instead of setting Frank straight on the fact that Trevor wasn't Logan's *fake* boyfriend anymore, Logan's response had confirmed Trevor's worst fears.

You're right, Frank... Trevor brought it out of me... Trevor's the one you have to thank for our numbers... Trevor made this whole campaign work...

Elliott remained silent and contemplative, but Ash was a different story. He scowled and crossed his arms, pacing in front of the couch.

"Does Logan know how you feel about him?" Ash asked. "Because I'm going to—"

"No," Trevor said, cutting him off. He shook his head. It wasn't Logan's fault. "It's my mistake. He doesn't know. We were supposed to be faking it, but it was so good. It felt real, and I... I guess I started wanting more."

"You deserve more," Elliott said loyally, which only made Trevor's eyes well up again.

It had *felt* like more. "It was just business to Logan," Trevor said, mostly to remind himself. Whatever he'd felt, he had to get over it. It was hard to believe that the Logan he knew now—*thought* he'd known—was the same man who used to present such a cold face to the world. Being with him, seeing him smile and making him laugh, teasing him and oh, God, the sex... it hadn't felt like business at all. Trevor swallowed, adding, "Well, not *just* business. We had fun, too, but... I'm just an idiot for forgetting what our deal was."

"Logan Carter? Fun?" Ash muttered, snorting in derision.

"You're *not* an idiot, Trevor," Elliott said, ignoring his fiancé's commentary. He patted Trevor's knee. "Emotions are complicated, and navigating new relationships can be scary. It's okay to feel hurt."

Ash's phone went off, the jingle muffled by Ash's pocket. He yanked it out, glanced down at the screen, then silenced it and put it away again.

"I only feel hurt *because* I'm an idiot," Trevor argued, closing his eyes and letting his head fall back. "Logan never said—"

Ash's phone rang again, and he pulled it out again, frowning.

"Who is it?" Elliott asked, mirroring his man's frown.

Ash shrugged, silencing it again. It rang again immediately. "What the hell?" he said. "Must be a wrong number, 'cause this is my private line, but it sounds like they're not going to give up."

He swiped to answer, his face going from vaguely irritated to pissed-the-fuck-off after he did so. "It's Logan," he said, covering the mouthpiece. "How did he get this number?"

Trevor's stomach clenched. How had Logan known where he'd be?

"Ash's number is unlisted," Elliott whispered to him as Ash listened to whatever Logan was saying on the line, responding with clipped, one-word answers as he watched Elliott and Trevor for direction. "No one would be able to find it through a search. Logan would have had to make a lot of calls to find someone willing to share it. Do you want to talk to him, honey?"

"No," Trevor said, sinking back and resting his head on Elliott's lap. Elliott ran his fingers through Trevor's hair. "I... can't."

He still didn't trust himself to go running back if Logan asked him to come home, or—worse—to *ask*, if Logan didn't.

"Tell Logan that Trevor's not here," Elliott whispered at Ash. "And that you don't know where he is."

Ash nodded at Elliott in acknowledgment. His responses to whatever Logan was saying came out in a tone laced with snark, and he continued to glower as he paced and talked.

"We *are* in town... mmm, nope... Oh, really?... No, Logan, we haven't heard from him at all... I didn't know anything had happened..."

Trevor watched from Elliott's lap as Ash wandered the

living room, going silent as he listened to something. The tender affection of Elliott's fingers moving through his damp, slightly-frozen hair was the balm his soul needed to start to calm down. As stupid as it was, knowing Logan was checking up on him helped, too.

Logan's primary interest in Trevor may have been in what he could do for bLoved, but, on some level at least, Logan obviously cared about him. Trevor blinked away tears, staring blindly at Ash. The fabric of his suit jacket hung perfectly; someone had obviously tailored it with care. When Trevor went back to Chicago, would that be his life again? Working at Ashby's full-time, tailoring on the side... oh, God. He didn't think he could bear it if Logan continued to come in for his monthly fittings.

If Logan expected them to go back to the way they'd been before.

Trevor squeezed his eyes closed.

"No, I don't think he knows anyone else in the city," he heard Ash say after a long silence. Then, "I'm not sure where he would go, either... we haven't talked to him all that much since he came to New York, he's been too busy with *you*... don't *you* know where he'd go? You're supposed to be his *boyfriend*, and— oh. Logan, I... uh-huh.... Okay... listen, I'm not going to... "

The venom in Ash's voice faded and Trevor opened his eyes again to see that Ash's face had softened as he nodded along with whatever Logan was saying. Trevor could hear the achingly familiar deep tones of Logan's voice coming from Ash's phone, too faintly to make out the words. He sighed, wishing he could just stop himself from caring.

"Okay, listen," Ash said forcefully, breaking in on whatever Logan was saying. "You don't need to do that. He's not going to do something stupid. I promise... no... *No*, Logan... He's here with me and Elliott, okay?"

Trevor shot upright. "Judas!"

Ash took the phone away from his ear and covered the receiver with his hand, looking sheepish. "He's almost in tears, Trevor, what am I supposed to do? The guy's totally torn up. If I were in his shoes, and it was Elliott who was missing, I'd just... I'd want to know that he's safe. It doesn't mean you need to talk to him."

"Do you want to?" Elliott asked quietly.

Yes. No. Trevor wasn't sure. He felt beat up inside.

"You need a little time," Elliott said decisively when Trevor didn't answer. He turned to Ash, and Ash nodded. He'd heard. He was still responding with one-word answers to Logan, but now they sounded sympathetic, rather than combative. After a moment, he left the room—phone still pressed to his ear—and barricaded himself in the bathroom.

Trevor stared after him, his heart beating a slow rhythm that felt heavy and dull in his chest. Why was Logan going through all the trouble of tracking Trevor down if he didn't love him? Was Trevor's contribution to the business really valuable enough that he'd go to the trouble of getting Ash's private number just to check in on him? Was it just a sense of responsibility, since he'd brought Trevor to New York?

No. Ash had said Logan had been close to tears. Trevor couldn't picture it, and couldn't bear to get his hopes up when his heart still felt so raw. He'd promised to fulfill his contract—he squeezed his eyes closed tightly to stop the damn leaking—and he *would* be at the television studio in the morning as promised. But until then... he wasn't in any shape to try and figure it out.

Trevor was so focused on staring at the distant bathroom door that he didn't notice when Elliott had left the couch. It wasn't until Elliott laid his hands on either side of Trevor's face and turned Trevor's head to face him that Trevor even realized he'd moved.

"Don't worry," Elliott said. "Ash isn't going to let Logan come here, so you'll have all the time you need to detox tonight. Trust me, Ash may have gone soft for a minute, but you can trust him. He cares about you."

Trevor nodded. He and Ash had become friends on their own, separate from his relationship with Elliott, and now that Elliott—one of Trevor's *best* friends—was engaged to Ash, that friendship had only strengthened. Knowing he could count on both Elliott and Ash had been the reason he'd come.

Elliott smiled at him, tugging him up from the couch. "Tonight, let's just curl up in bed, eat ice cream, and watch movies until we pass out, okay? I'll tell Ash to sleep on the couch."

"You really don't need to do that," Trevor said, remembering what he'd walked in on. "I'm okay."

"You are *not* okay." Elliott shook his head. "Tonight, you need ice cream, a friend, and some time to think. Tomorrow morning, when your head is clear, is soon enough to worry about talking to your man, okay?"

Trevor nodded, and followed Elliott into the kitchen, and truly, sincerely, appreciated his friend's caring.

But, still, he had to fight not to start crying a-fuck-ing-*gain*... because that was the thing, wasn't it? Logan *wasn't* his man. And even if, in the morning, Logan miraculously said he wanted Trevor back—wanted to make it *real*—a small, bitter, ugly part of Trevor's heart that he wasn't proud of would always wonder if he'd only done so to keep bLoved's numbers up.

But Trevor, fool that he was, was so damn in love with Logan, that he knew he'd say yes, anyway.

Which... sucked.

Chapter 20

LOGAN

Logan's eyes burned from lack of sleep. He rubbed at one of them, stifled a yawn, and began to slowly button his shirt. At the doorway to his bedroom stood Hiro, back turned. He tapped his foot impatiently.

"We're going to be late, Logan," Hiro chided. "I wasn't expecting a disaster this morning. I haven't even had time for my second coffee yet."

"I'll be ready when I'm ready," Logan insisted. He examined himself in the full-length mirror hanging near the closet. A royal blue tie Trevor had picked out for him hung, undone, around his neck. The color brought out his eyes, but did nothing to hide the bags beneath them.

Last night had been a disaster. His relief at knowing Trevor was okay had morphed into anger when Ash had refused to let Logan come get him, but he'd finally calmed down enough to trust Ash that it was for the best. Something he'd only been able to do since he'd had Trevor's promise to be at the studio this morning.

Logan had ended up talking with Ash for over an hour, uncharacteristically spilling his feelings out in an unstoppable tide to a total stranger. Logan would have thought that he'd regret it, but it had been... nice. There was no one else Logan could have talked to, but Ash both cared about Trevor, and had also been able to relate once Logan had admitted the depth of his feelings for Trevor.

Ash was just as in love with Elliott as Logan was with Trevor, and he'd acted as not just a confidante, but also an unexpected ally, promising to see to it that Trevor *did* show up at the studio in the morning. After the call had ended, Logan had spent the rest of the night thinking things through and making some calls. Sleep had been less important than making sure that when he finally had a chance to talk to Trevor at the studio, he'd be able to win him back.

And, even more importantly in Logan's mind, erase the hurt that he'd seen on Trevor's face during Frank's disastrous phone call.

"Something happened to you last night," Hiro said, leaning against the doorjamb.

Logan gave a humorless laugh at the massive understatement.

Hiro waited for a moment, but when Logan didn't offer any details, he pushed a little, his voice compassionate. "Did you not sleep? You're never this sluggish."

"No, but I'll be fine. We won't be late."

Hiro sighed, tapping his watch. "Logan..."

"I'm not leaving until I hear back from Kelly, Hiro."

He wasn't going to be able to salvage things with Trevor until he got in touch with his business partner, and with Kelly still in an undisclosed location with his bodyguard, the best Logan had been able to do was leave a series of messages for him.

"Kelly?" Hiro asked, sounding surprised. "Is he back? Have they caught the person who was threatening him?"

"No," Logan said, frowning.

The last update he'd received had been... disturbing. The police had apparently identified the man, but not before he'd gone off the radar. Logan hoped that the bodyguard entrusted with Kelly's care was as good as the police officer who'd recommended him had insisted he was. And that Kelly—headstrong and too mouthy for his own good at times—didn't do anything stupid to jeopardize his own safety.

"I need to speak to Kelly on a business matter before we do the show, Hiro. That's nonnegotiable. I'm waiting for his call now."

"Hmmm," Hiro said, restricting his commentary to that meaning-laden sound. After a moment, he asked, "And where is Trevor this morning?"

Logan couldn't help a glance at Trevor's empty side of the bed. The night had been long. Empty. Worse, in many ways, than the devastation he'd felt so many years ago when he'd discovered Ryan's infidelity. Back then, it had simply hurt, but without Trevor's warmth—not just of his body in the bed that was really too big for just one man, but also of his unquenchable spirit—Logan wasn't complete.

In the span of six short weeks, Trevor had turned his life around.

Logan couldn't recall the last time he'd laughed and actually meant it before that January. He'd had no reason to smile, and had grown out of the habit. Now, his only reason had left, and he felt the loss like a missing limb.

Logan finished buttoning his shirt and knotted his tie while Hiro patiently waited for an answer. He left the knot lower than usual, knowing that if Trevor were there, he would have adjusted it. Finally, he met Hiro's eyes in the mirror.

"Trevor will be at the studio," he said, knowing Hiro could see the truth in his face; that Trevor hadn't simply gone on ahead, but that they'd had a rift.

Logan's phone finally rang before Hiro could ask anything else, and he rushed to snatch it from the bedside table, answering without looking at the caller ID. "Kelly?"

Hiro slipped out of the room, allowing him some privacy.

"Hey, Logan," Kelly said, sounding lighthearted. "What's up? Sorry I missed your calls. Everything okay?"

"No," Logan said, pausing to take a breath as a surge of adrenaline rushed through him. There was no way Kelly would say no to his offer, but still, fixing things with Trevor was going to depend on his cooperation, and Logan wasn't used to relying on others. "I need your help, Kelly."

"Of course," Kelly said, sounding surprised. "Sorry I wasn't able to pick up when you called last night. Jase took my phone away." Kelly gave an odd laugh, not sounding all that disturbed about it, and Logan heard some kind of bird sound in the background. Was Kelly outdoors?

Logan hitched an eyebrow. "Jase is the bodyguard?"

Kelly laughed again. "He's... yeah. Yep. He's my, um, bodyguard. But he's also..." Kelly paused, clearing his throat, and when he continued, he didn't bother to finish the sentence. "So, your messages sounded urgent? I'm not too late to help, am I?"

"No, you're not. You're just in time." Logan took a deep breath and looked at himself one last time in the mirror, trying to see himself as Trevor would. Without Trevor there to fuss with the details, he was sure he didn't look as sharp as usual, but he was as put together as he was going to get. It would have to do. "Remember what you told me the first time you approached me about investing in bLoved, Kelly?"

Kelly laughed. "I was terrified, but yeah. *Everyone deserves love.*"

Logan smiled. At the time, he'd snorted cynically, and Kelly had gone pale, no doubt thinking he'd botched his chance. But the numbers had made sense, and... maybe something more. Kelly's vision had touched a part of Logan that he hadn't been willing to acknowledge back then, one that had held onto a tiny seed of hope that had never fully died, even after his heart had been broken.

Trevor had revived it, and now it was up to Logan to keep it alive.

"At last, my love has come along," Logan said, startling another laugh out of Kelly.

"Holy fuck, Logan," Kelly said, still laughing. "Did you just quote song lyrics at me? Who are you, and where's my business partner?"

Logan chuckled. "Those weren't lyrics—"

"Yes, they were."

"—just the truth. Kelly, here's what I need..."

"WE'RE *LATE*," HIRO MUTTERED AS THEY CUT ACROSS THE PARK-ing lot. He tsked. "We've never been late before. They're going to cancel our damn time slot. And you said Trevor would be here?"

"He will be," Logan said.

Despite the hurt between them, he trusted Trevor's word, and he trusted that Ash—who had once faced a similar anguish when he'd thought he'd lost Elliott—would do all he could to make it happen. After their talk the night before, Logan had a better understanding for who Ash was as a person, and how falling in love had changed him, too. Surprisingly, he was someone who Logan would like to have as a friend.

Hiro slipped on a patch of black ice just as they reached the studio. He stumbled, but braced himself against the door, pulling it open with an exasperated huff. The two of them were immediately beset upon by studio staff as they entered, and Logan was whisked toward the stage as a flurry of people worked to equip him with a sound pack and clip microphone and a series of urgent instructions.

The live taping had already begun, but Logan had a hard time caring about their urgency. Instead... he let out a sigh of relief, his heart surging as he finally caught sight of Trevor. He was waiting backstage by the wings, arms folded and expression distant, but still looking exactly like everything Logan could ever want.

Wearing a powder blue button-down shirt and brown slacks, he looked like he was ready to sit in the audience instead of on-stage. Logan didn't recognize the clothes, but he assumed they'd been provided courtesy of the Ashby Empire. He looked fantastic, hair styled with his usual flair and skin clear and fresh, as if he'd been able to get a good night's sleep. But up closer, Logan could still see the same hurt and doubt in his eyes that had appeared during Frank's phone call, and he was sorely tempted to screw the show and its production schedule and just pull Trevor aside and make things right between them.

"Mr. Carter, you have to stay still!" one of the production

assistants grumbled as Logan tried to make his way to Trevor. "We need to hook you up and get you on stage *right now*."

Trevor looked over at the woman's shrill words, meeting Logan's eyes for a split-second before he turned away, looking out at the stage. But not before Logan had seen the bright sheen of tears.

"I need to speak to my boyfriend," he said, pushing aside the hands grasping for him. Trevor's eyes weren't made to cry. They needed to be filled with laughter, or heat, or the sleepy, sexy contentment that filled them when Logan wrapped Trevor in his arms at night.

But a small crowd of production staff clustered around him, ignoring his words and fussing with his clothes, hair, *everything*, bringing Logan to a standstill as they finished prepping him for the stage.

"His hair is windswept," someone fretted.

"Yeah, and his cheeks are pink from the wind, but there's no time for hair and makeup. We've got to get him on set, *now*."

The cluster finally parted and Logan found himself shoved forward. Thankfully, in Trevor's direction. He could see Trevor's shoulders tense, but he refused to make eye contact again.

"Trevor," Logan said, stopping next to him despite the urgent whispers of the television staff. "Come with me. I need you on stage."

Trevor pressed his lips together, and he shook his head,

but Logan reached out and snagged his wrist, tugging him forward.

"Go out on stage!" one of the stage managers hissed at Logan. Logan ignored him.

"I need you," he repeated. "Please, Trevor."

"I can't put on a happy face, Logan, I'm sorry," Trevor said tightly.

"I don't need that. I just need *you*."

Trevor's expression started to thaw, but then he stiffened again. "Fine. But... this is the end of it, Logan. My last obligation under our contract."

Logan nodded, praying Trevor was wrong about the first part as he led him out on stage to the relieved sighs of the production staff. The show's hostess waited for them, beaming, and as they entered, the familiar melody of Etta James' *At Last* marked their entrance.

Logan's love truly had come along, and—with any luck—his lonely days *would* be over... and Trevor's words would be proven false. If Logan's plan paid off, this wouldn't be the end of it at all, but just the beginning.

Chapter 21

TREVOR

L OGAN LOOKED *HAPPY*. THE SMILE ON HIS FACE WAS ALL
Trevor could focus on, and after the night he'd spent
feeling crushed, it was like a stab in the heart.

Beneath the glow of Elliott's massive television screen,
stomach stuffed with too much cookie dough ice cream
to be comfortable, Trevor had stayed up all night either
silently crying while Elliott slept next to him, or curled up
in his friend's arms for comfort. Logan's long phone call
with Ash—about which Ash had been annoyingly close-
lipped—had given Trevor hope, but seeing Logan now, and
how epically un-devastated he was, shattered that.

Facing Logan through his heartbreak was one of the

toughest things Trevor had ever had to do, but he sucked it up and followed him on stage, telling himself that it was because he didn't want to risk any legal ramifications in terms of his contract. Definitely not because of what had happened to his foolish heart when Logan had said *I need you.*

There was a reason he'd always been so guarded with his heart, he realized. He'd always told himself it was the fear of getting trapped in a routine, of getting stuck living a life that was blah and boring, but the reality was that that didn't scare him as much as the simple fear of rejection. Hadn't his failure to pursue his dreams in New York been, really, about not wanting to be rejected, too?

All his life, Trevor had called the shots. He was the one who decided when his flings ended, what dates he went on, and what he did with his life. He may not have always been the one to end things, but he'd made damn sure he'd never cared enough to have someone else ending it *hurt.*

Before Logan.

He could feel the heat of Logan's thigh pressed against his own. The small couch on the talk show's set was plenty big enough that they shouldn't have had to sit so close together, but—as they'd done in every appearance—Logan had tugged Trevor down right next to him, placing a possessive hand on his knee while he chatted with the hostess.

Gone was the cold, awkward man who'd almost flubbed their first television appearance together. Today, Logan was doing a fine job of carrying the conversation, and the hostess trilled with laughter as he smiled at her with those amazing, cornflower-blue eyes.

Trevor, on the other hand, was having trouble tracking the conversation at all.

"Trevor, you're uncharacteristically quiet today," the hostess remarked. She leaned forward in her chair, a predatory gleam in her eyes as they darted between him and Logan. "Trouble in paradise?"

Trevor plastered a smile on his face that he hoped would pass muster, sensing that for all her friendly cheer, she'd pounce on the chance to break the news that Tregan was no more. "No trouble here," he lied, trying and failing to infuse his voice with the right amount of sincerity. He'd warned Logan that he wasn't up to maintaining the facade, but he'd still try his best. He took a deep breath, forcing his smile wider as she looked back at him with narrowed eyes.

"You and Logan aren't having... problems, are you?" she asked, tittering with the audience. "Certainly not on today of all days."

Valentine's Day. Right. "Um, no," Trevor said, covering Logan's hand with his own and feeling a little something shrivel inside him. He really sucked as an actor, didn't he? "There's no problem. Logan just—"

He'd planned on saying that Logan had kept him up all night—true, if not in exactly the way he hoped she'd take it—and that Trevor was exhausted—also true.

Before he could, though, Logan cut in. "Actually, there *is* a problem," he said soberly, turning his hand over underneath Trevor's so they were palm-to-palm and lacing their fingers together.

Trevor stiffened, sitting straighter in his chair. What the hell was Logan doing? Was this why he'd needed him on stage? Frank had said their breakup was scheduled for the next week, and Trevor wasn't ready. His eyes welled up with tears for the eighty millionth time, and he yanked his hand out of Logan's, swiping at them angrily. Couldn't Logan have waited? Or prepared him a little? *Anything* to save Trevor some of his dignity?

"Please don't do this," Trevor whispered, trying not to move his lips in the vain hope that the cameras wouldn't catch it.

Logan's eyes softened, and he reached out to wipe Trevor's cheeks for him. "The problem," he said, projecting his voice clearly the way Trevor had coached him on, so that the mics could pick it up and the audience could hear him clearly, "is that I did something stupid, and let the man who's more important to me than anything, think that he isn't."

What was he *doing*? Trevor was painfully aware of the cameras trained on them, but was Logan? Despite his publicity-oriented voice projection, it felt almost like he was speaking directly to Trevor. But they were here to sell bLoved—to sell *love*—and here Logan was, airing their dirty laundry in front of a live audience. Despite Trevor's own heartache, he didn't want to hurt bLoved.

"Logan," Trevor said, keeping his voice low as he shook his head slightly. "You don't want to—"

"I let him think that I valued work more than I valued him," Logan said, raising his voice enough to override Trevor's protest as he continued to look straight into his eyes.

Trevor's throat closed up, and he shook his head again—but this time, not to try to stop Logan. Just because he wanted to believe what he was hearing, but wasn't sure if he could.

Logan lowered his voice, too, taking both Trevor's hands in his. "I didn't tell him what he means to me, despite millions of chances to do it."

Trevor glanced from Logan to the cameras, then back at Logan again. It was so hard to tell what was business, and what wasn't. He'd been so sure he'd had it figured out before, but now, despite the apparent sincerity in Logan's words, a part of him still had to wonder whether Frank had advised Logan to act like this in order to plant the seed for their public breakup next week.

"I'm not very experienced in love, Trevor."

Despite the fact that every camera was trained on them and the studio was dead silent, Logan's attention stayed entirely on Trevor. He was doing the thing that always made it feel like they were the only two people in the world, and dammit dammit *dammit*, Trevor's eyes were welling up *again*.

"My heart shattered once before," Logan continued.

"And it almost destroyed me. Worse, it caused me to use business as a shield that kept me separated from the world. From getting close to anyone. From *you*. But you broke through, anyway, and it was my own fear of getting hurt again that almost—" he paused, looking away for a minute, before continuing in a voice lower and rougher with emotion, "—I'm hoping it's 'almost'... lost you."

Even with all the publicity work they'd done together, Logan had never turned into a talkative man. This was... out of character. So much so that it *had* to be either true, or a script.

"Trevor, I'm so sorry." Logan squeezed his hands. "It kills me that I didn't say what needed to be said, so that you could have laughed off last night. So that you would *know*..."

Tears streamed silently down Trevor's cheeks, but he refused to let his voice break. "Know what?"

"That I love you."

Just as he'd suspected the night before at Ash's, he could already tell he was going to give in to Logan's sweet words, but the poison of doubt was there, too, spreading underneath them. How many times had Logan told him that he loved him?

"Did Frank write that for you?" he asked, unable to stop the bitter question before it escaped.

"No," Logan said. "Frank doesn't work for me anymore."

Trevor's heart started racing. "You *fired* him?"

Logan shook his head, giving Trevor an odd smile. "That's up to Kelly. I fired *me*."

Trevor blinked, and behind Logan the hostess—who he'd all but forgotten about—sucked in a sharp breath. "W-what are you saying?" Trevor asked, having trouble making sense of it. Logan couldn't fire himself. He *owned* bLoved.

"I sold my shares of bLoved to Kelly this morning. I no longer have any affiliation with the company, Trevor."

The audience collectively gasped, but Trevor didn't so much as turn his head. His eyes were glued to Logan, and he could barely hear over the sudden pounding of his heart. "But... *why*? It was doing so well."

"Because, when I tell you I love you, Trevor, I need you to know it's true. I don't want there to be any doubt in your mind. I never want you to have to wonder why I'm saying it, or whether I really mean it. And, most of all—" his voice broke, and the pain in Trevor's heart evaporated as if it had never been, "—*most* of all, I'm hoping that without bLoved between us, you'll give me another chance to prove just how very, very much I do."

The hush that had fallen from the audience settled around him like a blanket, and despite the weight of knowing that every single pair of eyes in the studio was trained on them, the moment felt as private and intimate as if it really had been the two of them. The space in Trevor's heart that had been filled with a bitter wariness, now started to overflow with a crazy kind of happiness that could only be called *joy*.

Logan *loved* him, and his incredible gesture had wiped away Trevor's doubts as if they'd never been.

That bubbling joy inside him felt like champagne bubbles, and he clapped his hands over his mouth, trying to stifle the giddy laugh that threatened to break out. "You love me?" he asked, grinning so hard that his cheeks hurt.

"I do."

"So... you're saying that you love me."

Logan grinned, pulling Trevor's hands away from his mouth and leaning in to give him a toe-curling kiss. "I do. I love you, Trevor Rogers. And, if you'll let me, I always will."

The bubbling, joyful silliness inside him settled down into something warm and sweet and more wonderful than anything he'd ever imagined, and despite the sudden surge of sound around them—cheering and clapping from the audience, and rapid-fire questions from the hostess that Trevor paid not one single bit of attention to—Trevor had eyes only for Logan.

"I love you, too, you know."

"I was hoping so," Logan said, his lip quirking up.

Despite the teasing tone, Trevor saw real relief in his eyes, and his heart rolled over in his chest. Logan *loved* him, and he'd sold a who-knows-how-many-multimillion-dollar business just to make sure that Trevor knew it. His eyes, which apparently were made of water, spilled over as if they'd forgotten the meaning of the words "dry," not to mention "don't embarrass yourself in public."

Trevor plastered himself against Logan's chest, deciding then and there that he was perfectly content to stay there, well, basically forever.

"I love you," he said again, holding onto Logan's cheeks and making him meet his eyes. "I don't want you to doubt it, either. I think I have since the beginning... I was just too afraid to admit it to myself. I never wanted a relationship before, but I want *you*, Logan, and now that I, um, know you feel the same way—"

"We *all* do," the hostess interjected breathlessly, leaning forward in her seat.

Trevor laughed, but kept his eyes on Logan. "I'm not planning on letting you go."

"That... works for me," Logan said, leaning in to give him a chaste kiss before pulling back and smiling apologetically at the hostess. "As you heard, I no longer own bLoved, so I really have no place on this stage."

He tugged Trevor to his feet as the hostess squawked a protest.

"Wait," she insisted. "I wasn't told about this. We're scheduled for—"

"Love waits for no man," Trevor said cheekily, cutting her off with a grin. "And it's sure as hell not waiting for us."

Logan snickered and pulled him off-stage as the hostess yapped behind them.

"That's not going to hurt bLoved, is it?" Trevor asked, glancing behind them.

"How could it?" Logan said, laughing and looking carefree and gorgeous as he blew past a gawking—but smiling—Hiro. "After all, it was bLoved that brought us together."

"At last," Trevor quipped, flushing when he realized how cheesy quoting that sappy song from the app sounded. Exactly what he used to tease Jose about, back at Ashby's. But, when Logan swung him into his arms again and kissed him until he forgot his own name, Trevor decided... fuck it. Nothing wrong with a little cheese. It went well with love.

Especially on Valentine's Day.

Chapter 22

LOGAN

"I want you to move in with me," Logan said as the elevator doors slid shut.

"And I want you naked," Trevor retorted, doing his best to make that happen.

Logan's cock surged to life, and he laughed, having a sudden flashback as Trevor's hands made quick work of the buttons on his dress shirt and then reached for his belt.

"Something funny, baby?" Trevor asked, cocking an eyebrow at him as he gave up on the belt and just shoved a hand beneath the waistband of Logan's pants, wrapping it around him.

"Ashby's," Logan gasped, even though what he really

wanted to say was something more like *hallelujah*. He pushed Trevor back against the wall, tugging his head back so he could kiss the corner of his mouth... the edge of his jaw... the long line of his neck...

"Mm-hmm," Trevor said, snickering, even as he arched back to give Logan better access. "Ashby's is hilarious."

Logan smiled against Trevor's warm skin, pressing his cock against Trevor's palm as he said, "I was just remembering when you used to take my measurements—"

"*Please* finish that sentence with something naughty," Trevor interrupted him gleefully, wrapping one leg around Logan's hip and starting to grind against him in earnest. "Tell me that all those times I undressed you, you were secretly imagining I'd do something like... *this*."

Trevor's hand was pure magic, and Logan's eyes rolled back in his head as the incredible feel of... *that*... made it impossible for him to answer for a moment. He could feel the heat of Trevor's erection burning against his groin, and when he started whispering all the ways he wanted Logan to fuck him in his ear, Logan honestly wondered if he'd be able to make it all the way up to the penthouse.

He did, after all, like to give Trevor what he wanted.

But then a chime sounded, telling him they were already there, and he scooped Trevor up—not willing to break contact—and carried him down the hall while doing his best to inhale him. Trevor's mouth may have been dirty as sin, but it tasted like heaven. As soon as he made it to the bedroom, he gave it up for a moment, though—tossing

Trevor onto the bed and making sure he knew what was expected of him.

"Strip, Trevor. Now."

Trevor flopped backward, cock already tenting his pants and eyes sparkling with pure joy.

He was laughing.

He was *beautiful*.

He was... Logan's heart lurched in his chest as it hit him. Trevor was really *his*. And—even though, if Logan's cock had a voice at that moment, it would be telling him to pin Trevor to the mattress and find out just how fast he could make all that bubbling laughter turn into the hungry, whimpering moans that always drove Logan wild—his heart was telling him to slow down. He didn't want to miss a single moment with this man.

"I love you," he said, shrugging out of the shirt Trevor had already unbuttoned for him and making short work of the rest of his clothes.

"I know," Trevor said, grinning as he propped himself up on his elbows and took in the show appreciatively as Logan undressed.

"And," Logan said, doing his best to sound stern. "I believe I told you to strip."

Trevor cocked an eyebrow at him. "Oh? Now that you're really my boyfriend, you think you get to tell me what to do? Is that how it works?"

Logan was finally naked, and he crawled onto the bed, stalking up Trevor's body until it was trapped beneath him.

"Yes," he said, wondering if love felt like this for everyone. As if every moment was perfect—not because of what was actually happening—but simply because the one he loved existed.

...and loved him back.

The playful, horny glint in Trevor's eyes softened into something warmer. "Then I guess that means I need to say yes."

"Yes, you're going to strip?"

Trevor shook his head, reaching up to cup the side of Logan's face. "*Yes*, honey pop, I'll move in with you."

Logan squeezed his eyes closed as a fierce burst of emotion roared through him. It was so intense that the word *happiness* didn't really do it justice. Then Trevor moved beneath him, and Logan's eyes snapped back open. The sight of Trevor gazing up at him with everything Logan was feeling reflected back in his eyes, too, nearly took his breath away.

"Good," Logan said, dipping his head down to kiss the man who'd freed his heart. "Because everything you asked me for in the elevator? You're going to get it. Every day."

"Ooooh. Yes, please," Trevor said, a pink flush moving up his neck and coloring his face with arousal. He wiggled beneath Logan, managing to get rid of his clothes in record time. "How about we start with..."

Trevor let his voice trail off into a breathless laugh as Logan lowered himself on top of him, thighs and stomachs and chests all aligned. Every inch of their skin was in contact, and the natural lubrication that had already started pooling at the head of Logan's cock made the hot slide of their erections against each other feel incredible.

"Start with...?" Logan prompted Trevor, running a hand down his side and slipping it under his ass. Pulling them more tightly together.

"Everything," Trevor said, his breath coming faster as he arched up underneath him. "Oh, fuck, Logan. I want *you*. I want *everything*."

Logan smiled. He could do that.

He tipped Trevor's head back, kissing him deeply as he continued to rock his hips in a slow rhythm that he knew from past experience would either get Trevor to start begging soon, or bring out some of his dirtier promises. Trevor's hands clutched at his shoulders, then slipped lower, urging him on.

"Faster," Trevor panted, trying to make it happen.

"No," Logan said, grinning down at him.

Trevor laughed, slapping his ass hard enough to sting. "Fucker."

"We'll get to that, too," Logan promised, reaching around to grab Trevor's wrists and holding them firmly at his sides. "But first, I think we just agreed that I get to tell you what to do."

Trevor's cock, trapped between them, jerked against him, and his pupils dilated to the max. "*Logan*," he gasped, doing his best to fuck himself against Logan's body as he started panting in earnest. "That's only going to work if you tell me you want to make me come sometime around, um, *right now*."

"Weren't you the one who told me once that we should practice patience?" Logan teased, making sure Trevor was thoroughly trapped beneath him before dipping his head down to push his tongue against one of his hardened, overly sensitive nipples.

Trevor moaned, squirming beneath him as Logan sucked it between his lips, then bit down gently.

"Oh fuckohfuckoh fuck... *Logan*. Just... tell me what you want me to do."

"You're already doing it, sweetheart," Logan said, letting go of his hold on Trevor's wrists so he could move lower on the bed. He pushed Trevor's thighs apart, settling between them, then looked up at the gorgeous sight of his slender body spread out before him. "And, since I like making you happy, I *am* going to make you come... right... *now*."

"*No*," Trevor said, trying to surge upright.

Too late, though. Logan surged up over him, swallowing every inch of his mouthwatering cock and pushing him back against the mattress.

"Not... not *yet*, Logan," Trevor gasped, even as his hips jerked up against Logan's face. "Not... no... oh, *fuck*. Oh, yes... *yes*... *please*... ohfuckyesplease *yes*, Logan... oh my God, I'm going to... come... so... hard... oh my *God*."

Trevor's hands tightened almost painfully against the sides of Logan's head, and with a sharp gasp, he gave in to the relentless heat of Logan's mouth and did it. The warm, salty rush shot down Logan's throat as Trevor's entire body went taut for a long, drawn-out moment... then he relaxed, almost melting into the mattress underneath Logan.

"Dammit," Trevor murmured, running his hands softly through Logan's hair as Logan stretched out on top of him again, smiling down at him. "That was too fast. I wanted to fuck."

"Greedy," Logan teased, reaching toward the nightstand with one hand as his cock pulsed, trapped between them.

"For you?" Trevor agreed. "Always."

Logan kissed him, shifting his hips just enough to reach down and cover himself with the condom he'd grabbed, then lubing his fingers and pressing them home.

"Nnnnnghhh*ohhhh*," Trevor gasped into his mouth. Logan could feel Trevor's lips curving up under his own in one of those sassy, sexy smiles, even as his breath started to quicken again. "It's like that, is it? Haven't gotten enough of me yet?"

"Never," Logan said, meaning it.

Trevor's body was eager for him. A good thing, since Logan needed to be inside him like he needed to take his next breath. Not just for the sake of his cock—although oh *hell* yes, for that, too—but because the emotions welling up inside him required him to get as close as humanly possible to the man he loved.

"Wrap your legs around me."

Trevor did, and Logan pushed inside him easily, the familiar, tight heat like coming home.

"*This...*" Logan's throat tightened up with emotion even as pleasure surged through his body, and for a moment, he couldn't speak. He wanted this man so damn much. *Loved* him. And even though he'd wanted to draw this out, as soon as he was sheathed, he knew he wasn't going to be able to. Not this time.

He was still reeling from the roller coaster of emotion over the last twenty-four hours. Thinking he might have lost Trevor the night before, *knowing* he'd hurt him, and then, at last, the soul-deep relief of winning him back, his heart's rising euphoria with every "yes" Trevor had given him...

Logan tightened his arms around Trevor, holding him against his body, and snapped his hips forward again.

"This is perfect," he rasped. "Trevor... *you're*—"

"Perfect," Trevor said, the love shining from his eyes softening the cheeky tone. Then Logan changed his angle, obviously hitting him right where he needed it, because all of Trevor's sass instantly morphed into heat. "Oh... *fuck* Logan... *yes*... it really... it really *is*... keep... keep... *fuck*, please keep fucking me just... like... *that*."

Logan laughed. As if he'd be able to stop.

And then, despite the rising urgency driving him to do exactly what Trevor had just asked, he laughed even harder, because... laughing? During sex? Trevor was a gift. A miracle.

"I love you," Logan said, groaning as he drove himself deep.

"Oh, believe me, baby," Trevor panted, hands clutching Logan's ass as he urged him to go harder. "I... oh*fuck-fuckyes*... I *love* you... *really* love you, too..."

He kept going, his mouth running nonstop as Logan took him right back to the edge.

Logan lost track of time. His world narrowed to the sexy sounds that mixed with Trevor's soft declarations of love and the gasping, dirty pleas that tumbled out of his mouth; to the feel of Trevor's tight passage gripping Logan's cock as he fucked him with a relentless rhythm that he couldn't have stopped if he'd wanted to; to the sight of Trevor, gorgeous and flushed and panting, laughing and loving him and urging him to keep going... to go harder... to—

"*Come*, Trevor," Logan gritted out, needing it to happen before he could let himself go, even though neither one of them had touched Trevor's cock.

Didn't matter, though.

He felt a full-body tremor move through Trevor, and even if he hadn't felt the warm rush between them and the rippling spasms inside his body, the look of pure bliss on his face as he cried out and arched up against Logan would have told him that Trevor had given him what he'd asked for.

Logan's climax burst through him without warning at the sight, and his hips stuttered as his body took over.

"Watching you come is so sexy, sugar daddy," Trevor said, reaching up to smooth Logan's hair back from his forehead. "I could do it forever."

"Please do," Logan said, rolling them both to their sides but refusing to pull out quite yet. He brushed his lips against Trevor's, smiling.

"You've already missed your flight, so forever sounds good to me."

"Oh, shit," Trevor said lazily, his eyes still hooded and soft from his orgasm. "Guess I really will have to stay, hm? Whatever will we find to do with our time, now that you've sold bLoved?"

Logan laughed. "I *do* have a few other business interests to keep me occupied."

"Thank God," Trevor teased, pouting a little when Logan finally rolled away, pinching the base of the condom around his softening cock and heading into the bathroom to dispose of it. He raised his voice to be heard as Logan turned on the sink. "Because I'm not sure I could support you in the style you're accustomed to on my salary."

Trevor bit his lip as Logan returned to the bedroom, a momentary hint of uncertainty flashing across his face.

"What's wrong?" Logan asked, coming back to the bed and handing Trevor a warm cloth for cleanup.

"I'd love to move in with you—"

"I thought that was already decided," Logan said, frowning. Trevor *had* said yes in the heat of the moment, but it had still been a yes. If Trevor wasn't ready to come to New York, though, Logan had no problem with the idea of relocating to Chicago.

If Trevor wanted him there, that is.

"It *is*," Trevor said instantly, easing Logan's fear before it had a chance to take root. He sat up, scooting to sit next to Logan on the edge of the bed. "I mean, I want to, totally, Logan. And this last month or so with you has been amazing. You've spoiled me rotten, but... I guess I just want you to know I plan on pulling my own weight. We're in this thing together. I was just teasing with that 'sugar daddy' comment."

Logan's lips twitched, but Trevor looked so earnest that he bit his tongue.

"I'm sure I can get a transfer to the New York Ashby's, and eventually, find some tailoring clients here, too, and then—"

Logan kissed him.

"Logan, I don't expect you to—"

Logan laughed, putting a finger over Trevor's lips to shush him. "If you want to do that, that's fine, Trevor," he said. "But trust me, I'm not worried about it."

Trevor frowned. "I know you did well with Rise, Logan—and just so you know, that's *not* why I'm here—but I worry that you might have sold your bLoved shares prematurely? I mean, it was doing so well, and I appreciate the gesture. I really do, more than I can say, but..."

"Trevor," Logan said, lacing their fingers together and giving him a serious look, "I've got more money than God, and Kelly gave me exactly what I asked for, for my half of bLoved. It truly doesn't matter to me whether you want to work, or stay in bed all day, or run around in a French maid's costume—"

Trevor snickered. "Well, I *do* look good in ruffles."

Logan grinned, picturing it. He would definitely be down for a little role play, now and then...

"You *are* a kinky fuck, aren't you?"

Logan laughed. "The point is, I just want you to be happy, Trevor. So if you want to work at Ashby's, do it. If you want to keep tailoring, just let me know how I can help you get set up. Believe me, as long as you're here and doing something you love, I'll have everything I need."

Trevor looked away, blinking away a sudden sheen of moisture from his eyes. Then he looked back, grinning, and scrambled onto Logan's lap, straddling him and wrapping his arms around his neck.

"I really love you, you know," he said, leaning forward to rest his forehead against Logan's. "I really, really do."

"I know," Logan said, kissing him. "And it means everything, sweetheart."

Trevor kissed him back, then shook off his moment of mushiness and regained his usual cocky charm. "I hope so," he said, grinning. "Because after Tregan, bLoved is going to explode, and I don't want you to regret selling once you see all those future profits you'll be missing out on."

"Worth it," Logan said, slapping Trevor's bare ass when he wriggled against him. He winked. "Especially when you do that."

"I *will* wear you out," Trevor promised.

"You can try," Logan shot back, his heart swelling with love. He moved Trevor off his lap, standing up. "But maybe we should eat something first."

Trevor followed him toward the bedroom door. "I do like this eating naked idea," he said. "Is this going to be a regular part of living together?"

Logan laughed, but then realized Trevor was no longer behind him. He turned to see that he'd stopped near the dresser and was staring in shock at the screen of Logan's laptop. He'd left in a hurry that morning, eager to get to the studio as soon as he'd gotten Kelly's agreement and electronic signature, making the sale official.

"Logan," Trevor said, tearing his eyes away from the screen and giving him a look that Logan couldn't interpret. Trevor swallowed. "I bumped it, and the screen came on. Is this... tell me this isn't real."

Logan flushed. He hadn't meant for Trevor to know.

"One *dollar*?" Trevor asked incredulously. "bLoved must be worth millions, Logan."

"It's just money, Trevor."

"You get to say 'just money' when you lose a fiver," Trevor said, sounding stricken. "Not... oh my God, Logan. I can't believe you did this. You must have lost—"

"Nothing," Logan said firmly, crossing the room in two strides and pulling Trevor into his arms. "I *lost* nothing. And what I gained is worth infinitely more than a few million dollars. I love you, Trevor, and I needed you not to doubt that. *Ever.*"

Trevor shook his head. And then he nodded. And then

he laughed, covering his mouth to try to keep it in as his eyes welled up with tears again. "Oh my God," he whispered, the sound muffled by his hand.

"I love you," Logan said, wiping them away.

"I know," Trevor said, laughing again as his eyes sparkled with joy. He kissed Logan, beaming like the sun. "I *do*, Logan. I know. And I love you, too, baby."

Which absolutely, without a doubt, was worth far more than Logan's shares of bLoved. Trevor's love was priceless.

It was everything.

Epilogue

TREVOR

SKYLIGHT CLARKSON SQ LOOKED EVEN BETTER THAN IT HAD the year before. The plain white interior had been transformed, the space as sleek and glamorous as the event about to unfold in it. The white, lustrous runway was elevated from the first row seats so that spectators' heads would be at the level of the models' feet. Podiums had been installed, making each subsequent row of seats higher than the last, and the walls were covered in dark matte material that Trevor recognized as one designed to absorb light. The podiums and the seats were black as well, and the skylights above the runway were positioned in such a way that Trevor knew exactly what would happen.

He felt a frisson of excitement, not even remotely immune to the sheer fabulousness at attending his second
ever Fashion Week event.

Jean Marchand put on one hell of a show, and the icon-
ic designer always made sure the clothes were the star in
them. Today would be no exception. Once the show began,
the lights would cut out save for those illuminating the
runway, and in the total darkness, reflected off the lustrous
white finish, the models would shine.

Trevor and Logan were running late, and the house was
already packed.

After a year spent living together in Logan's luxurious
penthouse, Trevor knew Logan was used to how much time
Trevor spent getting ready to get out the door, and Trevor
had resigned himself to the peculiarities of New York traffic. Really, they *should* have been able to plan better.

But a year hadn't been even close to long enough to
diminish the desire that flared up each and every time they
were together.

Neither of them had planned on taking as long as they
had in the shower, but Logan's hand had strayed a little too
far down Trevor's front while they washed each other, and
Trevor had retaliated in kind, and now here they were, not
late late, but definitely not early enough to do anything but
head directly to their seats.

"Estelle Lowe arranged for this to happen?" Trevor
asked in a whisper as Logan led him through the crowd.
Trevor had been over the moon when Logan had told him

they'd be able to attend again this year, but he'd been far too busy constructing period piece clothing for the upcoming performance of *Les Miserables* to concern himself with details like those.

It turned out that being a social media presence—even briefly—came with all kinds of benefits. Having an influential boyfriend came with even more. Before Trevor had gotten around to putting in for the transfer to the New York Ashby's, Logan had taken him out to dinner with a *friend* who turned out to be Jo Quinlan, the celebrated Broadway producer. Logan refused to admit that it had been anything other than a social engagement, but despite his denials, there was no mistaking what he'd done for Trevor, and for his dream career.

Trevor, never shy or one to pass on an opportunity, had taken the introduction and run with it. It had paid off with the *Les Mis* opportunity, and now he was working his ass off to make sure the costume design was flawless.

Jean Marchand's event at Fashion Week was Trevor's first time away from work in close to a month, and as thrilled as he was to be finally living his dream, he was equally excited to step away from it for a day.

With *Logan*.

For *Fashion Week*.

Trevor still had to pinch himself some mornings, just to make sure that the crazy wonderful dream his life had turned into was really and truly *real*.

"I spoke with Estelle to get the passes," Logan confirmed,

smiling down at him. "She was happy to assist. I wanted to make sure we did something nice together for Valentine's Day."

Their anniversary. Trevor leaned against Logan as they walked, joy bubbling up from his core. It still struck him as hilarious that two men who had started out so staunchly opposed to love shared their anniversary on Valentine's Day. Life had proved them wrong, and their anniversary reminded Trevor of that more than ever.

He adored living with Logan. The routine he'd feared falling into had never come to pass. Between frequent week-long trips to Chicago to visit his family and his Ashby's friends, the costume design work he was now involved in, the many sights and attractions in New York, and the endless, playful, sexy creativity of his boyfriend at home, no day was like any other.

Trevor lived life limitlessly, and he loved it—not quite as much as he loved Logan, but close enough.

Logan led him to the front row, right at the end of the runway. The seats there were empty, and Logan sat in one of them. Trevor remained standing, staring at him.

"Well?" Logan asked. He gestured to the other empty seat.

"You're kidding."

"I'm not. When do I ever joke around?" Logan patted the seat beside him. Then, in his bossy voice—which despite their very recent shower play, instantly made Trevor's cock twitch—he added, "Sit down."

Was Logan for real? Trevor's heart raced. Front row seats right at the end of the runway? There was no way Estelle had the connections to hook them up with something that spectacular. Trevor didn't know her well, but he knew Fashion Week well enough to know it was an impossibility.

He narrowed his eyes. Logan had something else going on that he wasn't sharing. Trevor was almost sort of getting used to how much Logan liked to spoil him, but at the end of the day, there were still some things that money couldn't make happen.

He sat, eyeing Logan suspiciously.

Logan snorted at the look, his eyes sparkling. "What's wrong, sweetheart?"

Trevor turned in his chair, fixing Logan with a hard look. "You're up to something."

"Me?" Logan asked, trying and failing to look innocent. "Up to something? On our anniversary?"

There was playful mischief in his eyes, and it warmed Trevor's heart, even as it made it race. The man loved him, without a doubt. So much so that it often took Trevor's breath away.

"You're going to make the surprise I have waiting for you back at home look stupid, aren't you?" Trevor asked, crossing his arms and doing his best to look annoyed. Buying presents for a man worth billions of dollars wasn't easy, but he was pretty sure that the frilly apron he'd found online paired with the skills he'd learned from the cooking classes he'd talked Logan into taking with him a few months before were going to be a hit.

Logan grinned at him, looking nothing at all like the cold man who had first walked into Ashby's for a fitting a couple of years before. Trevor's heart did a slow roll in his chest.

Logan put the *man* in romantic.

If love had been a song, then Trevor's boyfriend was a full gospel chorus.

He was so head-over-heels for Logan that—

Trevor gasped as the lights suddenly cut off all at once, jolting him out of his mini love-fest. It was so dark that Trevor couldn't even see Logan's silhouette next to him, and if Logan hadn't had his customary, possessive hand placed on Trevor's thigh, he might seriously have wondered if everyone had disappeared when the audience fell utterly silent around him.

The air grew thick with anticipation, and then music pulsed through the sound system, shattering the tension. Trevor sat up straight in his chair, grinning madly as a light pierced the darkness from above. At the end of the runway, right in front of him, stood a single female model wrapped in a long black silk robe. Expression neutral, she loosened the belt and let the robe slip from her shoulders. Beneath, she was dressed in a nude-and-seafoam-green dress. The skirt was barely long enough to reach her thighs. The sleeves were long, draping loosely past her slender wrists, and it had a modest, boat neckline.

Stunning.

Trevor's eyes lit up, and he leaned forward, practically humming with excitement. The model looked out across the audience, eyes never focusing in one place for long, then turned sharply and strutted down the runway. The black robe slipped off the edge and pooled at Trevor's feet.

Whatever Logan might or might not be up to faded from Trevor's mind. Sitting in the audience at Fashion Week last year had been a tremendous milestone in his life, but it dimmed in comparison to what he experienced now. He was in heaven.

Model after model emerged, each of them wearing a design that was distinctly Jean Marchand. Lace and bold patterns were in vogue, and Trevor ate them up. Seafoam green was this year's *it* color, and Trevor couldn't get enough of it. Seeing the models up close, making out the details of the textiles and the artistry in their makeup, was beyond stunning. It was a dream come true.

The show finally wound to a close, but it felt like only minutes had passed. The final walk began and all the models paraded across the runway one last time as Trevor applauded wildly, totally enraptured.

"Oh my God, Logan," he whispered ecstatically. "Did you *see* that? The lacework was stunning!"

He rattled on, knowing Logan probably wasn't following half of it but loving him all the more for acting like he cared.

"I love you, Trevor," Logan whispered in his ear as Trevor

paused for breath. Upbeat, remixed pop music blared from the speakers, but Trevor heard every word.

He tore his eyes away from the climax of the show, looking at the man next to him. With every single part of his soul, he loved Logan, too. He was the one thing Trevor didn't ever want to do without. As amazing as their life together was, Trevor would give up any of it, even—he reached out and squeezed Logan's hand—passes to Fashion Week, before losing what they had.

Thank God he didn't think he'd have to.

"I love you, too, baby," he said, leaning over to kiss him. "Forever."

Logan smiled, but a flash of color drew Trevor's attention back to the runway. His brows lowered in confusion. The last three models at the end of the parade were wearing outfits Trevor hadn't seen yet.

The models made their way down the runway, each wearing royal blue. They wore faceless masks, their builds were irregular, and—while the clothes they wore were fashionable and well put-together—they definitely weren't Jean Marchand.

A murmur ran through the crowd as others noticed the same discrepancies.

"What the hell?" Trevor murmured, his eyes narrowing as he cocked his head to the side.

Jean Marchand's models disappeared backstage, but the three models in royal blue remained, stopping to pose at the very front of the stage, just inches from Trevor.

He gave a disbelieving laugh, Trevor recognizing them immediately now that they were so close.

"*Grace?* Elliott? *Jose?*"

With a synchronized motion that had to have been choreographed, they removed their masks, confirming that he was right. Grace, center stage, looked down at Trevor and winked.

"*Logan,*" Trevor whispered, voice rising as he twisted around in his seat to face his boyfriend.

This *had* to be his doing.

Next to him, Logan got up from his seat, but only the models—his best friends—on the runway were lit, and Trevor couldn't make out what Logan was doing in the dark. The murmuring of the audience was getting louder. Clearly, Trevor wasn't the only one for whom this was a surprise.

Overhead, a light suddenly flashed on, trained on Trevor and Logan.

Logan was down on one knee.

Trevor burst into tears.

"Jean Marchand would like to offer the next few moments of his show in service of true love," Grace announced to the audience, her voice carrying across the room and instantly silencing the rising whispers around them. Trevor, still seated, was trembling from head to foot, and waves of giddy excitement rippled through him as he stared into Logan's sparkling, cornflower-blue eyes.

"Over the past year," Jose said from the runway, his

voice ringing out, "the love between Trevor Rogers and Logan Carter has been growing strong. The three of us have witnessed it blossom into something just as stunning as any of the pieces in tonight's show."

"*Tregan,*" someone whispered excitedly from the still-darkened audience.

Trevor laughed, swiping at his cheeks, but Logan's hands were already there, wiping away his happy tears.

"I love you," Logan mouthed silently, making them start all over again.

Was this for real? How had Logan convinced Jean Marchand to let him commandeer his show like this? And how had he convinced Trevor's three best friends to walk the runway in front of so many influential people?

"So tonight, on behalf of true love—" even though Trevor had eyes only for Logan, he could easily hear the smile in Elliott's voice, "—we'd like to offer the world one last piece of beauty before the conclusion of the show."

Grace stooped down and handed Logan a small box. Trevor felt like his heart was going to burst, and when Logan took his hand, looking up at him that way he had— where it felt like they were the only two people in the whole world—time stood still.

Trevor didn't ever, *ever* want to forget this moment.

It was perfect.

"From the moment I met you, Trevor, my life started to change," Logan said, the words winding around Trevor's heart like an embrace. "You once promised to turn me into a person, and somehow, despite my doubt that it was possible, you managed to do it. The man I was before you didn't know love, didn't believe in it, but every morning when I wake up next to you, my heart shows me how wrong I was. You've not only brought out the best in me, Trevor, but you've filled every part of my life with color and love and joy and laughter. Loving you is the best part of every one of my days, and, if you'll have me, I want to spend all the rest of mine with you at my side.

"Trevor Rogers, will you marry me?"

Trevor nodded vigorously, his throat too tight to let the word that had been running through his mind ever since he'd seen Logan down on one knee come out.

Yes. YesyesyesyesyesyesyesohHELLyes.

Trevor's eyes had spilled over again, and he dashed away the moisture impatiently as Logan opened the lid of the box. A gorgeous, black cobalt band lay inside. Down its center, in a single line set flush with the metal, were dozens of tiny diamonds. The ring was masculine, but boasted exactly enough style that it screamed *Trevor*.

He reached for it, but Logan pulled it back, out of his reach, giving him a playful, loving smile. "Say yes, sweetheart," he said in his bossy voice. Then, with a flash of vulnerability, he added more quietly, "Please, Trevor. I love you."

"Yes," Trevor said, grinning from ear-to-ear. He launched himself at Logan, wrapping his arms around him as tightly as he could, laughing as Logan staggered under his weight, then pulled him close. Trevor hugged him tight as tears streamed down his cheeks, only remembering that they had an audience when the room around them burst into applause.

"Oh my *God*, Logan," Trevor said breathlessly as the lights came on around them, finally loosening his hold on his boyfriend—fiancé—long enough to let Logan slip the ring onto his finger. "How did you *do* this?"

"I have my ways," Logan said, winking and wrapping an arm around Trevor's waist as he accepted the congratulations of their friends.

Ash, Barry, and the guy Grace had just started dating were there, too, and their voices rose in an excited babble as the three "models" hopped down from the stage and joined them.

"Did I get it right?" Logan asked, leaning down to whisper the question into Trevor's ear with a smile. "You told me once you wanted a high-profile proposal; you wanted your friends involved; you wanted—"

"Logan," Trevor interrupted, shutting him up by kissing him soundly. "All I want is you."

"*All* you want?" Logan asked, pressing his lips together as if he were trying to hold back a smile.

Trevor grinned. "Well, fine. All I *need* is you. All of *this*..." He swept his arm out, the gesture encompassing everything Logan had done to make the moment special for him. His heart overflowed with a kind of happiness he honestly hadn't known could exist. Logan knew him so well, and every single thing he did, every day, proved it. "*This...* is perfect."

"I agree," Logan said, smiling down at Trevor like he was the only thing Logan could see. "Perfect."

And Trevor had no doubt that, with the two of them together, it always would be.

Also by Stella Starling

AVAILABLE NOW

All I Want (Elliott and Ash)

COMING SOON

Be Mine (Kelly and Jase, *At Last, The Beloved Series - Book Two*)

Be Loved (Brandon and Shane, *At Last, The Beloved Series - Book Three*)

About the Author

Stella Starling is the storytelling team of two M/M contemporary romance authors who have far too many stories to tell on their own, so decided it would be fun to tell a few of them together.

The authors bring their love for writing, romance, and sweet, steamy "happily ever afters" to every story, and hope that "their boys" will give readers a delicious escape into a world where love always wins.

CPSIA information can be obtained
at www.ICGtesting.com
Printed in the USA
LVOW12s1044271117
557656LV00004B/145/P